John Connolly is the author of the Charlie Parker mysteries. His
debut – EVERY DEAD THING – swiftly launched him right into th~~~
front rank of thriller writers, and all his subsequent novels hav~
Sunday Times bestsellers. BOOKS TO DIE FOR, which ~
with Declan Burke, was the winner of the 2013 Antho~
Macavity awards for Best Non-Fiction work. H~
American writer to win the US Shamu~ ~~~st
Irish writer to win an F~
www.johnconnollybo~

Praise for NIGHT MUSIC and John Connolly:

'An addictive and meticulously rendered collection of eerie, amusing
and achingly beautiful short stories.' *Sunday Business Post*

'A collection of supernatural fiction to rattle your cage . . . Connolly
never disappoints; his writing is always flawless, sympathetic and with
beautifully drawn characters . . . *Night Music* is a worthy follow-up to
Nocturnes, and there is much to enjoy here – and much to think about,
too. A must for John Connolly's many fans.' *Mass Movement*

'Connolly is a master of creating exquisite short stories . . . The stories
on offer range from charmingly whimsical to absolutely terrifying . . .
Read it with the lights down low, or by the light of the moon, but just
read it and revel in this macabre master storyteller.' *Starburst*

'Connolly knows how to unsettle, chill and outright terrify his readers
. . . *Night Music* is a good opportunity to watch him take full rein of
his supernatural enthusiasms, especially as the days shorten, tempera-
tures dip and a creepy tale read in the dark is most welcome.'
Portland Press Herald

'John Connolly's novels combine the supernatural with straightforward, if ingenious, crime, but his short stories come straight from
the bowels of Hell . . . a real master of the macabre gets to show us
how it's done.' *The Times*

Also by John Connolly

The Charlie Parker Stories
Every Dead Thing
Dark Hollow
The Killing Kind
The White Road
The Reflecting Eye (Novella in the Nocturnes Collection)
The Black Angel
The Unquiet
The Reapers
The Lovers
The Whisperers
The Burning Soul
The Wrath of Angels
The Wolf in Winter
A Song of Shadows
A Time of Torment

Other Works
Bad Men
The Book of Lost Things

SHORT STORIES
Nocturnes

The Samuel Johnson Stories (For Young Adults)
The Gates
Hell's Bells
The Creeps

The Chronicles of the Invaders (with Jennifer Ridyard)
Conquest
Empire
Dominion

Non-Fiction (as editor, with Declan Burke)
Books to Die For: The World's Greatest Mystery Writers on the
World's Greatest Mystery Novels

John Connolly

NIGHT MUSIC:
Nocturnes Volume 2

HODDER

First published in Great Britain in 2015 by Hodder & Stoughton
An Hachette UK company

First published in paperback in 2016

1

Illustrations by Jim Tierney

A CIP catalogue record for this book is
available from the British Library

B format ISBN 978 1 473 61974 6
A format ISBN 978 1 473 61975 3

Typeset by Hewer Text UK Ltd, Edinburgh
Printed and bound in Great Britain by Clays Ltd, St Ives plc

Hodder & Stoughton policy is to use papers that are natural,
renewable and recyclable products and made from wood grown in
sustainable forests. The logging and manufacturing processes
are expected to conform to the environmental regulations
of the country of origin.

Hodder & Stoughton Ltd
Carmelite House
50 Victoria Embankment
London EC4Y 0DZ

www.hodder.co.uk

For Seth Kavanagh

Contents

The Caxton Private Lending Library
& Book Depository

I

Let us begin with this:

To those looking at his life from without, it would have seemed that Mr Berger led a dull existence. In fact, Mr Berger himself might well have concurred with this view.

He worked for the housing department of a minor English council, with the job title of Closed Accounts Registrar. His task, from year to year, entailed compiling a list of those who had either relinquished or abandoned the housing provided for them by the council, and in doing so had left their accounts in arrears. Whether a week's rent was owed, or a month's, or even a year's (for evictions were a difficult business and had a habit of dragging on until relations between council and tenant came to resemble those between a besieging army and a walled city), Mr Berger would record the sum in question in a massive leather-bound ledger known as the Closed Accounts Register. At year's end, he would then be required to balance the rents received against those owed. If he had performed his job correctly, the difference between the two sums would be the total amount contained in the register.

Even Mr Berger found his job arduous to explain. Rare was it for a cab driver, or a fellow passenger on a train or bus, to engage in a discussion of Mr Berger's livelihood for longer than it took him to describe it. Mr Berger didn't mind. He had no illusions about himself or his work. He got on perfectly well with his colleagues, and was happy to join them for a pint of ale – but no more than that – at the end of each week. He contributed to retirement gifts, and wedding presents, and funeral wreaths. At one time it had seemed that he himself might become the cause

3

of one such collection, for he entered into a state of cautious flirtation with a young woman in Accounts. His advances appeared to be reciprocated, and the couple performed a mutual circling for the space of a year until someone less inhibited than Mr Berger entered the fray, and the young woman, presumably weary of waiting for Mr Berger to breach some perceived exclusion zone around her person, went off with his rival instead. It says much about Mr Berger that he contributed to their wedding collection without a hint of bitterness.

His position as registrar paid neither badly nor particularly well, but enough to keep him clothed and fed, and maintain a roof above his head. Most of the remainder went on books. Mr Berger led a life of the imagination, fed by stories. His flat was lined with shelves, and those shelves were filled with the books that he loved. There was no particular order to them. Oh, he kept the works of individual authors together, but he did not alphabetize, and neither did he congregate books by subject. He knew where to lay a hand on any title at any time, and that was enough. Order was for dull minds, and Mr Berger was far less dull than he appeared. (To those who are themselves unhappy, the contentment of others can sometimes be mistaken for tedium.) Mr Berger might sometimes have been a little lonely, but he was never bored, and rarely disconsolate, and he numbered his days by the books that he read.

I suppose that, in telling this tale, I have made Mr Berger sound old. He was not. He was 35 and, although in no danger of being mistaken for a matinée idol, was not unattractive. Yet perhaps there was in his interiority something that rendered him, if not sexless, then somewhat oblivious to the reality of relations with the opposite sex, an impression strengthened by the collective memory of what had occurred – or not occurred – with the girl from Accounts. So it was that Mr Berger found himself consigned to the dusty ranks of the council's bachelors and spinsters, to the army of the closeted, the odd, and the sad, although he was none of these things. Well, perhaps just a little of the latter:

although he never spoke of it, or even fully admitted it to himself, he regretted his failure to express properly his affection for the girl in Accounts, and had quietly resigned himself to the possibility that a life shared with another might not be in his stars. Slowly he was becoming a kind of fixed object, and the books that he read came to reflect his view of himself. He was not a great lover, and neither was he a tragic hero. Instead, he resembled those narrators in fiction who observe the lives of others, existing as dowels upon which plots hang like coats until the time comes for the true actors of the book to assume them. Great and voracious reader that he was, Mr Berger failed to realize that the life he was observing was his own.

In the autumn of 1968, on Mr Berger's 36th birthday, the council announced that it was moving offices. Its various departments had until then been scattered like outposts throughout the city, but it now made more sense to gather them all into one purpose-built environment and sell the outlying buildings. Mr Berger was saddened by this development. The housing department occupied a set of ramshackle offices in a redbrick edifice that had once been a private school, and there was a pleasing oddness to the manner in which it had been imperfectly adapted to its current role. The council's new headquarters, meanwhile, was a brutalist block designed by one of those acolytes of Le Corbusier whose vision consisted solely of purging the individual and eccentric and replacing it with a uniformity of steel, glass and reinforced concrete. It squatted on the site of what had once been the city's glorious Victorian railway station, itself now replaced by an unappealing bunker attached to a new shopping precinct. In time, Mr Berger knew, the rest of the city's jewels would also be turned to dust, and the ugliness of the built environment would poison the population, for how could it be otherwise?

Mr Berger was informed that, under the new regimen, there would be no need for a Closed Accounts Register, and he would be transferred to other duties. A new, more efficient system was to be put in place, although, as with so many other such initiatives, it would later be revealed as less efficient, and more costly, than the original. This news coincided with the death of Mr Berger's elderly mother, his last surviving close relative, and the discovery of a small but significant bequest to her son: her house, some shares, and a sum of money that was not quite a fortune but would, if invested carefully, enable Mr Berger to live in a degree of restrained comfort for the rest of his life. He had always had a hankering to write, and he now had the perfect opportunity to test his literary mettle.

So it was that Mr Berger at last had a collection taken up in his name, and a small crowd gathered to bid him farewell and good luck, and he was forgotten almost as soon as he was gone.

2

Mr Berger's mother had spent her declining years in a cottage on the outskirts of the small town of Glossom. It was one of those passingly pretty English settlements, best suited to those whose time on this earth was drawing slowly to a close, and who wanted to spend it in surroundings that were unlikely to unduly excite them, and thereby hasten the end. Its community was predominantly High Anglican, with a corresponding focus on parish-centred activities: rarely an evening went by without the church hall being occupied by amateur dramatists, or local historians, or quietly concerned Fabians.

It seemed, though, that Mr Berger's mother had rather kept herself to herself, and few eyebrows were raised in Glossom when her son chose to do the same. He spent his days outlining his proposed work of fiction, a novel of frustrated love and muted social commentary set among the woollen mills of Lancashire in the nineteenth century. It was, Mr Berger quickly realized, the kind of book of which the Fabians might have approved, which put something of a dampener on his progress. He dallied with some short stories instead, and when they proved similarly unrewarding he fell back on poetry, the last resort of the literary scoundrel. Finally, if only to keep his hand in, he began writing letters to the newspapers on matters of national and international concern. One, on the subject of badgers, was printed in the *Telegraph*, but it was heavily cut for publication, and Mr Berger felt that it made him sound somewhat obsessive about badgers when nothing could have been further from the truth.

It began to dawn on Mr Berger that he might not be cut out

for the life of a writer, gentleman or otherwise, and perhaps there were those who should simply be content to read. Once he had reached this conclusion, it was as though a great weight had been lifted from his shoulders. He packed away the expensive writer's notebooks that he had purchased from Smythson's of Bond Street, and their weight in his pocket was replaced by the latest volume of Anthony Powell's *roman-fleuve*, *A Dance to the Music of Time*.

In the evenings, Mr Berger was in the habit of taking a walk by the railway line. A disused path, not far from the back gate of his cottage, led through a forest and thus to the raised bank on which the railway ran. Until recently, trains had stopped four times daily at Glossom, but the Beeching cuts had led to the closure of the station. Trains still used the lines, a noisy reminder of what had been lost, but soon even the sound of them would disappear as routes were reorganized. Eventually, the lines through Glossom would become overgrown, and the station would fall further into disrepair. There were those in Glossom who had suggested buying it from British Railways and turning it into a museum, although they were unclear as to what exactly might be put in such a museum, the history of Glossom being distinctly lacking in battles, royalty, or great inventors.

None of this concerned Mr Berger. It was enough that he had a pleasant place in which to walk or, if the weather was conducive, to sit by the lines and read. There was a stile not far from the old station, and he liked to wait there for the passing of the last train south. He would watch the businessmen in their suits flash by, and experience a surge of gratitude that his working life had reached a premature but welcome end.

Now, as winter began to close in, he still took his evening strolls, but the fading of the light and the growing chill in the air meant that he did not pause to spend time with his book. Nevertheless, he always carried a volume with him, for it had become his habit to read for an hour at the Spotted Frog over a glass of wine or a pint of mild.

On the evening in question, Mr Berger had paused as usual to wait for the train. It was, he noticed, running a little late. It had recently begun to do so more and more which led him to wonder if all of this rationalization was really leading to any kind of improvements at all. He lit his pipe and looked to the west to witness the sun setting behind the woods, the last traces of it like flames upon the denuded branches of the trees.

It was at this point that he spotted a woman passing through the overgrown bushes a little farther down the line. He had noticed before a trail of sorts there, for the branches of shrubs had been broken in places, but it was a poor substitute for his own path, and he had no desire to damage his clothing or his skin on briars. The woman wore a dark dress, but what caught Berger's eye was the little red bag that she carried on her arm. It seemed in such stark contrast to the rest of her attire. He tried to see her face, but the angle of her progress concealed it from him.

At that moment he heard a distant whistle, and the stile beneath him started to vibrate. The express, the last train of the evening, was approaching. He could see its lights through the trees as it came. He looked again to his right. The woman had stopped, for she too had heard the sound. Mr Berger expected her to pause and wait for the train to pass, but she did not. Instead she hastened her steps. Perhaps she wishes to be across the track before it comes, thought Mr Berger, but that was a risky business. It was easy to misjudge distances under such circumstances, and he had heard tales of those who had caught a foot on a sleeper, or stumbled while rushing, and the train had been the end of them.

'Ho!' he called. 'Wait!'

Instinctively he stepped down from the stile and walked quickly towards her. The woman turned at the sound of his voice. Even from a distance, Mr Berger could see that she was beautiful. Her face was pale, but she did not seem distressed. There was about her an eerie, unsettling calm.

'Don't try to cross!' he shouted. 'Let the train pass.'

The woman emerged from the bushes. She hitched up her skirts, showing a pair of laced ankle boots, and proceeded to climb up the embankment. Now Mr Berger was running, but he continued to call to her, even as the express grew louder before passing him in a flash of noise and light and diesel. He saw the woman cast aside her red bag, draw her head between her shoulders and, with her arms outstretched, throw herself on her knees before the train.

Mr Berger flinched. The angle of the line meant that he did not witness the moment of impact, and any sounds of distress were lost in the roar of the engine. When he opened his eyes, the woman was gone and the train was continuing on its way.

Mr Berger ran to the spot at which he had last seen the figure in the dress. He steeled himself for the worst, expecting to find the track mired with gore and body parts, but there was nothing. He had no experience of such matters, though, and had no idea whether a train striking a person at such a speed would leave a great mess or none at all. It was possible that the force of it had sent fragments of the woman in all directions, or even that it had carried her broken frame farther down the track. After searching the bushes by the point of impact he followed the line for a time, but discovered no blood, and no sign of a body. He could not even find the woman's discarded red bag. Still, he had seen her, of that he had no doubt. He had not imagined it.

He was now closer to the town than he was to his home. There was no police station in Glossom, but there was one in Moreham, some five miles away. Mr Berger walked quickly to the public telephone at the old station house, and from there he called the police and told them of what he had witnessed. Then, as instructed, he sat on the bench outside the station and waited for the patrol car to arrive.

3

The police did much the same as Mr Berger had done, only with greater numbers and at greater expense in man-hours and overtime payments. They searched the bushes and the track, and inquiries were made in Glossom in case any female residents had gone missing. The driver of the train was contacted, and the train was kept on the platform at Plymouth for an hour while its engine and carriages were examined for any sign of human remains.

Finally, Mr Berger, who had remained seated on a stile throughout the search, was interviewed for a second time by the inspector from Moreham. His name was Carswell, and his manner when he confronted Mr Berger was colder than it had originally been. A light rain had begun to fall shortly after the search for a body had commenced, and Carswell and his men were now damp and weary. Mr Berger was also wet, and found that he had developed a slight but constant shiver. He suspected that he might be in shock. He had never witnessed a person's death before. It had affected him deeply.

Now Inspector Carswell stood in the growing dark, his hat jammed on his head and his hands thrust deep in the pockets of his coat. His men were packing up, and a pair of dogs that had been brought in to help with the search was being led back to the van in which they had arrived. The townspeople who had gathered to watch were also drifting away, but not without a final curious glance at the figure of Mr Berger.

'Let's go through it again, shall we?' said Carswell, and Mr Berger told his story one last time. The details remained the same. He was certain of what he had witnessed.

'I have to tell you,' said Carswell, when Mr Berger had finished speaking, 'that the driver of the train saw nothing, and was unaware of any impact. As you can imagine, he was quite shocked to hear that a woman had been reported as throwing herself under his wheels. He aided in the examination of the train himself. It turns out that he has some unfortunate experience of such matters. Before he was promoted to driver, he was a fireman on an engine that struck a man near Coleford Junction. He told us that the driver saw the man on the rails but couldn't brake in time. The engine made a terrible mess of the poor fellow, he said. There was no mistaking what had happened. He seems to think that, if he had somehow hit a woman without knowing, we'd have no trouble finding her remains.'

Carswell lit a cigarette. He offered one to Mr Berger, who declined. He preferred his pipe, even though it had long since gone out.

'Do you live alone, sir?' asked Carswell.

'Yes, I do.'

'From what I understand, you moved to Glossom fairly recently.'

'That's correct. My mother died, and she left me her cottage.'

'And you say that you're a writer?'

'Trying to be a writer. I've started to wonder if I'm really destined to be any good at it, to be honest.'

'Solitary business, writing, or so I would imagine.'

'It does tend to be, yes.'

'You're not married?'

'No.'

'Girlfriend?'

'No,' said Mr Berger, then added, 'Not at the moment.'

He didn't want Inspector Carswell to think that there might be anything odd or unsavoury about his bachelor existence.

'Ah.'

Carswell drew deeply on his cigarette.

'Do you miss her?'

'Miss who?'

'Your mother.'

Mr Berger considered it an odd question to ask, but answered nonetheless.

'Of course,' he said. 'I would visit her when I could, and we spoke on the telephone once a week.'

Carswell nodded, as if this explained a lot.

'Must be strange, coming to a new town, and living in the house in which your mother died. She passed away at home, didn't she?'

Mr Berger thought that Inspector Carswell seemed to know a lot about his mother. Clearly he had not just been asking about a missing woman during his time in Glossom.

'Yes, she did,' he replied. 'Forgive me, Inspector, but what has this got to do with the incident on the line?'

Carswell took the cigarette from his mouth and examined the burning tip, as though some answer might be found in the ash.

'I'm beginning to wonder if you might not have been mistaken in what you saw,' he said.

'Mistaken? How can one be mistaken about a suicide?'

'There is no body, sir. There's no blood, no clothing, nothing. We haven't even been able to find the red bag that you mentioned. There's no sign that anything untoward happened on the track at all. So . . .'

Carswell took one last drag on his cigarette, then dropped it in the dirt and ground it out forcefully with the heel of his shoe.

'Let's just say that you were mistaken, and leave it at that, shall we? Perhaps you might like to find some other way to occupy your evenings, now that winter is setting in. Join the bridge club, or take up singing in the church choir. You might even find a young lady to walk out with. What I'm saying is, you've had a traumatic time of it, and it would be good for you not to spend so many hours alone. That way, you'll avoid making mistakes of this nature again. You do understand me, don't you, sir?'

The implication was clear. Being mistaken was not a crime, but wasting police time was. Mr Berger climbed down from the stile.

'I know what I saw, Inspector,' he said, but it was all that he could do to keep the doubt from creeping into his voice, and his mind was troubled as he took the path back to his little cottage.

4

It should come as no surprise to learn that Mr Berger slept little that night. Over and over he replayed the scene of the woman's demise, and although he had not witnessed the moment of impact, still he saw and heard it in the silence of the bedroom. To calm himself, he had taken a large glass of his late mother's brandy upon his arrival home, but he was not used to spirits and the alcohol sat ill with him. He grew delirious in his bed, and so often did the woman's death play out before him that he began to believe that this evening was not the first time he had been present at her passing. A peculiar sense of déjà vu overcame him, one that he was entirely unable to shrug off. Sometimes, when he was ill or feverish, a tune or song would lodge itself in his mind. So entrenched would its hooks become that it would keep him from sleep, and he would be unable to exorcise it until the sickness had passed. Now he was having the same experience with his vision of the woman's death, and its repetitive nature was leading him to believe that he had already been familiar with the scene before he was present at it.

At last, thankfully, weariness overcame him and he was able to rest, but when he woke the next morning that nagging feeling of familiarity remained. He put on his coat and returned to the scene of the previous evening's excitement. He walked the rough trail, hoping to find something that the police might have missed, a sign that he had not been the victim of an overactive imagination – a scrap of black cloth, the heel of a shoe, or the red bag – but there was nothing.

It was the red bag that bothered him most of all. The red bag was the thing. With his mind unfogged by alcohol – although, in truth, his head still swam slightly in the aftermath – he grew more and more certain that the suicide of the young woman reminded him of a scene in a book: no, not just *a* scene, but perhaps the most famous scene of locomotive-based self-immolation in literature. He gave up his physical search, and decided to embark on a more literary one.

He had long ago unpacked his books, although he had not yet found shelves for them all, his mother's love of reading not matching his own, and thus leading to her preference for large swathes of bare wall that she had seen fit to adorn only with cheap reproductions of sea views. There was still more room for his volumes than there had been in his own lodgings, due in no small part to the fact that the cottage had more floor space than his flat, and all a true bibliophile needs for his storage purposes is a horizontal plane. He found his copy of *Anna Karenina* sandwiched in a pile on the dining-room floor between *War and Peace* and *Master and Man and Other Parables and Tales*, the latter in a nice Everyman's Library edition from 1946 about which he had forgotten, and which almost led him to set aside *Anna Karenina* in favour of an hour or so in its company. Good sense quickly prevailed, although not before he had put *Master and Man* on the dining table for further examination at a more convenient time. There it joined a dozen similarly blessed volumes, all of which had been waiting for days or weeks for their hour to come at last.

He sat in an armchair and opened *Anna Karenina* (Limited Editions Club, Cambridge, 1951, signed by Barnett Freedman, unearthed at a jumble sale in Gloucester and acquired for such a low price that Mr Berger had later made a donation to charity in order to salve his conscience). He flipped through the pages until he found Chapter XXXI, which began with the words 'A bell sounded . . .' From there he read on quickly but carefully, travelling with Anna past Piotr in his livery and top-boots, past the saucy conductor and the woman deformed, past the dirty hunchback *muzhik* until finally he came to this passage:

She was going to throw herself under the first car as its centre came opposite where she stood. Her little red travelling-bag caused her to lose the moment; she could not detach it from her arm. She awaited the second. A feeling like that she had experienced once, just before taking a dive in the river, came over her, and she made the sign of the cross. This familiar gesture called back to her soul a whole series of memories of her youth and childhood; and suddenly the darkness which hid everything from her was torn asunder. Life, with its elusive joys, glowed for an instant before her. But she did not take her eyes from the car; and when the centre, between the two wheels, appeared, she threw away her red bag, drawing her head between her shoulders, and, with outstretched hands, threw herself on her knees under the car. For a second she was horror-struck at what she was doing.

'Where am I? What am I doing? Why?'

She tried to get up, to draw back; but something monstrous, inflexible, struck her head, and threw her on her back.

'Lord, forgive me all!' she murmured, feeling the struggle to be in vain.

A little muzhik *was working on the railroad, mumbling in his beard.*

And the candle by which she had read the book that was filled with fears, with deceptions, with anguish, and with evil, flared up with greater brightness than she had ever known, revealing to her all that before was in darkness, then flickered, grew faint, and went out forever.

Mr Berger read the passage twice, then leaned back in his chair and closed his eyes. It was all there, right down to the detail of the little red bag, the bag that the woman on the tracks had cast aside before the express had hit her, just as Anna had thrown away her bag before she was struck. The woman's gestures in her final moments had also been similar to Anna's: she too had drawn her head between her shoulders and stretched out her

arms, as though the death to come was to take the form of crucifixion rather than iron and wheels. Why, even Mr Berger's own
memory of the incident had been couched in similar phrases.

'My God,' said Mr Berger to the listening books, 'perhaps
the inspector was right, and I have been spending too much
time alone with only novels for company. There can be no other
excuse for a man believing that he has seen the climactic scene
of *Anna Karenina* re-enacted on the Exeter to Plymouth
railway.'

He placed the volume on the arm of the chair and went to the
kitchen. He was briefly tempted to reach for the brandy again,
but no particular good had come of their previous shared
moments, and so he opted for the routine of making a big pot of
tea. When all was in place, he took a seat at the kitchen table and
drank cup after cup until he had drained the pot dry. For once he
did not reach for a book, nor did he distract himself with *The
Times'* crossword, still left untried at this late stage of the
morning. He simply stared at the clouds, and listened to bird-
song, and wondered if he was not, after all, going gently insane.

Mr Berger did not read anything else that day. His two examina-
tions of Chapter XXXI of *Anna Karenina* remained his sole
contact with the world of literature. He could not recall a day
when he had read less. He lived for books. They had consumed
every spare moment since the revelation in childhood that he
could tackle a novel alone without his mother having to read it
to him. He recalled his first halting encounters with the Biggles
stories of W.E. Johns, remembering how he had struggled
through the longer words by breaking them up into their individual syllables, so that one difficult word became two easier
ones. Ever since then, books had been his constant companions.
He had, perhaps, sacrificed real friendships to these simulacra,
because there were days when he had avoided his chums after
school or ignored their knocking on his front door when his parents' house was otherwise empty, taking an alternative route

home or staying away from the windows so that he could be sure that no football game or exploration of orchards would get in the way of finishing the story that had gripped him.

In a way, books had been partly responsible for his fatal tentativeness with the girl from Accounts. She seemed to read a little – he had seen her with a Georgette Heyer novel, and the occasional Agatha Christie mystery from the library – but he had the sense that it was not a passion with her. What if she insisted that they spend hours at the theatre, or the ballet, or shopping, simply because it meant that they would be 'doing things together'? That was, after all, what couples did, wasn't it? But reading was a solitary pursuit. Oh, one could read in the same room as someone else, or beside them in bed at night, but it rather presumed that an agreement had been reached about such matters, and the couple in question consisted of a pair of like-minded souls. It would be a disaster to find oneself embroiled with the sort of person who read two pages of a novel and then began humming, or tapping her fingers to attract attention, or, God help us, fiddling with the dial on the wireless. The next thing one knew, she'd be making 'observations' on the text in hand, and once that happened there would be no peace for ever after.

But as he sat alone in the kitchen of his deceased mother's house, it struck Mr Berger that he had never troubled himself to find out the views of the girl in Accounts on the subject of books or, indeed, ballet. Deep inside, he had been reluctant to disturb his ordered lifestyle, a world in which he rarely had to make a more difficult decision than selecting the next book to read. He had lived his life at one remove from the world around him, and now he was paying the price in madness.

5

In the days that followed, Mr Berger subsisted largely on newspapers and magazines of an improving nature. He had almost convinced himself that what he had seen on the track was a psychological anomaly, some form of delayed reaction to the grief he had experienced at his mother's death. He noticed that he was the object of peculiar looks, both poorly concealed and unashamedly open, as he went about his business in the town, but that was to be expected. He did hope that the town's memory of the unproductive police search might fade eventually. He had no desire to be elevated to the role of local eccentric.

But as time wore on, something odd happened. It is usual in the manner of experiences such as Mr Berger's that, as distance grows from the event in question, so too the memory of it becomes foggier. Mr Berger should, if the ordinary rules of behaviour were being obeyed, have become ever more certain of the psychologically troubling nature of his encounter with the young woman reminiscent of Anna Karenina. But Mr Berger found himself believing with greater and greater conviction that the opposite was true. He had seen the woman, and she was real, admittedly allowing for a certain latitude in one's definition of reality.

He began reading again, tentatively at first, but soon with his previous immersion. He also returned to walking the path that wound down to the railway line, and sitting on his stile to watch the trains go by. Each evening, with the approach of the express from Exeter to Plymouth, he would set aside his book, and watch the rougher trail to the south. It was darker now, and the trail was harder to see, but Mr Berger's eyes were still keen, and through habit he grew practised at picking out the difference in the density of the bushes.

But the trail remained undisturbed until February came, and the woman returned.

6

It was a cold but bracing evening. There was no damp in the air, and Mr Berger enjoyed the sight of his breath pluming as he took his evening constitutional. There was to be music in the Spotted Frog later: some form of folk revivalism, for which Mr Berger had a sneaking fondness. He intended to drop in for an hour or two, once he had watched the train go by. His vigil at the stile had become something of a ritual, and although he told himself that it was no longer connected to the business of the woman with the red bag, he secretly knew that it was. He was haunted by the image of her.

He took his seat on the stile, and lit his pipe. From somewhere to the east, he heard the sound of the approaching train. He glanced at his watch, and saw that it was just after six. The train was early. This was unheard of. If he had still been in the habit of writing letters to the *Telegraph*, he might well have popped off a missive announcing this turn-up for the books, much in the manner of those twitchers who liked to let the populace know of the appearance of the first cuckoo of spring.

He was already composing the letter in his head when he was distracted by a commotion to his right. Someone was coming down the trail, and in some hurry. Mr Berger dropped from the stile and began walking in the direction of the sounds. The sky was clear, and the moon was already silvering the undergrowth, but even without the aid of its light Mr Berger would have been able to pick out the woman rushing to meet the train, and the red bag that hung from her arm.

Mr Berger dropped his pipe, but managed to retrieve it. It was, after all, a good pipe.

While it would not be untrue to say that he had become obsessed with the woman, he had no real expectation of ever seeing her again. After all, people did not make a habit of throwing themselves under trains. It was the kind of act that tended to be performed once, or not at all. In the case of the former, any possible repeat of the incident was likely to be ruled out by the action of a heavy engine or, in the unlikely event of survival, sufficient recall of the painfulness of the first attempt to render most unwelcome any repetition of it. Yet here, without a shadow of a doubt, was the same young woman carrying the same red bag and making the same rush towards self-destruction that Mr Berger had previously witnessed.

It must be a ghost, thought Mr Berger. There can be no other explanation. This is the spirit of some poor woman who died long ago – for he saw that her clothing was not of this century – and she is doomed to repeat her final moments over and over until—

Until what? Mr Berger wasn't certain. He had read his share of M.R. James and W.W. Jacobs, of Oliver Onions and William Hope Hodgson, but had never come across anything quite like this in their stories. He had a vague notion that digging up a forgotten corpse and reburying it in a more appropriate location sometimes helped, while James tended to favour restoring ancient artifacts to their previous resting place, thereby calming the spirits associated with them, but Mr Berger had no idea where the young woman might be interred, and he had not picked so much as a flower while on his walks, let alone removed some old whistle or manuscript. All of this would have to be dealt with later, he realized. There was more important business to attend to.

The early arrival of the train had obviously caught the woman, spectral or otherwise, by surprise, and the branches seemed to be conspiring to keep her from her date with mortality. They caught at her dress, and at one point she took a tumble that sent her to her knees. Despite all of these hindrances, it was obvious to Mr Berger that she was still likely to make it to the track in time to receive the full impact of the train.

Mr Berger ran, and as he did so he screamed and shouted, and waved his arms. He ran faster than he had ever run before, so that he managed to reach the base of the trail some time before the woman did. She drew up short, apparently surprised to see him. Perhaps she had been so intent on her own demise that she had failed to hear his cries, but she was now faced with the physical reality of Mr Berger, and he with hers. She was younger than he, and her skin was unusually pale, although that might just have been the moonlight. Her hair was the blackest that Mr Berger had ever seen. It seemed to consume the light.

The woman tried to dart to her right, and then to her left, to avoid Mr Berger, but the bushes were too thick. He felt the ground vibrating, and the noise of the approaching train was deafeningly loud. He was aware of its whistle sounding. The driver had probably spotted him by the tracks. Mr Berger raised his right hand and waved to let the driver know that all was well. The woman was not going to get past him, and Mr Berger had no intention of throwing himself under any trains.

The woman clenched her fists in frustration as the train rushed by. Mr Berger turned his head to watch it go, some of the passengers staring at him curiously from the window, and when he looked back the woman was gone. It was only as the rattle of the train faded that he heard the sound of bushes rustling and knew that she was making her way back up the hill. He tried to follow, but the same branches that had previously hampered her progress now delayed his. His jacket was torn, he lost his pipe, and he even twisted his left ankle on a root, but he did not give up. He reached the road just in time to see the woman slip into a lane that ran parallel to Glossom's high street. The back gardens of a row of cottages lay on one side, and on the other the rear wall of what had once been the town's brewery but was now derelict and unused, although a faint smell of old hops still hung about it.

Eventually the lane diverged, with the path to the left connecting with the main street while the path to the right twisted into darkness. Mr Berger could see no sign of the woman to his left, for the high street was well lit. He chose instead to go right, and was soon among the relics of Glossom's industrial past: old warehouses, some still in use but most abandoned; a wall that announced the presence of a combined cooperage and chandlery, while the decay of the building behind it left no doubt that it had been some time since either barrels or candles had emerged from within; and, finally, a two-storey redbrick building with barred windows and grass growing by its doorstep. Beyond it was a dead end. As he drew nearer, Mr Berger could have sworn that he heard a door closing.

Mr Berger stood before the building and stared up at it. There were no lights burning, and the windows were so encrusted with dirt both inside and out that there was no possibility of catching a glimpse of its interior. A name was carved into the brickwork above the door. Mr Berger had to strain his eyes to read it, for the moonlight seemed to have no desire to aid him here. At last he made out the words 'Caxton Private Lending Library & Book Depository'.

Mr Berger frowned. He had asked in the town as to whether there was a library and had been told that there was none, the nearest, as with so much else that Glossom lacked, being in Moreham. There was a newsagent that sold books, but they were mainly detective stories and romances, and there was a limit to how many of either Mr Berger wished to read. It was, of course, entirely likely that the Caxton Private Lending Library & Book Depository was no longer in business, but if that was the case then why was the grass growing around its doorstep trampled flat in places? Someone was still entering and leaving it on a semiregular basis, including, if Mr Berger was not mistaken, a woman, or something phantasmagorical that resembled a woman, with an Anna Karenina fixation.

He took out his matchbook and lit a match. There was a

yellowed sign behind a small pane of glass to the right of the door. It read: 'For all enquiries, please ring bell.' Mr Berger used up three matches looking in vain for a bell of any kind. There was none. Neither was there a slot or box for post.

Mr Berger worked his way around the corner of the building to the right, for the wall barred any progress to the left. Here was a smaller lane, but it ended in another brick wall, and there were no windows on that side of the building, nor was there a door. Behind the wall was a patch of waste ground.

Mr Berger returned to the front door. He banged on it once with his fist, more in hope than expectation of an answer. He was unsurprised when none came. He examined the single key-hole. It did not look rusted, and when he put a finger to it, the digit came back moistened with a hint of lock oil. It was all most peculiar, and not a little sinister.

There was nothing else to be done for now, Mr Berger thought. The night was growing steadily colder, and he had not yet eaten. Although Glossom was a quiet, safe town, he did not fancy spending a long night outside a darkened lending library in the hope that a spectral woman might emerge so he could ask her what she thought she was doing, throwing herself repeatedly under trains. There were also some nasty scratches on his hands that could do with a spot of antiseptic.

So, with one final look back at the Caxton Library, and more perturbed than ever, Mr Berger returned home, and the Spotted Frog was deprived of his custom for that night.

7

Mr Berger returned to the Caxton Library shortly after 10.00 a.m. the next morning, on the basis that this was a reasonably civilized hour at which to appear, and if the Caxton was still in business then it was likely that someone might be about at such a time. The Caxton, though, remained as silent and forbidding as it had the previous evening.

With nothing better to do, Mr Berger began making inquiries, but to no avail. General expressions of ignorance about the nature of the Caxton Private Lending Library & Book Depository were his sole reward at the newsagent, the grocery, and even among the early arrivals at the Spotted Frog. Oh, people seemed to be aware that the Caxton existed, but nobody was able to recall a time when it was actually in business as a lending library, nor could anyone say who owned the building, or if any books remained inside. It was suggested that he might try the Town Hall in Moreham, where the records for the smaller hamlets in the vicinity were kept.

So Mr Berger got in his car and headed to Moreham. As he drove, he considered that there seemed to be a remarkable lack of interest in the Caxton Library among the townsfolk of Glossom. It was not merely that those to whom he spoke had forgotten about its existence until Mr Berger brought it up, at which point some faint atavistic memory of the building was uncovered before promptly being buried again; that, at least, might be understandable if the library had not been in business for many years. What was more curious was that most people seemed to be entirely unaware of its presence, and didn't care very much to investigate further once it was brought to their attention. Glossom was a close-knit community, as Mr Berger was only too well aware, for comments about hallucinations and train delays still followed him as he asked about the library. There appeared to be only two types of business in the town: everybody's business, and business that was not yet everybody's but soon would be once the local gossips had got to work on it. The older residents could provide chapter and verse on the town's history back to the sixteenth century, and every building, old or recent, had its history.

All, that is, except the Caxton Private Lending Library.

The Town Hall in Moreham proved to be a source of little illumination on the matter. The library building was owned by the Caxton Trust, with an address at a P.O. box in London. The trust paid all bills relating to the property, including rates and electricity, and that was as much as Mr Berger could find out about it. An inquiry at the library in Moreham was met with blank looks, and although he spent hours searching back issues of the local weekly paper, the *Moreham & Glossom Advertiser*, from the turn of the century onwards, he could find no reference to the Caxton Library.

It was already dark when he returned to his cottage. He cooked himself an omelette and tried to read, but was distracted by the fact of the library's apparent simultaneous existence and nonexistence. It was there. It occupied a space in Glossom. It was a considerable building. Why, then, had its presence in a small community passed relatively unnoticed and unremarked for so long?

The next day brought no more satisfaction. Calls to booksellers and libraries, including to the grand old London Library, and the Cranston Library in Reigate, the oldest lending library in the country, confirmed only a general ignorance of the Caxton. Finally, Mr Berger found himself talking to the British representative of the Special Libraries Association, an organization of whose existence he had previously been unaware. She promised to search their records, but admitted that she had never heard of the Caxton and would be surprised if anyone else had either, given that her own knowledge of such matters was encyclopaedic, a judgement that, after an hour-long history of libraries in England, Mr Berger was unwilling to doubt.

Mr Berger did consider that he might be mistaken about the mystery woman's ultimate destination. There were other buildings in that part of town in which she could have hidden to escape his notice, but the Caxton was still the most likely place in which she might have sought refuge and he was certain that he had heard a door closing. Where else, he thought, would a woman intent upon repeatedly re-enacting the final moments of Anna Karenina choose to hide but in an old library?

He made his decision before he went to bed that night. He would become a detective of sorts, and stake out the Caxton Private Lending Library & Book Depository for as long as it took for it to reveal its secrets to him.

8

As Mr Berger soon discovered, it was no easy business being a detective on a stakeout. It was all very well for those chaps in books who could sit in a car or restaurant and make observations about the world in a degree of comfort, especially if they were in Los Angeles or somewhere else with a climate noted for warmth and sunlight. It was quite another thing to hang around among dilapidated buildings in a small English town on a cold, damp February day, hoping that nobody one knew happened by or, worse, some passing busybody didn't take it upon himself to phone the police and report a loiterer. Mr Berger could just imagine Inspector Carswell smoking another cigarette and concluding that he now most definitely had some form of lunatic on his hands.

Thankfully, Mr Berger found a sheltered space in the old cooperage and chandlery that afforded a view of the end of the lane through a collapsed section of wall while allowing him to remain relatively concealed. He had brought a blanket, a cushion, a flask of tea, some sandwiches and chocolate, and two books, one of them a John Dickson Carr novel entitled *The Crooked Hinge*, just to enter into the spirit of the thing, and the other *Our Mutual Friend* by Charles Dickens, the only Dickens he had yet to read. *The Crooked Hinge* turned out to be rather good, if a little fantastical. Then again, Mr Berger considered, a tale of witchcraft and automatons was hardly more outlandish than apparently witnessing the same woman attempt suicide twice, the first time successfully and the second time less so.

The day passed without incident. There was no activity in the lane, the rustle of the odd rat apart. Mr Berger finished the

Dickson Carr and started the Dickens, which, being the author's last completed novel, meant that it was mature Dickens, and hence rather difficult by the standards of *Oliver Twist* or *The Pickwick Papers*, and requiring considerably more patience and attention. When the light began to fade, Mr Berger set aside the book, unwilling to risk drawing attention by using a torch, and waited another hour in the hope that darkness might bring with it some activity at the Caxton Library. No illumination showed in the old building, and Mr Berger eventually gave up his watch for the night, and took himself to the Spotted Frog for a hot meal and a restorative glass of wine.

His vigil recommenced early the next morning, although he chose to alternate Dickens with Wodehouse. Once again, the day passed with little excitement, the appearance of a small terrier apart. The dog began yapping at Mr Berger, who shooed it ineffectually until its owner gave a shrill whistle from nearby and the dog departed. Still, the day was warmer than the one before, which was a small blessing: Mr Berger had woken that morning with stiff limbs, and had determined to wear two overcoats if the new day proved as chilly as the last.

Darkness started to descend, and with it doubts on the part of Mr Berger about the wisdom of his course of action. He couldn't hang around lanes indefinitely. It was unseemly. He leaned into a corner and found himself starting to doze. He dreamed of lights in the Caxton Library, and a train that rolled down the lane, its complement of passengers consisting entirely of dark-haired ladies carrying small red bags, all of them steeling themselves for self-destruction. Finally he dreamed of footsteps on gravel and grass, but when he woke he could still hear the footsteps. Someone was coming. Tentatively he rose from his resting place and peered at the library. There was a figure on its doorstep carrying what looked like a carpetbag, and he heard the rattle of keys.

Instantly Mr Berger was on his feet. He climbed through the gap in the wall and emerged into the lane. An elderly man was standing before the door of the Caxton Library, his key already turning in the lock. He was shorter than average, and wore a long grey overcoat and a trilby hat with a white feather in the band. A remarkable silver handlebar moustache adorned his upper lip. He looked at Mr Berger with some alarm and hurriedly opened the door.

'Wait!' said Mr Berger. 'I have to talk to you.'

The old gent was clearly in no mood to talk. The door was wide open now, and he was already inside when he realized that he had forgotten his carpetbag, which remained on the ground. He reached for it, but Mr Berger got there at the same time, and an unseemly tug-of-war began with each man holding on to one of the straps.

'Hand it over!' said the old man.

'No,' said Mr Berger. 'I have some questions for you.'

'You'll have to make an appointment. You must telephone in advance.'

'There's no number. You're not listed.'

'Then send a letter.'

'You don't have a postbox.'

'Look, you must come back tomorrow and ring the bell.'

'There is no bell!' shouted Mr Berger, his frustration getting the better of him as his voice jumped an octave. He gave a final hard yank on the bag and won the struggle, leaving only a handle in the grip of the old man.

'Oh, bother!' said the old man. He looked wistfully at his bag, which Mr Berger was clutching to his chest. 'I suppose you'd better come in, then, but you can't stay long. I'm a very busy man.'

He stepped back, inviting Mr Berger to enter. Now that the opportunity had at last presented itself, Mr Berger experienced a twinge of concern. The interior of the Caxton Library looked very dark, and who knew what might be waiting inside? He was throwing himself on the mercy of a possible madman, armed only with a hostage carpetbag. But he had come this far in his investigation, and he required an answer of some sort if he was ever to have peace of mind again. Still holding on to the carpetbag as though it were a swaddled infant, he stepped into the library.

9

Lights came on. They were dim, and the illumination they offered had a touch of jaundice to it, but they revealed lines of shelves stretching off into the distance, and that peculiar musty smell distinctive to rooms in which books are ageing like fine wines. To his left was an oak counter, and behind it cubbyholes filled with paperwork that appeared not to have been touched in many years, for a fine film of dust lay over it all. Beyond the counter was an open door, and through it Mr Berger could see a small living area with a television, and the edge of a bed in an adjoining room.

The old gent removed his hat, and his coat and scarf, and hung them on a hook by the door. Beneath them he was wearing a dark suit of considerable vintage, a white shirt, and a very wide grey-and-white-striped tie. He looked rather dapper, in a slightly decaying way. He waited patiently for Mr Berger to begin, which Mr Berger duly did.

'Look,' said Mr Berger, 'I won't have it. I simply won't.'

'Won't have what?'

'Women throwing themselves under trains, then coming back and trying to do it again. It's just not on. Am I making myself clear?'

The elderly gentleman frowned. He tugged at one end of his moustache and sighed.

'May I have my bag back, please?' he asked.

Mr Berger handed it over, and the old man stepped behind the counter and placed the bag in the living-room before returning. By this time, though, Mr Berger, in the manner of bibliophiles everywhere, had begun to examine the contents of the nearest shelf. The shelves were organized alphabetically, and by chance Mr Berger had started on the letter 'D'. He discovered an incomplete collection of Dickens's work, seemingly limited to the best known of the writer's books. *Our Mutual Friend* was conspicuously absent, but *Oliver Twist* was present, as were *David Copperfield*, *A Tale of Two Cities*, *The Pickwick Papers*, and a handful of others. All of the editions looked very old. He took *Oliver Twist* from the shelf and examined its points. It was bound in brown cloth with gilt lettering, with the publisher's imprint at the foot of the spine. The title page attributed the work to 'Boz,' not Charles Dickens, indicating a very early edition, a fact confirmed by the name of his publisher and date of publication: Richard Bentley, London, 1838. Mr Berger was holding the first edition, first issue of the novel.

'Please be careful with that,' said the old gent, who was hovering nervously nearby, but Mr Berger had already replaced *Oliver Twist* and was now examining *A Tale of Two Cities*, perhaps his favourite novel by Dickens: Chapman & Hall, 1859, original red cloth. It was another first edition.

But it was the volume marked *The Pickwick Papers* that constituted the greatest surprise. It was oversized, and contained within it not a published copy but a manuscript. Mr Berger knew that most of Dickens's manuscripts were held by the Victoria and Albert Museum as part of the Forster Collection, for he had seen them when they were last on display. The rest were held by the British Library, the Wisbech Museum, and the Morgan Library in New York. Fragments of *The Pickwick Papers* formed part of the collection of the New York Public Library, but as far as Mr Berger was aware, there was no complete manuscript of the book anywhere.

Except, it seemed, in the Caxton Private Lending Library & Book Depository of Glossom, England.

'Is it –?' said Mr Berger. 'I mean, can it –?'

The old gentleman gently removed the volume from Mr Berger's hands and put it back in its place on the shelf.

'Indeed,' said the gentleman.

He was looking at Mr Berger a little more thoughtfully than before, as though his visitor's obvious appreciation for the books had prompted a reassessment of his probable character.

'It's in good company as well,' he said.

He gestured expansively at the rows of shelves. They stretched into the gloom, for the yellow lights had not come on in the farther reaches of the library. There were also doors leading off to the left and right. They were set into the main walls, but Mr Berger had found no doors when he had first examined the building. They could have been bricked up, but he had seen no evidence of that, either.

'Are they all first editions?' he asked.

'First editions, or manuscript copies. First editions are fine for our purposes, though. Manuscripts are merely a bonus.'

'I should like to look, if you don't mind,' said Mr Berger. 'I won't touch any more of them. I'd just like to see them.'

'Later, perhaps,' said the gent. 'You still haven't told me why you're here.'

Mr Berger swallowed. He had not spoken aloud of his encounters since the unfortunate conversation with Inspector Carswell on that first night.

'Well,' he said, 'I saw a woman commit suicide in front of a train, and then some time later I saw her try to do the same thing again, but I stopped her. I thought she might have come in here. In fact, I'm almost certain that she did.'

'That is unusual,' said the gent.

'That's what I thought,' said Mr Berger.

'And do you have any idea of this woman's identity?'

'Not exactly,' said Mr Berger.

'Would you care to speculate?'

'It will seem odd.'

'No doubt.'

'You may think me mad.'

'My dear fellow, we hardly know each other. I wouldn't dare to make such a judgement until we were better acquainted.'

Which seemed fair enough to Mr Berger. He had come this far: he might as well finish the journey.

'It did strike me that she might be Anna Karenina.' At the last minute, Mr Berger hedged his bets. 'Or a ghost, although she did appear remarkably solid for a spirit.'

'She wasn't a ghost,' said the gent.

'No, I didn't really believe so. There was the issue of her obvious substantiality. I suppose you'll tell me now that she wasn't Anna Karenina either.'

The old gent tugged at his moustache again. His face betrayed his thoughts as he carried on an internal debate.

Finally, he said, 'No, in all conscience I could not deny that she is Anna Karenina.'

Mr Berger leaned in closer, and lowered his voice significantly. 'Is she a loony? You know, someone who thinks that she's Anna Karenina?'

'No. You're the one who thinks that she's Anna Karenina, but she *knows* that she's Anna Karenina.'

'What?' said Mr Berger, somewhat thrown by the reply. 'So you mean she is Anna Karenina? But Anna Karenina is simply a character in a book by Tolstoy. She isn't real.'

'But you just told me that she was.'

'No, I told you that the woman I saw seemed real.'

'And that you thought she might be Anna Karenina.'

'Yes, but you see, it's all very well saying that to oneself, or even presenting it as a possibility, but one does so in the hope that a more rational explanation might present itself.'

'But there isn't a more rational explanation, is there?'

'There might be,' said Mr Berger. 'I just can't think of one at present.'

Mr Berger was starting to feel light-headed.

'Would you like a cup of tea?' said the old gent.

'Yes,' said Mr Berger, 'I rather think I would.'

They sat in the gentleman's living-room, drinking tea from china cups and eating some fruitcake that he kept in a tin. A fire had been lit, and a lamp burned in a corner. The walls were decorated with oils and watercolours, all of them very fine and very old. The style of a number of them was familiar to Mr Berger. He wouldn't have liked to swear to it, but he was fairly sure that there was at least one Turner, a Constable, and two Romneys, a portrait and a landscape, among their number.

The old gentleman had introduced himself as Mr Gedeon, and he had been the librarian at the Caxton for more than 40 years. His job, he informed Mr Berger, was 'to maintain and, as required, increase the collection; to perform restorative work on the volumes where necessary; and, of course, to look after the characters.'

It was this last phrase that made Mr Berger choke on his tea.

'The characters?' he said.

'The characters,' confirmed Mr Gedeon.

'What characters?'

'The characters from the novels.'

'You mean: they're alive?'

Mr Berger was beginning to wonder not only about his own sanity but that of Mr Gedeon as well. He felt as though he had wandered into some strange bibliophilic nightmare. He kept hoping that he would wake up at home with a headache to find that he had been inhaling gum from one of his own volumes.

'You saw one of them,' said Mr Gedeon.

'Well, I saw someone,' said Mr Berger. 'I mean, I've seen chaps dressed up as Napoleon at parties, but I didn't go home thinking I'd met Napoleon.'

'We don't have Napoleon,' said Mr Gedeon.

'No?'

'No. Only fictional characters here. It gets a little complicated with Shakespeare, I must admit. That's caused us some problems. The rules aren't hard and fast. If they were, this whole business would run a lot more smoothly. But then, literature isn't a matter of rules, is it? Think how dull it would be if it was, eh?'

Mr Berger peered into his teacup, as though expecting the arrangement of the leaves to reveal the truth of things. When they did not, he put the cup down, clasped his hands, and resigned himself to whatever was to come.

'All right,' he said. 'Tell me about the characters . . .'

It was, said Mr Gedeon, all to do with the public. At some point, certain characters became so familiar to readers – and, indeed, to many non-readers – that they reached a state of existence independent of the page.

'Take Oliver Twist, for example,' said Mr Gedeon. 'More people know of Oliver Twist than have ever read the work to which he gave his name. The same is true for Romeo and Juliet, and Robinson Crusoe, and Don Quixote. Mention their names to the even averagely educated man or woman on the street and, regardless of whether they've ever encountered a word of the texts in question, they'll be able to tell you that Romeo and Juliet were doomed lovers, that Robinson Crusoe was marooned on an island, and Don Quixote was involved in some awkwardness with windmills. Similarly, they'll tell you that Macbeth got above himself, that Ebenezer Scrooge came right in the end, and that D'Artagnan, Athos, Aramis and Porthos were the names of the musketeers.

'Admittedly, there's a limit to the number of those who achieve that kind of familiarity. They end up here as a matter of course. But you'd be surprised by how many people can tell you something of Tristram Shandy, or Tom Jones, or Jay Gatsby. I'm not sure where the point of crossover is, to be perfectly honest. All I know is that, at some point, some characters become sufficiently famous to pop into existence and, when they do so, they materialize in or near the Caxton Private Lending Library & Book Depository. They always have, ever since the original Mr Caxton set up the first depository shortly before his death in 1492. According to the history of the library, he did so when some of Chaucer's pilgrims turned up on his doorstep in 1477.'

'Some of them?' said Mr Berger. 'Not all?'

'Nobody remembers all of them,' said Mr Gedeon. 'Caxton found the Miller, the Reeve, the Knight, the Second Nun, and the Wife of Bath all arguing in his yard. Once he became convinced that they were not actors or lunatics, he realized that he had to find somewhere to keep them. He didn't want to be accused of sorcery or any other such nonsense, and he had his enemies: where there are books, there will always be haters of books alongside the lovers of them.

'So Caxton found a house in the country for them, and this also served as a library for parts of his own collection. He even established a means of continuing to fund the library after he was gone, one that continues to be used to this day. Basically, we mark up what should be marked down, and mark down what should be marked up, and the difference is deposited with the Trust.'

'I'm not sure that I understand,' said Mr Berger.

'It's simple, really. It's all to do with ha'pennnies, and portions of cents, or lire, or whatever the currency may be. If, say, a writer was due to be paid the sum of nine pounds, ten shillings, and sixpence ha'penny in royalties, the ha'penny would be shaved off and given to us. Similarly, if a company owes a publisher seventeen pounds, eight shillings and sevenpence ha'penny, they're charged eightpence instead. This goes on all through the industry, even down to individual books sold. Sometimes we're dealing in only fractions of a penny, but when you take them from all round the world and add them together, it's more than enough to fund the Trust, maintain the library, and house the characters here. It's now so embedded in the system of books and publishing that nobody even notices any more.'

Mr Berger was troubled. He would have had no time for such financial chicanery when it came to the Closed Accounts Register. It did make sense, though.

'And what is the Trust?'

'Oh, the Trust is just a name that's used for convenience. There hasn't been an actual Trust in years, or not one with a board of Trustees. For all intents and purposes, this is the Trust. I am the Trust. When I pass on, the next librarian will be the Trust. There's not much work to it. I rarely even have to sign cheques.'

While the financial support structure for the library was all very fascinating, Mr Berger was more interested in the question of the characters.

'To get back to these characters, they live here?'

'Oh, absolutely. As I explained, they just show up outside when the time is right. Some are obviously a little confused, but it all becomes clear to them in the days that follow, and they start settling in. And around the time that they arrive, so too does a first edition of the relevant work, wrapped in brown paper and tied with string. We put it on a shelf and keep it nice and safe. It's their life story, and it has to be preserved. Their history is fixed in those pages.'

'What happens with series characters?' asked Mr Berger. 'Sherlock Holmes, for example? Er, I'm assuming he's here somewhere.'

'Of course,' said Mr Gedeon. 'We numbered his rooms as 221B, just to make him feel at home. Dr Watson lives next door. In their case, I do believe that the library received an entire collection of first editions of the canonical works.'

'The Conan Doyle books, you mean?'

'Yes. Nothing after Conan Doyle's death in 1930 actually

counts. It's the same for all of the iconic characters here. Once the original creator passes on, then that's the end of their story as far as we, and they, are concerned. Books by other authors who take up the characters don't count. It would all be unmanageable otherwise. Needless to say, they don't show up here until after their creators have died. Until then, they're still open to change.'

'I'm finding all of this extremely difficult to take in,' said Mr Berger.

'Dear fellow,' said Mr Gedeon, leaning over and patting Mr Berger's arm reassuringly, 'don't imagine for a moment that you're the first. I felt exactly the same way the first time that I came here.'

'How did you come here?'

'I met Hamlet at a number 48B bus stop,' said Mr Gedeon. 'He'd been there for some time, poor chap. At least eight buses had passed, and he hadn't taken any of them. It's to be expected, I suppose. It's in his nature.'

'So what did you do?'

'I got talking to him, although he does tend to soliloquize so one has to be patient. Saying it aloud, I suppose it seems nonsensical in retrospect that I wouldn't simply have called the police and told them that a disturbed person who was under the impression he was Hamlet was marooned at the 48B bus stop. But I've always loved Shakespeare, you see, and I found the man at the bus stop quite fascinating. By the time he'd finished speaking, I was convinced. I brought him back here and restored him to the safe care of the librarian of the day. That was old Headley, my predecessor. I had a cup of tea with him, much as we're doing now, and that was the start of it. When Headley retired, I took his place. Simple as that.'

It didn't strike Mr Berger as simple at all. It seemed complicated on a quite cosmic scale.

'Could I—?' Mr Berger began to say, then stopped. It struck him as a most extraordinary thing to ask, and he wasn't sure that he should.

'See them?' said Mr Gedeon. 'By all means! Best bring your coat, though. I find it can get a bit chilly back there.'

Mr Berger did as he was told. He put on his coat and followed Mr Gedeon past the shelves, his eyes taking in the titles as he went. He wanted to touch the books, to take them down and stroke them like cats, but he controlled the urge. After all, if Mr Gedeon was to be believed, he was about to have a far more extraordinary encounter with the world of books.

In the end, it proved to be slightly duller than Mr Berger had expected. Each of the characters had a small but clean suite of rooms, personalized to suit their time periods and dispositions. Mr Gedeon explained that they didn't organize the living areas by authors or periods of history, so there weren't entire wings devoted to Dickens or Shakespeare.

'It just didn't work when it was tried in the past,' said Mr Gedeon. 'Worse, it caused terrible problems, and some awful fights. The characters tend to have a pretty good instinct for these things themselves, and my inclination has always been to let them choose their own space.'

They passed Room 221B where Sherlock Holmes appeared to be in an entirely drug-induced stupor, while in a nearby suite Tom Jones was doing something unspeakable with Fanny Hill. There was a brooding Heathcliff, and a Fagin with rope burns around his neck, but like animals in a zoo, a lot of the characters were simply napping.

'They do that a lot,' said Mr Gedeon. 'I've seen some of them sleep for years, decades even. They don't get hungry as such, although they do like to eat to break the monotony. Force of habit, I suppose. We try to keep them away from wine. That makes them rowdy.'

'But do they realize that they're fictional characters?' said Mr Berger.

'Oh, yes. Some of them take it better than others, but they all learn to accept that their lives have been written by someone else, and their memories are a product of literary invention, even if, as I said earlier, it gets a bit more complicated with historical characters.'

'But you said it was only fictional characters who ended up here,' Mr Berger protested.

'That is the case, as a rule, but it's also true that some historical characters become more real to us in their fictional forms. Take Richard III: much of the public perception of him is a product of Shakespeare's play and Tudor propaganda, so in a sense *that* Richard III *is* a fictional character. *Our* Richard III is aware that he's not actually *the* Richard III but *a* Richard III. On the other hand, as far as the public is concerned he is *the* Richard III, and is more real in their minds than any products of later revisionism. But he's the exception rather than the rule: very few historical characters manage to make that transition. All for the best, really, otherwise this place would be packed to the rafters.'

Mr Berger had wanted to raise the issue of space with the librarian, and this seemed like the opportune moment.

'I did notice that the building seems significantly larger on the inside than on the outside,' he remarked.

'It's funny, that,' said Mr Gedeon. 'Doesn't seem to matter much what the building looks like on the outside: it's as though, when they all move in, they bring their own space with them. I've often wondered why that might be, and I think I've come up with an answer of sorts. It's a natural consequence of the capacity of a bookstore or library to contain entire worlds, whole universes, and all situated between the covers of books. In that sense, every library or bookstore is practically infinite. The Caxton takes that to its logical conclusion.'

They passed a pair of overly ornate and decidedly gloomy rooms, in one of which an ashen-faced man sat reading a book, his unusually long fingernails gently testing the pages. He turned to watch them pass, and his lips drew back to reveal a pair of elongated canines.

'The Count,' said Mr Gedeon, in a worried manner. 'I'd move along if I were you.'

'You mean Stoker's Count?' said Mr Berger. He couldn't help but gawp. The Count's eyes were rimmed with red, and there was an undeniable magnetism to him. Mr Berger found his feet dragging him into the room as the Count set aside his book and prepared to welcome him.

Mr Gedeon's hand grasped his right arm and pulled Mr Berger back into the corridor.

'I told you to move along,' he said. 'You don't want to be spending time with the Count. Very unpredictable, the Count. Says he's over all that vampiric nonsense, but I wouldn't trust him farther than I could throw him.'

'He can't get out, can he?' asked Mr Berger, who was already rethinking his passion for evening walks.

'No, he's one of the special cases. We keep those books behind bars, and that seems to do the trick for the characters as well.'

'But some of the others wander,' said Mr Berger. 'You met Hamlet, and I met Anna Karenina.'

'Yes, but that's really most unusual. For the most part, the characters exist in a kind of stasis. I suspect a lot of them just close their eyes and relive their entire literary lives, over and over. Still, we do have quite a competitive bridge tournament going, and the pantomime at Christmas is always good fun.'

'How do they get out, the ones who ramble off?'

Mr Gedeon shrugged. 'I don't know. I keep the place well locked up, and it's rare that I'm not here. I just took a few days off to visit my brother in Bootle, but I've probably never spent more than a month in total away from the library in all of my years as librarian. Why would I? I've got books to read, and characters to talk to. I've got worlds to explore, all within these walls.'

At last they reached a closed door upon which Mr Gedeon knocked tentatively.

'*Oui?*' said a female voice.

'*Madame, vous avez un visiteur,*' said Mr Gedeon.

'*Bien. Entrez, s'il vous plaît.*'

Mr Gedeon opened the door, and there was the woman whom Mr Berger had watched throw herself beneath the wheels of a train, and whose life he felt that he had subsequently saved, sort of. She was wearing a simple black dress, perhaps even the very one that had so captivated Kitty in the novel, her curly hair in disarray, and a string of pearls hanging around her firm neck. She seemed startled at first to see him, and he knew that she recalled his face.

Mr Berger's French was rusty, but he managed to dredge up a little from memory.

'*Madame, je m'appelle Monsieur Berger, et je suis enchanté de vous rencontrer.*'

'*Non*,' said Anna, after a short pause, '*tout le plaisir est pour moi, Monsieur Berger. Vous vous assiérez, s'il vous plaît.*'

He took a seat, and a polite conversation commenced. Mr Berger explained, in the most delicate terms, that he had been a witness to her earlier encounter with the train, and it had haunted him. Anna appeared most distressed, and apologized profusely for any trouble that she might have caused him, but Mr Berger waved it away as purely minor, and stressed that he was more concerned for her than for himself. Naturally, he said, when he saw her making a second attempt – if attempt was the right word for an act that had been so successful the first time around – he had felt compelled to intervene.

After some initial hesitancy, their conversation grew easier. At some point Mr Gedeon arrived with fresh tea, and some more cake, but they barely noticed him. Mr Berger found much of his French returning, but Anna, having spent so long in the environs of the library, also had a good command of English. They spoke together long into the night, until at last Mr Berger noticed the hour, and apologized for keeping Anna up so late. She replied that she had enjoyed his company, and she slept little anyway. He kissed her hand, and begged leave to return the next day, and she gave her permission willingly.

Mr Berger found his way back to the library without too

much trouble, apart from an attempt by Fagin to steal his wallet, which the old reprobate put down to habit and nothing more. When he reached Mr Gedeon's living quarters, he discovered the librarian dozing in an armchair. He woke him gently, and Mr Gedeon opened the front door to let him out.

'If you wouldn't mind,' said Mr Berger, as he stood on the doorstep, 'I should very much like to return tomorrow to speak with Anna, if that wouldn't be too much of an imposition.'

'It wouldn't be an imposition at all,' said Mr Gedeon. 'Just knock on the glass. I'll be here.'

With that the door was closed, and Mr Berger, feeling both more confused and more elated than he had in all his life, returned to his cottage and slept a deep, dreamless sleep.

12

The next morning, once he had washed and break-fasted, Mr Berger returned to the Caxton Library. He brought with him some fresh pastries that he had bought in the local bakery in order to replenish Mr Gedeon's supplies, and a book of Russian poetry in translation of which he was unusually fond, but which he now desired to present to Anna. Making sure that he was not being observed, he took the lane that led to the library and knocked on the glass. He was briefly concerned that Mr Gedeon might have overnight spirited away the contents of the premises – books, characters, and all – fearful that the discovery by Mr Berger of the library's true nature might bring some trouble upon them, but the old gentleman opened the door to Mr Berger's knock on the glass, and seemed very pleased to see him.

'Will you take some tea?' asked Mr Gedeon, and Mr Berger agreed, even though he had already had tea at breakfast and was anxious to return to Anna. Still, he had questions for Mr Gedeon, particularly pertaining to the lady.

'Why does she do it?' he asked, as he and Mr Gedeon shared an apple scone between them.

'Do what?' said Mr Gedeon. 'Oh, you mean throw herself under trains?'

He picked a crumb from his waistcoat and put it on his plate.

'First of all, I should say that she doesn't make a habit of it,' said Mr Gedeon. 'In all the years that I've been here, she's done it no more than a dozen times. Admittedly, the incidents have been growing more frequent, and I have spoken to her about them in an effort to find some way to help, but she doesn't seem

49

to know herself why she feels compelled to relive her final moments in the book. We have other characters that return to their fates – just about all of our Thomas Hardy characters appear obsessed by them – but she's the only one who re-enacts her end. I can only give you my thoughts on the matter, and I'd say this: she's the titular character, and her life is so tragic, her fate so awful, that it could mean both are imprinted upon the reader, and herself, in a particularly deep and resonant way. It's in the quality of the writing. It's in the book. Books have power. You must understand that now. It's why we keep all of these first editions so carefully. The fate of characters is set for ever in those volumes. There's a link between those editions and the characters that arrived here with them.'

He shifted in his chair, and pursed his lips.

'I'll share something with you, Mr Berger, something that I've never shared with anyone before,' he said. 'Some years ago, we had a leak in the roof. It wasn't a big one, but they don't need to be big, do they? A little water dripping for hours and hours can do a great deal of damage, and it wasn't until I got back from the picture house in Moreham that I saw what had happened. You see, before I left I'd set aside our manuscript copies of *Alice in Wonderland* and *Moby-Dick*.'

'*Moby-Dick*?' said Mr Berger. 'I wasn't aware that there were any extant manuscripts of *Moby-Dick*.'

'It's an unusual one, I'll admit,' said Mr Gedeon. 'Somehow it's all tied up with confusion between the American and British first editions. The American edition, by Harper & Brothers, was set from the manuscript, and the British edition, by Bentley's, was in turn set from the American proofs, and there are some six hundred differences in wording between the two editions. But in 1851, while Melville was working on the British edition based on proofs that he himself had paid to be set and plated before an American publisher had signed an agreement, he was also still writing some of the later parts of the book, and in addition he took the opportunity to rewrite sections that had already been set for America. So which is the edition that the library should store: the American, based on the original manuscript, or the British, based not on the manuscript but on a subsequent rewrite? The decision made by the Trust was to acquire the British edition and, just to be on the safe side, the manuscript. When Captain Ahab arrived at the library, both editions arrived with him.'

'And the manuscript of *Alice in Wonderland*? I understood that to be in the collection of the British Museum.'

'Some sleight of hand there, I believe,' said Mr Gedeon. 'You may recall that the Reverend Dodgson gave the original ninety-page manuscript to Alice Liddell, but she was forced to sell it in order to pay death duties following her husband's demise in 1928. Sotheby's sold it on her behalf, suggesting a reserve of four thousand pounds. It went, of course, for almost four times that amount, to an American bidder. At that point, the Trust stepped in, and a similar manuscript copy was substituted and sent to the United States.'

'So the British Museum now holds a fake?'

'Not a fake, but a later copy, made by Dodgson's hand at the instigation of an agent of the Trust. In those days, the Trust was always thinking ahead, and I've tried to keep up that tradition. I've always got an eye out for a book or character that may be taking off.

'So the Trust was very keen to have Dodgson's original *Alice*: so many iconic characters, you see, and then there were the illustrations too. It's an extremely powerful manuscript.

'But all of this is beside the point. Both of the manuscripts needed a bit of attention – just a careful clean to remove any dust or other media with a little polyester film. Well, I almost cried when I returned to the library. Some of the water from the ceiling had fallen on the manuscripts: just drops, nothing more, but enough to send a little of the ink from *Moby-Dick* on to a page of the *Alice* manuscript.'

'And what happened?' asked Mr Berger.

'For one day, in all extant copies of *Alice in Wonderland*, there was a whale at the Mad Hatter's tea party,' said Mr Gedeon solemnly.

'What? I don't remember that.'

'Nobody does, nobody but I. I worked all day to clean the relevant section, and gradually removed all traces of Melville's ink. *Alice in Wonderland* went back to the way it was before, but for that day every copy of the book, and all critical commentaries on it, noted the presence of a white whale at the tea party.'

'Good grief! So the books can be changed?'

'Only the copies contained in the library's collection, and they in turn affect all others. This is not just a library, Mr Berger: it's the *ur*-library. It has to do with the rarity of the books in its collection and their links to the characters. That's why we're so careful with them. We have to be. No book is really a fixed object. Every reader reads a book differently, and each book works in a different way on the individual reader. But the books here are special. They're the books from which all later copies came. I tell you, Mr Berger, not a day goes by in this place that doesn't bring me one surprise or another, and that's the truth.'

But Mr Berger was no longer listening. He was thinking again of Anna and the awfulness of those final moments as the train approached, of her fear and her pain, and how she seemed doomed to repeat them because of the power of the book that bore her name.

But the contents of the books were not fixed. They were open not only to differing interpretations, but also to actual transformation.

Fates could be altered.

13

Mr Berger did not act instantly. He had never considered himself a duplicitous individual, and he tried to tell himself that his actions in gaining Mr Gedeon's confidence were as much to do with his enjoyment of that gentleman's company, and his fascination with the Caxton, as with any desire he might have harboured to save Anna Karenina from further fatal encounters with locomotives.

There was more than a grain of truth to this. Mr Berger did enjoy spending time with Mr Gedeon, for the librarian was a vast repository of information about the library and the history of his predecessors. Similarly, no bibliophile could fail to be entranced by the library's inventory, and each day among its stacks brought new treasures to light, some of which had been acquired purely for their rarity value rather than because of any particular character link: annotated manuscripts dating back to the birth of the printed word, including poetical works by Donne, Marvell, and Spenser; not one but two copies of the First Folio of Shakespeare's works, one of them belonging to Edward Knight himself, the book-holder of the King's Men and the presumed proofreader of the manuscript sources for the Folio, and containing his handwritten corrections to the errors that had crept into his particular edition, for the Folio was still being proofread during the printing of the book, and there were variances between individual copies; and what Mr Berger suspected might well be notes, in Dickens's own hand, for the later, uncompleted chapters of *The Mystery of Edwin Drood*.

This latter artifact was discovered by Mr Berger in an un-catalogued file that also contained an abandoned version of the final chapters of F. Scott Fitzgerald's *The Great Gatsby*, in which Gatsby, not Daisy, is behind the wheel when Myrtle is killed. Mr Berger had glimpsed Gatsby briefly on his way to visit Anna Karenina. By one of the miracles of the library, Gatsby's quarters appeared to consist of a pool house and a swimming pool, although the pool was made marginally less welcoming by the presence in it of a deflated, bloodstained mattress.

The sight of Gatsby, who was pleasant but haunted, and the discovery of an alternate ending to the book to which Gatsby, like Anna, had lent his name, caused Mr Berger to wonder what might have happened had Fitzgerald published the version held by the Caxton instead of the book that eventually appeared, in which Daisy is driving the car on that fateful night. Would it have altered Gatsby's eventual fate? Probably not, he decided: there would still have been a bloodstained mattress in the swimming pool, but Gatsby's end would have been rendered less tragic, and less noble.

But the fact that he could even think in this way about endings that might have been, confirmed in him the belief that Anna's fate might be recast and so it was that he began to spend more and more time in the section devoted to Tolstoy's works, familiarizing himself with the history of *Anna Karenina*. His researches revealed that even this novel, described as 'flawless' by both Dostoevsky and Nabokov, presented problems when it came to its earliest appearance. While it was originally published in instalments in the *Russian Messenger* periodical from 1873 onward, an editorial dispute over the final part of the story meant that it did not appear in its complete form until the first publication of the work as a book in 1878. The library held both the periodical version and the Russian first edition, but Mr Berger's knowledge of Russian was limited, to put it mildly, and he didn't think that it would be a good idea to go messing around with the book in its original language. He decided that the library's first English language edition, published by Thomas Y. Crowell & Co. of New York in 1886, would probably be sufficient for his needs.

The weeks and months went by, but still he did not act. Not only was he afraid to put in place a plan that involved tinkering with one of the greatest works of literature in any language, but Mr Gedeon was a perpetual presence in the library. He had not yet entrusted Mr Berger with his own key, and still kept a careful eye on his visitor. Meanwhile, Mr Berger noticed that Anna was becoming increasingly agitated, and in the middle of their discussions of books and music, or their occasional games of whist or poker, she would grow suddenly distant and whisper the names of her children or her lover. She was also, he thought, taking an unhealthy interest in certain railway timetables.

Finally, fate presented him with the opportunity he had been seeking. Mr Gedeon's brother in Bootle was taken seriously ill, and his departure from this earth was said to be imminent. Mr Gedeon was forced to leave in a hurry if he was to see his brother again before he passed away and, with only the faintest of hesitations, he entrusted the care of the Caxton Private Lending Library & Book Depository to Mr Berger. He left Mr Berger with the keys, and the number of Mr Gedeon's sister-in-law in Bootle in case of emergencies, then rushed off to catch the last evening train north.

Alone for the first time in the library, Mr Berger opened the suitcase that he had packed upon receiving the summons from Mr Berger. He removed from it a bottle of brandy, and his favourite fountain pen. He poured himself a large snifter of the brandy – larger than was probably advisable, he would later accept – and retrieved the Crowell edition of *Anna Karenina* from its shelf. He laid it on Mr Gedeon's desk and turned to the relevant section. He took a sip of brandy, then another, and another. He was, after all, about to alter one of the treasures of nineteenth century literature, so a stiff drink seemed like a very good idea.

He looked at the glass. It was now almost empty. He refilled it, took a large strengthening swig, and uncapped his pen. He offered a silent prayer of apology to the god of letters, and with three swift dashes of his pen removed a single paragraph.

It was done.

He took another drink. It had all been easier than expected. He let the ink dry on the Crowell edition, and restored it to its shelf. He was, by now, more than a little tipsy. Another title caught his eye as he returned to the desk: *Tess of the d'Urbervilles* by Thomas Hardy, in the first edition by Osgood, McIlvaine and Co., London, 1891.

Mr Berger had always hated the ending of *Tess of the d'Urbervilles*.

Oh well, he thought: in for a penny, in for a pound.

He took the book from the shelf, stuck it under his arm, and was soon happily at work on Chapters LVIII and LIX. He worked all through the night, and by the time he fell asleep the bottle of brandy was empty, and books surrounded him.

In truth, Mr Berger had got a little carried away.

14

In the history of the Caxton Private Lending Library & Book Depository, the brief period that followed Mr Berger's 'improvements' to great novels and plays is known as the 'Confusion', and has come to be regarded as a lesson in why such experiments should generally be avoided.

The first clue Mr Gedeon had that something was amiss was when he passed the Liverpool Playhouse on his way to catch the train, his brother having miraculously recovered to such an extent that he was threatening to sue his physicians, and discovered that the theatre was playing *The Comedy of Macbeth*. He did a quick double take, and immediately sought out the nearest bookshop. There he found a copy of *The Comedy of Macbeth*, along with a critical commentary labelling it 'one of the most troubling of Shakespeare's later plays, due to its curious mixture of violence and inappropriate humour bordering on early bedroom farce.'

'Good Lord,' said Mr Gedeon aloud. 'What has he done? For that matter, what *else* has he done?'

Mr Gedeon thought hard for a time, trying to recall the novels or plays about which Mr Berger had expressed serious reservations. He seemed to recall Mr Berger complaining that the ending of *A Tale of Two Cities* had always made him cry. An examination of a copy of the book in question revealed that it now ended with Sydney Carton being rescued from the guillotine by an airship piloted by the Scarlet Pimpernel, with a footnote advising that this had provided the inspiration for a later series of novels by Baroness Orczy.

'Oh God,' said Mr Gedeon.

Then there was Hardy.

Tess of the d'Urbervilles now closed with Tess's escape from prison, engineered by Angel Clare and a team of demolition experts, while *The Mayor of Casterbridge* had Michael Henchard living in a rose-covered cottage near his newly married stepdaughter, and breeding goldfinches. At the conclusion of *Jude the Obscure*, Jude Fawley escaped the clutches of Arabella and survived his final desperate visit to Sue in the freezing weather, whereupon they both ran away and went to live happily ever after in Eastbourne.

'This is terrible,' said Mr Gedeon, although even he had to admit that he preferred Mr Berger's endings to Thomas Hardy's.

Finally he came to *Anna Karenina*. It took him a little while to find the alteration, because this one was subtler than the others: a deletion instead of an actual piece of bad rewriting. It was still wrong, but Mr Gedeon understood Mr Berger's reason for making the change. Perhaps if Mr Gedeon had experienced similar feelings about one of the characters in his care, he might have found the courage to intervene in a similar way. He had been a witness to the sufferings of so many of them, the consequences of decisions made by heartless authors, the miserable Hardy not least among them, but his first duty was, and always had been, to the books. This would have to be put right, however valid Mr Berger might have believed his actions to be.

Mr Gedeon returned the copy of *Anna Karenina* to its shelf, and made his way to the station.

15

Mr Berger woke to the most terrible hangover. It took him a while even to recall where he was, never mind what he might have done. His mouth was dry, his head was thumping, and his neck and back were aching from having fallen asleep at Mr Gedeon's desk. He made himself some tea and toast, most of which he managed to keep down, and stared in horror at the pile of first editions that he had violated the night before. He had a vague sense that they did not represent the entirety of his efforts, for he dimly recalled returning some to the shelves, singing merrily to himself as he went, although he was damned if he could bring to mind the titles of all the works involved. So ill and appalled was he that he could find no reason to stay awake. Instead he curled up on the couch in the hope that, when he opened his eyes again, the world of literature might somehow have self-corrected, and the intensity of his headache might have lessened. Only one alteration did he not immediately regret, and that was his work on *Anna Karenina*. The actions of his pen in that case had truly been a labour of love.

He rose to sluggish consciousness to find Mr Gedeon standing over him, his face a mixture of anger, disappointment, and not a little pity.

'We need to have words, Mr Berger,' he said. 'Under the circumstances, you might like to freshen up before we begin.'

Mr Berger took himself to the bathroom, and bathed his face and upper body with cold water. He brushed his teeth, combed his hair, and tried to make himself as presentable as possible. He felt a little like a condemned man hoping to make a good impression on the hangman. He returned to the living-room, and smelled strong coffee brewing. Tea, in this case, was unlikely to be sufficient for the task at hand. He took a seat across from Mr Gedeon, who was examining the altered first editions, his fury now entirely undiluted by any other emotions.

'This is vandalism!' he said. 'Do you realize what you've done? Not only have you corrupted the world of literature, and altered the histories of the characters in our care, but you've also damaged the library's collection. How could someone who considers himself a lover of books do such a thing?'

Mr Berger couldn't meet the librarian's gaze.

'I did it for Anna,' he said. 'I just couldn't bear to see her suffer in that way.'

'And the others?' said Mr Gedeon. 'What of Jude, and Tess, and Sydney Carton? Good grief, what of Macbeth?'

'I felt sorry for them too,' said Mr Berger. 'And if their creators knew that, at some future date, they might take on a physical form in this world, replete with the memories and experiences forced upon them, would they not have given some thought to their ultimate fate? To do otherwise would be tantamount to sadism!'

'But that isn't how literature works,' said Mr Gedeon. 'It isn't even how the world works. The books are written. It's not for you or me to start altering them at this stage. These characters have power precisely *because* of what their creators have put them through. By changing the endings, you've put at risk their place in the literary pantheon, and by extension their presence in the world. I wouldn't be surprised if we were to go and inspect the lodgings to find a dozen or more unoccupied rooms, with no trace that their occupants ever existed.'

Mr Berger hadn't thought of that. It made him feel worse than ever.

'I'm sorry,' he said. 'I'm so very, very sorry. Can anything be done?'

Mr Gedeon left his desk and opened a large cupboard in the

corner of the room. From it he removed his box of restorer's equipment: his adhesives and threads, his tapes and weights and rolls of buckram cloth, his needles and brushes and awls. He placed the box on his desk, added a number of small glass bottles of liquid, then rolled up his sleeves, turned on the lamps, and summoned Mr Berger to his side.

'Muriatic acid, citric acid, oxalic acid, and tartaric acid,' he said, tapping each bottle in turn.

He carefully mixed a solution of the last three acids in a bowl, and instructed Mr Berger to apply it to his inked changes to *Tess of the d'Urbervilles*.

'The solution will remove ink stains, but not printer's ink,' said Mr Gedeon. 'Be careful, and take your time. Apply it, leave it for a few minutes, then wipe it off and let it dry. Keep repeating until the ink is gone. Now begin, for we have many hours of work ahead of us.'

They worked through the night, and into the next morning. Exhaustion forced them to sleep for a few hours, but they both returned to the task in the early afternoon. By late in the evening, the worst of the damage had been undone. Mr Berger even remembered the titles of the books that he had returned to the shelves while drunk, although one was forgotten. Mr Berger had set to work on making *Hamlet* a little shorter, but had got no further than Scenes IV and V, from which he had cut a couple of Hamlet's soliloquies. The consequence was that Scene IV began with Hamlet noting that the hour of twelve had struck, and the appearance of his father's ghost. However, halfway through Scene V, and after a couple of fairly swift exchanges, it was already morning. When Mr Berger's excisions were discovered many decades later by one of his successors, it was decided to allow them to stand, as she felt that *Hamlet* was quite long enough as it was.

Together they went to the lodgings and checked on the characters. All were present and correct, although Macbeth appeared in better spirits than before, and remained thus ever after.

Only one book remained unrestored: *Anna Karenina.*

'Must we?' said Mr Berger. 'If you say "yes", then I will accept your decision, but it seems to me that she is different from the rest. None of the others are compelled to do what she does. None of them is so despairing as to seek oblivion over and over. What I did does not fundamentally alter the climax of the novel, but adds only a little ambiguity, and it may be that a little is all she requires.'

Mr Gedeon considered the book. Yes, he was the librarian, and the custodian of the contents of the Caxton Private Lending Library & Book Depository, but he was also the guardian of its characters. He had a duty to them and to the books. Did one supersede the other? He thought of what Mr Berger had said: if Tolstoy had known that, by his literary gifts, he would doom his heroine to be defined by her suicide, might he not have found a way to modify his prose even slightly, and thus give her some peace?

And was it not also true that Tolstoy's ending to the novel was flawed in any case? Rather than give us some extended reflection on Anna's death, he chose instead to concentrate on Levin's return to religion, and Koznyshev's support for the Serbs, and Vronsky's committal to the cause of the Slavs. He even gave the final word on Anna's death to Vronsky's rotten mother: 'Her death was the death of a bad woman, a woman without religion.' Surely Anna deserved a better memorial than that?

Mr Berger had crossed out three simple lines from the end of Chapter XXXI:

The little muzhik *ceased his mumblings, and fell to his knees by the broken body. He whispered a prayer for her soul, but if her fall had been unwitting then she was past all need of prayer, and she was with God now. If it were otherwise, then prayer could do her no good. But still he prayed.*

He read the preceding paragraph:

And the candle by which she had read the book that was filled with fears, with deceptions, with anguish, and with evil, flared up with greater brightness than she had ever known, revealing to her all that before was in darkness, then flickered, grew faint, and went out forever.

You know, thought Mr Gedeon, Chapter XXXI could end just as easily there, and it might mean peace for Anna.

He closed the book, allowing Mr Berger's change to stand.

'Let's leave it, shall we?' he said. 'Why don't you put it back on its shelf?'

Mr Berger took the book reverently, and restored it gently, lovingly to its place in the stacks. He thought about visiting Anna one last time, but it did not seem appropriate to ask Mr Gedeon's permission. He had done all that he could for her, and he hoped only that it was enough. He returned to Mr Gedeon's living-room and placed the key to the Caxton Library on the desk.

'Goodbye,' he said. 'And thank you.'

Mr Gedeon nodded but did not answer, and Mr Berger left the library and did not look back.

16

In the weeks that followed Mr Berger thought often of the Caxton Library, and of Mr Gedeon, and of Anna most of all, but he did not return to the lane, and he consciously avoided walking near that part of the town. He read his books, and resumed his walks to the railway track. Each evening he waited for the last train to pass, and it always did so without incident. Anna, he believed, was troubled no more.

One afternoon, as summer drew to its close, there came a knocking on his door. He answered it to find Mr Gedeon standing on his doorstep, two suitcases by his side, and a taxi waiting for him at the garden gate. Mr Berger was surprised to see him, and invited him to step inside, but Mr Gedeon declined.

'I'm leaving,' he said. 'I'm tired, and I no longer have the energy that I once had. It's time for me to retire, and bequeath the care of the Caxton to another. I suspected as much on that first night, when you followed Anna to the library. The library always finds its new librarian, and leads him to its door. I thought that I might have been mistaken when you altered the books, and I resigned myself to waiting until another came, but slowly I grew to understand that you were the one after all. Your only fault was to love a character too much, which caused you to do the wrong thing for the right reasons, and it may be that we both learned a lesson from that incident. I know that the Caxton and its characters will be safe in your care until the next librarian comes along. I've left a letter for you containing all that you need to know, and a number at which you can contact me should you have any questions, but I think you'll be just fine.'

He held out to Mr Berger a great ring of keys. After only a

moment's hesitation, Mr Berger accepted them, and he saw that Mr Gedeon could not stop himself from shedding a tear as he entrusted the library and its characters to the new custodian.

'I shall miss them terribly, you know,' said Mr Gedeon.

'You should feel free to visit at any time,' said Mr Berger.

'Perhaps I will,' said Mr Gedeon, but he never did.

They shook hands and Mr Gedeon departed, and they did not meet or speak again.

17

The Caxton Private Lending Library & Book Depository is no longer in Glossom. At the beginning of this century the town was discovered by developers, and the land beside the library was earmarked for houses, and a modern shopping mall. Questions started to be asked about the peculiar old building at the end of the lane, and so it was that one evening a vast fleet of anonymous trucks arrived driven by anonymous men, and in the space of a single night the entire contents of the Caxton Private Lending Library & Book Depository – books, characters and all – were spirited away and resettled in a new home in a little village not far from the sea, but far indeed from cities and, indeed, trains. The librarian, now quite old and not a little stooped, liked to walk on the beach in the evenings, accompanied by a small terrier dog and, if the weather was good, by a beautiful, pale woman with long, dark hair.

One night, just as summer was fading into autumn, there came a knock on the door of the Caxton Private Lending Library & Book Depository, and the librarian opened it to find a young woman standing on the doorstep. She had in her hand a copy of *Vanity Fair*.

'Excuse me,' she said, 'I know this may sound a little odd, but I'm absolutely convinced that I just saw a man who looked like Robinson Crusoe collecting seashells on the beach, and I think he returned with them to this' – she looked at the small brass plate to her right – '*library*?'

Mr Berger opened the door wide to admit her.

'Please come in,' he said. 'It may sound equally odd, but I think I've been expecting you . . .'

The Blood of the Lamb

She looked at her husband, who had just placed a mug of tea on the good dining table, the one she'd spent an hour polishing to a high sheen, and him not even bothering to pick up a coaster along the way, and she despaired. Sometimes she wondered if he wasn't going soft in the head.

'Jesus, what are you doing?' she asked.

'What? I'm having a mug of tea. Can't a man have a mug of tea in his own house without asking permission?'

She scuttled past him, picked up the offending item, and placed it on the mantelpiece instead.

'Aren't I only just after cleaning that table? You'll leave a mark on it.'

She squatted before the table, peering along the length of it.

'Ah, look,' she said. 'I can see it. I can see the mark.'

She retrieved her cloth from under the kitchen sink, and went to work again. Her husband put his hands in his trouser pockets. The ironing board still stood in the centre of the room, in front of the television. It reminded him uncomfortably of a funeral bier, the kind that Clancy's undertakers used for the resting of the coffin at a wake. She'd forced him to buy a new shirt, even though his old shirts were perfectly fine, and then insisted on ironing it to get the creases out, no matter that he promised he'd keep his jacket and cardigan on over it, so that even the Lord Himself wouldn't be able to tell whether it was creased or not.

He wasn't sure that he wanted his tea now. It would taste of polish. The whole house smelled of polish and soap and bleach. It hadn't been this clean in years – and his wife was a house-proud woman, so it was no small matter. He was nearly afraid to walk on the floor, even though he was only wearing slippers. In fact, he suspected that he was making his own home look untidy just by being in it.

'It's grand,' he said.

'It isn't grand. Nothing is grand. Nothing.'

She started to cry. He took his hands out of his pockets and patted her awkwardly on the back, as though she'd just had a piece of bread go down the wrong way. He was no good at this kind of thing. He loved his wife dearly, but he wasn't one for hugging and holding hands, and he never knew what to do with her when she cried. It was seldom that she did it, but it was still too often for his liking.

'Come on, now,' he said. 'Come on. There's no need for that.'

And she knew that he was right, but wrong as well. She wasn't crying over the table. It was everything else. Really, she didn't know what to think. They'd be here tomorrow, and she'd never had anyone so important in her house before, never even thought that she would. It was bad enough when Father Delaney came, but these others . . . God, it might as well have been the Pope himself who was coming to call.

She found a tissue somewhere in the folds of her apron, and wiped her eyes and nose with it.

'Look at the place,' she said. 'I'm ashamed to let anyone see it in this state.'

He bristled now. He'd worked hard for this house. He was still working hard for it, and would be for a few years yet. It was no palace, but it was theirs, and he wasn't about to be made to feel embarrassed about it, especially not after his wife had been breaking her back getting it ready for the visitors, her and their daughter both working at it until their hands were raw.

The thought of the girl upstairs was like a punch to the gut.

'Don't say that,' he said. 'They'll never set foot in a cleaner house than this one, nor one more loved either.'

She stood and rubbed at his right arm, feeling the muscles of him, the heat. God, she loved him, fool that he was for loving her.

'You're right,' she said. 'I'm just . . .'

But she didn't have the words for it, and neither did he.

'I know,' he said, and that was enough. But she kept her hand on his arm, drawing strength from him just as he drew it from her, although he'd never have confessed as much to his wife, and she'd have dropped dead on the spot if he did.

'What if they tell us that there's something wrong with her?' she asked. 'What if they take her away?'

'Why would they do that?' he replied. 'And there's nothing wrong with her. She's just different, that's all. Special. Whatever she has is a gift from God.'

'I wish He'd given it to someone else, if it is. I wish He'd left her alone, and let her be a normal girl. Maybe they can get rid of it, the priests. Maybe they can, I don't know, say a prayer, and send it back where it came from.'

'I think that's an exorcism you're talking about, and she doesn't need one of those.'

'Are you sure?'

Now it was his turn to hold her. He took one of her thin arms in each of his meaty hands, hard enough to hurt, if he squeezed.

'Don't you say that,' he told her. 'Do you hear me?'

She nodded dumbly. The tears started again. Jesus, he thought, she's like a waterworks, and here were the two of them taking the Lord's name in vain, her aloud and him in his head, and the men from the Vatican on their way. Not like they'd know it, of course. It wasn't as though they had a radar that told them when someone had been breaking a commandment, although he wouldn't have put it past Father Delaney, who had an eye cold as a crocodile's when he chose, and knew every voice that spoke to him from the dark of the confessional, which was as good a reason as any to avoid it, except at Christmas when it was proper for a man to unburden himself of his sins, even if a wise one made sure to gloss over the worst of them with 'for these and all my other sins I am heartily sorry', leaving Father Delaney with a couple of admissions of lying and swearing and lustful thoughts in order to hold to the spirit of the thing, and keep the priest happy.

He glanced at the clock on the mantelpiece. Just after nine. Their daughter had gone to bed early, telling them that she wanted to get a good night's rest in preparation for the day to come. She didn't seem nervous at all, but she'd been quiet at dinner, and hadn't eaten much. He'd asked her if she was all right and she'd told him that she was, but he thought there was a sadness to her. Still, she was often that way, and had been ever since her gift had first started to manifest itself. Even though he would never have admitted it to either of them, he thought that his wife might well be right, and it would have been better if the Lord had bestowed this particular boon on another, for some gifts were no better than curses.

It had started to rain, a heavy downpour that belaboured the roof with a sound like coins dropping in a tin cup. He was glad that he wasn't out in it. It wasn't weather fit for man or beast.

'Your tea will be going cold,' she said.

'Ah, I don't know why I made it.'

'I was thinking that. You don't usually have tea so late.'

'It was for want of something to do with my hands,' he said.

She put her arms around his waist and drew in the smell of him. Her head only came to his chest, for he had a good foot on her. Despite all that was happening, and all that was to come, she felt the warmth spreading through her. It might be nice, she thought, to lose herself beneath the weight of him, and forget their troubles for a while in the pounding of him.

'I can think of something you can do with them,' she said, and was pleased to see the look of shock on his face.

'Jesus, and the priests on our doorstep!'

'Don't be saying "Jesus",' she scolded.

'You said it not five minutes ago.'

'I did not!'

'You did so.' He smiled at her. 'You're a terrible woman.'

And then they heard the knock at the door.

The three men on the step were already soaked from their walk up the path, their hair – or the hair of those who had it, for one of them was entirely bald and another wouldn't be lording it over him for much longer on that count – plastered to their heads, their black jackets stained darker over the shoulders and back. Two of them were wearing collars. The third, the one with the big red beard, wore an old sweater, and the top button of his black shirt was unbuttoned. He had the hair of a mountain man, and the face and body to match. *Weathered*. A hard man, in his way.

'Mr Lacey?' said the bearded one, and Lacey nodded a yes. He was briefly struck mute, and all he could think was that he'd bought himself a new shirt for no good reason now.

He found his tongue.

'Yes,' he said. 'Are you—?'

But he didn't finish. Of course they were. I mean, who else would they be?

'I'm Father Manus. These are my colleagues, Father Faraldo and Father Oscuro.'

The other two priests nodded greetings at the mention of their names. Faraldo was the oldest of the trio, Oscuro the youngest, with a bald spot spreading over the back of his head that you couldn't have covered with a saucer. Oscuro didn't smile, and he made Lacey uncomfortable. He had the eyes of a man who didn't trust in much, and believed in less. His path to the priesthood must have been difficult, Lacey thought.

'We weren't expecting you until the morning,' said Lacey. 'That's when Father Delaney told us you'd be coming.'

His wife appeared beside him, wringing her hands, her apron hurriedly tossed aside before she came to the door. He could feel the waves of nervousness, and worse, rolling off her. There was a word for it, he knew. He'd read it somewhere. 'Obsequiousness', was that it? Yes, he believed so. He wanted to take her aside for a moment and tell her to calm herself, that these were men, only men.

'Perhaps we can explain ourselves inside?' said Father Manus. Water was dripping from the drain above, pattering on his shoulder. Lacey thought that he'd have to get a ladder and take a look at it, once the rain had stopped and there was light to see.

His wife took charge now, pushing him gently aside with her hip, forcing him to open the door wider.

'Of course,' she said. 'You're very welcome, no matter the time. Come in, please. Can I offer you a cup of tea, or something to eat? You must be exhausted after your long journey.'

They trooped inside, careful first to wipe their feet on the mat. Lacey peered into the darkness, but couldn't see their car. He supposed that it was out there somewhere. Had they driven themselves? He thought the diocese would have sent someone to collect them, given how important they were. Then again, they'd probably flown into Dublin and driven down from there, but that was a long old road, and it was easy to go astray if you didn't know the way. He thought that he had better ask, just in case someone was out there needing a cup of tea in his hand to warm himself, and maybe a sandwich or a biscuit, too.

'Did you drive yourselves, Fathers?' he asked.

'No, a driver picked us up at the airport,' said Father Manus.

'And he'd no trouble finding us?'

'Clearly not.'

His accent was hard to place. There was a bit of Irish in it – Cork, or south Kerry – but all the edges had been knocked from it, and it was more neutral than anything else.

'I'm glad,' said Lacey. 'Does he need anything, your driver?'

'I shouldn't think so. I believe he's capable of looking after himself.'

Lacey took one more look into the night, still straining to pick out their car, then closed the door. His wife was trying to steer the priests into the good room, but Father Manus insisted that he was always more comfortable in a kitchen.

'We lived around the kitchen table when I was young,' he explained. 'I never knew where to sit when we had visitors in the living-room.'

Lacey slipped ahead of them to put away the ironing board, just in case they did decide to move to the living-room at some point, and when he returned his wife already had a kettle boiling, and was putting plates down on the table, and cutting the barmbrack she'd baked earlier that day. The priests took off their jackets, and Lacey hung them in the airing cupboard to dry. They made small talk about their trip from Rome, Manus doing most of the talking, the other two remaining silent except when Faraldo thanked Lacey's wife for the tea, and accepted sugar and milk. His accent was thick, and he smiled all the time. He tucked into his slice of brack with relish, slathering it with butter first.

Oscuro, by contrast, communicated mostly by gesture: shakes and nods, and small movements of his right hand. He picked at his brack in an effort at politeness, but Lacey could see that it wasn't to his taste. He was already establishing a picture of the three priests and how they might operate: Manus the glad-hander, the personable one, but clever with it; Faraldo the quiet, genial one, the repository of knowledge; and Oscuro the sceptic, cold and dispassionate, the closest in spirit to Doubting Thomas, his hand poised to explore the wound in his Saviour's side, heedless of the pain that the action might cause.

'I should call Father Delaney and let him know that you've arrived safely,' said Lacey, but Manus raised a hand to stop him.

'I'd prefer if you didn't just yet,' he said.

'He'll be sore annoyed,' said Lacey.

This was Father Delaney's fiefdom, and he wouldn't take it well if he was left out of anything to do with the visit from the Vatican. Father Delaney didn't suffer fools gladly. He didn't suffer anyone gladly.

'I'll explain my reasons to him in time, just as I'm about to explain them to you. Will you sit with us, please, Mr Lacey?'

Lacey sat. His wife positioned another cup of tea in front of him to replace the mug that was still standing cold on the mantelpiece. At the rate they were going, the whole house would be filled with cups of tea before they were done.

'Your daughter?' asked Manus.

'She was upstairs asleep, though I'm sure she's awake now,' said Mrs Lacey. 'Do you want me to bring her down?'

She was surprised that Angela hadn't appeared yet. She must have heard the commotion of the priests' arrival. Perhaps she was just listening upstairs. Sound carried through the house, and who knew what business Angela had been privy to over the years, either intentionally or accidentally. It was why her parents had learned to make love in silence.

'No,' said Oscuro. 'Perhaps later we might like to see her, just for a minute or two.'

Lacey was shocked to hear the young priest speak so much. His voice was soft, and not unpleasant, but almost as heavily accented as Faraldo's. Lacey didn't know what nationality he might be. Was Oscuro an Italian name, or a Spanish one?

'We came early,' said Manus, 'out of experience.'

'I don't understand,' said Lacey.

Manus sipped his tea. Droplets of it hung in his beard, and although he couldn't have seen them, he wiped them away with his right hand. Experience again, thought Lacey, who had never grown a beard for precisely the reason that he'd have spent his life wondering if there was anything caught in its bristles.

'You must understand that we have to approach all cases such as this one with great care,' said Manus. 'We must be open to miracles, to the hand of God at work, yet at the same time be watchful for deception. I mean to cast no aspersions on your honesty, or that of your daughter, but there have been . . . *incidents* in the past.'

'What kind of incidents?' asked Mrs Lacey, before her husband could pose the same question.

'Unfortunate,' said Oscuro. 'Very bad.'

Manus shifted uncomfortably in his seat. It was clear that he would have preferred it if Oscuro hadn't dived straight in at the deep end, but now the words had been spoken. Unfortunate. Very Bad.

'Go on,' said Lacey. 'We'd be happier if you were open with us from the start.'

Manus gave a little grimace of understanding.

'Last year, we were sent to Padua—' he began.

'In Italy,' said Oscuro.

'I know where Padua is,' said Lacey. Fuck's sake. It came out sounding testier than he'd intended, but he didn't want these three thinking he was an ignorant man. He wasn't about to be patronized in his own home.

'My apologies,' said Oscuro, but he didn't sound as though he meant it.

'Anyway,' said Manus. He cast a meaningful glance at Oscuro, as if to say, For the love of God, can you not show an ounce of common sense? 'We went to Padua because a child there, a little girl, was showing signs of the stigmata.'

'The wounds of Our Lord from the Cross,' said Mrs Lacey, to avoid any confusion, and to show that she, too, was no idiot, for she was also fully aware of the location of Padua, after St Anthony of Padua. She could have given them chapter and verse on St Anthony, having done a series of essays on him while at school, and also because she was forever losing things and promising him a shilling if he found them for her. St Anthony, she thought, must spend his days peering under mattresses and rugs.

'Indeed,' said Manus. 'She had open wounds on her hands and feet. They bled on Sundays, and holy days, and any time the girl received Communion. They were also said to produce a pleasant, perfumed smell – the Odour of Sanctity, as it's sometimes called. Word reached us, and we came to investigate.'

'We had our suspicions from the start, though,' said Oscuro. 'Because of the nature of the wounds.'

Lacey looked puzzled. 'In what way?'

'The wounds appeared on the palms of her hands, and the tops and soles of her feet,' said Manus, 'just as they do in most depictions of the Crucifixion. But the nails in a Roman crucifixion were driven in through the wrists, because the palms of the hands couldn't support the weight of the body, and might be pulled free if the nails were hammered through their soft flesh. In the same way, the legs would probably not have hung down in the way we see on the crucifix. They'd have been pulled up and sideways, like this' – he demonstrated awkwardly, assuming a position in his chair that was close to kneeling – 'with the nails driven in closer to the ankle.'

'So why was she bleeding from her palms?' asked Lacey.

'Because her parents' knowledge of crucifixion came from what they had seen in church, and in the illustrated Bible they kept in their home, so they cut their daughter in those places?'

'They *cut* her?' said Mrs Lacey. 'Her own mother and father?'

'With a blade,' said Oscuro, 'then used a screwdriver to widen the injuries. But it was the mother who did it.'

'The girl was a deaf-mute,' said Manus. 'She could not talk of what was taking place, and she lived in fear of her mother. Her father was a weak man. He turned a blind eye to what was happening.'

'And the smell from her wounds?' asked Lacey.

'Cheap perfume poured into them,' said Manus. 'The pain must have been terrible.'

'But why do such a thing?' asked Mrs Lacey.

'They were poor, and people brought them offerings of food and money in the hope of securing their daughter's intercession in matters of health, marriage, wealth,' said Manus. 'Mostly, though, her mother wanted to be important, to be noticed, and her daughter's stigmata gave her a position of authority in the town.'

Lacey and his wife exchanged a look. Both of them had rarely been forced to raise a hand to Angela, because that was just the kind of girl she was, and they always regretted it afterwards when they did. They couldn't even conceive of torturing their own flesh and blood.

'We arrived in Padua a day before we were expected,' said Oscuro, 'and prevented the parents from gaining access to their daughter, so that we could speak to her without interference. Father Faraldo examined the wounds, and saw that they were infected. In cases of true stigmata, the wounds show no such septicity. He also detected signs of the introduction of a foreign object into the girl's flesh. Finally, we brought a woman from Vigonza who knew sign language, and through her we were able to establish the truth, and expose the imposture. Now the mother has been instructed never to hurt her child again on pain of arrest and imprisonment.'

'The poor girl,' said Mrs Lacey. 'I hope you don't think we'd ever do such a thing to our daughter.'

'I don't believe for a moment that you would,' said Father Manus.

Lacey wondered how true that was, and if Manus had said precisely the same words to the parents of the girl in Padua, all the while looking at them and thinking, Yes, I know just what you're capable of doing. Lacey glanced at Oscuro. Now there was a man who saw the worst in everyone. The problem with his kind was that they caused badness to manifest itself, as though their distaste for the failings of others fanned them into flame.

'And Angela, from what we hear, has shown no trace of stigmata,' said Manus. 'It is statues that bleed when she is near, is that not correct?'

They were drawing close to it now. Mrs Lacey turned to her husband, giving her consent for him to speak on their behalf. He did so, leaving nothing out, describing how, when Angela had turned twelve, the statue of the Holy Virgin in Saint Bernadette's had begun to weep from the eyes when Angela passed it after taking Communion. At first, there was talk of it being a prank, but the statue was examined and no trace of interference could be found. It wasn't even clear who might be causing the phenomenon, and it was only when Father Delaney took it upon himself to sit close to the statue, and allowed his curate to give out Communion alone while he kept an eye on all who walked by, that he detected the link to Angela.

And then, on the occasion of her Confirmation, Christ on the cross above the altar bled from His wounds, and blood and water gushed from the hole in His side, drenching the wall. The stain was still there, and nothing could remove it. Not that Father Delaney had tried very hard: he might have been a difficult man, but he had faith, and any doubts he originally entertained about Angela had long been cast aside. That was why the three priests from the Vatican were sitting in the kitchen.

It was in the days after the bleeding of Christ that people began to come to Angela, asking for her blessing and pleading with her to pray on their behalf. Lacey and his wife had tried to discourage them, but her daughter instructed her parents to let the people come, and had spoken with such authority and conviction that they were unable to refuse.

In the beginning, the miracles – if miracles they were – seemed minor: an ache relieved here, a sickly child improved there. But then Irene Kelly had brought her youngest daughter, Kathleen, the one who'd been diagnosed with cancer and whose hair was now entirely gone, her eyes sunk into her head and a smell coming off her like meat that had gone on the turn in the sun. Angela had touched Kathleen, placing the index finger of her right hand on the girl's tongue, and immediately after had announced that she was feeling unwell, and couldn't see anyone else that day. Angela went to bed, and in the middle of the night her parents heard her vomiting in the bathroom. When they went to see what was the matter they discovered her lying on the floor, the tiles covered with bile and blood, and pieces of what looked like rotten, blackened flesh that stank of decay.

Her father carried her back to bed, and they called Dr French, but by the time he arrived Angela was sleeping soundly, and her skin was cool and dry to the touch. He examined her, but could find nothing wrong. They showed Dr French what they'd found on the bathroom floor, and he put some of it in a jar and sent it off to Dublin to be tested, but by the time the results came back everyone in the village knew what it was: Kathleen Kelly's cancer, drawn from her body by Angela Lacey and then later vomited out onto clean tiles. Kathleen Kelly began to recover that very night, and now the doctors could find no trace of the disease that had been eating away at her internal organs. The child was still weak, but her hair had started to grow back, and that awful smell was entirely gone.

There had been other cures since then, but none as dramatic as Kathleen's. People continued to come to the door to ask for Angela's help. Some even waited for her at the school gates, or congregated outside the church doors after Mass on Sunday, and she never declined to touch them, or pray for them. But in recent weeks Father Delaney had made it clear that Angela was to be left in peace for a while, and rumours began to circulate about the arrival of priests from the Vatican who would talk with Angela and try to discover the nature of her gift. Father Delaney had asked her about it, of course, but she could give him no explanation. She had experienced no visions, seen no flickering images of Our Lady at night. No voices spoke to her from the dark, and she was untroubled by angels.

Or so she said.

Now here were the priests, drinking tea, eating brack, and each in his own way considering what he was being told. Faraldo was tugging at his chin, from which a few wisps of beard hung like pale, trailing ivy on old stone, yet his smile remained in place, and his eyes were placid. But Oscuro looked troubled, and even Manus had lost something of his joviality.

'Has your daughter been threatened by anyone?' asked Manus.

'What?' said Lacey. 'Why would anyone threaten her?'

'People can act strangely when confronted with something that they don't understand,' said Manus. 'Fanaticism takes many forms.'

'Not in this village,' said Lacey. 'No one would ever wish any harm on Angela. God, I think some of them would be willing to lay down their lives to protect her, especially after what she did for Kathleen Kelly.'

'If what you tell us is true,' said Oscuro, 'her fame is already spreading. It will attract others: the desperate, the lost. There will be some who might hurt her without meaning to, and others who will arrive with only that intention in mind.'

'Oh Lord,' said Lacey's wife. Clearly this was a possibility that she had never considered. She put her right hand to her mouth, and her husband held her left, rubbing it gently.

'Zacatecas,' said Oscuro, and the word appeared to cause him pain.

'Yes, Zacatecas,' said Manus.

'What is that?' asked Lacey.

'A city in Mexico,' said Oscuro. 'A child, José Antonio, emerged from one of its suburbs.'

'Enough,' said Manus.

'No,' said Lacey, 'let him speak. I told you already. We have a right to know these things, if they may affect Angela.'

Oscuro looked to Manus for permission to go on, and it was granted with a tired wave of a hand.

'José Antonio was said to have gifts not unlike those now being associated with your daughter,' said Oscuro. 'He healed the sick, and caused water to flow from under stones in barren desert. He had the stigmata too, but only on his wrists. The local bishop requested the assistance of the Vatican to corroborate what were already being described as miracles, but Mexico is a long and arduous trip, and it was almost a year before a Curia team could be dispatched. When the investigators arrived, the boy was gone, and nobody could say where he was. He was an only child who lived with his father, but their home was now uninhabited, even though many of the family's possessions remained in place. The local police were of no help, and the parish priest confessed himself baffled by their disappearance.

'On the evening before the investigators were due to return to Rome, there came a knock on the door of the small inn at which they were staying. An old peasant stood before them – a vagabond, an outcast. He was covered in dust, and tired and filthy from the road. He said that he had walked many miles to find them, and claimed to know the fate of the boy and his father. The next morning, just after dawn, the investigators had their driver take them into the desert, with the peasant guiding them. He led them first to a cairn of stones, beneath which he said were the remains of the boy's father. The driver dug, and sure enough, bones were exposed, but the investigators could not have said how long they had been down there, or whose bones they might have been.

'Then the peasant guided them up a rocky incline to a cave. They had to crouch to enter, and had the peasant not instructed them to bring torches, then they would have been entirely blind, for no light entered the space beyond the first few feet.

'And there they found José Antonio. He had been mummified and placed in an alcove surrounded by fetishes: statues, carvings, jewellery, even alcohol and cigarettes. The peasant showed them the hole in his skull where it had been fractured by a heavy blow.'

'He was murdered?' said Lacey.

'Yes.'

'But who would do that to a child?'

'His own people,' said Manus. 'Or that's what we think. Maybe his gifts were so frightening to them that they felt they had to kill him, or were so great that it was believed he should be returned to God. Either way, he died, and that was the end of it.

So perhaps now you understand why we arrived in secret and at night, and why care must be taken when it comes to Angela. We live in troubled times, and even the innocent are not immune from threat.'

Then Manus leaned across the table and gripped Lacey and his wife each by a shoulder, his big hands heavy upon them.

'I'm sorry,' he said. 'This conversation has taken a dark turn. All may be well, though, and you should pray that it will be so. It's time that we were on our way, and let you go to your bed. Tomorrow may bring illumination. But before we go, Father Faraldo and I would like to speak with Angela.'

'She's in her room,' said Mrs Lacey. 'I'd say she's awake. I'm surprised that she hasn't made an appearance already, to be honest with you. I'll go and call her.'

'I'd prefer if we went up to see her,' said Manus. 'It would be good to meet her first in her own environment. Such things, we've come to realize, are important.'

Mrs Lacey stood. 'I'll make sure that she's decent and let her know that you're on your way.'

Manus thanked her and she left. The four men remained at the table and did not speak until Mrs Lacey returned.

'Angela's awake,' she said. 'You can go up and see her now.'

If Manus and the others had been expecting a girl out of the ordinary, they were destined to be disappointed. Angela Lacey was tall for thirteen, and bordering on pretty, but was otherwise unexceptional. Her bedroom betrayed nothing of the gifts that they had come to investigate, apart from a small, luminous statue of the Blessed Virgin on the windowsill. The room was small and furnished with a single bed, a bedside cabinet, a wardrobe and matching chest of drawers, and a small desk beneath the window. The walls were brightly painted in shades of yellow and blue, and decorated with posters of bands and pop stars that only Manus could name, for the other two had no interest in such matters: ABBA was well represented, and he saw one of the detective fellows off the television – David Soul, that was him.

Angela was sitting up in bed, wearing a dressing gown over her nightclothes. She looked curiously at the two priests who crowded into her room with her parents, but said nothing.

Father Manus introduced himself and his colleague, then asked Angela's parents for permission to speak alone with their daughter for a few minutes. He assured the Laceys that they would not be long, and would leave the door open just in case they might have any concerns. But those were more innocent times, and the Laceys did not give a second thought to the presence of two clerics in their daughter's room, especially as the more forbidding Oscuro would not be joining them. He remained in the kitchen, and the Laceys went back down to join him.

Father Faraldo took the small chair beside Angela's desk, while Manus remained standing.

'I knew you were coming,' said Angela. They were the first words she had spoken since the priests entered her room.

'Well, it was no secret,' said Manus.

'No, I knew you were coming *tonight*. I sensed it.'

Manus glanced at Faraldo, who merely nodded and smiled as though this, too, he had anticipated. He was counting the beads on his rosary, feeding them through his thumb and index finger like a man shelling peas.

'Your parents have told us a lot about you,' said Manus. 'It sounds like you're a very special young woman. You wouldn't be fooling people now, would you, or playing tricks?'

'I ate Kathleen Kelly's cancer,' said Angela. 'It tasted like old liver. I took the ulcers from Tommy Spance's stomach, and turned them into pips that I spat into the toilet. They were no tricks.'

'Then children like you are rare,' said Manus. 'Very rare.'

Angela regarded him with eyes that were more knowing than any teenager's eyes should be.

'It won't make any difference, you know,' she said.

'What won't?'

'What you're going to do. You think you can stop it, but you can't.'

'You're just a child, Angela. You have no idea what we can and cannot do. Aren't you afraid?'

'No,' said Angela, as Faraldo rose from his chair, the beads shining like dark eyes in the lamplight. 'I'm not afraid.'

Manus and Faraldo came down the stairs and returned to the kitchen. Manus looked grimmer than before, and Faraldo's smile had faded. They asked for more tea, and for the next half hour they detailed to the Laceys the likely course of their investigation. This would probably be the first visit of many. There would be more doctors who would examine those who claimed to have been cured by Angela. Panels of clerics and theologians would be assembled. It might even be the case that Angela would be required to travel to Rome, he said, and when Mrs Lacey replied that they couldn't afford to go to Rome, something of Manus's old spirit returned, and he grinned and told her the Vatican would pay for it all, and they would be well looked after.

'Do you think we might meet the Pope?' she asked.

'We'll arrange for you to be part of a general audience,' Manus replied, 'and we can take it from there.'

Mrs Lacey glowed.

It was shortly after eleven when the priests finally left. The rain had eased off a little, and a car was waiting for them at the end of the lane: a black Mercedes, with a man in a suit sitting behind the wheel. Lacey offered them the use of a couple of umbrellas to keep them dry until they got to the car, but Manus politely declined.

'It's only a few yards,' he said. 'We won't melt. We'll see you in the morning, and thank you again for your hospitality.'

The Laceys watched them get into the car and drive away. Mrs Lacey went to check on her daughter, but Angela was already asleep, so she said a quiet prayer for her and followed her husband to their bed.

Dawn came, bringing with it clear blue skies, although the morning was cold, and a dampness hung in the air. Lacey woke first, and washed and shaved. He dressed in his new shirt, knotted a tie, and slipped into a cardigan to keep out the chill. He put the kettle on to boil as he heard his wife moving around upstairs. They had slept later than normal, so it was already after eight when he began laying the table for breakfast. He'd bought some fresh bacon, and thought that he might fry some eggs with it. They usually only had a fry on Saturdays, but this was likely to be a long, busy old day, and he thought Angela might appreciate a little treat. He'd just put the bacon in the pan when he heard the knock at the door. He removed the pan from the gas ring and went to see who was there. He hoped that it wasn't the three priests back already, maybe with Father Delaney in tow. He didn't have enough bacon and eggs for all of them, and he was looking forward to his breakfast.

He opened the door, and the tubby form of Father Delaney looked up at him from the porch step. Behind him stood two unfamiliar middle-aged men wearing black suits and clerical collars, each carrying a leather briefcase.

'Francis,' said Father Delaney, 'I hope we're not too early. This is Father Evans and Father Grimaldi. They're the priests from the Vatican.'

Upstairs, Lacey's wife began to scream.

A Dream of Winter

When I was a boy, I attended a school that stood by a cemetery. Mine was the last desk, the one closest to the graveyard. I spent years with my back to the darkness of it. I can remember how, as autumn neared its end and winter gathered its strength, I would feel the wind begin to blow through the window frame and think that the chill of it was like the breath of the dead upon my neck.

One day, in the bleakness of January, when the light was already fading as the clock struck four, I glanced over my shoulder and saw a man staring back at me. Nobody else noticed him, only I. His skin was the grey of old ash long from the fire, and his eyes were as black as the ink in my well. His gums had receded from his teeth, giving him a lean, hungry aspect. His face was a mask of longing.

I was not frightened. It seems strange to say that, but it is the truth. I knew that he was dead, and the dead have no hold over us beyond whatever we ourselves surrender to them. His fingers touched the glass but left no trace, and then he was gone.

Years passed, but I never forgot him. I fell in love, and married. I became a father. I buried my parents. I grew old, and the face of the man at the school window became more familiar to me, and it seemed that I glimpsed him in every glass. Finally, I slept, and when I awoke I was no longer as I once had been.

There is a school that stands by a cemetery. In winter, under cover of fading light, I walk to its windows and put my fingers to the glass.

And sometimes, a boy looks back.

The Lamia

The worst part of the aftermath was that she kept seeing him: when she walked down the street; when she went to buy a newspaper, or milk; when she managed to work up the courage to leave the house for any length of time – to read in a café, to catch a movie, even simply to take a stroll in the park before the sun set, because she no longer liked being out after dark. She began to believe that she might be going mad. Surely he couldn't be in all those places, not unless he was actively stalking her, but in her calmer moments she understood that this was a small city, and it was just bad luck that the person one most despised in the world, the man whom one least wished to see, should be he whose path seemed destined to repeatedly cross one's own.

The trial had come close to breaking her, leaving her almost as bruised and humiliated as the original assault. Oh, the police had been kind to her, and the prosecution barrister had gone over all of it with her in advance – how she wanted to see him behind bars just as much as Carolyn did (although that couldn't have been true, not unless he'd raped the barrister as well), how she would do all in her power to ensure that this was the ultimate outcome, but, you know . . .

And Carolyn did know, because after it happened – after he'd watched her dress, her tights laddered, her panties ripped, while he smoked a cigarette and asked if they could see each other again, I mean, Jesus Christ – she'd done the worst thing possible: she'd gone home and taken a shower, because more than anything else she wanted to rid herself of every trace of him, to scour him from her, inside and out. She'd still been a little drunk too, but not so much that she didn't realize what had just happened to her. She'd told him 'No' over and over again, and fought him as best she could, but he was bigger and stronger than she was, and treated it like it was some kind of game, smiling all the while, whispering that he liked a girl with a bit of fight in her.

It was so strange, at least to her, but it was clear that he didn't think he'd done anything wrong, or perhaps he'd simply convinced himself this was the case in order to live with his actions. She couldn't believe that, though. She'd seen it in his eyes all through the trial, and heard it in his testimony: he felt himself to have been truly wronged. He used the word 'consensual' over and over, spinning to the jury a version of what had occurred that had credibility because he imbued it with his own credence. In the end, it came down to his word against hers, and the jury chose to believe him. That was how Carolyn saw it, even if the barrister tried to convince her otherwise as Carolyn wept in an anteroom after the verdict, a soft voice explaining that it was a matter of reasonable doubt, and there simply hadn't been enough evidence to convict.

Now Carolyn was drifting through the wreckage of her life, tossed on grey seas, prey to tides of anger and depression. She was on leave of absence from work, assured that her job would be waiting for her when she decided she was ready to return, but the office was growing impatient, and she was being gently pressured either to come back or accept a pay-off. The latter would be the end of her, she thought, because she still retained the hope that she'd be able to resume her previous existence. The weekly therapy sessions helped maintain what was rapidly coming to seem like a fiction, but only for a day or two, and then she'd begin to drift again. Her parents were dead, so she couldn't turn to them for support, and her only sister lived in Australia. They spoke regularly over Skype, but it wasn't the same, and so Carolyn's isolation grew.

He, on the other hand, remained unaffected by it all. He'd

been cleared in court, although some residual taint from the trial still adhered, but he'd kept his job, and she'd heard that he now had a girlfriend, too. She wondered if the girl knew about the trial. Probably not or, if he had been forced to disclose it, he'd surely have presented himself as the victim, falsely accused of a terrible crime by an unhinged woman, because that was the kind of bastard he was. Sometimes Carolyn thought about calling his girlfriend and telling her the truth. Carolyn knew her name, and where she worked.

God, she hated him. She hated him so much.

The card arrived on the first day of November. It was made of expensive stock, and came in a matching envelope with rough edges, the kind of stationery that cost more than a book. The note was handwritten. It read:

I can help you

Below it, written in the same clear hand, was an address in the south of the city. No contact number, no e-mail: only the address.

Carolyn stared at the card for a moment before tearing it up and throwing it in the bin. She'd had her share of weird post since the trial. Her identity was supposed to be secret, but sometimes she thought that every dog in the street must have been barking her name. She'd received printed quotations from the Bible, most of them alluding to the immorality of pre-marital sex, and implicitly suggesting that she'd got what she deserved. Those, at least, were marginally better than the ones that *explicitly* stated she'd got what she deserved, and added words like 'whore' and 'slut' just in case the message wasn't getting through. A few letters of support found their way to her as well, often from women who'd been through what she had, offering to meet her for a coffee and a chat, if she thought it might help, but those she put in the bin along with all the rest. She didn't think about the expensive card again, not even when she poured another half-eaten meal over it later that evening before taking a sleeping pill and embracing oblivion.

One week later, a second note, identical to the first, arrived in the post. That, too, went into the bin, although only after a slightly longer period of hesitation.

When the third appeared on her mat, she did not destroy it.

The house was part of a pretty row built at the end of the nineteenth century, all well maintained and with new, or relatively new, cars parked outside. The houses had no front gardens, just narrow stone terraces that most of the residents had brightened with planters or ornamental trees, all except whoever lived at number 65, before which Carolyn now stood, taking in the clean windows behind which the curtains were drawn, and the red front door with the paint that had just begun to peel.

She opened the gate, walked up the short path and rang the doorbell. She heard no sound inside and wondered if the bell might be broken, but within seconds the door was opened by a tall, sickly woman with prematurely white hair and a face that appeared to be composed of skin without any flesh for support. It clung so tightly to the shape of her skull that Carolyn could see the whiteness of the bone beneath, as though her sharp cheekbones might at any moment erupt bloodlessly through their covering. Her eyes were grey-blue, and protruded from their sockets like pale bubbles about to burst.

Carolyn wasn't sure what to say. She produced the card, and began to introduce herself, but the woman simply stepped back and gestured with her left hand, inviting Carolyn to enter. The hallway beyond was dark, lit only by a lamp with a thick yellow shade that absorbed more light than it dispersed. The red and white wallpaper was the kind of flock found in old bars, and the patterned carpet was so thick that it swallowed the soles of

Carolyn's shoes. Somewhere a clock ticked, but otherwise all was silent.

Carolyn stepped inside, and the door closed behind her.

Only then did she become aware of the smell.

It was later, once she had returned home, put her clothes in the wash, and showered to get the stink from her skin and hair, that she managed to place the odour. She recalled visiting the zoo with her parents, and the peculiar stench of the reptile house with its lizards and snakes, and the alligators that lay as still as stones in their ponds. That was the smell that pervaded number 65, but she had no time to think about it while she was there, for the thin woman led her to a back room of the house dominated by a big bed, the adjustable kind found in hospitals. Beside it, in a wheelchair, sat another, younger woman, her legs covered by a tartan rug. The room was very warm, and Carolyn began to sweat.

The woman in the chair wasn't beautiful, but she was striking. Her hair was long and dark, and streaked with silver on one side. Her eyes were green, and her skin almost as white as that of her companion, but touched with spots of red at either cheek. Only her mouth detracted from her looks, for it was very wide, and the lips were so narrow as to be barely visible.

'Hello, Carolyn,' she said. 'My name is Amelia. The lady behind you is my nurse, Miss Bronston. We were hoping you'd come. Please, take off your coat and make yourself more comfortable. I'm sorry about the heat. I feel the cold terribly. May we offer you tea, or something else?'

Carolyn consented to some iced water. She thought that it might help her to cope with the temperature. The room really was stifling. Miss Bronston poured a glass of water from a jug in a corner. Carolyn sipped it and felt a little better. She cupped her hands so that her wrists rested against the glass. She'd read somewhere that it helped to cool the body.

'I'm not sure why I'm here,' said Carolyn.

'You're here because you received the note.'

'Yes, but I don't know what it means.'

'It means what it says. I can help you.'

'With what?'

'With your problem. With David Reese. Please, sit.'

Behind Carolyn, Miss Bronston pushed an upright chair into position. Once Carolyn was seated, Miss Bronston turned and left the room, pulling the door closed behind her.

'How do you know about him?' asked Carolyn.

'I followed the case in the media.'

She waved a lazy hand at a pile of newspapers on the floor to her right. Beside her, on a small table, lay a folder of cuttings. Carolyn recognized the one on the top, which dealt with her rapist's acquittal. Weeks had passed before she'd been able to read it herself.

'I monitor a lot of such incidents,' said Amelia. Her voice was so soft that Carolyn had to lean forward to catch every word. It was like listening to a message formed by the hiss of escaping gas. 'It wasn't hard to find out his name, and yours. I'm sure I'm not the first person to have contacted you about it. People are resourceful, particularly when driven by the desire to torment another.'

She caught Carolyn's look of surprise.

'Don't worry, I haven't been reading your post,' Amelia assured her. 'But there is a pattern to these events, and I'm not the only one with an interest in cases like yours. There are men – and women, too, I regret to say – who take a great deal of pleasure in taunting the victims of sex crimes. If I could, I would wipe them from the earth, each and every one of them.'

The tone of her voice changed, and Carolyn heard the rage in it. In that moment, she wondered if this woman had once suffered just as she had, but Carolyn didn't care. It had been a mistake to come here. Amelia just wanted company, someone with whom to share her misery, but Carolyn's pain was her own. She wasn't inclined to mix it with another's.

'Your note promised that you could help me,' said Carolyn. 'How: by talking? I already have a therapist. She doesn't help much, but I don't need another, paid or unpaid.'

Carolyn stood, and placed the now empty glass by the jug.

'Thank you for the water,' she said, 'but I think I should leave.'

'Sit down,' said Amelia. Her eyes held Carolyn, and it was almost as though she had risen from her chair and physically restrained her visitor.

And Carolyn sat.

'How angry are you?' asked Amelia.

'With David Reese?'

'Who else?'

'Very.'

'That's not good enough. I need more. How much do you hate David Reese?'

'More than I've ever hated anyone in my life. I wake up hating him, and I go to bed hating him. He took everything from me, but his life goes on. He's happy. He has a good job. He has a girlfriend. It's as though what he did to me never happened. He raped me, and he got away with it.'

'Do you want to see him punished?'

'Yes, more than anything.'

'Then we can punish him. You only have to say the word.'

'Punish him how?'

'What does it matter? You hate him, and want to see him suffer. That can be arranged.'

'Are you talking about hurting him, or—?'

Carolyn didn't finish the question. She'd spent enough time dealing with police and barristers, and sitting in a courtroom, to have learned caution.

'Let's just say that we don't deal in half measures,' said Amelia, 'and he will never again do to another woman what he did to you.'

Could Amelia be serious? Now that the possibility of retribution had been raised, Carolyn shied away from it.

'I don't know,' she said.

'Of course you don't,' said Amelia. 'But this is not an open-ended offer. The world has no shortage of men like David Reese, or women who've suffered at their hands. If you don't accept our offer, someone else will.'

'Are you serious?'

'Yes. Serious as death.'

Carolyn's head was swimming. If anything, the room seemed to be growing warmer, and that smell . . .

'I really would like to go now,' she said, and she felt that she was asking permission.

'Then go,' said Amelia. 'Nobody is stopping you.'

Carolyn got to her feet again. She swayed, but managed to keep her balance. The door opened behind her and Miss Bronston entered to show her out. Carolyn wondered if she'd been listening at the keyhole.

'A lot of thoughts will go through your head over the coming days,' said Amelia. 'Among them may be an urge to talk to a lawyer, or even the police. I would advise against it. If you decline our offer, then we ask only that you enable another to accept, should the situation arise, and we wouldn't like to be forced to protect ourselves. Anyway, who would believe you? They didn't believe that you'd been raped, did they? Why should they give credence to anything else you might tell them?'

Amelia smiled, and her mouth grew thinner yet.

'Go, Carolyn, and consider what we've discussed.'

Amelia turned her face to the light streaming through the window behind her, basking in its warmth, and a pale tongue popped from her mouth and licked at her cracked, dry lips.

Carolyn drove home, and the farther she got from Amelia, and Miss Bronston, and number 65, the more absurd it all began to seem until, by the time she had showered, and poured herself a glass of wine, the whole encounter had taken on the complexion of a dream. She tried to watch some television, but found herself unable to concentrate on the screen. Eventually she gave up and went to bed. She poured herself some water so that she could take her sleeping pill, and the coldness of the glass against her skin brought her back to that warm bedroom. She looked at the small white object in her hand, and for the first time in months she set this crutch aside.

That night, she dreamt that David Reese was raping her again. When she woke, the sleeping pill was in her hand and on its way to her mouth almost before she realized what she was doing. It took all of her will not to drop it on her tongue and swallow. Again, she laid it on her bedside table, but she did not go back to sleep. She was too frightened of what might be waiting for her in her dreams.

The next day passed in an awful blur of tiredness and nerves. She did not leave the house, did not even shower and dress, and the memory of David Reese, and the pain of what he had done, returned more strongly than ever. That night, she held the bottle of pills in her hand as she lay in bed, and she knew that she would either take none, or all. She sometimes dozed, but she did not sleep long, and her body jerked her into wakefulness as soon as she began to dream.

The next morning she showered, dressed, made some toast and coffee, then returned to number 65. Miss Bronston opened the door before Carolyn even had a chance to ring the bell, and Amelia was waiting for her in her chair, wearing the same clothes, the same blanket over her legs, and the same smile.

'Yes,' said Carolyn. 'Do it.'

This was how it would unfold. Carolyn was to contact Reese – she could decide for herself how best to make the initial approach: by phone from a public call box would be best, Amelia said, and she should avoid e-mail because it left a trail – and admit that she had been wrong to pursue the case against him.

Immediately Carolyn baulked, even though Amelia had only just begun to speak.

'Admit *what*?' said Carolyn. 'I can't do that. I can't give him that satisfaction.'

'There will be worse to come before all this is over,' said Amelia. 'Not only will you apologize for dragging him into court, but you'll tell him that you enjoyed what he did to you, and your shame at these feelings caused you to make your accusations against him. You'll ask him to come back to your apartment with you. You'll ask him for more of the same.'

'No,' said Carolyn. Her stomach turned at the thought, and she felt that she might be sick. Speaking to Reese would be bad enough, but she wasn't sure that she'd be able to get those other words out of her mouth. As for the possibility of inviting him back to her apartment, and having him defile with his presence the only place in which she felt safe . . .

But that wasn't really true, was it? She didn't feel safe there. Only the pills helped prevent Reese from invading her dreams, and hurting her all over again.

She slumped in the chair. She'd been fooling herself. She'd hoped that Reese's punishment might be inflicted without her direct involvement, without having to do anything more than read about it later in the newspapers, but it was just the natural instinct of the coward: Let someone else do the dirty work. I don't want to see or hear anything that might disturb me. I don't want to smell blood.

This thought caused her to notice that the stench in the room wasn't as strong today, or maybe she was simply getting used to it. Even the heat wasn't bothering her as much. She wondered what was wrong with Amelia. Cancer, probably. Everybody seemed to be getting cancer these days.

'How do you know that he'll even agree to meet?' Carolyn asked. 'Surely he'll run a mile at the first sight of me.'

'He'll agree because he's arrogant and deluded,' said Amelia. 'He'll agree because you'll only be confirming what he already believes: that he was falsely accused, that you lied to the court, and what you want more than anything else is another taste of him.'

It seemed inconceivable to Carolyn that Reese could see rape in those terms, but then she recalled the look on his face in the courtroom, and the way in which he had described what he termed as their 'encounter'. If he really felt he was the injured party in this, then he deserved everything that was coming to him.

'He has a girlfriend,' said Carolyn, but even to her own ears it sounded like a hollow protest, a last gasp of excuse.

'When has that ever stopped a man like him from taking his pleasures elsewhere?' asked Amelia, and that was the end of it. She instructed Carolyn to make a copy of the keys to her building, and the apartment itself, and told her that Miss Bronston would be in touch.

'Just get him back to your place,' were Amelia's last words to Carolyn, as she prepared to leave. 'We'll take care of the rest.'

It was easier than Carolyn had anticipated, but harder than Amelia had suggested. She called Reese's mobile from a phone by the toilets in a shopping mall. It had taken all of her powers of persuasion to prevent him from killing the connection within the first ten seconds, but somehow she managed to get the necessary words out without stumbling or choking on them. She'd been practising for days, and she thought that she sounded almost convincing. He agreed to meet her for coffee the next day in one of those greasy spoon cafés in which he wouldn't ordinarily have been caught dead, but which meant that the chances of him being seen with her by someone he knew were virtually nil. That suited her just fine.

She arrived at the café early, and ordered a horrible milky coffee. It didn't matter. She took one mouthful and knew that she wasn't going to finish it, and her hand trembled so much when she picked up the cup that most of the coffee ended up in the saucer anyway.

She jerked in her chair when she saw him appear, and something clicked painfully in her back. He was wearing a blue suit that was cut slightly too narrow for him, but then he had always dressed a little young for his age. He was handsome in a very conventional way, like a model from a cheap catalogue. Watching him now, she couldn't think what had ever attracted her to him to begin with. He wasn't even her type, for God's sake. She blamed it on the wine, but that was all she would blame on it. The rest was his alone.

He ordered a tea, and took the seat across from her.

'It's nice to see you again,' he said. 'And under better circumstances than last time.'

He gave her a grin, the one she remembered from their first meeting, the one he probably thought made him look boyish and cute. She wanted to throw her coffee in his face, then break her saucer in two and grind the sharp edges into his eyes. Beneath the table, she dug the nails of her left hand into her thigh.

'Yes,' she said. She swallowed, and found the appropriate words. 'I'm so sorry about what happened – about all of it.'

It was simple after that. They talked, she managed a couple of facsimiles of smiles, and he agreed to meet her for a drink the following Friday. She could already see him picturing in his head how the evening might progress, and where it might lead. She saw a flicker of disgust pass over his face. She wanted to believe that it was disgust at himself, but she knew better.

He made a show of paying for her coffee, and then, as they left the café, he gave her a peck on the cheek. That was the point at which she almost lost it, but she retained enough self-control simply to turn away so he wouldn't see how much she hated him. She used a wet wipe to clean her cheek once he was out of sight, and was so distracted that she bumped into someone as she turned the corner. She looked up to see Miss

Bronston. The tall woman said nothing, but simply raised an eyebrow in inquiry.

'Friday,' said Carolyn. Miss Bronston reached out a hand, and Carolyn dropped the copied keys in her palm before continuing on her way.

Carolyn and Reese arrived almost simultaneously at the Asian-themed bar, far away from their own regular haunts. They ordered finger food, and he tried to ply her with booze, but she carefully nursed a single glass of wine. When he asked her why she wasn't drinking more, she told him that she wanted to keep a clear head. She reached out and touched his hand.

'I want to enjoy it,' she said. 'You know, later. I don't want to miss any of it.'

He took her hand in his, and lazily inscribed circles on her palm with the tip of his index finger. He leaned over and kissed her on the mouth. His tongue probed at her lips, and she opened them wide enough to allow it to enter, just enough not to raise his suspicions, just enough to make sure that he was hooked.

They took a cab back to her apartment, his hand working to part her legs. She slapped it away a little more forcefully than he might have liked, then threw him a smile to soften the blow. He grew more insistent once they got inside and took off their coats. She gave in to his kisses, and allowed his hands to wander for a while before pushing him away.

'I need to go to the bathroom,' she said. She took him by the hand and led him into her bedroom. She undid his tie, and unbuttoned his shirt, and kissed him on the chest.

'You do the rest,' she said. 'I'll be out in a moment.'

As she walked away, she reached behind her and let him see her start to unzip her skirt. Then, as she had been instructed to do, she went into the bathroom, and locked the door. She sat on the toilet seat, and waited.

*　　*　　*

Reese stripped down to his underwear. He'd hold off on that until she came back from the bathroom, then let her witness the grand unveiling. He knew what he wanted to do to her. He was going to screw her six ways till Sunday, then spit in her face for what she'd put him through. If she came near him again, he'd report her to the police as a stalker.

He sat on the bed and glanced at himself in the mirror of her dressing-table. He sucked in his gut, then released it. He didn't care how he looked to her. He wasn't trying to impress her. If anything, he wanted her to feel degraded by him. It was the only time in his life that he wished himself fatter and uglier than he was. He willed her to hurry up. At least her bed was big. That was good.

A sound came from behind him. He hadn't heard the bathroom door open, but he'd been lost in thoughts of what he would soon be doing to her. He looked over his shoulder, but the door was still closed. There was that sound again. It was coming from the floor. Did she have a cat? He hated cats. And what was that smell?

He had shifted position to check, climbing on all fours so that he could lean across the mattress, when a woman's face appeared from the other side of the bed. Her hair was dark, her face mostly pale, and her mouth almost lipless. Christ, thought Reese, she must have been hiding under the bed. A flatmate? Was this some kind of kinky sex thing? He didn't mind, but it would have been nice to be asked.

The woman's hands grasped the mattress and she pulled herself on to the bed. Her upper body was naked. Her breasts were small, and dry skin flaked from them.

'Who the f—'

Reese glimpsed the swell of her buttocks, and then whatever else he might have wanted to say died in his mouth.

The woman had no legs. Instead her skin darkened and mutated from white skin to reddish-black scales at the small of her back, and her thighs were fused below the cleft of her buttocks to form a single hard, jointed limb that tapered to the thickness of a man's arm. It resembled a scorpion's tail, right down to the dark, curved stinger at its tip.

The woman moved closer to him, dragging herself across the mattress. Reese wanted to get away, but his body wouldn't respond. The woman's eyes fixed him in place as surely as if he were pinned like a dead insect to a board. That dark tail arched over her back, and a drop of clear liquid dripped from the end.

'Please,' he said, and he wasn't sure what he was asking her to do, beyond letting him live. 'Please.'

The stinger struck, catching him on the top of the chest, in the same spot on which Carolyn had kissed him only minutes before. Instantly he felt the venom spreading through his system, like a fire burning inside. His body shuddered, and his mouth opened so wide that he both heard and felt his jaw dislocate. He looked up at the stinger and saw it bifurcate, the bony carapace splitting to reveal a sharp pink organ covered in small, glistening hairs.

The woman gripped him hard by the torso, and he smelled her breath upon him. She forced him onto his back, and her body arched at an impossible angle so that the stinger was poised above his mouth. She made a sound that might have been pain or pleasure, and Reese heard her vertebrae crack as the spike shot into his mouth and slowly began to force itself down his throat.

Carolyn heard Reese's final words, followed by a thrashing on the bed. She wanted to look. She wanted to see. She'd been told not to, but after what he had done to her, she wanted to know.

She opened the door and stared at the composite creature on her bed. Amelia was crouched over Reese's body, most of her lower half lost between his jaws. There was blood on his face where his mouth had torn as the metasormal segments of her tail had pushed themselves inside. Her eyes locked on Carolyn's, and her upper half shuddered as she strived to force herself deeper still into the expiring man.

Before Carolyn could react, a figure appeared from the right.

Miss Bronston pressed a pad against her mouth, and the image of the monstrosity faded from Carolyn's mind just as the life died in Reese's eyes.

Carolyn woke in her own bed. Reese's body was gone. So too were Amelia and Miss Bronston. She might almost have dreamed it all were it not for the faint reptilian smell that hung in the room, and the fact that the sheets on the bed had been changed.

She pulled the covers over her head, and tried to sleep.

Months went by before Carolyn returned to number 65. She half-expected to find the house unoccupied, but the same Miss Bronston answered the door, and the same Amelia sat in her wheelchair in her uncomfortably warm room, her lower body covered by a blanket.

'I came to thank you,' Carolyn told Amelia.

'No regrets?'

'None. But I was wondering . . .'

'Yes?'

'. . . if there was anything I might do for you in return?'

Amelia looked past her to where the fading Miss Bronston stood, listening to their exchange.

'Not now,' said Amelia, 'but later, perhaps, I may have a proposal for you.'

Amelia gave a final snip of the scissors, and handed the article to the waiting Carolyn.

It was winter. Miss Bronston had been dead for three months. Carolyn had been with her when she passed away. By then, Miss Bronston had told her all that she needed to know.

'This one,' said Amelia.

Carolyn read the article before taking a small notebook from her pocket. She knew the case. She flicked through the pages until she found the name and address she was looking for, then sat at the old desk in the corner and removed an expensive blank card and matching envelope from the drawer. In clear, careful script, she wrote:

I can help you.

The Hollow King

Once upon a time, in a distant island realm, there lived a king and queen of great renown, admired as much for the devotion of the one to the other as for the wisdom and mercy of their rule. The king was handsome, the queen beautiful, and only the absence of children shadowed the perfection of their life together. Instead they lost themselves in their love, and it consumed them, body and mind.

After many years of peace, rumours reached them of a threat from the north: a great mist that spread itself over the land, engulfing farms, villages, and entire towns. Nothing that it touched survived, and nothing that entered it ever emerged again. The people fled before it, and the stream of refugees became a torrent, all seeking safety in the stronghold by the sea, only to reach it and find that there was nowhere left to run, and they must turn at last and face the entity that was pursuing them. Those who came told the king of strange beasts glimpsed in the mist – creatures with jaws in their bellies, women with the bodies of serpents, and men with two heads who rode upon the backs of flightless dragons.

The king listened, and he was afraid. He sent scouts to the northern edges of his realm, the better to warn him of the mist's approach, but none returned, and in time, from the battlements of his castle by the sea, he saw the first grey tendrils invade the distant forests, and within hours his kingdom was lost from sight. Some took to boats in an effort to reach other lands, but the mist was on the sea, and none escaped it, and all died unseen.

But the murk did not descend upon the castle, and the plain

between the walls and the forest remained open and clear. Yet the halt brought no comfort, for the white fog was alive with alien screeches and roars and the cries of those who had been unable to flee in time to the safety of the castle walls. The king listened as they called out to him for help, and the pitch of their screams rose in accordance with their suffering, until, one by one, they were silenced by the mercy of death.

The king could stand by no longer. He summoned his knights and his infantry, armed all those within his walls who could fight, and set out to do battle. His queen did not try to stop him, and would have gone with him had he allowed it, but he told her to take care of those left behind, and rule in his absence. She kissed him once, and said: 'I shall not rest until you return, and I shall not weep until you do, for I will shed no tears of sorrow for you.'

The queen watched from the highest battlement as the king led his army into the mist, and it swallowed the thousands entire.

In the days that followed there came the sounds of distant combat, of trumpets calling and weapons clashing, and then all was silence that continued for a month and a day, until at last the mist began to recede. A single horseman emerged from the woods now revealed once more, and the queen watched as her king approached. The gates were opened for him, and he was welcomed and hailed, although his face was haggard, and his skin pale. He was but a shadow of the man he once had been, seated on an emaciated horse with its flesh scorched and torn, its eyes rolling in madness and terror. As soon as the king was helped from his saddle, the poor beast fell dead upon the ground.

The queen led the king to his chambers, and removed the remnants of his bloodied armour. She bathed the wounds on his body, and as he stood naked and vulnerable before her, she shed a single tear. The king kissed it from her cheek and drank it down, and something of the old light appeared in his eyes.

From that moment on he grew stronger, and became more like his former self, but he did not speak, as though the silence that descended after the battle had somehow infected him, rendering him mute. He ruled as once he had, but now through signs and writing, and he lay each night with the queen in her bed.

But the mist had not vanished: it had merely retreated to the very edges of the kingdom, and the queen felt it as a coldness in her bones, and glimpsed it as a dimness in the corner of her vision.

One year after his return, the king appeared in his courtyard, mounted on his finest charger and clad in his armour. When the queen enquired where he was going, he pointed north, and she knew that he was returning to the mist. But when she asked him why, he simply shook his head, and she told him for the second time: 'I shall not rest until you return, and I shall not weep until you do, for I will shed no tears of sorrow for you.'

This time, the king returned after a single night, once more thin and enshadowed, and riding a horse driven mad by what it had endured. And the queen shed one tear, and the king kissed it away, and was made whole again.

And so this continued for nine years: each year a journey, each year a return, each year a tear. The kingdom grew prosperous again, and traders journeyed from the lands beyond the mist, skirting the great forest in which it had made its stand, and from which no sounds came. Neither did birds fly through it, nor deer emerge from its reaches, and anyone foolish enough to risk an exploration was never seen again.

But on the tenth year the queen could contain her curiosity no longer, and she sent one of her most trusted and courageous courtiers to follow the king, and brave the mist, if he would. To protect the courtier, she gave him the most powerful talisman that she possessed: a vial of blood from the only child she had brought to term, a girl born dead from the womb.

So the courtier pursued the king, who did not look back, and in time they came to the forest. The courtier's heart grew cold at the sight of the mist that enveloped it, but he loved his queen, and could not have lived with his shame were he forced to return and tell her that he had failed at the first obstacle. The wall of mist parted for the king, and came together in his stead.

The courtier opened the vial of the dead child's blood and smeared a little on his forehead and on the brow of his horse, as the queen had instructed him to do, and instantly they were rendered invisible. With blood trickling from skin and hide, man and beast advanced into the mist.

All of the trees in the forest were dead, their branches bare, their trunks grey, so that they appeared almost as insubstantial as the mist itself. The courtier could see only a few feet ahead of him, but he was able to follow the path cut by the king. He came across bones of men scattered so thickly upon the ground that they resembled drifts of snow. He passed the remains of a two-headed giant, impaled by a spear against the split trunk of a great oak, and the withered husk of a creature with the torso of a woman and the legs of a spider, an axe buried in its back.

Worst of all, he descried the features of men on the tree trunks, and believed them the play of shadow upon bark, until he drew closer and saw that they were the shrivelled faces of those whom he had known in life – knights, squires, soldiers – torn from their corpses and nailed to the wood.

But he neither saw nor heard one sign of life.

At last he came to the edge of a clearing, and in the heart of it stood the king. The mist was less dense here, but the courtier thought that he caught sight of figures forming and vanishing in the clouds, and there came a whispering from all around.

'*All hail the Hollow King.*'

The king dismounted and walked towards the body of a

man that hung from the thick branch of a sycamore tree. It was entirely skinless, its exposed flesh in a state of slow decay, its ribs visible through the holes in its chest. Only the ornate helm on its head gave any clue to its identity, for it bore the royal insignia.

As the courtier watched, the king on the ground shed his boots, and then his clothing, and finally his skin and the flesh beneath, the two halves falling away like the membrane of a snake. Standing in the clearing was no longer the king but a being with a wretched, twisted body, and a deformed skull, and a nose that was more like the beak of a carrion bird than the organ of a man.

And though the courtier had never before laid eyes on this creature, still he knew his name, for every land had heard tales of the Crooked Man. Some claimed that he was the union of an old, violent god and a human woman, and had torn his way out of his mother's womb at the time of his birth, killing her in the process. Others said that he had no such origin, but had come into existence with the dark stuff of the universe. He had always been, they whispered, and would always be. In the end, all that was certain about the Crooked Man was the harm he meant to living things, and the joy he took in their torment.

Beside him, his horse began to shy and whinny in panic, terrified by the transformation, for all creatures fear predators, and the Crooked Man was the greatest predator of all. The horse was tied to a tree, and could not escape, and so its terror increased. The Crooked Man paid it no heed, but its cries served to hide the distress of the courtier's own mount. The Crooked Man's black eyes gleamed with all of the wickedness in this world as he bowed low before the dangling man.

'Your Majesty,' he said. 'Why, you look almost good enough to eat!'

And with that he tore a strip from the decaying body, and jammed it into his mouth.

'Ah,' he added, chewing on the carcass, 'if only you tasted as good as you look. And if only your queen would shed more than a single tear . . .'

And as he ate, he spoke.

> *One tear for a year,*
> *One bite for a coat,*
> *Flesh for a wall,*
> *And blood for a moat,*
> *All to possess a pretty queen,*
> *All to restore a Hollow King.*

He swallowed the last of the meat, and a new body began to take shape over his own: blood and bone, muscle and fat, and finally a layer of skin, until at last he once again resembled the old king. Then, exhausted by his efforts, the Crooked Man collapsed to the ground and fell into a deep sleep.

The courtier needed to see and hear no more. He turned his horse and galloped for the castle.

The queen was asleep when the gates were opened to the courtier, but she had left instructions that she was to be woken as soon as he appeared. He came to her alone in her chamber and told her of all that he had witnessed. When he had finished, the queen instructed him to wait for her in an anteroom, and to speak to no one. She went to her window and stood in silence, and did not move from her vigil until a figure on horseback appeared in the distance. Only then did she summon her courtier to her, and as he knelt before her she took a blade from her sleeve and stabbed him through the right ear, killing him instantly. She tore her gown and cried to her guards for help, screaming that the courtier had attacked her.

And all the time, the Hollow King drew nearer.

This I know to be true: there are those who would rather choose false hope over true grief, who would embrace the counterfeit of love before the reality of loneliness. Perhaps the queen was such a person, but who knows to what madness great sorrow may drive us, or the thousand ways in which a heart may be broken?

When the Hollow King returned to her, the queen took him by the hand and led him to her bed.

And as he embraced her, she wept, and wept, and wept . . .

The Children of Dr Lyall

Even amid rubble and dust, there was money to be made.

The German bombers had reduced whole streets to scattered bricks and memories, and Felder couldn't see anyone coming back to live in them soon, not unless they fancied taking their chances with the rats. Some areas were still so dangerous that their previous occupants hadn't even been permitted to scour the ruins for any salvageable possessions. Instead they could only stand behind the cordons, weeping for what had been lost, and pray that something might yet be recovered when the buildings were at last declared safe, or when the walls and floors were either pulled down or collapsed of their own volition.

'Buried treasure', that's what Felder called it: money, jewellery, clothing – anything that could be bartered or sold, but you had to be careful. The coppers didn't look kindly on looters, and in case Felder and his gang needed any reminders on that score they had only to visit Pentonville Prison, the Ville, where Young Tam was doing five years, and they'd be five hard years, too, because one of the coppers had broken Tam's right leg so badly that he'd be dragging it behind him like a piece of twisted firewood for the rest of his life.

For the most part, though, the Old Bill weren't up to much any more, weakened as they were by the demands of war, and Felder and his boys could outrun most of them. Young Tam was just unlucky, that was all. Even then, it could have gone much worse for him: rumours abounded that Blackie Harper over in Seven Dials had been shot by a soldier while stealing suits from a bombed-out gentleman's outfitters, but the details of the killing were hushed up for the sake of morale, it being bad enough having Germans slaughtering Londoners without our own boys giving them a helping hand. It was also said that Billy Hill, who was carving a reputation for himself as the leading figure in London's criminal underworld, was very interested to know the name of the soldier who fired the fatal bullet, for Blackie Harper had been an associate of Billy's, and good staff were hard to come by in wartime.

But Billy Hill and his kind operated on another level from men like Felder, even if Felder ultimately aspired to similar heights. Felder, Greaves and Knight: they sounded like a firm of solicitors, but they were just bottom-feeders, scouring the dirt for food while trying to avoid being eaten alive by the bigger fish. All three, along with the unfortunate Young Tam, had, in a sense, been liberated by the Germans at the start of the war, when the prisons freed any man with fewer than three months left to serve, or any Borstal boy with six months under his belt. Knight, Greaves and Young Tam fell under the latter category. Felder was older, and already on his third conviction for receiving stolen goods when he was released in 1939. He was spared conscription because he had lost his left eye to a catapulted stone when he was eight years old, and was careful to exaggerate the paucity of vision in his remaining organ.

Young Tam, meanwhile, was a mental defective, and Knight had come over from Northern Ireland to find work in London only a few weeks before he was locked up in Borstal for assault, and was therefore technically ineligible for conscription, although he hadn't bothered to present himself to the relevant authorities in order to clarify his status. Finally, Greaves had spectacularly flat feet. All four, even Young Tam, should have been required to perform civilian work under the terms of their exemption, but they did their best to remain below His Majesty's radar, for they would not grow wealthy digging potatoes or cleaning up after the sick and dying in one of the city's crowded hospitals. Quite the little band they were, Felder sometimes thought: a one-eyed man; an idiot; a flatfoot; and a Belfast Protestant with an accent so thick that he might as well have been speaking Swahili for all the sense he made to anyone but his closest associates. It seemed that Billy Hill, high on his throne, needed to have few concerns about them for the time being.

And now they were three. It was a blessing, in a way, that Young Tam was no longer with them. True, he would always do as Felder told him, and was strong, and good with his fists, but Felder's ambitions did not allow for one as slow as Young Tam. Billy Hill had no idiots working under him, because idiots wouldn't make a man rich. Early in the war, Hill's gang had used a car to break into Carrington's of Regent Street and nab £6000 worth of jewels, a sum that boggled Felder's imagination even now. Hill was selling everything from silk to sausage skins, and it was whispered that the war had already made him a millionaire. By contrast, Felder's biggest score had come in 1941, when he and Knight had been fortunate enough to find themselves only streets away from the Café de Paris on Coventry Street when its supposedly secure basement ballroom was blown to pieces by a pair of German bombs that descended down a ventilation shaft, killing more than 30 people. Felder and Knight had stripped the dead and dying of rings, watches and wallets under the guise of evacuating the wounded. They'd made hundreds on that one night, but things had never been as good for them since.

Now Felder and Knight stood on a patch of waste ground that had once been a redbrick terrace, and stared at a house brushed by moonlight. It stood like a single jagged tooth in the ancient mouth of the street. Its survival had no logic to it, but then Felder had long ago learned that, like the mind of God, the nature of bombs was ultimately unknowable. Some hit and did not explode. Some took down one house or shop while sparing all else around, or, as the unfortunate patrons of the Café de Paris had learned, struck with uncanny accuracy at the only vulnerable point in an otherwise secure structure.

And then there were bombs that annihilated whole

communities and left, as in this case, a single residence standing as a monument to all that once had been. The house was slightly larger than the ones that had been lost, but not unusually so: a middle-class residence in an otherwise working-class street, perhaps. But Felder had cased it after his keen eye spotted the quality of the curtains at the windows, and a quick glance into the front room had revealed what looked like original paintings on the walls, nice rugs on the floor, and, most enticing of all, a sideboard full of polished silverware. Discreet enquiries established that it was the home of a widow, Mrs Lyall, who lived alone, her husband having departed to the next world during the final days of the last war.

As a rule, Felder tried to avoid burgling occupied houses: it was too risky and brought with it the likelihood of a confrontation if one of the occupants awoke. Felder wasn't above inflicting violence but, like any clever man, he avoided it when he could. Still, times were hard, and growing harder by the day. Despite his ambitions, Felder had resigned himself to the fact that he needed to form allegiances if he were to improve his position in life, and Billy Hill's gang seemed to offer the best opportunities for wealth and promotion. Hill would require an offering, though, a token both of Felder's potential and his esteem for the crime boss. That was why, after some thought, Felder had elected to cut Greaves out of the evening's work – in fact, to cut him loose for ever. Greaves was weak and too good-natured for the likes of Billy Hill. He also had principles, to the extent that he had refused to accept a cut of the Café de Paris proceeds offered as a gesture of goodwill by Felder, even though Greaves had not been present on the night in question. Robbing the houses of the dead was one thing, it appeared; stripping their bodies was another. Felder had no time for such sensitivities, and he doubted that Billy Hill had either.

Felder carried a cosh in his coat pocket, Knight a knife and a homemade knuckle-duster fashioned from wood embedded with screws and nuts, which he preferred to the more traditional models easily available on the street, Knight being a craftsman of sorts. The weapons were only for show. Neither man anticipated much trouble from an elderly widow, but the old could be stubborn, and sometimes the threat of violence was required to loosen their tongues.

Felder turned to Knight.

'Ready?'

'Aye.'

And together the two men descended to the house.

Later, as he was dying – or rather, as one of him was dying – Felder would wonder if the house and its occupants had been waiting for him; if, perhaps, they had always been waiting for him, understanding that the laws of probability, the complex cross-hatching of cause and effect, suggested his path and theirs must surely intersect eventually. He didn't consider Knight's part in the process. Knight did as he was told, and so Felder's decision to target this particular house was the moment at which the die was cast. But Knight could have made a determination of his own at any of a hundred, a thousand, forks in the road between Felder's conversation with him about the house and the moment that they entered it. After all, thought Felder, as he bled from wounds unseen, wasn't that the old woman's point? Not one, but many. Not infinite, but as close to infinity as made no difference to a man like Felder, especially not at that most crucial juncture of all, the line between living and dying, between existence and nonexistence.

And, yes, some small consolation might have been derived from the knowledge that this was the end for only one Felder, had it not been the end for the only Felder he had known, and would ever know.

But all that came later. For now there was only the house, its windows hooded, like the eyes of a hawk, by the ubiquitous blackout curtains. They did not enter by the front but climbed the still-intact wall that surrounded the back garden and found, not entirely to their surprise, that the door there was unlocked. Once inside, they saw that the tidy little kitchen, with its pine table and two chairs, was lit by a candle encased in a glass lamp, and similar candles illuminated the hall. Beneath the stairwell was a locked door, leading down, they assumed, to a cellar. They heard no sound but the ticking of an unseen clock.

It was Knight who first noticed the patterns on the walls in the hall, taking them initially to be some strange manner of floral wallpaper and then, as he drew nearer, deciding – still erroneously – that what he was seeing was a network of cracks in the plaster, almost like the craquelure on the surface of a painting. Knight had shared little of his background with Felder and the others. Equally, they did not trouble themselves to enquire into another man's business if it did not concern them, especially when the man in question gave no sign that such an intrusion would give him great pleasure in any case, but Felder had come to realize that Knight knew something of art and literature, and was better educated than his thick accent might have led one to believe. In fact, Knight came from a house filled with paintings, and a family that talked easily of abrasure and blanching, gesso and glair. Had he been privy, before he died, to the insights gifted to Felder, then he might have appreciated more the story told by the patterns on the walls.

Both men drew closer, Felder's fingers reaching out to trace what was gradually revealed to be ink work on the otherwise unadorned walls of the house, an intricate design that resembled most closely the thin branches of some form of creeping briar, as though the interior had been invaded by a pestilential vegetation, its greenery now lost to the harsh breath of winter, had it ever enjoyed such foliage to begin with. The effect was further enhanced by the addition of red dots at apparently random points, like fruits somehow clinging to a dead bush. Beside each red sphere was a pair of initials: E.J., R.P., L.C., but never the same combination of letters twice.

And although it was impossible to find a logic to the entirety of the tracery, it seemed to Felder and Knight that, on an individual level, its creator began with a single line which then split after an inch or so, one channel continuing on to divide again while the other terminated in a horizontal dash over the vertical, like a dead end. Yet even here deviations from the norm sometimes occurred in the form of a series of dashes that, on occasion, eventually found their way back to the main thread. Similarly, numbers were appended to certain lines, which Felder took to be dates or, in particularly involved cases, hours, minutes and seconds. The designs entirely covered the walls, a few even extending onto the ceiling itself: a stepladder by the front door permitted access. The tracery continued along the wall beside the stairs and, Felder presumed, up to the floor above their heads. The kitchen, by contrast, appeared devoid of any adornments, largely because it was barely spacious enough to accommodate its cupboards, sink, and a four-ring gas cooker, until Knight, in a fit of curiosity, returned there and opened one of the cupboard doors, revealing a further network of bifurcating branches drawn, and sometimes even cut, into the interior panelling.

Again, waiting for death – *a* death – to approach, Felder perceived another crucial moment here, a point in events when lives might have been saved, when both men could have turned and left the house, for although they had not yet spoken, still their mutual unease was evident on their faces. Then Felder thought of Billy Hill, and a share in the wealth that the war was bringing to those ruthless enough to seize opportunities when they were offered. Hill would not have faltered in the face of such inky manifestations of madness. Instead, he would have reckoned the creator more vulnerable still to his predations, and honed in on easy pickings.

Beyond the kitchen lay a dining-room, empty and dusty, with a closed pair of interconnecting doors leading to the front room. As with the hall, the walls were covered with lines.

Only now did Felder become aware of a presence in the front room, the one in which he had earlier glimpsed the rugs and paintings and, most interesting of all, the glass-fronted silver-ware cabinet. It was the merest shifting of shadow against shadow, and the slightest exhalation of breath. A chair creaked, and Felder recognized the sounds of a sleeper responding to some small disturbance, such as the unfamiliar noise created by two men entering a house that was not theirs. Footsteps shuffled on carpet. The door began to open.

Knight reacted first. He was past Felder before the older man could even make a determination of the situation. Knight pushed hard against the door. There was a single shout – a female voice, old and querulous – and then a series of muffled impacts beneath which Felder discerned the breaking of fragile bones, like a quail being consumed behind closed lips.

Felder entered the room to find Knight straddling an old woman on the floor, one knee on her chest, his fist raised to strike, her eyes already assuming the strange vacancy of shock. Felder gripped Knight's wrist before he could hit her again.

'Stop!' he said. 'For Christ's sake, you'll kill her!'

He felt the downward pull of Knight's right hand, the urge to harm, and then the tension went out of the younger man. Knight rose slowly and wiped his hand across his face. Knight rarely acted in this way, with heat and anger. He was, by nature, a cold being, and seemed startled by his own rage.

'I—' said Knight. He looked down at the old woman and shook his head. 'I—' he repeated, but nothing more came to him.

Felder knelt and gently took the woman beneath the chin, turning her head so that she was facing him. Her nose was broken, that much was clear, and her left eye was already closing. He thought that Knight might also have broken her left cheek-bone, maybe even damaged the eye socket itself. Her mouth was bloodied, the upper lip split, but, as with Knight, something of her true self was now returning after the attack. Her right eye grew bright. She tried to rise. Felder helped her to her feet, aided by Knight, even though the woman weighed little more than the clothing she wore, and they almost carried her between them to the armchair in which she had been dozing.

'Get her some water,' said Felder, 'and a cold cloth.'

Knight did as he was told. Tenderly, Felder brushed a length of grey hair back from the woman's face and tucked it behind her right ear.

'I'm sorry,' he said. 'That wasn't meant to happen.'

The woman didn't respond. Her single undamaged eye merely regarded Felder with a kind of disappointment.

Knight returned, a dripping tea towel in one hand, a cup in the other. From the right pocket of his jacket, Felder noticed, peeked a bottle of brandy. Felder reached for the cloth, but Knight paused at the door, his eye fixed on the wall in which the window lay. Felder followed his gaze: more lines, more forks, more patterns, more red, inky berries. On three sides the walls were filled with bookcases and cabinets. Only here, around the window, was there space to continue the house's peculiar decoration.

'Never mind all that,' said Felder. 'Give me the towel.'

His words broke the spell, and Knight handed over the wet cloth and the cup of water. Felder cleaned away some of the blood. He had hoped that a little pressure might also keep the swelling down on the damaged eye, but when he touched the towel to the area the woman gave a pained yelp, and Felder knew that his initial suspicion had been correct: Knight had broken some of the bones in her orbital rim. Felder forced her to take water, then emptied the rest onto the rug and indicated that Knight should fill the cup with brandy instead. Knight opened the bottle, took a long draught for himself, and then poured two fingers of brandy into the cup. Felder made the woman drink once more, and used the cloth to wipe away the trickle that dribbled down her chin.

'It'll help,' he said.

He hooked her hand around the cup. Her respiration was shallow, as though it pained her to take deep breaths. Felder saw again Knight's left knee buried in the woman's tiny, flat chest. He held his hand over the spot, not wanting to touch her breast.

'Does it hurt here?' he asked.

She gave a small nod. Felder looked away.

'You should go,' said the old woman. She spoke the words on an exhalation, wheezing them out.

'What?' said Felder.

'You should go. They won't like it.'

'Who?'

'You told me that she lived alone!' said Knight. A clean blade appeared in his hand, extending itself like tempered moonlight.

'Shut up,' said Felder, his attention fixed on the woman. 'Who?' he asked again, but she did not reply, and her right eye flicked away from him to the bookshelves over the fireplace.

Felder stood. He turned to Knight.

'If anyone else lived here we'd have heard from them with that racket you made,' he said. 'Still, search the house. We're in this now, and we may as well milk it for all we can. Jewellery, money, you know the drill.'

'Why don't you ask her where she keeps it all?'

'Have you seen the size of this house? It's not Buckingham Palace. There can't be more than a few rooms upstairs.'

'I know, but—'

'Maybe you want to hit her again, see if you can kill her this time.'

Knight had the decency to look ashamed.

'What are you going to do?' he asked.

Felder reached under his coat and untied the strings that held the sack in place. He indicated the silverware with his chin.

'I'll take care of that lot. Now get a move on.'

Knight appeared to be on the verge of saying something more, but he knew better than to argue with Felder, especially with the old woman bleeding before him. Felder would take him to task later for his loss of control, once they were safely away from here. Knight left the room, and Felder heard his heavy tread as he ascended the stairs. When he looked back at the old woman, she was smiling at him.

'Thank you,' she said.

'For what?'

She coughed, and a spray of red blood shot from between her lips.

'For killing me.'

Under the gaze of the old woman, Felder emptied the silverware into his sack. It was good stuff. He'd been a little worried that it might turn out to be plate, although his expert eye, in that first short glance through the window, had told him otherwise. The weight was considerable, but the sack was thick and strong, and had not let him down yet. His only concern now was to get it all to safety without being stopped by the police or the wardens, for there would be no explaining away a sack full of silver.

Felder had chosen to ignore the woman's recent words to him. She'd taken a couple of blows to the head, and who knew how badly it had scrambled her thoughts? Once the cabinet was empty he made a cursory search of the shelves and drawers, but found only a few florins and half crowns wrapped in a handkerchief, and a gent's gold pocket watch engraved with three initials and a date in 1912. He considered putting it in the sack as well, but then slipped it into his own jacket pocket for fear that it might be damaged amid the silverware. From upstairs he heard the sounds of Knight rummaging through wardrobes and drawers.

Felder lit a cigarette and took in his surroundings. During his search of the room he couldn't help but notice the nature of the books on its shelves. None of them were titles that he recognized, not that Felder was much for reading, but most appeared to be scientific volumes.

'Were these your husband's?' he asked the woman. 'A son, maybe?'

The bright right eye fixed itself upon him.

'Mine,' she said.

Felder raised an eyebrow. In his world, women didn't read books on science. They hardly read anything at all. Like rumours of lost tribes in Africa, and monsters in Scottish lochs, Felder had heard of women scientists, but had yet to meet one himself, and so remained uncertain of their actual existence.

'You a scientist, then?'

'Once.'

'What kind?'

'A physicist, although I have qualifications in chemistry too.'

'What are you, then: Professor Lyall?'

If she was surprised that he knew her name, she did not show it.

'Doctor Lyall,' she said.

'Doctor Lyall the physicist. And all this' – Felder gestured at the patterns on the wall – 'is physics?'

Lyall gave another cough, but there was only a little blood this time. Her breathing seemed to have eased somewhat. It might have been a sign that her condition was improving, but Felder doubted it. He suspected that it was her body relaxing into death. He wanted Knight to hurry up. Once they were away from the house, they'd find a telephone box and call for an ambulance. It might not be too late to save her.

'Quantum physics,' she said.

'What's that, then?'

'The study of the universe at the smallest levels.'

'Huh.' Felder took another drag on his cigarette, and moved closer to the wall. 'But what does it all mean?'

He saw her almost smile.

'You want science lessons from me?'

'Maybe, or it could be that I just want to keep you talking, because if you're talking then you're awake, and alive. We'll get help for you, I promise. It won't be long now. But just try to stay conscious.'

'It's too late for that.'

'No, it's not. Talk to me. Tell me about these quantum physics.'

She took another sip of brandy.

'There is a theory,' said Lyall, 'that there are an infinite number of possible existences, and each time we make a decision, one of those possible existences comes into being. But equally, alongside it may exist all other possible, or probable, existences too. It's more complex than that, but I'm keeping it as simple as I can.'

'Because you think I'm stupid?' He said it without rancour.

'No, because I'm not even sure that I fully understand its implications myself.'

Felder tried to follow the pattern of the lines on the wall.

'So each of these forks represents a decision?' said Felder.

'That's correct.'

'It's your life,' he said, and there was a hint of wonder in his voice. 'All of these lines, these forks and dead ends, they're decisions you've made. You've mapped them out, all of them.'

'Yes.'

'Why?'

'To understand.'

'Understand what?'

'Where I went wrong,' she said. She took as deep a breath as she dared, readying herself for a longer speech. 'Because some decisions, some actions, have more damaging consequences than others. And I think, perhaps, that if they're repeated often enough, the fabric of reality is altered. I call it "confluence". If I'd lived long enough, I might even have published a paper on it.'

'Confluence.' Felder repeated the word, liking the sound even if he didn't understand it. 'But what kind of bad things could an old woman like you have done?'

She frowned, and her voice rose slightly.

'I don't regard them as bad. Some might, but I don't. Still, they had repercussions that I could not have foreseen. Confluence occurs at extremes, and nothing is more extreme than the possibility that, by one's actions, the nature of existence is altered. I did nothing wrong. I helped. But all paths fork, and some paths may lead into shadow. And things wait in the shadows.'

'What are the red dots supposed to be?' asked Felder.

He received no answer. Turning, he saw that Dr Lyall had closed her eyes.

'Hey,' he said. 'Hey.'

He did not move, but watched as her breathing grew softer and softer before ceasing entirely. The cup of brandy fell from her hand and bounced on the tiles of the fireplace.

And suddenly Felder noticed that he could no longer hear Knight moving above his head.

The house had four rooms upstairs: an indoor toilet – quite the luxury, as far as Knight was concerned – and two bedrooms, along with a third room so tiny that Knight couldn't quite figure out why it had been put in to begin with, since it was too small to take a bed and resembled more closely a telephone box than an actual inhabitable space. It was piled high with the detritus of the house: broken suitcases, old newspapers, the frame of a lady's bicycle, and more books. Books also occupied the two bedrooms, and even the loo, but unlike in the living-room downstairs, they stood in teetering columns on the floor, the better to free up wall space for more of those infernal branching lines.

Knight was still struggling to understand why he had attacked the old woman – not that it was beyond him to strike a lady, or even the odd girl who in no way resembled a lady at all, but it was the ferocity of his assault that surprised him. For a few seconds he had been overcome not only by an anger that burned like a wound, but also a deep and abiding sense of fear. The patterns on the walls alone could not have caused him to act in this way. They were odd, and unsettling, but no more than that. Knight wondered if he might be coming down with something, but he had been fine until he and Felder had entered the house.

There was a miasma to this place, he felt, as though the very air were polluted, even if it smelt no better or worse than any other house he knew in which an old woman was living – or slowly dying, depending on one's point of view.

Nevertheless, his looting of the rooms had not proved unproductive. In the main bedroom he discovered an assortment of jewellery, most of it gold, including an ornate pendant studded with rubies and diamonds, and a tin box which, when opened using the blade of his knife, was found to contain just over £100 in notes, and a small roll of gold sovereigns. Knight immediately liberated two of the sovereigns and stashed them in the lining of his coat. He was aware of Felder's plan to hand over to Billy Hill most of the proceeds of the night, and largely approved of it, but that didn't require them to abandon common sense entirely. The possibility existed that Hill might simply relieve them of their offerings and throw them back on the street, perhaps with a beating to remind them of the extent of their delusion if they thought they could buy their way into his favour. If nothing else, the sovereigns would ease the pain of rejection, both physical and metaphorical, and provide Knight with some security if he chose to abandon Felder in the aftermath. And if Billy Hill accepted them, well, then all to the good: the sovereigns would form the basis of greater wealth to come.

Knight was just storing the loot in his various pockets when he heard footsteps on the floor outside the bedroom door. Felder, he thought at first, but the steps were too light, and Felder would have known better than to approach him without warning in a strange house. Knight turned just in time to see what appeared to be a small child's bare left foot and leg disappear from sight, as though the child had been watching him and now feared being caught. A boy, Knight thought, although he had caught just the merest glimpse. But where could the child have been hiding? There was nowhere to conceal oneself in the downstairs rooms, and Knight had searched this floor thoroughly. Could the boy somehow have secreted himself among the rubbish in the tiny spare room? It was possible, but unlikely, not unless he had actively conspired to bury himself beneath the books, bags and cases.

Then it came to him: the cellar. They had checked it and found it locked, but Knight could not recall seeing a key. Perhaps the boy had spotted them as they entered the house and, in fear, slipped into the cellar and locked the door behind him. Yes, that was it. There could be no other explanation. Somehow the boy had managed to get past Felder and come upstairs, although Knight wondered why he had not instead left the house and gone to find help. But who could understand the thought processes of a frightened child?

By now Knight was already in pursuit. He wrenched open the bedroom door, stepped onto the upstairs landing, and stopped.

It was no longer the same house. The landing was dark, the walls entirely unadorned except for patches of faded wallpaper that hung stubbornly to the plaster, hints of funeral lilies beckoning to Knight in the dimness. He could see no inked lines, no initialled dots. The floor was still lit by candles, but everything was now part of a much larger structure, and Knight counted at least eight doors in the extended hallway before it ended at a flight of stairs. One of those doors, halfway along on the right, was slowly closing before Knight's eyes.

'Felder?' he called. 'Felder, can you hear me?'

But there was no reply.

Knight reached into one of his pockets and once again withdrew his knife. It was of Japanese manufacture, and among his most prized possessions, as well as being one of the few items he had taken from his childhood home before fleeing it for the mainland. He kept the blade keen, and even to touch it carelessly was to risk the kind of wound that would require stitches to heal. Opening the old woman's lock-box had not left even a scratch on the steel. Holding it in his hand gave Knight some small sense of reassurance, even as his mind struggled to comprehend how he could enter a room in one house and apparently emerge from it into another entirely.

'Felder?'

This time his cry elicited some response. It came in the form of a childish giggle, and then a hushing sound. Not just one child, then. Two, at least.

Knight moved silently along the landing, testing the doors as he went. All appeared to be locked, except that door on the right, which stood slightly ajar. As he drew nearer he heard the sound of running from behind it, as of children moving farther into its reaches. The footfalls echoed slightly before they faded away, as though the room beyond was very long, and its ceiling very high.

Knight stood before the door. He reached out his left hand and pushed. The door opened without a noise. Ahead of him was a wall inset with a series of large windows, although he could see nothing through them because of the blackout curtains. Below the windows stood a line of children's cots, all apparently unoccupied. Knight stepped into the room and saw more cots lined up against the wall opposite the windows. A single lamp on a nightstand by the door provided the only illumination. Knight counted twelve cots on either side and then, as his eyes grew more accustomed to the dark, yet more stretching away into the darkness. He could not even begin to guess the size of the room, or the height of its ceiling, which was taller than that of the landing outside.

The windows drew his attention again. Yes, there was blackness beyond them, but surely that meant the curtains had been hung *outside* the windows. He approached them, the knife still clutched firmly in his right hand. He glimpsed his reflection in the glass, a marooned spectre of himself. He touched his fingers to the pane. The glass was painfully cold, although the room itself was tolerably warm.

And what he felt, as his reflected self stared back at him, and his fingertips grew numb, was that the blackness beyond the window was not caused by drapes, or natural dark, but by a kind of nothingness given form, as though all the stars had been plucked from the night sky and hidden away, and the house was floating in the void. Knight was overcome by a sense of terrible loneliness, of a hopelessness that only oblivion could bring to an end. Hypnotized by the vacuum, he understood that a man might stand here and allow the emptiness beyond to drain him slowly and methodically, leaving only a husk that would, in time, fall to the floor and crumble slowly like the desiccated form of a fly sucked dry by a spider.

Knight heard movement far above his head: a soft scuttling. He began to tremble. He feared that, in envisaging a spider and its prey, the great room had taken the image and given it substance. Slowly he raised his face to the ceiling. The lamp by the door grew brighter, its light spreading outwards and upwards, until it was reflected at last in a multitude of black eyes like flecks of obsidian embedded in the plaster. Knight saw movement, too; pale, naked forms intermingling, clinging to the ceiling with fat, truncated limbs; and now descending along the walls, crawling like insects, their gaze fixed on Knight.

They were infants, hundreds of them, each no more than a few months old and each alive yet not alive, their bodies mottled slightly with corruption. Knight stared at them as they came, flowing down the walls. Behind him, and unseen, a small hand reached out and touched a finger softly to the back of the neck. Knight felt a sting, a spider's kiss. The blade fell from his hand and he followed it, dropping to his knees as the venom took hold. He collapsed on his right side, his eyes open, unable to move, to speak, even to blink. They came to him, hands reaching for his nose, his mouth, his eyes, exploring, testing, more and more of them, until he was lost beneath their bodies and died in stillness among creatures that basked in the novelty of his fading warmth, and wept when it was gone.

*   *   *

Felder went to the door of the living-room and called Knight's name. When no answer came, he stepped into the hall. The stairs to the bedroom were still there, but now they ended in blackness, with nothing beyond. Where once had stood a front door, there was only a wall upon which hung a long mirror. The kitchen, too, was gone, and another mirror had taken its place, so that Felder stood trapped between infinite reflected versions of himself. He looked back at the body of the old woman, but that too was now changed – or, the thought struck him, unchanged, for her face was unmarked, and she appeared to be sleeping. She moved in her dreams, the chair squeaking, her mouth emitting a small snore, but she did not wake, and no Knight appeared to pummel her with his fists. Only as the door began to close in front of Felder did she open her eyes, but he could not tell if she saw him or simply dreamed him before she was lost to his sight. He heard a key turn in the lock as, in the mirrors, all reflections disappeared, and the wall before him began to crack. He watched the cracks advance – forking, diverging, progressing, ending – and saw the ink dry against the plaster as the pattern of his life was drawn for him.

And as one door was locked, so another was opened. He heard the cellar door creak, and light footsteps descending its stairs. Felder did not rail. He did not fight, or scream. He simply followed the sound.

Knight was in the cellar. He sat slumped in a chair, his head back, his eyes, now just ruins in their sockets, staring sightlessly at the ceiling. The walls of the cellar were lined with jars, none of them empty.

They won't like it.

On a workbench rested a bag, and beside it a set of bright, clean surgical instruments. Felder saw unmarked potions in bottles, and powders and pills ready for use. He looked again at the jars, and at what they contained, floating in preservative. He had heard of women like Dr Lyall. Young unmarried girls with reputations to protect, wives who could not explain away a new child when their husbands were fighting in foreign fields, mothers with bodies so worn that another baby would kill them, all came to Dr Lyall or others of her kind, and they did what the medical doctors would not. Felder had never considered the price that might have to be paid, the burden to be carried. She had marked them all on her wall, the red dots of her visitations.

Thank you.

Confluence. Existence and nonexistence, tearing at the fabric of reality, at the walls between universes.

For killing me.

One more mirror stood in the cellar. Felder saw himself reflected in it: this Felder, this moment, fixed by the decisions and actions that had led him to the house. The walls drew away from him, leaving only shadows behind, and out of those shadows emerged children, some little more than crawling newborns, but others older and more watchful. Their rage was a cold thing, for there is no rage quite like that of children. He experienced it as a multitude of surgical hooks and blades cutting into his flesh. His reflected self began to bleed, and he supposed that he must have been bleeding too, although he could see no wounds. He could feel them, though, deep inside.

He died slowly, or one of him did, the only version that he would ever know. In the logic of his dying he understood that, in another universe – in many universes – the torment of Dr Lyall by her children would continue, but in this one it had concluded, just as his own must surely, mercifully end.

As the life faded from him, a line of ink moved inexorably across the filthy wall, then faded away to nothing.

The Fractured Atlas – Five Fragments

1. The Dread and Fear of Kings

Couvret was waiting at *het Teken van de Eik*, the Sign of the Oak, for the ship that would take him at last to England. He had been at the inn for weeks, and was growing uneasy. Rumours of impending Catholic retribution were reaching the ears of Huguenot refugees, and Couvret did not believe that he was safe in Amsterdam. Only when he had put the North Sea between the Continent and himself would he feel any sense of ease.

His wife and child were dead, taken by the red plague. The news had reached him at almost the same time that Henry of Navarre had broken his siege of Paris and retreated before the advance of the Spanish-Catholic relief army under the Duke of Parma. Couvret had fled with the rest, and had not looked back. It was said that Henry's siege had caused the deaths of a quarter of the city's population. The Catholics would make someone pay for it, but it would not be Henry. Already there were whispers that he was considering converting, and overtures had been made to Rome on his behalf.

But Henry's situation had been complicated by the death of Sixtus V shortly before the lifting of the siege, and the subsequent failure of his successor, Urban VII, to live for longer than twelve days after his election. Sixtus's passing would probably have been welcomed by Henry, Couvret thought: the former Felice Peretti was a fierce opponent of the Reformation, and had sanctioned Philip II's ultimately doomed plan to invade England. Since Urban's demise, the cardinals had elected Nicolò Sfondrati to the papacy as Gregory XIV, but Gregory was frail. The Spanish cardinals had arranged his election in order to strengthen their position against France, further constricting Henry's room for manoeuvre. If Henry were not a Catholic by Christmas twelvemonth, Couvret would himself become a Jew.

God, Amsterdam was cold – almost as cold as the Dutch themselves. Couvret had no love for the Calvinists, but his enemy's enemy counted as his friend, and the ongoing conflict between the Spanish and the Dutch was the only reason that he had come so far. But this was a dangerous city: the Calvinist suppression of Catholicism had succeeded only in inspiring a virulent strain of Counter-Reformist zeal in the Low Countries, and now seminaries were reopening, and Catholic missionaries were reestablishing footholds in Protestant districts. As one of Henry's legal advisers, Couvret was a wanted man. If his true identity became known to any of the Catholic zealots lurking in the shadows, his life would be forfeit.

The English ship's captain had assured him of safe passage in the interests of their shared Protestant brotherhood, although those bonds were less strong than the demands of commerce, and Couvret was being forced to pay a small fortune for his berth. He didn't care. There was nothing left for him here, and he would find work in London. He had in his possession letters of introduction to two lawyers at the Inns of Court, and he had been assured of a warm welcome from both.

But for now he was forced to wait at the Oak until word came to him that the ship was ready to sail. He kept mainly to his room, and tried to speak as seldom as possible when away from the precincts of the inn, for fear that his accent might draw the wrong kind of attention. Instead he ate and drank in solitude, studied his Geneva Bible, and thought on his lost wife and daughter.

Yet, even for one in Couvret's circumstances, the need for human company – if only to bask in its reflected warmth – was sometimes overwhelming, and so it was that he found himself in a corner of the Oak, far from the fire and the greater mass of those who had come to that place. He had dined on *hutspot* for the fourth night in a row, for it was both filling and cheap. Before him was a glass of *jenever*, and beside it some sugar and a spoon. He listened discreetly to the conversations going on around him. He had only a little Dutch, but the Oak attracted men of many nations, mostly of the wealthier kind and connected to the business of shipping. The common sailors ate and drank elsewhere.

A hunted man – if he is to survive the ordeal – learns to anticipate the approach of his pursuers, but may also develop a sense for others who are themselves the object of a hunt. So it was that Couvret's attention was drawn to a figure seated to his right, who kept to the shadows and did not converse beyond what was necessary to secure food and drink. Couvret simply registered his presence without drawing him into conversation, and contented himself with his own company. It was, then, with some surprise that he was distracted from his thoughts by the appearance of a full bottle of *jenever* on his table, held in the left hand of the stranger.

'May I offer you a drink?'

Couvret looked up at the questioner. He was a man of exceptional thinness and pallor, his hair long but fine, so that his scalp was visible through the strands. His clothes struck Couvret as well made, but cut for a larger physique. Either they had once belonged to another, or the role as quarry ascribed to him by Couvret had taken its toll on him as much physically as psychologically, for Couvret had no doubt now that this man was living in fear of his life. His eyes were those of a rabbit who sees the shadow of the hawk, and whatever alcohol he might already have taken had failed to still the trembling of his hands.

'No, thank you,' said Couvret. 'I was about to retire for the night.'

He might have wished for company, but not such as this, for fear of drawing the same pursuers down upon both of them.

'You are Couvret,' said the man.

Couvret managed to hide his shock. Even the English captain did not know him by that name.

'You are mistaken. My name is Porcher.'

He rose to leave, but the man placed a hand on his shoulder. He might have been reduced in both body and spirit, but he was still strong. Couvret could have struggled against him, of course, and prevailed, but the action would almost certainly have drawn attention to them.

'You are no swineherd, nor do you come from such humble beginnings. You don't have to fear me. I will not reveal your secret. My name is Van Agteren, and I ask only for a little of your time. In return, I promise you a share in this bottle, and a tale.'

'Again, I tell you that you are mistaken.'

'Perhaps. Then let you be Porcher, and I shall remain Van Agteren. The offer stands. Come, we are both in need of conversation and companionship. Your room will still be waiting for you in an hour, and will be no less empty for the delay in its occupation.

'And,' added Van Agteren, 'I would consider it an act of Christian fellowship, and after you have heard my tale you will understand the value of such a service. So, may I sit?'

Couvret appraised the Dutchman. His training in the law had convinced him of his ability to judge a man's character within minutes of meeting him, and he detected in Van Agteren no signs of malice or hostility, only a deep fear kept under control by an act of will. Yes, a predator circled above him, but Couvret lived under a similar threat, and he was lonely, and tired of his own company.

'Sit,' he said at last, 'and I will listen to your tale.'

Van Agteren was a native of Tilburg, in the south of the country. His family lived in the shadow of St Joseph's Church, or the Heuvelse Church as it was known to the people of that town, which explained the origins of his name, for Van Agteren meant 'from behind' in his language, and referred to one born in the vicinity of a great building. He was a clever boy, and at an early age he began to train as a clerk to the famous Dutch scholar

Cornelis Schuyler, a man particularly learned in arithmetic, geometry, and astrology.

Tilburg was a strange town in which to find one such as Schuyler: it had grown up around a 'herd place', the shared pasturelands for sheep, and was filled with weavers and looms. Schuyler lived in a small, cluttered house close by the Kerkpad of the Church of St Dionysius, called the Heikese Church, and he rarely left its precincts. He would tell Van Agteren that all he needed for his work was contained 'out there' – gesturing to the papers that took up every shelf space in the house – and 'in here', tapping his head. Of course, this was not entirely true, and a steady stream of visitors came to Schuyler bearing documents and maps, and scientific instruments the purposes of which were unknown to Van Agteren, indeed obscure to all but a handful of the most brilliant of men, his master among them.

Schuyler was a widower, with only one daughter, Eliene. She took after her father, and was a more able assistant to him even than Van Agteren, although her sex required her to be discreet about her gifts, and retiring in the presence of the old men who came to visit her father. A degree of affection gradually arose between Eliene and her father's clerk, and the subject of marriage was broached, but only in private. Schuyler was fiercely possessive of his daughter, but also fond of Van Agteren, and it seemed to the young lovers that a match between them might meet all of their needs, for it would assure the scholar of the continued presence of Eliene, Van Agteren not wishing to leave Schuyler's employ.

One night, in the winter of 1589, a knock came upon the door of Schuyler's house, and it was put to Van Agteren to answer it. A labourer stood on the step, a package under his arm, and asked if the gentleman was home, for he had found something that he believed might be of interest to him. It was late, but Van Agteren admitted the man and brought him to meet Schuyler, who was engaged in the dissection of the body of a monkey sold to him by the sailor who had owned the little creature until its death. The sailor had wept as he pocketed Schuyler's coin.

The labourer explained that he was engaged in work in the vicinity of the Heuvelse Church. A house nearby had collapsed, and another, larger one was to be raised in its place. The labourer was one of those responsible for digging the foundations, and while doing so he had come upon the item that he now presented to Schuyler.

It was a book, of a most unusual and expensive character, bound in a hide unfamiliar to Schuyler or Van Agteren, upon which scars and traces of vein were visible. It was deep red and reminded the younger man uncomfortably of fresh meat. Schuyler made as if to open it and inspect its contents, and the labourer laughed.

'I wish you better luck than I had, *mijnheer*,' he said.

The book would not open. It was as though its pages had been smeared with glue and then stuck together. Schuyler took a thin blade and gently tried to separate the leaves, but it was no use. The book would not yield its secrets to him.

'Perhaps it is a false book,' said Van Agteren.

'What do you mean?' asked Schuyler.

'At Utrecht I once saw a volume of the *Tetrabiblios* which looked to the naked eye like any other, but was revealed to be only the imitation of the work. It was more box than book. The scholar who owned it used it to hide gold from thieves who would have no interest in his library.'

Schuyler ran a thumb along the tops of the pages.

'Yet this feels like paper to my hand,' he said. He tapped the cover all over, listening for changes in tone that might reveal a hollow interior, but heard none. 'I believe this to be a true book,' he concluded, 'but how it has been so closely sealed, I cannot tell.'

The collapsed house belonged to one Dekker, a most ignorant man. It was highly unlikely, therefore, that the book belonged to him. The labourer confirmed this by informing Schuyler that he only discovered the volume after breaking through a thin layer of rock and stone far below the level upon which Dekker had built his original house.

'Strange, too, *mijnheer*,' said the labourer, 'is that one moment the book was not present, and then it was. I did not uncover it. I simply turned, and saw it before me. As you can see, it is not even stained or damaged in any way.'

This was true. The book was without blemish, which was extraordinary for something that had presumably been lying in the ground for so long. Schuyler wondered aloud if it were not possible that the book had been dropped there by a passing other, or had fallen from a window, but the labourer assured him that the plot was not overlooked in a way that could have allowed for the latter, and he was entirely alone when he discovered it, which ruled out the former. And yet the third option, that the book might have been buried, seemed beyond belief, given that the labourer had been breaking through a layer of ancient stone when it was found.

One final possibility did present itself: the labourer had stolen the book, and was now trying to make a little money from the only man in Tilburg who might appreciate the value of such an item. But Van Agteren knew the labourer and his family, and had no reason to believe that he was anything but honest. He whispered the same to Schuyler, for he was by now adept at telling the direction of the old scholar's thoughts.

Finally, Schuyler consented to give the labourer some coin for his trouble, and promised him more if the book proved to be of unusual value once opened. To Van Agteren's surprise, the man did not try to haggle, and neither did he object to the small sum handed over to him by the scholar. He simply pocketed it and left, doing so almost with a sense of relief.

Van Agteren escorted the labourer to the door and took his arm on the step.

'You could have got much more for that book had you taken it to Eindhoven or Utrecht,' said Van Agteren.

'I know that,' said the labourer. 'In truth, I had considered making the journey to Eindhoven, but now I am glad that I did not. I just wanted to be rid of the book, and had I the wealth to do so, it is I who might have paid your master to take it off my hands.'

'Why do you say this?' asked Van Agteren.

'You have not yet touched it,' said the labourer, 'nor held it in your grip. It is like being in contact with a living thing. It pulses, and smells of blood. I found it just today, but I did not want it to remain a night under my roof. Even your master's coin may end up in the coffers of the Heuvelse Church, for I fear that any food or drink bought with it might end up poisoning my family and me. And—'

'Yes, what is it?'

The labourer was looking out into the night, as though expecting to see someone emerge from the mist.

'Before I left my home to come here, I glimpsed a shape in the fog – a man, but larger than any man that I have ever seen, yet also indistinct. He was watching the house, and I am certain that he followed me here. I thought that I could hear his footsteps under the sound of my own, but when I looked back, I saw nothing, and I can find no trace of him now. Perhaps I was mistaken.'

With that, the labourer left and Van Agteren never saw him alive again. A wall collapsed on him the following day and he was dead by the time his colleagues retrieved him from under the stones.

Van Agteren returned to Schuyler's study and found him examining the book, testing its spine and covers for some concealed mechanism that might cause the volume to open.

'Extraordinary,' said Schuyler, stroking the cover of the book. 'Feel it, Maarten. It is warm to the touch, like living flesh.'

Van Agteren had no desire to lay a hand on the book, not after what the labourer had told him. He shared the details with his master, but Schuyler just laughed, remarking that the fog often played games with his own perceptions.

Van Agteren departed, closing the study door behind him. In the hallway he met Eliene carrying a candle.

'Who was that who came here so late?' she asked.

'A labourer. He found a book in the ground, and brought it to your father for examination.'

'A book? What kind of book?'

'I don't know,' said Van Agteren.

'But you saw it?'

'Yes, and I cannot say why, but already I wish that I had never laid eyes on it.'

Eliene stared at him.

'Sometimes,' she said, 'I think that you are most peculiar.'

'And if you love me, then you are most peculiar too.'

'Yes, I suppose I am.'

Her lips parted, and he kissed her.

'My father—' she said.

'Is lost in the examination of his book.'

'It is almost my time of flowers,' she said. 'But you can come to my bed.'

And he did.

Van Agteren did not stay with Eliene for the night. A pair of elderly servants tended to the needs of the house, and he wanted to give them no more cause for gossip than they already had. He also respected Schuyler, although not so much that he was above sleeping with his daughter. He did not know how much the old man suspected of his relationship with Eliene, but he wanted to give him no reason to act on any suspicions that he might have.

The study door was open when Van Agteren awoke. He knocked before entering, but received no reply. The room was empty, and the little compartment in which Schuyler slept was unoccupied. Neither was Schuyler in the kitchen or elsewhere in the house, but the front door was unlocked, which meant that he had left either very early or very late. The servants were already preparing breakfast and had not seen their master. It was most odd.

Eliene rose, but had no more idea of her father's whereabouts than anyone else. She was not concerned for him, though. He was a man of capricious moods, even if they rarely led him to take to the streets at unusual hours. But Van Agteren was uneasy. After eating a hurried breakfast, he went in search of his master.

And although Tilburg was a small town, he could find no trace of him.

At the Sign of the Oak, Van Agteren poured Couvret another glass of *jenever*.

'I admit that you have me intrigued,' said Couvret, 'although I still don't understand why you have chosen to share this tale with me.'

'Oh, there is more to come,' said Van Agteren. 'And far less pleasant it is, too.'

Van Agteren excused himself to make water, leaving Couvret alone. The inn had grown stuffy and warm, and Couvret had drunk more than he might have wished. He felt the need for some air. He went to the front door and stepped outside. A boy was clearing the snow from behind the inn so that its customers might have an unobstructed path, but already fresh flakes had begun to fall. Beyond him, Couvret saw a massive figure in black walking in the direction of the Nieuwe Kerk, although it appeared to be more shadow than man, a consequence, perhaps, of the poor light and descending snow.

'Do you know that man?' Couvret asked the boy.

'What man?'

'The one who passed by just moments before I came out.'

'You must be mistaken, *mijnheer*,' said the boy. 'No one has passed since I started clearing this snow. You can see for yourself that there are no fresh prints on the ground.'

The boy was right. The new snow had partially filled the old footprints, and there were none more recent.

Despite the cold, Couvret moved past the boy and walked to where he had seen the man, but even here there was no sign of the presence of another, and Couvret's were the only marks that led from the inn.

He returned to find Van Agteren seated at the table, waiting for him.

'Where did you go?' asked Van Agteren.

'To take some air,' Couvret replied.

'You're a braver man than I. I didn't even venture outside, but put most of my piss on the steps. Forgive me, but you seem troubled.'

Couvret took a sip of *jenever*.

'I thought that I saw someone walking, but I was wrong,' he said.

Van Agteren regarded him carefully.

'When you say "someone", what precisely do you mean?'

'A figure in black. A huge man, I think, but almost a shadow against shadows. Yet when I went in pursuit of him I could find no sign that he had passed this way.'

Van Agteren looked to the door, as though the subject might make himself apparent, summoned by their discourse. Whatever animation the Dutchman had demonstrated up to that point voided itself in an instant, and he seemed to be on the verge of weeping.

'Then I have not much time left for my tale,' he said. 'Listen . . .'

Schuyler had not returned to his house by the time Van Agteren reached it. By now even Eliene was starting to fear for his safety, and one of the servants had been sent to instruct the local militia to keep a watch for Schuyler.

Van Agteren found Eliene in her father's study. She was sitting at his desk, the book that the labourer had brought the night before lying open in front of her. Van Agteren could not contain his surprise.

'How did you unlock it?' he asked.

'Unlock it?' replied Eliene. 'I found it this way when I came to see if my father had left any indication of where he might have gone. It's odd: only one page will open. The rest appear to be sealed.'

Van Agteren stood over her and watched as she demonstrated. The pages were made from what might have been vellum, with only one side of the parchment used, the roughness of the other betraying the animal origins of the material.

'Here it is,' she said, revealing what Van Agteren took to be a map of constellations, except none were familiar to him, and the markings beside them were in an unknown alphabet. An expert hand had created the map. Van Agteren could not recall ever before seeing such perfection in illustration.

'It's beautiful,' he said.

'But no night sky looks like this,' said Eliene. 'It is an invention.'

Although he could not interpret the markings, Van Agteren believed that they might be mathematical calculations, for among them were diagrams familiar to him from Euclidian geometry. Why would someone go to such trouble to indulge a fantasy?

'Wait!' said Eliene. 'I think another page has freed itself from whatever substance was used to seal the whole.'

She used two hands to turn a number of folios, such was the weight of the book.

'What's this?' she said. 'It cannot be.'

Revealed to them was an intricate drawing of Schuyler's study and its contents – his instruments, his books, his shelves and furniture – but the word 'drawing' did not do justice to the execution. Rather, what was contained in the book was a perfect copy of the room, as though the page were not made from paper but was instead a mirror without tarnish. The skill with which it had been created was beyond even the greatest artist. It was impossible to comprehend how it might have been done, or how long it must have taken to complete.

Van Agteren licked his finger and pressed it against the page. It came back without a trace of ink or paint. He gazed at the drawing. The angle of depiction was unusual. It was almost as if . . .

Van Agteren turned and squatted behind the desk, so that he was facing Eliene.

'What are you doing?' asked Eliene.

'I could not swear to it, but the one who did this could only have produced it by using a glass to reflect the room back to him at the same angle as the book. But why?'

'When did you say this book came to my father?'

'Last night.'

'And where was it found?'

'Buried deep beneath the foundations of the old home of Dekker, or so the man who brought it to us claimed.'

'You must find him and bring him back here. He may have more to tell.'

'I promise you that he does not. He is a simple man, but an honest one. He wanted only to be rid of the book.'

'And did you go by Dekker's plot when searching for my father?'

'Yes. I asked after him this morning, but was told that he had not been seen there.'

'Will you try again?'

'Of course.'

She held his hand in hers and kissed the knuckles, one by one.

'Thank you.'

'We will find him,' said Van Agteren. 'I shall not rest until he is with us again.'

It was growing dark, and by the time Van Agteren reached the Dekker plot all work had ceased, and the workmen had gone. He found Dekker and his family staying at his father's house while work continued on their own, but the thatcher had not seen Schuyler in days. Neither did he have any knowledge of a book, but he demonstrated considerable interest in any possible value it might have, and was quick to claim ownership of it and to curse the just deceased labourer who had brought it to Schuyler. It was left to Van Agteren to remind Dekker that anything found on the land was ultimately the property of the lords of Tilburg, and it might be better for all if Dekker did not make a fuss until more could be learned about the book. Dekker assented, but only reluctantly.

As Van Agteren was leaving, Dekker asked him, 'Tell me, who was that who walked here with you?'

'I came alone,' said Van Agteren. 'There is no other.'

'But I would swear that I saw a man following in your footsteps. Big he was, all dressed in black. I might almost have taken him for a priest.'

Van Agteren denied it again, and left Dekker to puzzle over the mystery without him. But he was reminded of what the unfortunate labourer had told him the previous night, and on the walk back to Schuyler's dwelling he spent as much time looking behind him as ahead.

He was met at the door by Eliene. Only the candlelight gave life to her face. Otherwise, it resembled a porcelain mask.

'Nobody has seen your father,' he said.

But the only reply she made was 'Come', as she led him upstairs to the study.

Another page of the book was open. It showed a detailed anatomical drawing of her father's face, split evenly down the middle, rendered in a manner that would have incited the envy of Vesalius himself. One side depicted him as he was in life, except that his mouth was open wide, as though caught in the act of screaming. The other, the left, was without skin, and some unknown insects writhed in the exposed flesh, four claws visible around the maw of their mouths, and the pincers of an earwig jutting from the end of their lower abdomens. One was forcing itself out of the hollow socket of Schuyler's left eye.

'Someone is playing a cruel game,' said Eliene, and Van Agteren thought that he caught a hint of suspicion directed at him.

'Not I!' he said. 'I have not even been here.'

Eliene instantly relented.

'I'm sorry,' she said, and clasped herself to him. 'I don't know why I should have thought such a thing. But I don't understand what is happening. I came into the study after you'd left, and the book was open at this page. The servants claim to know nothing about it, and I believe them. They never come into this room, not even to clean. They know better than to disturb my father's work.'

Van Agteren closed the book, hiding that dreadful version of Schuyler. For a moment, as he touched his hand to the cover, he felt it pulse in an unpleasant way.

'It is the book,' he said. 'It should have been left in the ground.'

'Then what do you propose to do with it? Return it there?'

'No,' said Van Agteren. 'I'm going to burn it.'

The fire in the kitchen was already blazing when Van Agteren and Eliene arrived with the book. They sent the servants out, and Van Agteren added more wood to the blaze, until even to approach it was to feel one's skin begin to prickle. Finally, when he was satisfied, he threw the book on it, but the stench that immediately arose was so terrible that they could not stay in the kitchen. Even outside the room, the smell was foul, like the rotting carcass of an animal that had been set to roast. It filled the house, and Eliene became violently ill. They heard a knock on the door, and their neighbour, Janzen, was found to be standing before them, come to complain about the stink. The whole street was filled with it, and Van Agteren had no choice but to remove the book from the fire. It was slightly damaged on one side, but no more than that. The cover had blistered like skin.

Van Agteren placed the book in a sack, added bricks to it, then walked to the canal and threw it in the water. He watched it sink before returning to the Schuyler home.

The smell remained in the house and the servants were burning sage to get rid of it. Van Agteren sat with Eliene, and their only visitor was a militiaman who came to confirm that Schuyler had not returned. He told them that a search would be organized at first light.

Van Agteren did not sleep with Eliene that night. She wanted to be alone. He smelled nutmeg, which he knew she used during her time of flowers.

Van Agteren went to his room and worked by candlelight, transcribing some of Schuyler's untidy notes. He only ceased his labours when his eyes began to ache. He dipped his quill in water to clean it and watched the ink spread through the liquid, turning it from clear to dark.

He lay on his narrow cot and thought of the book.

It was still dark when he woke. A sound had pulled him out of sleep. He heard a creak, and saw his door closing, although it remained sufficiently ajar to enable him to discern a figure in the shadows beyond.

'Eliene?' he said.

There was no reply.

He climbed from his cot and went to the hall. He looked to his left and saw Eliene enter her father's study. He followed her. A light burned inside the study. He could see it under the bottom of the door.

He put his hand on the handle. It was warm. He pushed, and the door opened.

Eliene stood naked, her back to him. It took Van Agteren a moment to realize that her feet were not touching the floor, and she was instead hanging suspended. In the shadows behind her was a greater darkness, a thing of substance like a statue made from black glass, and within it Van Agteren glimpsed an infinite number of angles, and the lights of multitudinous stars. And while the being before him was physically present, yet it also appeared hollow, for there was embryonic movement inside it, and a cluster of eyes peered back at Van Agteren from within.

And on Schuyler's reading stand lay the book, the same one that he had last seen sinking into the dank waters of the canal.

Eliene's body rotated in the air. She turned – or was turned – to face him.

Her eyes were gone, her face cracked around their empty

sockets like a child's doll to which a hammer had been taken in a fit of rage. It seemed as though an unseen blade were being used upon her flesh, for her body began to bleed: her belly, her breasts, her thighs. Van Agteren glimpsed patterns forming on her skin, and he thought that they resembled the coastlines of unfamiliar continents, and maps of unknown constellations.

And all the time the glass being, the obsidian man, stood unmoving behind her.

Eliene spoke.

'Maarten,' she said. 'The book contains worlds.'

She stretched out her arms, then her legs. From behind her came a sound like the grinding and shattering of glass.

The entity exploded, sending shards of darkness splintering through Eliene, then freezing them in place, so that for just an instant she was a being of both flesh and mineral, her body petrified at the moment that her soul departed. Then once again all was movement, and Van Agteren instinctively shielded his face with his arms and waited for the fragments to pierce him, but nothing happened.

He opened his eyes, and there was only blood.

The *jenever* was gone. Van Agteren's story was nearly complete.

'Do you believe me?' he asked.

And Couvret heard himself answer 'Yes' before the word even formed in his head.

'What did you do?'

'I fled,' said Van Agteren. 'They would think me a murderer, or a sorcerer, after what had befallen Eliene. Even now, they are at my heels, but they will never take me.'

'Why? Will you leave the country?'

'No, I will never leave here. Another comes. Wherever Eliene may be, there too shall I also be before this night is out. I feel it.'

'That figure I saw outside . . .'

'Yes.'

'What is it? What do you believe it to be?'

'You served Henry of Navarre, did you not?'

'I did.'

'Did you fear him?'

'Sometimes.'

'And Henry is not even a great king,' said Van Agteren. 'Perhaps someday he may be, but not now. He was forced to run from Paris or be annihilated by a more powerful force. Every king, if he looks, will see another who threatens him – a king in name, or a king in waiting. Only God has no fear of kings, or so I once believed.

'But does God fear the Devil? Does he fear the King Below? This I now wonder. Because if He could, would God not wipe from existence the creature that took Eliene? Would He not have destroyed that book, or prevented it from ever being found? Is God cruel, or careless, or are there beings that threaten even His rule?'

'That is heresy,' said Couvret.

'And you are an expert on that, Huguenot,' said Van Agteren.

'Perhaps I am. And what of the book?'

'Gone,' said Van Agteren.

'Where?'

'You saw what is coming for me,' said Van Agteren. 'Do you really wish to know?'

Couvret did not answer. There was no need.

Van Agteren stood.

'Where will you go now?' asked Couvret.

'I will walk, and I will breathe the air while I still can. Thank you for listening to my tale.'

'I still do not understand why you chose to share it with me,' said Couvret.

'I think you do,' said Van Agteren. 'I chose you because you smell of the hunted, just like me. And maybe,' he added, 'I chose you because you are unlucky.'

Couvret watched him leave. A flurry of snowflakes entered in his stead, and melted on the floor.

He never heard of Van Agteren again.

* * *

Early the next morning, word reached Couvret that his ship would depart for England at noon. He repacked what little he had removed from his trunk and paid the innkeeper to have it taken in a cart to the port. Couvret ate a good breakfast, and arrived at the quayside an hour before the ship was due to depart. The vessel was a crayer, a single-masted merchant ship designed not for speed but to carry the maximum amount of cargo in its hold. Couvret's berth was a board and pillow against the hull, sectioned off from the rest of the hold by a piece of sacking hung from nails. He was the only passenger. He stood on the deck as he left the Continent behind, never to return.

The crossing was long and slow. Fully loaded, the crayer was capable of making about two miles an hour, and the distance from Amsterdam to London was almost three hundred miles. Couvret spent much of the voyage sleeping and reading. The food was poor, but filling. He was a good traveller, which helped.

On the last night of the crossing, just as darkness was falling, he woke from a nap to see that the sacking on the empty berth across from his own had fallen, obscuring the interior. Previously he had been able to see its hard pillow and narrow board from his own. Now he could not, and he thought that he detected signs of movement from behind the sacking.

He stood, holding on to the edge of his bunk for support until he was certain that he had his sea legs. He moved towards the other berth, and black smoke began to rise from behind it. No, not smoke: oil, or ink, spreading from behind the sacking, adhering to the ceiling and hull and bulkhead, smothering all, darkness upon darkness . . .

Couvret woke for a second time, emerging so suddenly from his nightmare that he banged his head painfully on the deck above his head. When he had stopped seeing stars, he sat on the edge of his board and looked at the opposite berth.

Its sacking hung in tattered ribbons, as though torn apart by gunshot.

Or splinters.

Couvret found the book at the bottom of his trunk, wrapped in a shirt that was not his. It was, as Van Agteren had noted, warm to the touch. Through the white muslin it resembled meat from a butcher's block.

When had he passed it on, Couvret wondered? Before they had even met, while Couvret was eating alone at the inn? When he went to make water? It didn't matter. Getting rid of it hadn't saved him, because when Couvret unwrapped the book it would open only at one page. It showed Van Agteren, his mouth agape, with flames emerging from his throat. Wherever he now was, Van Agteren was burning.

Destroying the book would do no good. Van Agteren had tried fire and water, both to no avail. But Couvret had something that Van Agteren did not.

Couvret had faith.

He took his Bible and placed it on top of the book. Then he wrapped both in the muslin shirt, and tied the parcel with rope from the hold. He examined the ship's cargo until he found a Dutch oak chest with a second baseboard laid within it for extra strength. He ascended to the main deck, and managed to remove some tools from the rigger's box without being seen. Then he went to work and when he was done, the book and Bible were safely hidden in the chest. It was not a perfect job, but would pass a cursory inspection.

Couvret left the hold and spent the rest of the voyage on the main deck with the captain. He was cold and wet by the time the crayer entered the Thames, but he did not care. When he disembarked, his letters of introduction in hand, no shadow followed him from the ship.

And London swallowed him up.

2. The Djinn

Maggs: no first name, or none that anyone could remember, or cared to use. Maggs: redolent with the whiff of poorly dried clothes and old paper, a parcel of books always to hand. Maggs: ready to buy, readier still to sell.

They said that he did not love books, not really, but this was not true. He simply had few sentimental attachments to them. They were useful for the knowledge that they contained, or the money they might bring him. Some were aesthetically interesting, but most were not. He kept a small library in his rooms, containing volumes of particular rarity or attractiveness, although even these he was not above selling for the right price. But most of the books that passed through his living space did so for only the briefest of periods, for they were on their way to other hands. Those for which a buyer could not be found were of no use to him, and so were offloaded by weight, or, as a last resort, left on the steps of a public lending library. Whatever his other flaws, Maggs could not bring himself to destroy a book.

He kept an eye on the obituary columns, and it was said of him that only flies could beat him to a bibliophile's corpse. He haunted estate sales and preyed on the relatives of collectors who were too numbed by grief to pay close attention to the disposal of assets like books, or had little or no understanding of the worth of a collection to begin with. He was adept at haggling over volumes of minor value in order to distract attention from those that really interested him and regarded it as a sorry day indeed if he were forced to pay more than half of a book's true price. His every waking moment was consumed by covers and pages, and they haunted his dreams by night.

Maggs specialized in what was often euphemistically described as 'esoterica', a term capable of encompassing everything from the erotic to the occult. He was a sexless being, so the former did not interest him, and also a committed atheist, which meant that the latter did not frighten him. Rather, he regarded the buyers of both as depraved in similar ways and endeavoured to spend as little time as possible in their company. If forced to make a distinction, Maggs might have opined that the collectors of pornography were less inclined to quibble over price, and, although clearly the possessors of polluted minds, were less sinister than the occultists, whose connection to the ordinary tenets of humanity was tentative at best.

There were exceptions, of course, for the ranks of the occultists numbered some for whom money was no object at all, as long as they got what they wanted. Unfortunately for Maggs, they tended to seek volumes of extreme rarity, most of them private printings, or even manuscript copies of otherwise singular works. In addition, some of the books on their wish lists had been consigned to the flames by various clerics over the centuries and now existed only as smoke-tinged rumours.

Still, Maggs was occasionally lucky, although his good fortune was a consequence of his tenacity and perseverance. Twice in recent years he had mined valuable occult gems from otherwise ordinary collections, the relatives of the deceased – and, possibly, the deceased themselves, given the solitary nature of the finds – quite unaware of the uniqueness of the dusty, battered old works in question. At other times, he had been alerted by his network of lesser book scouts and minor informants to the existence of noteworthy assemblages in the estates of gentlemen collectors – for they were almost exclusively gentlemen – who were so discreet in their interests as to have bypassed Maggs's attentions entirely. But he also retained meticulous lists of his own private customers, so that, upon their demise, he might be in a position to buy back, for pennies on the pound, the books that he had sold them in life.

The bibliophilic possessions of one such customer – Sandton, late of Highbury, interested in illustrated volumes from the Far East, mostly seventeenth and eighteenth century, floral, but occasionally with a mild erotic bent – now lay in boxes on the floor of Maggs's modest rooms. Some he had himself sold to Sandton, and he welcomed them back like old debtors with bankers' notes in their pockets. Others were less familiar to him, but he had been able to make a shrewd estimate of their value based on his knowledge of similar items. Unfortunately, Sandton's son was no fool, and Maggs had been forced to pay more for the choicer items in the collection than he would have liked, even if he were still certain of eventually turning a profit from the whole business.

Maggs carefully examined each book, noting the nicks and tears, checking the binding and the edges, shaking his head over any recent foxing. Sandton had been more careful than most, but a number of volumes betrayed signs of ill use. Maggs was inclined to blame the son.

His work took him into the small hours and it was only as he was repacking the books that he spotted, lying in a corner of one of the boxes, the shape of a small volume wrapped in cloth. He couldn't recall handling it during the negotiations with Sandton's son, and he certainly hadn't paid any money for it. The boxes had been empty when he brought them to Highbury to transport the books, and he had packed everything himself in order to prevent any accidental damage. He couldn't imagine how this interloper had contrived to gain passage, unless Sandton had added it when he wasn't looking, although Maggs could understand neither why nor how Sandton might have done such a thing, for he had kept his distance from Maggs throughout the entire process, appearing to regard it as a dull necessity destined to yield only a small profit, and doing little to hide his distaste for the book scout.

Now Maggs unwrapped the book. It had a brown leather binding – relatively undamaged, although clearly of considerable antiquity – and an unusual locking device consisting of a pair of concentric silver rings, each marked with tiny symbols, and each capable of being turned independently. Maggs took a magnifying glass from his desk drawer and examined the lock and its inscriptions. He then went to his shelves, removed one volume of an encyclopedia, found the reference that he sought and returned to his desk with the book. Yes, the symbols were Arabic-Indic numerals, and Eastern – in all likelihood Persian or Urdu: he could tell by the differences in the designs of the four, five and six numerals. What he was looking at was an early combination lock of a kind that he had never encountered before.

He spent a few minutes experimenting with the dials, to no avail, before putting the book aside. He would look at it again in the morning. It was curious, though. He wondered if he should return it to the younger Sandton, and decided to sleep on the matter. The testy negotiations over the purchase of the books still rankled. Had he been a man of faith, Maggs might have chosen to view the little volume as a gift from God, a way of making up for some of his lost profit. He brought the book to his bedroom and placed it on his bedside table. It was the last thing that he saw before he turned off the light and closed his eyes.

That night, Maggs dreamed that he was working on the lock. His fingers moved in his sleep – testing, turning. When the click came, it was so slight that it did not disturb his rest.

Maggs slept late the next morning. He woke feeling fractious and unsettled, and barely glanced at the leather book by his bedside, for there was money to be made. He went to the window, checked the sky and saw no sign of rainclouds. He dressed hurriedly, stuffed a slice of buttered bread into his mouth for sustenance, then placed two boxes of Sandton's choicest books on his little trolley and headed out.

Most of Maggs's business was conducted with the bookshops

that lined Charing Cross Road. His dealings with them followed an established pattern. He would divide up his hoard, determining which books were best suited to each individual dealer, and then, once a week, he would pay them all a visit: this one on Monday, these two on Tuesday, that fellow on Wednesday. He preferred not to try to sell books towards the end of the week, when the booksellers' coffers might already have been emptied by other scouts, and a good price would be harder to obtain as a consequence. Then again, Maggs was not above offering to buy a drink come close of business on Friday in order to draw in a buyer, especially if he felt that he had a nice prize with which to bait his hook.

But most of the dealers were not particularly sociable, regarding Maggs and his kind as an unfortunate necessity in the trade and one that was best left publicly unacknowledged. Some – the ones who regarded themselves as 'gentlemen booksellers' – refused even to have him on their premises for longer than it took him to drop off a parcel of books for examination, and then parted only reluctantly with money when they found something they liked, as though doing Maggs a favour by consenting to accept the volumes, let alone pay for the pleasure. Maggs preferred dealing with those who, like himself, were not afraid to get dusty and dirty and sniffed after treasures with all the grubby energy of pigs seeking truffles in a French forest.

Atkinson was just such a dealer. He owned one of the smaller bookshops on Charing Cross Road, although nobody could ever have accused him of not using the premises to its fullest advantage. He had fitted out the shop himself, and any space capable of containing books had been adapted for shelving. He appeared to own only one shirt, or multiple versions of the same: a red-and-white-striped affair that, in fabric and hue, reminded Maggs of a deck chair. In fact, since Atkinson closed his shop for one week each August in order to take the sun at Brighton, it wouldn't have surprised Maggs to learn that, somewhere in the town, one or more such chairs had been reduced to wooden slats in order to serve the bookseller's sartorial needs.

Atkinson didn't allow smoking on his premises, as he claimed that it damaged the books. He refused to drink tea anywhere but in the little office behind the counter, for fear that an accidental spillage might ruin a volume, and even then he sipped directly from a Dewar flask and always replaced the lid between mouthfuls. There was, it was said, a Mrs Atkinson, although nobody had seen her in years, possibly not even Mr Atkinson, whose place of business was the first on the street to open each morning and the last to close again at night. Even then, Atkinson could still be glimpsed inside, examining books by lamplight, or just sitting in his little office, reading and sipping tea.

Atkinson's particular areas of interest included the kind of Asian volumes contained in Sandton's collection. His knowledge of the subject was greater than Maggs's and his list of potential buyers for such items commensurately larger. Maggs wanted to turn the books around as quickly as possible, for he had his eye on an estate sale in Bath the next month, and he trusted Atkinson more than any other dealer in London. Even allowing for Atkinson's percentage on the sale, Maggs would still be comfortably in the black on the Sandton collection and the money would be in his hands more quickly than if he tried to sell its contents himself.

But Atkinson was busy when he reached the shop – he was on the verge of offloading half a shelf of nautical volumes for at least twice what they were worth and ten times what he had paid for them – and Maggs knew better than to distract him from such a windfall, especially when he was about to ask for Atkinson's assistance. Furthermore, if Atkinson did well out of the nautical volumes then he might be inclined to settle for a smaller cut on the Sandton collection. So Maggs simply dropped off the boxes, and told Atkinson that he'd call on him again the next day to discuss their value. With that done and his burden lightened, he wheeled his trolley down to the Corner House on the Strand, where he treated himself to a hearty late breakfast in anticipation of the influx of funds that would soon be coming his way.

Maggs spent the rest of the day scouting for books and discovered a nice underpriced first edition of *The Water Babies* at Marks & Co, which he then sold to a young bookseller at Sotheran's for a considerable profit. (Both Marks and Cohen, proprietors of the former establishment, had trained at the latter, and would have been galled to learn of the oversight.) With his pockets heavier than when he'd started that morning and the promise of more money to come, it was a cheerful Maggs who returned to his rooms as darkness fell.

He had forgotten about the little volume until he spotted it lying on his bedside table. He instantly saw that the two interlocking silver rings had separated and the volume was now unlocked. He had a vague memory of dreaming about the book, but that was all. It had certainly been secure when he went to bed, and he was sure that nobody had been in his rooms since he left that morning. He could only suppose that either his efforts of the night before had inadvertently led him to stumble across the correct combination, and the lock had been so stiff with age that it had taken a while for the mechanism to respond; or the lock was long past its usefulness, and the simple act of fiddling with it had caused it to yield.

Maggs examined the damage of the years, and the exposed parts of the boards and binding. He thought the headband might have been worked at the same time that the book was sewn, and cord used instead of catgut. At a guess, he was prepared to date it to the fifteenth century, or earlier, which made it quite the gem. As before, he could still find no trace of decoration on the cover, or any indication of its contents.

He dug up a pair of cotton gloves before opening the book. If it was valuable, he did not want to risk having the dirt and oils from his skin transferring to the paper and staining it. The pages were of a linen fibre mix – he could tell just by looking at them – with rough edges. The first four were entirely blank. The rest – perhaps 50 in all – were covered in script, although rendered in an alphabet and language that Maggs did not recognize. The ink was reddish purple and had not faded in the slightest over the years, so that the pages might have been filled that very morning. The volume was also palimpsestic, so that a turn on the diagonal might reveal a different communication to one familiar with its language of origin.

Maggs's first impression was that the book had been written with a sense of some urgency, for the calligraphy had none of the beauty and elegance of even the more modest European manuscript copies that had passed his way. It seemed to Maggs that what he was holding was a notebook, but it struck him as unusual that a creation such as this – a leather-bound book, constructed with enough skill to survive relatively intact for five or six centuries at least, its pages of the finest quality – should contain only a palimpsest rendered in untidy script.

He spent an hour going through his encyclopedia, consulting examples of alphabets ancient and modern, trying to find a comparable model for the scribbles. He had no success and finally set the book aside, but not before wondering once again about the extraordinary vibrancy of its ink. He carefully touched it with a gloved finger, half-expecting it to stain the tip, but the material came away clean.

He decided that Atkinson might know of someone willing to buy it, earning Maggs a nice little windfall. Then again, he could always take it to the British Library and ask someone there to examine it first. Yes, that might be for the best. After all, he reasoned, he could have in his possession the notebook of some Arab genius, an Eastern da Vinci, although an Arab would surely have written in Arabic, and the book's only connection to that civilization appeared to be its lock. Could the lock have been a later addition? Possibly, but Maggs was no more expert in locks than he was in the lost languages of the East.

He went to his window and listened to the sound of a man singing in the pub at the end of the lane, a piano tinkling in accompaniment. The song was unknown to Maggs, but not to the babble of voices that joined in the chorus. He felt no urge to join them. He was, by nature, a solitary being.

It was a warm, close night, so he left the windows open to allow some air to circulate, even though not the lightest of breezes disturbed the stillness. He stripped to his underclothes and went to bed, where he read a couple of pages of *The Octopus*. He had a weakness for books about railways. It came from childhood, he knew, when he would watch the trains pass along the track that ran below his family home. He had wanted to become a train driver, imagining that there could be no finer vocation, but the closest he had ever come to his wish was a seat in a third-class carriage. Instead, he was a single man of indeterminate age, who smelled of damp clothes and dry paper, and would not be mourned when he died, except perhaps by the handful of dealers who could be bothered to close up their shops for the duration of the funeral.

The singing in the pub stopped, and he heard time being called. He closed *The Octopus*. Tomorrow he would meet with Atkinson, and they would discuss an appropriate price for the books. As he nodded off to sleep, he heard a sound as of the pages of a book being turned. He put it down to the wind, for he was too tired to recall the calmness of the night.

The following morning he again woke later than usual, and his renewed sense of being poorly rested was not entirely unjustified, for the night had remained very humid, and it seemed that he spent most of it twisting and turning in an effort to find a cool spot on his narrow bed. He shaved, nicking himself painfully in the process, and headed for Charing Cross Road and his meeting with Atkinson. Only when he was more than halfway there did he realize that he had forgotten the little notebook, but he was in no mood to return for it. The British Library would still be standing tomorrow, and Maggs was more interested in Atkinson's valuation of the illustrated volumes and in discovering how quickly he could sell them on.

Atkinson was on his stool by the window, carefully erasing the pencilled price on a modest set of Austen. Beside him were the two boxes that Maggs had delivered the day before, still containing the books. Perhaps Atkinson hadn't got round to looking at them yet, but that would have been unusual for the bookseller, who was generally quick off the mark when it came to making a few quid. But the boxes were in the place where Atkinson habitually placed assortments in which, for whatever reason, he was not interested, there to be collected by their soon-to-be disappointed owner. But it wasn't conceivable that Atkinson was uninterested in those volumes, thought Maggs. They couldn't have been closer to hard cash if they bore the king's head on them.

'All right?' said Maggs. 'Warm one out there.'

'Warm one in 'ere and all,' said Atkinson.

The sweat was dripping from his brow and his underarms were already stained with patches of damp. Maggs was sure that his own shirt was pasted to his back beneath his coat. He should have left it at home, but his coat was as much a part of him as his eyes and ears. He could fit a lot of books into the pockets of that coat, inside and out.

'So,' said Maggs. 'You take a look at 'em yet?'

Atkinson seemed puzzled. He peered at Maggs through his thick spectacles. They were slightly fogged with condensation, so he took them off and wiped them with a handkerchief, then put them on again. It did nothing to alter his expression. If anything, now that he could see Maggs clearly, he appeared more puzzled still.

'Didn't you look at them yoursel' before you dragged them all the way over 'ere?' asked Atkinson. 'If you didn't, you ought to 'ave done. Might have saved yoursel' some trouble.'

'What do you mean?' said Maggs. 'Them's good books. I sold some of 'em to old Sandton myself, and he was no fool, so don't try telling me you've no interest in 'em. I could throw a stone on Charing Cross and hit half a dozen gentlemen who'd be prepared to take them off my hands for more than I paid for 'em and no questions asked. I was doing you a favour by offering 'em to you first.'

'Well, why don't you go off and start flinging stones, then, and best of luck to you. If you call it a favour to waste a man's time, then you did me a good 'un, make no mistake.'

Something of Maggs's genuine distress rubbed off on Atkinson, and his attitude softened.

'Seriously, Maggsy, didn't you examine 'em before you brought 'em to me?' he said.

'Of course I did,' said Maggs. 'What do you take me for?'

'Then you must have seen it.'

'Seen what?'

'How they was all vandalized,' said Atkinson. 'Broke my 'eart to open the first of 'em, and then it broke a dozen or more times again before I was done. How someone could do something like that to those lovely books, I do not know. It troubles me to think that you'd have brought 'em to me in that condition. We've known each other a long time, you and me, and I'd 'ate to think that you was tryin' to pull a fast one. You wouldn't do that, now, would you, Maggsy? I thought that was true, and you and me might 'ave a fallin' out.'

Maggs was no longer listening. He reached for the first, and most valuable, of the books in the box – a seventeenth-century set of early colour woodblock prints known as *The Ten Bamboo Studio Collection of Calligraphy and Pictures*, published in 1633 by Hu Zhengyan – and removed its wrapping. He placed it on the counter and used the edge of the cloth to open the cover and begin turning the pages.

'You don't need to be gentle with it,' said Atkinson. 'It's long past caring. You could open it with your boots if you 'ad a notion.'

Maggs let out a small cry of shock. The first page of the set was covered with a familiar reddish-purple scrawl. So too were the second and the third. He flicked through the volume and saw that every page – every painted orchid and flowering plum, every delicately lettered section – had been similarly defaced. He closed the book and reached for another, with the same result. He did not stop until each volume had been removed from the boxes and examined from cover to cover.

'It's not possible,' said Maggs. 'They were perfect when I brought 'em here. I sat up half the night checking 'em.'

He turned on Atkinson.

'You must have let 'em out of your sight!' he shouted. 'Someone must have come in 'ere while your back was turned and gone through 'em, markin' 'em all, defacin' 'em, because when I laid 'em 'ere yesterday they was near as perfect as the day they was made. You owe me, Atkinson. I'll 'ave you up before the magistrate. You see if I don't!'

Any tolerance vanished from Atkinson's face.

'You get out of 'ere now, Maggs, and don't you return, not until you learn to keep a polite tongue in your 'ead, or till you get your reason back. Don't come tryin' that on me. I been in this game far too long for it, and if any man knows that, it should be you. Go on, on your way. And take your poxy books with you!'

Maggs returned the books to their boxes. His face burned. It had to be Atkinson's fault. What other explanation could there be? Yet, in his heart, Maggs knew that Atkinson would have treated the volumes as carefully as if they had been his own, and nothing happened in his shop of which he was not aware. Also, it would have taken hours to reduce the books to their present condition. Perhaps someone had sneaked in during the night, and ruined them while the shop was closed. He tried to suggest the same to Atkinson, but the words came out wrong, and a bad situation was made worse, until Maggs found himself on the footpath, the boxes of books at his feet, and no way to transport them back to his rooms. And then there was the not insignificant matter of the money that he'd spent on them, investing a considerable amount of his available funds in the hope of multiplying them. What about Bath? What about the estate sale?

He caught hold of a barrow boy and paid him a few coppers to take the books back to his rooms, although he did not know why he should hold on to them now. They were worthless – worse than worthless, because he could do nothing at all with them. They were fit only for the furnace. He followed on behind the boy, trying to make the connection. It was clear that the writing in the defaced volumes was the same as that in the notebook by his bed, but as far as he knew, he was the only one to have unlocked it and seen what was inside.

No, wait! What about young Sandton? Maggs hadn't liked the look of him from the start, hadn't liked him at all. Could this be some cruel trick on his part? But to what end? Maggs had paid him for the books, and had Sandton wished to hold on to them and seek a better price, there was nothing Maggs could have done to stop him. He hadn't cheated Sandton. He'd named a price, had it rejected, named another, and heard it accepted. Sandton couldn't complain, and even if he had subsequently learned that the books were worth more than Maggs paid for them, the difference was only a drop in the ocean compared to what Sandton was destined to inherit from his old man's estate once all the paperwork was completed. It would be like haggling over pennies. Could Sandton possibly be so deranged as to have sent someone to follow Maggs, learn his plans for the books, and then break into Atkinson's in order to reduce those plans to naught? It made no sense, but Maggs could find no other explanation.

They reached Maggs's lodgings. He convinced the boy to carry one of the boxes up the stairs for him, but if he was expecting another coin for his trouble, he was destined to be disappointed. Maggs fumbled for his keys, opened his door, and used his right foot to push the first of the boxes inside. He didn't look up until the second box was over the threshold. His response to what he saw was to fall back against the door, knocking it closed and almost losing his footing in the process.

The floor was covered in books, all lying open, all defaced. His shelves were entirely empty: not one volume had escaped the carnage. He picked up a copy of *Sketches by Boz* that was resting by his left foot. The words were almost invisible beneath the layers of reddish-purple ink, and such was the ferocity of the attack upon the book that a hole had been dug through the first fifty pages, as though a nail had been driven into them. Maggs moved through his rooms, examining damaged volumes and discarding them, until finally he lay down on his bed and started to weep.

His sobs stopped almost as soon as they had started. He stared up at the ceiling. So concerned was he at the destruction of his library and his stock that he had failed to notice the plaster above his head had been similarly vandalized, its yellow-white paint now almost entirely covered in writing. He pulled the curtains – Maggs always kept them drawn to protect his books from the sun, so his living space was a place of gloom and lamplight – and the beams shone on the old, dark wallpaper of his bedroom. What he had at first taken to be shadows was more writing covering the pattern of the paper. He picked up a book from the floor, and a part of the cheap linoleum unprotected by rugs was revealed to him.

Words, all written in that same infernal alphabet.

Maggs dashed into his living-room, almost losing his footing again on the books lying beneath his feet. He began flinging volumes behind him, searching for one book, and one alone. He discovered the notebook lying in a corner, not even close to where he had left it the night before. He examined it, comparing its lettering to that which now covered his rooms and every book in them that meant anything to him at all. There could be no mistake: it was the same writing, the same ink. He tested a word on the wall nearest him, rubbing at it with a finger. The finger came back entirely dry. He licked the same finger, and tried again, but the ink appeared indelible.

In a fury he tried to pull the notebook apart, but it would not give. He took a page in his hand, and wrenched, but the cord held, and the paper barely wrinkled. Then he spotted the box of matches on the mantelpiece. He set a fire, got it burning and without a second thought cast the notebook into the flames. He waited for it to burn, but it would not. He pushed at it with the poker, trying to move it to where the fire was burning strongest, but it made no difference. The pages did not even brown. Finally, he used the poker to pull the notebook from the blaze and sat on the floor, staring at it, willing it to disappear. When it showed no signs of doing so, he swore at it.

This wasn't a matter for the British Library. This was much stranger. And Maggs knew just the woman who might be able to provide an answer.

The bookselling firm of Dunwidge & Daughter was notorious, even by the standards of occultists. Dunwidge himself was a rude old sod, but his daughter was actively unpleasant, and those who moved in such circles whispered that she was a witch, or even a demonist. Maggs tried to have as little as possible to do with her or her father, but sometimes contact was unavoidable for commercial reasons. Such meetings were made marginally more palatable by the fact that Eliza Dunwidge paid well for what she wanted. She even seemed to have some grudging respect for Maggs, though Maggs felt that her business was less an end in itself than part of a larger, stranger purpose. Eliza Dunwidge was as much a collector as a dealer – perhaps even more the former than the latter. This was not uncommon in the book trade, particularly among sellers of her stripe, yet Eliza's collecting was both selective and obsessive, and involved some very foul books indeed. Maggs had located a handful of such books for her and been well rewarded for his troubles, but whatever he dug up, she demanded more: darker, viler, rarer, each more transgressive than the last.

What she wanted most of all was the book that she called the *Atlas Regnorum Incognitorum*, or the *Fractured Atlas*, even if Maggs wasn't convinced that it even existed. As far as he was concerned, it was a myth, but one with a price to match its status. If it was real, and he were to find it, he would be a wealthy man – wealthier even than young Sandton would soon be, and Sandton's inheritance guaranteed him a life of pleasure and indolence. But, unlike Eliza, Maggs was not a believer in very much at all, and to conceive of the reality of the existence of a book like the *Fractured Atlas* required a faith that he simply did not have.

On the other hand, Maggs knew that books had a power, one that was real yet often indefinable, but came down to a capacity to alter individuals, societies, nations. If nothing else, he now understood that, in the notebook, he had somehow come into possession of a volume that was powerful and dangerous beyond his range of knowledge, and Eliza Dunwidge knew about odd books of every stripe. He was unable to come up with any answer as to how the script in its pages had managed to impose itself on his environment and possessions, but Eliza might be able to offer some suggestions. Perhaps he could convince her to take it off his hands. Yes, that would be the ideal solution. He was even prepared to give it to her for nothing, so anxious was he to be free of it.

He wrapped the notebook in a clean tea towel and slipped it into the pocket of his coat. He could feel the heat of it against him and wondered if it might be radiating some of the warmth of the fire, but it had been cold to the touch when he took it up. He locked the door of his rooms, took the Underground to Walham Green, then walked the short distance to the house at World's End occupied by Dunwidge & Daughter, identifiable only by a brass plate on the front door, decorated with a pair of interlocking 'D's.

He rang the bell, but nobody answered. He considered trying again, then decided that it might be best just to leave the book on the doorstep, with a note. He was searching in his pockets for a pencil and a scrap of paper when a light came on in the hall, and he saw the shape of Eliza Dunwidge against the glass.

'It's Maggs, Miss Dunwidge,' he said. 'I'd very much like to talk to you.'

'What have you brought with you, Maggs?' came the voice, muffled but still understandable, from the other side of the door.

'A book, Miss,' he said. 'It's an odd one.'

'It's a dangerous one, Maggs. I can smell it. I can *hear* it. It whispers. You ought not to have come to me with it.'

Maggs felt that he might be going mad. What was this? She could smell it, hear it?

'I don't understand what you mean, Miss,' he said.

'I think you do. You want to get rid of it on me, but I don't want it.'

Now Maggs was growing frightened. He hadn't realized how badly he had wished for Eliza Dunwidge to take the book until she refused to do so.

'I need your advice,' said Maggs. 'I don't know what to make of it.'

'Why, Maggs? What's it done to you? Be honest, now. Tell me true.'

'It'll sound like madness, Miss Dunwidge, but it's filled with writing that I can't read, and that writing has transferred itself to the other books in my lodgings, even to the walls themselves. It's like a disease, spreading . . .'

'And you brought it here, to a house full of books?' Her voice rose to a shriek of panic.

'I didn't know what else to do. I didn't mean no harm by it, but I'm right scared. Tell me what to do. How do I make it stop?'

There was a thoughtful silence before Eliza Dunwidge asked him to describe the notebook for her, and he was aware of a kind of curiosity in her voice. She *does* want it, he thought. Why wouldn't she, given the books that she collects? But she's wary of it, and so she should be.

Maggs told her everything through the closed door, from the discovery of the notebook amid the contents of Sandton's library, to his efforts to destroy it earlier that day.

'You say it came wrapped in a cloth?' said Eliza.

'That's right,' said Maggs. 'Just an old rag. Clean, though. And old.'

'I think you'll find that it was more than a rag, Maggs. Did you notice any patterns on it, any writing or symbols?'

'To be honest, I didn't examine it that closely, but it seemed plain to me.'

'Look harder. You must find that cloth. You say that the notebook was in the same box as the Sandton collection, but those volumes were undamaged when you first examined them, and it was only when you removed the notebook from its wrapping that the trouble started? You're a careless man, Maggs. You'd better hope that you haven't lost that cloth.'

'Why? Tell me!'

'I'd say it's a shield of some sort, maybe a spell or a hex. Call it what you want, but it restrained whatever lived in the pages of that book, and now it's free.'

'What is? What's free?'

Eliza laughed, and the sound of it made Maggs tremble. It was the laugh of someone who found the suffering of others infinitely amusing.

'I think you've gone and found yourself a djinn, Maggs,' said Eliza, 'and a nasty one, too. The djinn is the book, and the book is the djinn. The problem for you is that all djinns have a purpose, and you'll have to let this one run its course. You'll know when it's done with you. Then you find that cloth, you wrap up the book and you bring it to me. And no games, Maggs: you make sure that it's the same cloth. You try any trickery and I'll see you burn. Now get away from here. You're a plague rat.'

Maggs did as he was told. He wasn't about to argue with

Eliza Dunwidge, and he wanted to find that cloth. He wanted to find it more than anything else, maybe even more than Eliza wanted to find her precious atlas. He was so anxious to return home as quickly as possible that he hailed a cab, an extraordinary extravagance for one as parsimonious as he. On the way he considered what he'd been told. A djinn: could it be true? He knew nothing of such things beyond stories of lamps and wishes in the *Thousand and One Nights*. And what did Eliza mean by a 'purpose'? As far as Maggs could tell, if this thing did have an aim, it was simply the defacing of books, and there were no books of his left to ruin. Surely, if Eliza was right, then it had done its worst already?

Once back in his rooms, Maggs began throwing volumes aside, trying to recall where he'd put the cloth. He was sure that he'd left it on the table, but there was no sign of it now. Where was it? Where was the blasted thing?

A movement caught his eye, and he saw the cloth moving towards the still warm ashes of the fire, as though propelled there by a breeze. He made a leap for it and caught it in the air. It seemed almost to wriggle in his fingers, but he clenched his fist and held it tight. He went to his bedroom and closed the door, fearful of the consequences if the cloth slipped from his grasp and ended up in the fireplace. His bedroom window was shut, because he wasn't so much of a fool as to leave it open while he was out. He laid the cloth on the bed, placed the notebook on it and folded the material around it. Now he needed some string to seal it, but there was none to hand. He knew that he had a ball of twine in the kitchen drawer and—

A sudden lassitude overcame him. He felt weary and nauseous. The bedroom swam before him. And the heat! God, he couldn't remember ever being so warm. He looked at the notebook. The cloth covered it entirely. And he was tired, so very tired . . .

He stripped down to his sleeveless union suit, unbuttoning the top down to his waist to cool his back and chest, and lay on the bed. He reached for the window in order to open it and air the room, but his strength failed him at the last. He closed his eyes and was instantly asleep.

Maggs dreamed that fleas were biting him. The little beggars were hopping all over him, nipping at his arms and his chest. He tried to brush them off, but his hands would not move. The pain grew deeper, and he felt like fangs were being driven deep into his flesh. No fleas inflicted bites like these.

Maggs opened his eyes.

A figure was squatting by his bed. It wore a dark, wet cloak of purple that flowed down from its head and over its body, congealing in damp waves upon the floor. But as Maggs's vision cleared, he realized that he was looking not at a cloak but at folds of skinless flesh, like the offal dumped in a corner of a slaughterhouse after an animal has been butchered for its meat. On the front of its head, where its features should have been, were only two dark, lidless eyes, and below them the hint of a circular mouth, like a wound gouged with a blunt blade. A pair of thin arms, the exposed flesh hanging from the bones with a kind of solid viscosity, protruded not from its shoulders but from the front of its chest. One ended in a splayed claw that now lay upon Maggs's naked torso, while the other tapered to form a single bony member, more like the leg of an insect than a digit. It terminated in a sharp nib, and it was this nib that was now cutting at Maggs's belly, scratching at his skin, forming patterns that he could not see for blood but which he knew must surely resemble the writing in the notebook.

The creature's movements briefly ceased. It removed its nib from Maggs's skin and then, like a scribe dipping a nib in an inkwell, it dug at a pustule in its own flesh, and the wound streamed reddish-purple fluid. Once its member was dripping with the liquid, it returned to its work: writing, always writing.

Only then did Maggs find the strength to scream.

*   *   *

He woke to darkness, lying on bloodstained sheets. He staggered from his bed, searching the shadows for any sign of his tormentor, but there was none. He stood before the mirror on his dresser. The creature might have been gone, but the evidence of its presence remained on Maggs's torso. His face had been spared. That, at least, was something. His own calmness surprised him, but in recognizing it he realized it was all that stood between himself and insanity.

He walked to the kitchen and found the twine. The notebook lay on the bedroom floor, its cover visible where a corner of the cloth had come away. He must have knocked it over during the night. As he reached for it, he felt that tiredness again, but this time he fought it. He took up the notebook, forced its twin silver locks back into place and turned the dials. He had forgotten to do so earlier, for he had thought the lock less important than the hex. Perhaps that had been his mistake. He wrapped the book in the cloth and tied it so securely with string that a blade would have been needed to reveal its contents.

When all was complete, he filled a bowl with water and washed the dried blood from his body. The lettering remained, though, tattooed on him by the entity: the djinn, if that was what it truly was. He wondered if he would ever learn the meaning of the words on his body. He suspected not, and thought that might be for the best.

Finally, he took the Underground back to Walham Green. This time, Eliza Dunwidge opened the door to him before he even managed to ring the bell. She was wearing a red robe and her feet were concealed by yellow slippers.

'So you found the cloth, then?' she said.

'Yes, I found it.'

He extended the notebook to her and for a moment she appeared to doubt the wisdom of taking it. Then her hand closed upon it, and the volume vanished into the folds of her robe.

'I don't hear it no more. That's good.'

'What did you hear?' asked Maggs. 'Tell me.'

'I heard it calling your name, Maggsy. It wanted you. What did it do to you, in the end?'

'It doesn't matter,' said Maggs.

'No,' said Eliza, 'I expect it doesn't.'

'Will it come back?'

'Not as long as it remains sealed in here, and I'm not likely to be letting it out.'

'What will you do with it?'

'Put it in the collection. Keep it safe, and far from careless hands.'

'You're sure it won't return?'

'Why should it?' She smiled. 'I don't believe that you'll forget it, will you?'

She extended a hand and touched the front of his shirt. Maggs looked down. He had sweated through the material, and beneath it could be glimpsed the letters of an unknown alphabet.

'It's left its mark on you, Maggsy,' she said. 'Might even be that it's done you a favour, because you believe now, don't you? You understand that there's books, and more-than-books.'

She leaned forward and whispered in Maggs's ear.

'So find me *my* book, Maggs. Find me the *Atlas* . . .'

3. Mud

You get all kinds of mud, you know. People – city folk, mostly – dismiss it as one and the same. To them it's just wet dirt, something that stains their shoes and their clothes. But to a farmer, or a gardener, it's soil, not dirt, and things grow in soil. Flowers. Shrubs. Weeds.

Beautiful things.

Frightening things.

The criticism had begun to get to the General. One could see it on his face and in his bearing. It wore him down. There was a name, he told me, for what they were doing to him. 'Revisionism', they called it: changing history to suit themselves, damaging a man's legacy for their own ends, shredding a reputation with a thousand cruel cuts. That was why he had decided to write down what really happened, he said, his shadow falling over me as I pruned the wisteria. It's worth pruning wisteria in summer. I know there are those who don't hold with summer pruning at all, but wisteria is a great plant to prune in July or early August. You train in your horizontals, shorten back the side shoots – although not as far as in winter, when you don't want more than four buds from the main frame. Same with espalier apples, to form fruit buds. And you ought to prune walnuts and vines in late summer too, because they're bleeders, and I don't like seeing sap leaking from cuts in February.

So I listened to the General while I worked. His wife was up in London and didn't show any sign of returning before the autumn. He probably shouldn't have married her. It's not for me to say, but I always thought that they were ill suited from the start. The General, if I'm being honest, wasn't the wisest of men. He had a knighthood, but that doesn't mean anything. Most folk called him 'Sir William', but to me he had always been the General and I think that, in his heart, he preferred to be acknowledged by his rank. That was probably why the revisionism business hurt him so. He'd entered the army through the Oxford militia, commissioned as a second lieutenant. He didn't train at Sandhurst or the Staff College, and he always felt that his peers looked down on him because of it. He was knighted in 1915, the same year that he received his promotion to lieutenant general. They say that was as good as his war ever got, because after 1915 he had blood on his hands, but I'm no soldier or military historian. The official inquiry into Cambrai exonerated all of the formation commanders and found fault with the subordinate officers and lower ranks. The General told me so, just like he told me that Barter was responsible for what happened at High Wood.

But now 'meddlers' and 'German sympathizers' were trying to undermine England's already fragile postwar morale by raising questions about the competence of the senior staff in the last conflict. The General wasn't having any of it. He'd commenced writing a memoir, an attempt to set the record straight. It even had a title. It was to be called *The Devils in the Woods*. It was a play on words, said the General, a reference to the Battle of Delville Wood, which preceded that business with the tanks at High Wood. But the devils in the woods were also the Germans, the Hun. They were the real devils, according to the General, and it was only the South Africans who kept them at bay in Delville, losing four out of every five of their men while doing it. They started out with more than 3000 officers and men on 14 July, 1916 and finished up four days later with just over 600 still standing. Then came High Wood, and another 4500 men dead or wounded, and they blamed the General for that, or tried to.

The General convinced Haig to dismiss Barter in the

aftermath, but the whispers never really went away. They even found physical form in a man named Soter, a former soldier who had been at High Wood. Soter had come to the house, demanding to speak with the General. Thankfully the General wasn't at home when he arrived and Soter didn't get farther than the gate. I made sure of that myself. Soter didn't get rough or kick up, but he made it clear that he was unhappy with what he was hearing about the General's proposed memoir. He told me that he'd lost friends at High Wood, good men who might still be alive if the General had done his job right. I informed him that I didn't want to hear it and sent him on his way, but I have to admit to feeling pity for the man. It was hard to see how anyone could have returned from that slaughter without being damaged in some way. Even the General was not unharmed by it, or so I would come to learn.

If anything, the story of Soter's visit simply confirmed the General in his aim of writing his story of the war in order to silence the naysayers. He was doing it for England, he said, not for himself. Doubt was the enemy; doubt, and men like Soter.

That was when the mud began to appear.

The first I knew of it was when the General called me to the house. I was up a ladder, pruning those espalier apples I mentioned earlier, when I heard him calling my name. I got there as fast as I could and smelled it almost before I saw it. It had a nasty odour; most particular. As I said before, there's all kinds of mud, some cleaner than others. This stank like animals had lived and died in it, bleeding and excreting at the last. It smelled like an abattoir yard. The mud itself was grey, and great wet clumps of it had been traipsed across the floorboards and up the stairs to the bedrooms, the imprints of a boot clear upon it. The General was red in the face, and howling blue murder about how Lady Jessie would have someone's guts for it. He turned on me as soon as I appeared, accusing me of coming into the main house without permission, of failing to remove my footwear and destroying his home. He told me I'd be jailed for it and I'd never work again, or some such nonsense. It took the housekeeper to calm him down and point out that I'd been over in the orchard and she'd been watching me herself, and I'd never come near the house. I showed him my boots, which had barely a trace of soil upon them. We'd been having a dry summer and the ground was hard. I was wishing for rain, but none had come.

Well, as soon as the General recovered himself and accepted that I hadn't caused the damage, the question was raised as to who might be responsible and, more to the point, whether the individual in question might still be around. The General was a hunter and had served in the Uganda protectorate against the Banyoro and the Nandi. He took his old Africa shotgun from the cabinet, and I picked up a stout walking-stick from the hall. Together we searched every room in the house, but we found no trace of an intruder, and the mud petered out somewhere near the General's bedroom, halfway along the upstairs hallway. As far as the General could tell, nothing had been touched and nothing taken, but it was a queer business. The footprints only went up, not down. I mean, I suppose that by the time whoever it was arrived upstairs, most of the mud had probably dropped off his boots, but I would have expected some traces of it to appear on the way down too, certainly if they'd been that muddy to begin with.

The General called the police, and a constable came along to take a statement. There wasn't much that he could do except promise to keep an eye out for suspicious characters and advise the General to ensure that his doors and windows remained locked for the time being. I helped the housekeeper to clean up the mud, and filthy stuff it was. I wouldn't have eaten anything that grew out of it, not even if it had been boiled to within an inch of disintegration.

I offered to sleep in a chair outside that night, just in case our visitor tried to come back, but the General told me not to be silly. He liked his own company, the General. I think he was secretly glad that Lady Jessie had chosen to stay in London. I kept working in the garden until darkness fell, though, and I walked the housekeeper to her home, just in case.

That night, the General was woken by a frantic scratching at his bedroom door. He was still half-asleep when he opened it, and a white-and-brown form shot by his feet. It was the cat, Tiger, a big, lazy old beast that had once been the terror of every bird and small mammal within a square mile of the house, but now spent most of his time napping and swatting at flies. The General hadn't seen him move so fast in years, but something had clearly frightened Tiger enough to cause him to relinquish his place in a basket at the foot of the stairs and make his way up to the General's bedroom. Tiger climbed onto the headboard of the bed and stood against one of the posts, hissing at the open door, every hair on his body raised in fright.

The General had brought his shotgun to bed with him, something Lady Jessie would never have permitted had she been present, not even if the whole German army had been threatening to invade through the rose garden and annex the vegetable patch. Now he grabbed the shotgun and called out a warning, but received no reply. That smell was back, though, that stench of filthy, polluted mud, and he could hear movement in the darkness of the hallway, low against the wall. Even at the risk of exposing himself further, he turned on the lights.

A rat was running along the carpet by the sideboard, but it was no ordinary rodent. This creature was bigger than the cat, its pelt caked with mud, its belly swollen with carrion. As it sensed the General's approach, it raised itself on its hind legs and sniffed at the air. It had no fear of him, not even as he levelled the shotgun at it. In fact, just before he pulled the trigger, the General felt certain that the thing was about to launch itself at him. Then he fired, and the rat was no more. But even when I saw it the next day in its ruined state (for the General had let it have both barrels, leaving little of it but fur and regrets) I could tell what a monster it had been. The tail was enough of a gauge. It was as long as my forearm.

But what I remember most about that day is the stink of mud. It had permeated the entire house. You couldn't take a breath but that you smelled it, and you couldn't put a bite in your mouth but that you tasted it. The carpet and floorboards kept their own memory of it too, for even after all of our efforts they retained the marks of footprints upon them. I feared that even a professional would be hard-pressed to do much about the damage. The carpets would, in all likelihood, have to be replaced, and the boards sanded down and varnished again. That might get rid of the smell too, although it wasn't any worse if you got down low and sniffed at the marks. It was just there, in the air, and every door and window left wide open failed to rid the house of it.

The General returned to work on his memoir. If anything, the events of the previous 24 hours seemed only to spur him on to greater efforts. I glimpsed him through the window, writing furiously. He'd rubbed a little clove oil under his nose to help with the stench.

As for myself, I disposed of what was left of the rat, but I still had no idea where the mud on its fur might have come from – or, indeed, the origins of the creature itself, for I had never before seen one so big, dead or alive. It was only as I was dumping it among the trees near the house – for the insects and birds would do a better job of ridding the world of it than I ever could – that it struck me how little blood there had been in the aftermath of its destruction. Now that I thought of it, I couldn't recall seeing any blood at all, only bone and fur and some unidentifiable grey matter. I examined the remains more closely and it seemed to me that the fur wasn't quite of a whole, for it was not uniform, even through the mud congealed upon it. After a while, I became convinced that the patches of fur were not even from the same animal. Similarly, the bone fragments appeared to be of different ages – I could tell by their colour – and as I began laying them out I thought I discerned what might have been part of a bird's wing, and an upper jawbone that belonged more correctly to a smaller mammal: a squirrel perhaps, or even a bat, for I saw that it had two short fangs in the centre with two longer ones at either side, and no rat that I had ever seen bore such teeth.

I sat back on my heels and considered the problem. It was, I thought, as though a rat had somehow been assembled from whatever pieces of other deceased animals might be found in the undergrowth or the soil, the fur and bones formed into a whole that, from a distance, might well resemble a large rodent but would not bear closer inspection. Yet how could such a thing be animated? Surely the General must have been mistaken in believing that he had seen it run, for this was a dead thing formed of other dead things. Someone must have been playing a nasty trick upon him, perhaps the same individual responsible for tracking muddy footprints through his house.

And as my thoughts returned to the mud, so I made a kind of connection. I rose and walked through the trees to the pond at the heart of the woods. It wasn't much of a body of water, even when swelled by rain, and the level was now as low as I could ever recall. Had I made my way to its deepest point, I doubt that I would have been submerged above my waist. The water was cloudy and the bank was dry. I looked for traces of footprints, but could find none. Flies filled the air: nasty black brutes that went for my ears and eyes.

I caught a smell. It was fainter than the odour at the house, but I thought that I could detect it nonetheless. Then again, the stink of the mud at the General's residence had attached itself to my clothing, my hair, and my skin, or so it felt to me, and I couldn't be certain that what I was smelling had its source at the pond or had simply been carried there with me. I admit to feeling uneasy, though. I can't say why. A kind of stillness, I think: a sense that something, somewhere was holding its breath.

* * *

I met the General when I was on my way back to the house. He was carrying his shotgun, and I wondered if he had been thinking along the same lines as I. But no good could come of making the trek to the pond, for the day was unpleasantly warm and those flies annoyingly persistent. I told him I'd been out to take a look and that the banks were caked hard by the sun. He appeared content to take my word for it and we returned to the house together. I was glad of his company until we cleared the woods. Again, I can't say why, except that the smell faded the farther we got from the pond, and then grew more noticeable again as we reached the garden. The General returned to his study to write, and I locked up my tools and went home.

I have what happened next only from the General himself. I saw nothing of it and can bear no witness. All I can tell you is what he told me after I found him out by the pond just as the rain began to fall.

He had remained in his study until after dark. His hopes of writing a memoir were, he realized, excessively optimistic, and he had instead determined to produce a piece for *The Times* or *Telegraph*, revisiting again the events at High Wood and offering the truth of them, as he saw it. He immersed himself in his work, regularly smearing his upper lip with more clove oil to keep away the smell until his moustache was soaked in the stuff. Eventually, though, even the clove oil no longer worked and he could only conclude that, somehow, the stench was getting worse, if such a thing were possible. The window before him was slightly ajar, but all of the other doors and windows in the house were secured. He set aside his pen, poured himself a glass of whisky, then remembered the blasted clove oil. He could have one or the other, but not both, and he determined to wash the oil from his moustache and make do with the Scotch.

He stepped from his office, and his foot slipped in mud. The front door remained closed, but muddy footprints led from it to his study – where they appeared to have paused, as though someone outside had listened for a time to the scratching of the General's pen – then made their way left to the dining-room and the kitchen, and across the hall to the drawing-room, and upstairs to the bedrooms. The footprints crossed one another, and even in the dim lamplight he could see that they were not one set, but many, for the feet were of different sizes, and the tread marks were not the same.

And the smell! God, the smell!

He followed the prints as if in a daze, heedless now of whom he might find, seeking only an answer to the mystery of their presence. In the drawing-room he found smeared finger marks upon a photograph of his wife. The taps in the bathroom were clogged, the sink stained with dirt and, he thought, dark smears of blood. There were blemishes upon the wallpaper in the halls, and mud dripped from the handles of the doors. The linen on his bed was no longer white, as though someone caked in filth had been overcome by the urge to rest upon it. Every room, with the exception of the study that he had occupied, bore traces of intrusion, but of the intruders themselves he found no sign.

The front door was open when he returned downstairs, and moonlight shone near bright as day on the lawn and the muddy tracks upon it, all now leading away from the house and into the trees. He walked in those footsteps, and the woods closed around him, drawing him deeper and deeper into themselves, until at last he found himself by the banks of the pond. He stared into the water at its base, the dankness of it seeming to swallow the moonlight, and as he did so, the water level sank, seeping away until all that was left in the pond was foul grey mud.

And in the mud, something moved.

The General caught sight of a shape ill defined, a figure that appeared both of the mud and yet a thing apart. It forced itself up from the mire, its back bent, its hands and knees braced against the bed of the pool. Fragments of old wood and rotting vegetation partly concealed its head, like the hood of a shroud, but he caught a glimpse of pale features, like the face of a second moon, and clouded eyes that turned towards him yet did not see, not truly.

Now all was movement, the mud in a state of slow yet constant turmoil as more and more men emerged, and the General had a vision of an immensity of bodies being forced up from below, a great eruption of the dead, hundreds of thousands of them, all with names to whisper, all with stories to tell, a generation of the lost that would give the lie to his every word of self-justification and crack the hollow shell of each excuse.

Because he had known. He had always known.

He sank to his knees, and prepared to join their number.

That was where I found him the next morning, his clothes caked with grey mud, his body shaking from something more than cold. As I raised him to his feet the rain came, washing him clean, and the pond began to fill again. The General babbled as I half-carried him home, and I thought him unhinged. Even then, he seemed unsure of what was mud, and what was not mud. He thought, he said, as he shivered against me, that what he saw that night might not have been men at all but merely the memory of them given form by whatever substance was closest to hand.

He never told the tale again, and never mentioned it to another soul, as far as I know. He's gone now, of course. He died in 1941, just as another generation was facing the guns. As for his great rebuttal, I never heard him speak of it again, and I believe that he burned to ash what he had put down.

I'm not a scientific man, but I can read and write, and I retain a curiosity about the world. I have learned that we contain billions of atoms in our bodies and all of those atoms at one point formed part of other human beings, so that each one of us carries within us a trace of every man and woman who has ever walked this earth. It is to do with the law of averages, as I understand it. If it is true of us, then is it true also of other things?

Like mud, I mean. Ten million soldiers died in the Great War, most of them laid to rest in mud and soil. Ten million, each containing billions and billions of individual atoms. If each human being can contain within himself every other, could not something of those dead men be retained in the very ground, a kind of memory of them that can never be dispelled?

There are all kinds of mud, you know.

All kinds.

4. The Wanderer in Unknown Realms

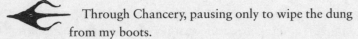 Through Chancery, pausing only to wipe the dung from my boots.

Through Chancery, to the chambers of the lawyer Quayle.

There are men of wealth and power who wish others to know of their position in society. They eat at the best restaurants and stay in the finest hotels; they revel in ostentation. Even those who serve the interests of men more important than themselves are not immune from grand gestures, and so it is that the Harley Street physicians who tend to the ailments of the great will acquire suites of rooms fitted with antique furnishings, as if to say 'See! I am as good as you. I can demean myself in displays of wealth just as readily as you can.' It should be said, of course, that it is somehow less noble to have bought your possessions with money earned than it is simply to inherit, and *arrivistes* who try to compete will always be looked down upon by those whose wealth was acquired so long before that the effort of its acquisition, the filth and the sin of it, have since been erased from memory.

Then there are those who understand that wealth and power are weapons and should be used carefully, and not without fore-thought. They disdain ostentation in themselves and in other men. In a way, they may even be ashamed of their privileged position. They have learned, too, that if those who look after their affairs – the physicians, the lawyers, the bankers – work in lavish surroundings, then someone, somewhere is paying more than a shilling extra on his bill in order to provide such comforts. The man who looks after one's money should know its value, and be as parsimonious with his particular funds as he is with one's own.

So it was that the lawyer Quayle worked out of a courtyard in a part of Chancery that had changed little since Quayle's near neighbours, the esteemed legal tailors Ede & Ravenscroft, had established their business on Chancery Lane as the seventeenth century was drawing to its close. A narrow arch led into a space not much larger than a bed-sitting-room, its cobbles always slick with damp even in the driest of weather, the surrounding buildings craning over as though to peer down disapprovingly on interlopers, the old crown glass of the windows distorting the view of the world from both within and without. There was a smell of cooking to the place on that November morning, although none lived here, and none cooked, unless one counted the tea that Quayle's clerk, Mr Fawnsley, kept stewing on a little stove outside his master's lair. In a moment of weakness, I had once consented to take a cup, and had not made a similar mistake since. Workmen applied tar to the roads that was tastier and less viscous.

A brass plate – somewhat tarnished by the years, not unlike the man whose services it advertised – was set beside a solid black oak door to the left of the courtyard. None of the other doors bore similar efforts at identification, and I had never seen any of them put to use. They appeared as permanently closed as the tombs of the ancients: were one to have been forced open, it would not have been a surprise to find the mummified forms of generations of advocates stacked behind it like grey kindling, while the papers from forgotten cases slowly decayed and fell like snow upon their heads.

A bell tinkled above me as I opened Quayle's door, the sound of it incongruous in the gloom of the interior. It smelled of musty files and melting wax. A lamp burned on the wall, casting yellow light and flickering shadows over stairs that ascended, unevenly and unsteadily, to the floor above, where Quayle conducted his business. I had long since learned not to be shocked by the banister rail that seemed ready to give way beneath my hand, nor by the creaks from the steps that suggested an imminent collapse. Quayle was too canny to allow any mishap to befall his clients, and the most illustrious of London's citizenry had been climbing these stairs without incident for centuries, ever since some distant relative of the current Quayle had formed a partnership of sorts with a fellow lawyer, a Huguenot refugee and widower named Couvret whose experiences in France had weakened his mind, and who subsequently fell prey to the curse of gin. Couvret was found robbed and near-gutted in Spitalfields, not far from the home of a pretty silk weaver named Valette with whom he was reputed to be having a discreet love affair. Once, over a lunch of braised lamb, a reward for an investigation concluded by me to his benefit, the current Quayle gave me to understand that family lore suggested his ancestor had grown weary of Couvret, and the unfortunate man's robbery and murder had been arranged to remove him from the business of law entirely. In this, the action appeared to have succeeded admirably.

Mr Fawnsley was at his desk when I reached the top of the stairs. Not to have found him there would have been a surprise on the scale of the Second Coming, for where Quayle lingered so too did Fawnsley lurk, at least during business hours, like the pale sickly shadow of his master. What the man did in his own time, I could not say. I often suspected that, at five o'clock on the dot, Quayle turned a dial on Fawnsley's neck, sending him into a stupor, then laid him carefully in the alcove behind his desk, there to remain until eight the following morning when the necessity of resuming business required his reanimation. Fawnsley was a man who seemed incapable of ageing, which might have been said to be a good thing were it not for the fact that the actions of the years had ceased for Fawnsley not in relative youth, but in unhealthy late middle-age, so he bore the aspect of a man who was perpetually teetering on the cliff edge of mortality.

Fawnsley looked up from his scribbling and regarded me resignedly. It didn't matter to him that his master had summoned me to his presence. Everything was an inconvenience to Fawnsley, all men jesters sent by the gods to try him.

'Mr Soter,' he said, tipping his head sufficiently to allow a small cloud of dandruff to fall from his pate and mix with his ink.

'Mr Fawnsley,' I said, placing my hat on an understuffed chair. 'I believe he's expecting me.'

Fawnsley's look gave me to understand that he considered this to be a serious lapse of judgement on the part of Mr Quayle, and consequently he took his time about laying down his fountain pen.

'I'll let him know that you're here.'

He rose from his chair as one being pulled from above rather than impelled from below. His feet barely made a sound on the boards, so thin and light was he. He knocked at the door behind his desk and waited on some muffled permission to enter before cautiously poking his head through the gap like a man trying out a guillotine for size. There was a hushed exchange and then, somewhat reluctantly, Fawnsley stepped aside and invited me to enter the inner sanctum.

Quayle's chambers were smaller than might have been expected and darker than seemed wise if their occupant was intent on preserving what was left of his eyesight. Thick red drapes hung over the windows, held back at the sides by bronze loops to allow a triangular pattern of light to fall through the glass and onto Quayle's desk. The room was lined with shelves of books, and carpets of Persian manufacture absorbed the sound of my footsteps. There was not a speck of dust to be seen anywhere, although at no time during my visits to Quayle's chambers had I ever encountered a cleaning woman. There was only Fawnsley, and try as I might, I could not picture him teetering on a ladder with a duster in his hand. It was quite the mystery.

Quayle's desk was an enormous construction of wood so old that it had turned to black. Generations of Quayles had sat behind it, mulling over ways in which to work the law to the benefit of their clients and, by extension, themselves, and justice be damned. It was likely that, at this very desk, the fate of the unfortunate Monsieur Couvret had been decided, with one such as Fawnsley dispatched with coin to ensure the safe conduct of the whole grisly business.

Quayle himself was a surprisingly elegant man of 60 winters or more. (One might equally have said '60 springs' or '60 summers', but that would have been inaccurate, for Quayle was a man of bare trees and frozen water.) He was six feet in height, and one of the few men I knew who could look me in the eye, although I had only a distant memory on which to rely for this, as Quayle rarely stood. His hair was very dark and smelled faintly of the boot polish that he used to keep the grey at bay. His teeth were too white and even, and his skin was so pale as to be almost translucent, so that, in better light, one might have been able to discern his circulatory system in all its delicate glory. Instead, in the murk of his chambers, there was only the faintest hint of veins and arteries, like the shadows of branches cast on snow. Half-spectacles, rimmed in black, caught something of the sunlight, hiding his eyes from me.

There was another man seated in the red leather armchair to Quayle's left. He was somewhere in his twenties, I would have said, and dressed in the manner of a gentleman, but I could see that his shoes, although polished, were worn at the soles, and his suit was just a year out of fashion, with a carnation in his button hole to serve as a distraction. Moneyed, then, but struggling: he had enough to pay a man to polish his shoes, but not enough to replace them until the need became pressing. To tell the truth, I disliked him on sight. His eyes were vapid, and his chin was almost as one with his neck. Never trust a man who, by his presence in a room with two others, brings down the average number of chins by a third.

'Welcome, Mr Soter,' said Quayle. 'Let me introduce you to Sebastian Forbes. His uncle, Lionel Maulding, is a client of mine.'

Forbes rose, and shook my hand. His grip was firmer than I had anticipated, although I sensed that he was putting a little more effort into it than usual.

'Delighted to make your acquaintance, Mr Soter,' he said. He spoke in the manner of some of his kind, as though the statement had rather too many syllables for his liking, and so he had decided to dispense with those deemed surplus to requirements and skate as quickly as possible over the rest.

'Likewise, sir,' I replied.

'Mr Quayle tells me you served with some distinction in the recent conflict,' he said.

'I served, sir. I can't say any more than that.'

'Who were you with?'

'The Forty-Seventh, sir.'

'Ah, the Londoners! Stout men. Aubers Ridge, Festubert, Loos, the Somme.'

'Did you serve, sir?'

'No, sadly not. My knowledge is based purely on my reading. Too young to enlist, I'm afraid.'

I looked at him and thought that I had fought alongside men who, had they lived, would still have been younger than he was now, but I said nothing. If he had found a way to avoid the whole bloody mess, then I wasn't about to begrudge him. I'd been through it, and had I known going in what I was about to face, I'd have run and never looked back. I'd have deserted and left all of the bastards to it.

'You chaps were at High Wood, weren't you?' continued Forbes.

'Yes,' I said.

'Bloody business.'

'Yes,' I said, again.

'They relieved Barter of his command after what happened, didn't they?'

'Yes, sir, for wanton waste of men.'

'He was a fool.'

'Not as big a fool as Pulteney.'

'Come, come, now. Sir William is a fine soldier.'

'Sir William is an ignorant man, and led better men to their deaths.'

'I say, now, Jessie Arnott was a friend of my late mother's . . .'

I seemed to recall that Pulteney had married one of the Arnott women. I must have read about it in the society pages, probably just before I lost any appetite for my breakfast.

Before the conversation could deteriorate further, Quayle gave a dry cough.

'Please take a seat, Mr Soter. And you, Mr Forbes.'

'I demand an apology,' said Forbes.

'On what basis?' asked Quayle.

'This man insulted a hero of the realm, and a friend of my mother's.'

'Mr Soter merely expressed an opinion, and gentlemen must agree to differ on such matters. I'm sure Mr Soter meant no offence to your mother. Is that not correct, Mr Soter?'

Quayle's tone suggested that it might be wise if I were to make some gesture of amends. I could have refused, of course, but I needed the work, whatever it was. I wasn't fussy. There was little enough of it to go around, and it seemed that every street corner had its veteran with his trouser legs pinned up over his thighs, the better to show his missing limbs, or a cup held in one hand while the sleeve of his other arm dangled emptily. It was the hatred for ex-soldiers on the part of those who had not fought that I could not understand. They wanted us to disappear. There were no more parades now, no more kisses on the cheek. Soldiers were no more than beggars, and nobody likes a beggar. Perhaps we made them feel guilty by our presence. They might have preferred it had we all died in the mud and been buried far from England in places we had not even learned to pronounce properly before we perished.

'I apologize for any offence I might have caused,' I said. 'I meant none.'

Forbes nodded his acceptance. 'These are emotional matters, I know,' he said.

He resumed his seat, and I took mine. Quayle, having refereed the bout to his satisfaction, turned to the matter at hand.

'Mr Forbes is concerned about his uncle,' he said. 'Apparently, he has not been seen for a number of days, and has left no indication of his whereabouts.'

'Perhaps he's taken a holiday,' I said.

'My uncle is not in the habit of taking holidays,' said his nephew. 'He finds comfort in familiar surroundings, and rarely ventures farther than the local village.' He thought for a time. 'Actually, I think he went to Bognor once, but he didn't much care for it.'

'Ah, Bognor,' intoned Quayle solemnly, as though that explained everything.

'If you're worried about his safety, then shouldn't the police be informed?' I asked.

Quayle arched an eyebrow, as I knew he would. Like most lawyers, he found the police to be something of an inconvenience to the proper pursuit of legal ends. The police were useful only when he could be certain that they would do his bidding, and no more than that. He tended to worry when they showed signs of independent thought and therefore made it his business to have as little as possible to do with them unless absolutely necessary.

'Mr Maulding is a very private man,' said Quayle. 'He would not thank us for allowing the police to intrude into his affairs.'

'He might if he has come to some harm.'

'What harm could he come to?' asked Forbes. 'He hardly leaves the house.'

'Then why am I here?' I said.

Quayle sighed in the manner of a man for whom the world holds the capacity for infinite disappointment, the only surprise being the variety of its depths.

'Mr Forbes is Mr Maulding's only living relative and the principal beneficiary of his estate should any harm befall him. Naturally, Mr Forbes hopes that this is not the case in the present circumstance, as he wishes his uncle many more years of happiness and good health.'

Forbes looked like he might be about to differ on that point, but common sense prevailed and he provided a grunt of assent.

'With that in mind,' Quayle continued, 'it would obviously contribute greatly to Mr Forbes's peace of mind if the well-being of his uncle could be established as quickly as possible, and without recourse to the intervention of the police, a fine force of men though they might be. *That* is why you are here, Mr Soter. I have assured Mr Forbes of your discretion in all matters, and he has been informed of the positive outcomes you have secured for my clients in the past. We should like you to find Mr Lionel Maulding and return him to the safe and loving embrace of his family. That is a fair summation of the situation, is it not, Mr Forbes?'

Forbes nodded enthusiastically.

'Safe and loving embrace, absolutely,' he said. 'Unless, of course, he's dead, in which case I'd rather like to know that as well.'

'Indeed,' said Quayle, after a pause that spoke volumes. 'If there's nothing else, Mr Forbes, I shall apprise Mr Soter further of the necessary details and, rest assured, we shall be in touch in due course.'

Forbes stood. The door opened at that precise moment and Fawnsley appeared holding a coat, a hat, and a pair of gloves. He could not have been more prompt had he been listening at the keyhole to every word, which he might well have been. He helped Forbes into the coat, passed him the hat and gloves, then stood waiting with a reserved impatience for him to leave, like an undertaker faced with a prospective corpse that simply refuses to die.

'In the matter of payment . . .' Forbes began, in the tone of one who finds the whole business of money rather distasteful, especially when he doesn't have enough of it to go around.

'I am sure that Mr Maulding's funds will cover any expenses,' said Quayle. 'I cannot imagine that he would begrudge expenditure incurred on his own behalf.'

'Very good,' said Forbes, with some relief and bade us farewell. He paused for a final time at the door, almost causing Fawnsley to walk into his back.

'Mr Soter?' he said.

'Yes, Mr Forbes?'

'I'll look deeper into what you said about Pulteney, and we can talk of it again.'

'I look forward to that, Mr Forbes,' I said.

It didn't matter, of course. I'd watched 40 men being buried in a shell crater at High Wood. I was there. Forbes wasn't.

And neither was General Sir Bloody William Pulteney.

Quayle asked if I would like some tea. Although he had a drinks cabinet behind his desk, I had never known him to offer anything stronger than Fawnsley's tea, possibly on the grounds that there wasn't anything stronger than Fawnsley's tea.

'No, thank you.'

'It's been a while since we've seen you, Mr Soter. How have you been?'

'I've been passing well, thank you for asking,' I replied, but he had already returned to rearranging the papers on his desk, and the state of my health had ceased to be of any interest to him, relative or otherwise. He licked his right index finger, used it to turn a page, and paused as if a thought had only just struck him, although I well knew that Quayle was not a man to be stricken by sudden thoughts. He planned too far ahead for that.

'What did you think of Mr Forbes?' he said.

'He's young.'

'Yes. There's a lot of it about, it seems.'

'Not as much as there used to be.'

'War does tend to have that effect,' said Quayle. 'You really ought to learn to hold your tongue, you know.'

'In front of my betters, you mean?'

'In front of anyone. For a man who prides himself on his reserve, you have an unfortunate habit of giving rather too much of yourself away when you do choose to speak.'

'I'll bear that in mind. I'm grateful to you for pointing it out.'

'Were you always so sarcastic?'

'I believe I was, yes, but only in certain company. As you say, it's been a while since we met.'

That almost brought a smile from Quayle, but his facial muscles were unfamiliar with the action, and it collapsed somewhere between a grin and a sneer.

'Mr Forbes lives beyond his means,' said Quayle. 'His uncle's bequest represents the best possible opportunity to rectify that situation as quickly as possible.'

'He could try working for a living.'

'What makes you think that he hasn't?'

'He wasn't dressed for any job that I could see, unless it involved advertising carnations.'

Quayle gave another of his weary sighs.

'His mother left him a small annuity, and I believe that a little money trickles in from investments. Were he wiser and less profligate, he could probably live comfortably on what he has – well, comfortably for one such as myself, and most certainly for one such as you. But he has a fondness for wagers, and one could probably clothe an entire village with the suits in his wardrobe. If he were to get his hands on his uncle's money, it would inevitably slip through his fingers like sand, and he would find himself in a similar situation to the one he is in now, albeit with a few more suits to his name.'

'Do you suspect him of doing away with the old man, and covering his tracks by coming to you?'

'You are very blunt, Mr Soter.'

'I say what others think, especially in the confines of a Chancery chamber.'

Quayle, who couldn't hold a shiny new guinea in his hand without seeking the tarnish upon it, or look upon a beautiful woman without picturing the hag that she would become, acknowledged the truth of what I had said with a gentle inclination of his head.

'In answer to your question, no, I don't believe that Forbes has done his uncle some injury. He's not the kind, and had he commissioned someone to act on his behalf, then I would know about it. But there is a mystery here: Lionel Maulding is among the most private of men and begrudges any time spent away from his home. He comes to London to discuss business once a year, and even that is a great chore for him. I make sure that there are adequate funds in his accounts to meet his needs, and I look after his investments in order that this may continue to be the case.'

Look after them, I thought, and charge a fat fee and a fine commission in the process. Now we came to it. If Maulding were dead, then his nephew would be on that money as soon as the corpse was identified. It would vanish in fineries and fripperies, and Quayle's income would be diminished accordingly. Quayle didn't look like he spent much, but he was fond of coin, and didn't relish the thought of anyone reducing the flow of it into his purse.

'What do you want me to do?' I asked.

Quayle slid a manila folder across his desk.

'Find him. All of the information that you'll need is here, along with a photograph of Maulding. I'll pay your usual fee plus any expenses, and there'll be a bonus in it if you can close this business quickly. Fawnsley will advance you a week's pay, and some money for your pocket. Naturally, you'll provide receipts.'

'Naturally.'

'There's an inn at Maidensmere, which is the nearest village to Maulding's place, although I hear that his house has enough rooms to accommodate a battalion. If you choose to stay there, the housekeeper will make up a bed for you. She doesn't live in the house, but arrives first thing in the morning and departs after dinner, or she did while Maulding was still in residence. It was she who raised the alarm. She'll look after you, and it might save us a shilling or two if you stayed elsewhere than at the inn. Look through Maulding's papers. Find out if there are any unusual patterns of expenditure. Examine his correspondence. I trust you. I know that you'll keep your mouth shut, unless someone raises the issue of errant lieutenant generals.'

I stood.

'And what if I discover that something has happened to him after all?' I asked. 'What if he's dead?'

'Then find a resurrectionist,' said Quayle, 'because I want Lionel Maulding brought back alive.'

II

Maidensmere lay close to the eastern extreme of the Norfolk Broads, an area of about 120 square miles, much of it consisting of navigable waterways, both rivers and lakes, or 'broads' in the local parlance. The village was equidistant from the towns of West Somerton and Caister-on-Sea and close to Ormesby Broad, but by the time I arrived it was late in the evening, and the waters were only patches of silver in the moonlight. There was no one to meet me at the station, and I spent some of Quayle's money on the relative luxury of a night at the Maidensmere Inn. As Quayle had indicated, a room was available for me at Bromdun Hall, Maulding's home, but I had decided to wait until the morning before taking up residence there. I ate a good meal of roast lamb and allowed myself an ale or two before bed, but I did so as much for the company as the taste of the beer. For a man in my line of work, there is much to be learned of a new place by talking a little, and listening more, and Maidensmere was small enough for a stranger to be of passing interest to the locals.

When I was asked my business in Maidensmere, as I inevitably was, I told the truth, more or less: I was there to do some work on behalf of Lionel Maulding, and I would be staying at Bromdun Hall until that work was completed. News of Maulding's disappearance did not appear to have circulated as yet, a testimony to the loyalty of his housekeeper, Mrs Gissing, and Maulding's solitary ways. It appeared that Maulding was rarely seen in the village and was regarded, at worst, as harmlessly eccentric by his neighbours. But then, this was the old kingdom of East Anglia, and had always regarded itself as somewhat different from the rest of England. There was a tolerance for separateness, for otherness. If Lionel Maulding wanted to maintain a private existence, then there were many others like him in these parts, sharing his outlook if not his wealth. I saw no meaningful glances exchanged at the mention of his name and nobody skulked away into the night, his features clouded with guilt. Such giveaways were the stuff of the Sexton Blake stories in the *Union Jack*, which was why you only had to pay tuppence for them. The real world was grey with complexity.

There was only one reference to Maulding that I failed to understand, although it amused the assembled locals.

'You a bookkeeper, then?' asked the landlord, all muttonchop whiskers and red-faced good cheer, when I told him of my purpose. He tipped the wink to his audience. 'A bookkeeper, aye, lads?'

They all laughed, and then laughed the harder when it was clear that I did not understand the reference.

'You'll see, sir,' said the landlord. 'No harm meant, but you'll see.'

And off he went to call time, and off I went to my bed.

I slept little that night, which made it no different from any other. I could not recall the last time I had slept soundly from darkness until dawn. I liked to think that I had learned to survive on less rest than others needed, but surviving and living were not the same. It was only shortly before sunrise that I managed at last to snatch a few hours of uninterrupted sleep. I dozed through breakfast, but the landlord's wife had set aside some ham and eggs for me, kept warm over a pot of boiling water that she then used to make tea. She talked as I ate and I was content to listen. She was much younger than her husband, and had lost a brother at the Somme. Someday, she said, she hoped to visit his grave. She asked me what the countryside looked like, over there.

'It wasn't much to see when I left it,' I said, 'but I expect that the grass has grown back now, and there are flowers in the meadows. Perhaps some trees have survived. I don't know. But it won't be the same as it was before, not for anyone.'

'And you?' she asked gently. 'You must have lost someone too?'

But she already sensed the answer. She would not have asked otherwise. Women have a way of detecting absences.

'We all lost someone,' I said, as I stood and wiped my hands and mouth.

I could see that she wanted to enquire further, but she did not. Instead she said, 'Pain and loss are so strange, are they not?'

'I'm not sure that I know what you mean.'

'I mean that we have all suffered in the same war, and we all have spaces in our lives now that were once filled by people whom we loved, but none of us experiences it in exactly the same way,' she said, and her gaze was set far from me, and far from the inn. 'When we talk about it – if we talk about it – nobody quite understands what we're saying, even when we're speaking to someone who is also living with such loss. It's as if we are speaking versions of the same language, but the most important words have slightly different meanings to each one of us.

Everything has changed, hasn't it? It's just as you said: the world can never be the same as it was before.'

'Would you want it to be?' I said. 'The seeds of the war were sown in the old world. Perhaps the only good thing to come out of it all is that those seeds have been blasted from the earth, and will never grow again.'

'Do you really believe that?' she said.

'No.'

'I don't either. But we have to hope, don't we?'

'Yes,' I said, 'I suppose we do.'

Mrs Gissing came to the inn shortly after. She was a small, dour woman of indeterminate age, but probably somewhere between 40 and 50, and dressed entirely in black. The landlord's wife had told me that Mrs Gissing had lost two sons in the war, one at Verdun and the other at Ypres, and was now entirely alone, having been widowed when her boys were still infants. It was about a mile or so to Bromdun Hall, and Mrs Gissing informed me that she usually walked to and from there, so I walked with her.

We had to pass through the village to reach Bromdun Hall, and there were the usual greetings given and received, although nobody asked me my name or my business, and I could only assume that those who did not know did not care, and those who did care already knew from the men who had kept me company at the bar the night before. At the centre of the village was a small green, and on it stood a war memorial. There were fresh flowers laid at its base. Mrs Gissing kept her face to the road, as if she could not bear to look at the monument. Perhaps I should have kept quiet but, as Quayle pointed out, I had a perverse habit of speaking my mind, and the landlord's wife had set me to thinking.

'I was sorry to hear of your loss,' I said to Mrs Gissing.

Her features tightened for a moment, as though reacting to a physical pain, then resumed their previous expression.

'Twelve boys left this village and never came back,' she said.

'And the ones who did return lost something of themselves over there in the mud. I still don't understand the point of it all.'

'I was there, and I don't understand the point of it either,' I said.

She softened at that: just a little, but enough.

'Were you at Verdun, or Ypres?' she asked. There was a kind of hope in her voice, as though I might have been able to tell her that I knew her sons, and they had spoken of her often, and their deaths were quick, but I could tell her none of those things.

'No. The war ended for me at High Wood.'

'I don't know where that is.'

'The Somme. The French call it Bois des Forcaux. It has something to do with pitchforks. There was a place called Delville Wood nearby, but the men I served with always called it Devil's Wood. They didn't clear it after the war. They say thousands of bodies are still buried beneath it.'

'You left friends there?'

'I left everything there. I don't suppose it matters, though. The dead are past caring.'

'I don't know if that's true,' she said. 'I talk to my boys, and I feel them listening. They listen, the dead. They're always listening. What else is there for them to do?'

And she said no more.

Bromdun Hall was a huge, rambling pile set on about five acres, and every inch of the house spoke of slow decay. It was falling into disrepair, and I could feel the draughts as soon as we were in sight of the place. I couldn't imagine that one small woman would be able to maintain a house of that size, even with some help from its resident, but Mrs Gissing said that most of the rooms were used for storage and nothing else. Her main duties consisted of cooking three meals a day, doing laundry, and keeping a handful of rooms in a clean and habitable condition. Mr Maulding, it seems, made few other demands upon her. She displayed considerable fondness towards him, though, and seemed genuinely concerned for his welfare. When I asked if she had considered calling the police at any point, she replied that Mr Quayle in London had expressly ordered her not to do so. It was, it seemed, to Quayle that she had first reported her concerns about her master. Maulding's nephew, Mr Forbes, had only learned of his absence later, when he called at the house, as he was occasionally wont to do when he needed money, and Mrs Gissing was forced to inform him of the situation.

What I did learn was that Maulding had made a number of sojourns into London in the months before his disappearance, trips of which Quayle appeared to have been entirely unaware, for he had not mentioned them to me. Mrs Gissing had been surprised by this change in her master's routine, but had made no comment upon it. On such occasions, a cab would collect him at the door first thing in the morning, deliver him to the station and then return him to his home following the arrival of the last train from London. He had made three such trips and had always informed Mrs Gissing the day before of his intention to travel.

'Is it possible that he might have gone to London without your knowledge, and simply not have returned?' I asked.

'No,' she said, and her tone brooked no contradiction. 'He always got the same driver to take him to the station and bring him home after, and he always made his timetable known. He's a delicate man, Mr Maulding. He had polio as a boy, and it left him with a twisted right leg. He can't walk very far without it causing him pain. It's one of the reasons why he has travelled so rarely. There's just too much discomfort in it for him.'

'And do you have any idea where in London he might have been going, or whom he might have been seeing?'

'He didn't share such matters with me,' she said.

'Had he any enemies?' I asked.

'Lord, no,' she said. 'He had no friends, neither – not because there was anything wrong with him,' she hastened to add. 'He just had all that he needed here.'

She gestured to the house, which was now looming above us.

'This was—' She corrected herself. 'This *is* his home. He didn't want to go out into the world, so he found a way to bring the world to him.'

It was an odd thing to say, and I didn't comprehend her meaning until I entered the house itself, and then I understood.

There were books everywhere: on the floors, on the stairs, on furniture both built for that purpose and constructed for other ends entirely. There were bookshelves in the main hallway, in the downstairs rooms and in the upstairs rooms. There were even bookshelves in the bathroom and the kitchen. There were so many volumes that, had it been possible to extract the skeleton of the house, its walls and floors, its bricks and mortar, and leave the contents intact, then the shape of the building would still have been visible to the observer, but constructed entirely from books. I had never seen anything like it. Even the reading rooms of the British Library itself seemed to pale beside it. Standing among all those books it was possible to believe that there was no other space in the world so crammed with manifestations of the printed word than Lionel Maulding's home.

As I walked through the house, Mrs Gissing at my heels, I examined the titles. There were books on every subject, and in every major language. Some were so large that special tables had been made to hold them, and to move them safely would have required two men. Others were so small that they lived in glass cases, a magnifying glass hanging beside them on a chain so the microscopic print within could be made legible.

'Astonishing,' I said.

'Every day more arrive,' said Mrs Gissing. 'I've left the new ones in the library for Mr Maulding's return.'

For the first time, she showed some sign of distress. Her voice caught, and her eyes grew moist.

'You will find him, sir, won't you? You will bring him back safely to his books?'

I told her that I would try. I asked if the grounds had been searched, and she told me that they had. There was a groundsman, Ted Willox, who knew the property intimately. He and his sons were the only other people in the village aware of Lionel Maulding's disappearance. Willox had engaged his sons to help him search Maulding's land and they had gone over it, every inch. They had found no trace of the master of the house.

Willox was away that day, visiting a sister who was ill, but was due to return to Maidensmere the following morning. I told Mrs Gissing to send him to me as soon as he arrived. I was, I confess, surprised at the loyalty of Gissing and Willox to Maulding, and their willingness to protect his privacy even as they feared for his safety. Mrs Gissing seemed to sense this, for as she showed me to my room, she spoke once more.

'Mr Maulding is a good and kind man. I just want you to know that, sir. He's always been generous to me. My boys, my lovely boys, they're buried in the cemetery here, and I get to speak to them every day. There are always fresh flowers for them, no matter the season, and the weeds are kept at bay. Mr Maulding arranged that, sir. He spoke to the generals in London, and they brought my boys home for me, each of them in turn. I've never wanted for anything, Mr Willox neither. All Mr Maulding asks in return is for his meals to be prepared, his clothes to be cleaned, and his bed to be made, and otherwise to be left in peace with his books. There is no harm to the man, and no harm should come to him.'

I wanted to tell her that such was not the way of the world until I remembered that she had buried two sons, and was thus more conscious of the world's true workings than any of us. Our arrival at my room saved me from uttering any further foolishness, and she left me to unpack the small bag that I had brought with me, and to explore my environs alone. There was a bathroom next door to my room, with a fine claw-toed bathtub. I could not recall when last I had enjoyed a bath that didn't involve a tin tub and saucepans of water with which to fill it, and I promised myself the luxury of a lengthy immersion that evening.

None of the other rooms was locked. As Mrs Gissing had intimated, most were being used for storage, and the only items that Lionel Maulding desired to store were books. I began to grasp a sense of the house's arrangement for it was, in truth, simply one large library: here were volumes on geography, there on history. Three adjoining rooms gathered together studies on biology, chemistry and physics respectively, with a series of shelves in the final room being given over to more general works that touched on all three aspects of the sciences. There were many rooms for fiction, and almost as many for poetry and drama. One sizeable area was given over to beautiful books of art reproductions, some of them very old and probably very expensive. A few were of an erotic nature, but did not appear to have been perused any more closely than the others.

In time I came to Maulding's bedroom. Once again, there were books on every surface, and each wall was furnished with shelves, floor to ceiling, except for the wall above his bed, although even here a single shelf had been placed to accommodate those works that were clearly occupying Maulding's attention at any particular time. Bookmarked on that shelf were a volume of Tacitus, a study of beekeeping, a guide to growing one's own vegetables, and two oddities: *A Lexicon of Alchemy* by Martin Rulandus the Elder, dating from 1612; and a single-volume edition of Henry Cornelius Agrippa's *Three Books on Occult Philosophy*. The Rulandus bore a leather bookmark in the 'Supplement to the Alchemical Lexicon', and two paragraphs had been heavily underscored. A pencil lay beside the book, so I took it that Maulding had made the marks. The two entries, one beneath the other, were:

ANGELS – The chemical Philosophers sometimes gave this name to the Volatile Matter of their Stone. They then say that their body is spiritualized, and that one will never succeed in performing the Grand Work unless one corporifies spirits, and spiritualizes bodies. This operation is philosophical sublimation, and it is certain that the fixed never becomes sublimated without the assistance of the volatile.

ANGLE – The thing which has three angles – a term of Hermetic science. The Philosophers say that their matter, or the Philosophical Mercury, is a substance having three angles as regards the substance of which it is composed, of four as regards its virtue, and of two in respect of its matter, while in its root it is one. These three angles are salt, sulphur, and mercury; the four are the elements; the two are the fixed and the volatile, and the one is the remote matter, or the chaos from which all has been produced.

These final words – '*the chaos from which all has been produced*' – had been more heavily underlined than the rest, although I could make no more sense of them than I could of anything else that I had read there. I completed the search of Maulding's room, but found nothing that might help in discovering his whereabouts. I then continued my examination of the house, until I came at last to the kitchen where Mrs Gissing was preparing enough food to last a whole family for a week, as I had informed her that it would not be necessary for her to come to the house every day while I was there. My needs, I explained, were probably even fewer than her master's.

'Where does Mr Maulding spend most of his time?' I asked.

'In his study, sir.'

Hardly surprising: I should probably have guessed that for myself. I had poked my head into it on the way to the kitchen, and the only thing to distinguish it from the rest of the house was that it contained marginally more books than any other room, although it was a close-run thing.

'Where would I find his papers, and the household accounts?'

'In his desk, I should imagine.'

'Does he keep it locked?'

'Why would he do that?' she asked. She seemed quite surprised at the question.

'Well, some men are rather private about the matters of their finances.'

'But what kind of person would pry into the affairs of another?'

'A person like me,' I replied.

She didn't have an answer to that, or not one that she felt inclined to speak aloud, so I left her to her pots and pans and made my way to the study.

III

It took me some time to make sense of Maulding's filing system, in part because there wasn't one, as such: there were simply piles of paper, some older than others, separated loosely into invoices and receipts, and all relating to the year in hand. Some digging behind three sets of encyclopediae produced binders containing details of his income and expenditure in previous years. Most of his purchases were made by personal cheque, but sometimes in cash, and he kept notes of expenses, major and minor, in a small ledger. So, over the course of the afternoon, and fuelled by tea and sandwiches from Mrs Gissing, I became familiar with the processes by which he maintained order in his finances. I could find little personal correspondence, some begging letters from his nephew apart, as any post that he received related almost exclusively to the purchase and, very occasionally, the sale of books. He appeared to deal with booksellers throughout Britain and, indeed, a number on the Continent and in America.

Still, it was the most recent of his acquisitions that interested me and gave some clue as to his purpose in travelling to London. It appeared that he had begun dealing with two new suppliers of books in the months preceding his disappearance: Seaford's, the specialists in scientific literature in Bloomsbury; and an antiquarian establishment, of which I had previously been unaware, called Dunwidge & Daughter. I counted at least 30 receipts from Dunwidge, all acknowledging cash payments for books, the nature of which were detailed on the documents themselves. There was *The Hermetic Museum*, which appeared to relate to something called 'the Philosopher's Stone', a first English translation from 1893 of a work apparently originally published in Latin in 1678; *The Art of Drawing Spirits in Crystals*, undated, by Johannes Trithemius; the *Grimorium Imperium*, alleged to be a copy of a work originally owned by the alchemist Dr John Dee, published in Rome in 1680; *The Theatre of Terrestrial Astronomy* by Edward Kelly, Hamburg, 1676; and assorted others in a similar vein. I could not claim to be an expert on such matters, but it seemed to me that Lionel Maulding had spent a great deal of time, effort and money to begin acquiring a library of the occult, and Dunwidge & Daughter had been the principal beneficiaries of this new enthusiasm. Unlike the better-known Seaford's, though, Dunwidge & Daughter had not appended a contact address to their receipts, merely the name of their business.

I paused in my perusals. Something had been nagging at me ever since I had begun reading this list of esoteric volumes. Slowly, I retraced my steps through the house, examining shelves and taking note of the divisions and subdivisions of subjects. It took me some hours, and by the time I was done the light had begun to fade. My back ached and my eyes could barely focus, but I was certain of this: I could find no trace of a section devoted to occult literature in Maulding's home, the two volumes on the shelf above his bed excepted. Neither could I find any trace of the books that he had apparently purchased from Dunwidge & Daughter. Naturally, it was entirely possible that I might have missed them, or that they had been misfiled, but the former seemed to me more likely than the latter, for Maulding struck me as a meticulous cataloguer of his collection. I determined to make a second search the following day, just to be sure. Maulding had no telephone in his house, so I asked Mrs Gissing to send a telegram to London on my behalf on her way home, asking Quayle's assistant Fawnsley to ascertain the location of the business known as Dunwidge & Daughter, and to reply by return of telegram the following morning, which Mrs Gissing would collect and bring to the house.

It was by now well past six o'clock. Mrs Gissing had prepared an eel pie, which I ate accompanied by the best part of a bottle of Bordeaux from Maulding's cellar. When I was done, Mrs Gissing ran a bath for me before departing for the night. I thanked her for her kindness, and then I was alone in Bromdun Hall for the first time.

I checked the bath, but the water was still too hot to bear. I had no desire to boil myself like a lobster, so I returned to my room and poured the last of the red wine while I waited for the water to cool. I had taken some books from the shelves for my own amusement, among them McNeile's recently issued *Bulldog Drummond*, published under the pseudonym 'Sapper'. McNeile had fought at Ypres, and I'd admired his stories for the *Daily Mail* and *The War Illustrated*, even if he had sugared the pill more than I liked. Then again, he was writing while the war was still ongoing, and had he dwelt upon the true horror of the fighting at the time, then none of his stories would have seen the light of day.

I had read about two pages of the novel when I heard the sound of splashing from the bathtub.

'Mrs Gissing?' I called.

Perhaps she had returned to the house for some reason and felt compelled to check the water while she was there, but I had not heard the front door opening, and the stairs leading up to the bedrooms creaked and moaned like souls in torment. Neither did the sounds coming from the bathroom resemble those of a hand being briefly swished through water in an effort to gauge its temperature. Instead, the splashing was intermittent, yet consistent with the noise a person might make while washing in a tub.

Mrs Gissing had set a fire in my bedroom before her departure. I grabbed a poker from the fireplace and, gripping it tightly, made my way to the bathroom. The door was slightly farther ajar than I had left it, although that might simply have been my nerves playing tricks on me. The difference was marginal at best. As I drew nearer the door the splashing increased in tempo before ceasing altogether, as though someone inside had become aware of my approach and was now listening for me.

I used the poker to push the door open to its fullest extent. The bathtub was empty and there appeared to be only the faintest hint of disturbance on the surface of the water. That water, though, had changed in colour. When I had left the room it was relatively clear, with only the faintest hint of brown to it. Now it was a sickly, unpleasant yellow, like curdled milk, and held a faint scum upon it. There was a smell, too, as of fish on the turn.

I stood above the tub and, feeling faintly foolish, used the poker to probe the water, half-expecting to feel soft flesh give beneath it and a torrent of bubbles to rise to the surface as the force of the poker expelled the air from whomever might be hiding below. No such bubbles appeared, however, and the only obstacle the poker encountered was the porcelain of the tub itself. There was nowhere else in the bathroom where anyone might have hidden.

I called Mrs Gissing's name again, the sound of it echoing from the bathroom tiles, but there was no reply. I wrinkled my nose at the smell from the water. Perhaps what I had heard was some emission from the taps, an expulsion of pollutants from the pipes that had tainted the water. I had no intention of bathing in it now, but I was still intent upon a bath. Mrs. Gissing had assured me that there was plenty of hot water to be had so, almost without thinking, I reached into the tub to pull the plug.

Something moved against my hand. It was hard, and jointed, reminiscent of the carapace of a lobster. I withdrew my hand with a shout, the chain of the plug still grasped in my fist, and watched as the water began to drain. Down, down it went, leaving a layer of yellow residue on the sides like foam on a beach after the tide has departed. When there was barely six inches of water left, there came a sudden flurry of movement from the vicinity of the plughole, and a form briefly broke the surface. I had a brief impression of an armoured body, pinkish-black in colour, with many, many legs. I caught a glimpse of pincers like those of an earwig, except larger and wickedly sharp, before the creature somehow forced itself into the small plughole and exited the tub, even though its body had seemed far too wide to be accommodated by such a small means of escape. There were noises from the pipes for a time, and then all was unsettlingly quiet.

Unsurprisingly, I did not take my bath after all. After immediately restoring the plug to the plughole, I did the same thing with every bath and sink I could find, more for some false peace of mind than out of any real hope that a plug of metal could stop such a creature from emerging again, should it have chosen to do so.

I sat up in my bed, wondering. What could it be, I thought: some crustacean of the Broads, unfamiliar to me but a commonplace sight to those who lived in these parts? Had I mentioned it in the Maidensmere Inn, might the landlord have tipped the wink once again to his customers and announced that what I had seen was merely X, or Y, and that fried with some cream sauce, or boiled in a pot with a little white wine vinegar, it was actually most palatable? Somehow, I suspected not. My fingers tingled unpleasantly where they had touched the thing, and they looked red and irritated in the lamplight.

Eventually I dozed. I dreamed of Pulteney's tanks rolling ineffectually towards High Wood, great rumbling silhouettes moving through the darkness until picked out by the light of flares and the explosion of shellfire. Then the shape of them began to change and they were no longer constructions of metal but living, breathing entities. They did not roll on heavy tracks, but propelled themselves on short, jointed legs. Turrets became heads, and gun barrels were transformed into strange, elongated limbs that spat poison from orifices lined with curved teeth. The flares were bolts of lightning, and the landscape they illuminated was more terrible yet than the wasteland between the trenches, even as it seemed almost familiar to me. I picked out in the distance the ruins of a village, and realized that I was looking at the Norfolk Broads, and what was left of Maidensmere, the steeple of its sixteenth-century chapel still somehow intact amid the rubble. But it was another town too, a place not far from High Wood, where bodies lay broken in the ruins, killed by shellfire: old men, women, little children. We were told that everyone had fled, but they had not.

I woke with a start. It was still dark, and only the ticking of a clock disturbed the silence.

But there was no clock in the room.

I sat up. The sound was coming from the other side of the bedroom door, which I had closed – and, yes, I admit it, locked – before going to bed. As I listened, it became clear that it was more a clicking than a ticking. I lit my lamp and gripped the poker, kept close at hand for any such eventuality. I climbed from the bed and padded across the floor as softly as I could. The sound began to increase its tempo until, just as I reached the door, it stopped, and I heard what appeared to be footsteps moving swiftly away. I unlocked the door and pulled it open. Before me there was only the empty hallway, illuminated by my lamp as far as the stairs. Beyond was darkness. I squinted into the gloom, but could discern nothing.

I looked at the door. The wood around the lock had been picked away, leaving it splintered and white, as though someone had been trying to expose its workings. I reached down and rubbed a finger against it. A splinter caught on my flesh, causing me to gasp. I took it between my teeth and pulled it loose, then spat it on the floor. A tiny jewel of blood rose from the wound.

From the shadows, there came the sound of sniffing.

'Who's there?' I said. 'Who are you? Show yourself!'

There was no reply. I moved farther into the hallway. The darkness retreated a little with each step that I advanced, and I was reminded uncomfortably of the bathwater slowly disappearing from the tub until the creature in the water had no option but to expose itself before fleeing. Two steps, four, six, eight, the shadows before me giving way to light, the shadows behind me growing, until, when I reached the stairs, the darkness made its stand. It seemed to me that there was a deeper blackness apparent, and this did not move. It was much larger than a man, and slightly hunched. I thought that I could discern the shape of its head, although the flickering of the lamp made it difficult to tell, and its form blurred into the shadows at its edges, so that it was at once a part of them and apart from them. Within it were the reflections of unseen stars. It turned, and where its face should have been I had an impression of many sharp angles, as though a plate of black glass had dropped and been frozen in the first moment of its disintegration. I felt blood trickle from the cut in my finger and drop to the floor, and the sniffing commenced again.

I backed away, and as I moved the shadows advanced once again, and the dark entity moved with them. Faster now they came, and my light grew increasingly ineffectual, the darkness encroaching upon its pool of illumination, slowly smothering it from without. Soon it would be but a glimmer behind the glass, and then it would be gone entirely.

I flung the poker. I acted without thinking, operating purely on instinct, aiming for that mass of shards and angles. The poker spun once in the air, and the heavy handle struck at the centre of the black form. There was a sound like a million delicate crystals shattering in unison, and the shadows rippled in response to some concussive force. I was thrown backwards and struck my head hard against the floor, but before I lost consciousness I thought I saw that deeper blackness collapse in upon itself, and a hole was briefly ripped in the fabric of space and time. Through it I glimpsed unknown constellations, and a black sun.

And the face of Lionel Maulding, howling into the void.

IV

Mrs Gissing arrived shortly after seven, an older man behind her whom I took, correctly as it turned out, to be Mr Willox. They found me awake and seated at a table in the library, a cup of tea steaming before me, and more in the pot nearby. Mrs Gissing seemed rather put out by this, as though in venturing to provide for myself I had usurped her natural place in the universe and, more to the point, threatened her livelihood, for if men began to make cups of tea for themselves then soon they might well attempt to cook meals, and do laundry, and next thing poor Mrs Gissing and her kind would find themselves out on the streets begging for pennies. As if to ensure that this would not come to pass without a struggle, she prepared to bustle her way to the kitchen to make bacon, eggs, and toast, even though I assured her that I was not hungry.

'Did you not sleep well?' she asked.

'No, I did not,' I said, then ventured a question. 'Have you ever spent the night in this house, Mrs Gissing?'

I should, perhaps, have phrased the question a little more delicately, as Mrs Gissing appeared to feel that her reputation as a widow of good standing was being impugned. After some awkward apologies on my part, she chose to take the question in the spirit in which it was asked, and confessed that she had never spent a night under Mr Maulding's roof.

'Did he ever complain of noises, or disturbances?' I asked.

'I'm not sure what you mean, sir.'

I wasn't sure what I meant either. The mind plays odd tricks, often to protect itself from harm, and it had already begun the process of consigning the events of the previous night to that place between what we see and what we dream.

'There was something in my bathtub last night,' I said. 'It was a creature of some sort.'

Willox spoke for the first time.

'A rat?' he said. 'We've had them, sir. They find ways into old houses like this. I'll lay down some poison.'

'No, it wasn't a rat. To be honest, I'm not sure what it was. It fled down the plughole as the water level dropped. It was more of a crustacean, I think.'

'A crustacean?'

'Like a crab, or a lobster.'

Mrs Gissing looked at me as though I were mad, as well she might have done. Willox appeared uncertain, and could have been considering whether people in London might enjoy a sense of humour different from, and stranger than, his own.

'Who would put a lobster in your bath?' said Mrs Gissing. 'Certainly not I.'

She seemed ready to take umbrage once again, so I assured her that I was not accusing her of being in the habit of putting lobsters in the bathtubs of strange men.

'And then,' I continued, 'I was woken by what appeared to be a presence in the house.'

'A . . . presence?' said Willox.

'Yes. I can't describe it any better than that.'

'Are you talking about a ghost, sir?'

'I don't believe in ghosts,' I said. 'Did Mr Maulding believe in ghosts?'

'I can't recall him ever mentioning the subject to me.' He turned to Mrs Gissing, who shrugged and shook her head.

'I ask because he seems to have recently begun building a library of the occult, which suggests that something might have excited his interest in such matters. He never mentioned disturbances in the house to you?'

'No.'

'Did he appear distressed in recent weeks, or seem tired and anxious?'

'No.'

'Do you think I'm mad, Mrs Gissing?'

For the first time, she smiled. 'I couldn't possibly say, sir. But this is a big, old house, and big, old houses are filled with creaks and groans that can seem strange to those who aren't used to them. I'll go and make you that breakfast, sir, and you'll feel better for it.'

'What about you, Mr Willox?' I said. 'Do you doubt my sanity?'

'I don't know you well enough to be certain, sir, but you look sane enough to me. But, like Mrs Gissing says, it takes time to get used to a strange house, especially one as old as this. Even I sometimes find myself looking over my shoulder when I'm alone in it. It's the way of such places, isn't it? They wear their history heavily.'

I asked him about Mr Maulding, but he could add nothing to what Mrs Gissing had told me. He did ask about his wages, and I told him that I'd arrange for Mr Quayle to make the payments. He seemed satisfied with this, although he might not have been had he known Quayle personally. Quayle rarely paid quickly, and Maulding's financial obligations to his domestic staff would have been very low on the lawyer's list of priorities. The fact that he had paid me money in advance was a sign of just how anxious he was to ensure Maulding's safe return.

Willox departed to work on the grounds. I heard the sound of bangs and crashes from the kitchen, and the smell of frying bacon began to waft, not unpleasantly, into the library. Surrounded by these noises and scents, these indicators of normality, I became less and less certain of what I had witnessed the previous night. It was not unnatural. The undisturbed mind will tend to seek the most rational explanation for an occurrence: to do otherwise is to sow the seeds of madness. I had a troubled mind, fractured by experience, but I was not yet ready to surrender entirely to disquiet.

It was about this time that there came a knock on the door. Mrs

Gissing being otherwise occupied, I answered it myself and found the boy from the post office waiting with a telegram for me. I gave him a shilling for his efforts, having nothing smaller, and sent him on his way. I wondered if I could claim the shilling from Quayle as an expense. Perhaps I should have asked for a receipt.

The telegram was from Fawnsley. Its brevity made it clear that he was paying by the word, and counting every one. There was no greeting, merely an insincere expression of regret that no confirmed address could be found for Dunwidge & Daughter, although he had heard that they operated from somewhere near the King's Road in Chelsea, and a final, terse addition:

```
large withdrawal made from maulding funds
last month stop ten thousand pounds stop not
approved by quayle stop investigate stop
```

£10,000 was more than a small fortune. There was a safe in Maulding's library, but I had no way of accessing its contents. It was possible that the money was still in there, but if Maulding had withdrawn it without going through Quayle, as he was perfectly entitled to do, even if it were not according to his habit, this suggested that the funds were required for some purpose that he did not wish to share with his lawyer, and one with a hint of urgency to it.

In my experience, unusual patterns of spending gave rise to certain speculations about the reason for them. For example, a gradual seepage of money, slowly rising in quantity and instances of occurrence, might lead one to suspect a gambling problem; larger but more consistent sums suggested a newfound interest in a woman, or a tart. A single significant payment, particularly the kind that a man chose not to share with his lawyer, might be the consequence of an investment opportunity of dubious legality, or an effort to make a problem go away.

But from what I knew of Lionel Maulding, he had no particular interest in gambling or women, and therefore was unlikely to be troubled by the problems that might arise from over-indulgence in either. No, £10,000 suggested a purchase of some kind, but Maulding already had one huge house: he didn't need another. Neither was there a sudden proliferation of motor cars or yachts in the immediate vicinity of Bromdun Hall.

So: on what did Lionel Maulding spend his money as a matter of habit?

Lionel Maulding spent his money on books.

What kind of book, or books, would cost a man £10,000?

A rare book. A *very* rare book.

I ate my breakfast, confirmed the times of trains with Mrs Gissing and prepared to return to London.

V

I had rarely, if ever, darkened the door of Seaford's, mainly because there was nothing in there that I felt qualified to read. I also feared that this would be recognized the moment I crossed its threshold, and some officious clerk would appear from behind a counter piled high with works on physics and the nature of the atom, politely steer me back out the door, and point me in the direction of a news stand liberally stocked with illustrated weeklies. Instead, a very polite young man with the build of a good front row rugby player showed me to a seat in a cluttered office, and listened as I explained my purpose. I had brought with me some of the receipts for Maulding's recent purchases, but the handwriting on them was abysmal, and those words that I could read meant nothing to me.

The young man, who introduced himself as Richards, could have made a decent career out of the interpretation of ancient Sanskrit if the bookselling or science didn't work out, for the errant handwriting gave him not a moment's trouble.

'That's Old Mr Blair's hand,' he explained. 'I've come to know it well over the years.'

'Is Mr Blair available?' I asked.

His face assumed an awkward expression.

'I'm afraid Old Mr Blair passed away some weeks ago.'

'I'm sorry to hear that.'

'He was ninety-two.'

'I'm still sorry to hear it.'

'The original Mr Seaford gave Mr Blair his job,' Richards explained. 'He was the last link to the store's foundation. His handwriting was always terrible, though.'

He returned his attention to the list.

'There's a definite pattern to these purchases,' he said.

'In what way?'

'Well, you have a copy of the Liebniz-Clarke correspondence, first published in English in 1717, although this is obviously a later edition. The main interest in it for most readers is a dispute over the nature of space and, indeed, time. Here's Mach's *The Analysis of Sensations* from 1897. Mach suggested that only sensations were real, and nothing else, if I understand him right, although it's not entirely my area.'

He read out some more names that meant little to me – 'Planck. Einstein – quite the coming chap' – and then frowned.

'Hullo,' he said. 'He ordered various works by William James. Some of these are a bit outside our usual remit: *Proceedings of the American Society for Psychical Research, Volume 3; The Varieties of Religious Experience; The Will to Believe and Other Essays in Popular Philosophy*. That's a curious one. Not uninteresting, but certainly odd.'

I waited. Sometimes, my own patience astounded me.

Richards smiled apologetically. 'Sorry. Fascinating stuff. James refers to something called the "multiverse", a hypothetical set of possible universes, of which this universe is just one part.'

'And what does he think is in these other universes?'

'I'm not sure he's got that far, but I can't confess to being an expert on James. Judging from Mr Maulding's list, though, I'd guess that he'd become interested in the nature of reality. Complex business, especially for the general reader.'

I thanked him. I wasn't sure that there was any more to be learned here, or any more that I might have a chance of understanding.

'By the way,' I said, 'have you ever heard of a bookseller called Dunwidge, or Dunwidge & Daughter, in Chelsea?'

'Can't say that I have,' said Richards. 'We can ask Young Mr Blair, though. He knows every bookseller in London.'

He led me up various flights of stairs to a small section devoted entirely to works of psychology. A slight man in a dark suit, who must have been 80 if he was a day, was snoozing quietly behind a till.

'Old Mr Blair's brother?' I enquired.

'Strangely enough, no,' said Richards. 'They weren't even related, and they didn't get on at all. Young Mr Blair wouldn't even contribute to the wreath.'

Mr Richards gently woke Young Mr Blair, who took the disturbance well. In fact, he seemed rather pleased that somebody wanted to talk to him. Perhaps he was just glad to have woken up at all. At his age, he was close to the time when the line between a short nap and the eternal rest was but a thin one.

'This is Mr Soter, Mr Blair. He has a question about a bookseller.'

Young Mr Blair smiled and mumbled a string of words, out of which I managed to pick two, 'delighted' and 'help', which boded well.

'I was wondering if you knew anything of a bookseller in Chelsea named Dunwidge?' I asked.

Young Mr Blair's face darkened. He scowled. He shook his head. An index finger appeared and was waved in an admonitory manner. Another string of muttered words emerged from his lips, blending into one long caw of disapproval. Eventually, spotting that I was somewhat at a loss to make any sense of what he was saying, he managed to force out some coherent, if short, sentences.

'Dreadful man,' he said. 'Daughter worse. Umm . . . Occultists! Fire and brimstone sorts. Quite. Quite. Old books. *Nasty* books. Not science. Not science at all.'

He leaned forward and tapped his finger on the counter.

'Mumbo-jumbo,' he said, enunciating each syllable carefully.

'I need an address for them,' I said. 'I've been told they're in Chelsea, perhaps on the King's Road.'

Young Mr Blair returned to his mutterings, but he found a scrap of paper and, in elegant copperplate, wrote down an address for me. I thanked him for his help and prepared to leave, but he stood and gripped my arm with a surprisingly strong hand.

'Stay away from 'em,' he urged. 'Bad sorts, both of 'em, but the daughter most of all!'

I thanked him again, and he released his grip and returned to his seat. His eyes closed, and he returned to his slumbers.

Richards was quite impressed.

'You know,' he said, 'I haven't seen him that excited since Old Mr Blair died.'

VI

I went next to Chancery to report my progress, or lack thereof, to Quayle, but he was not in his chambers. Only Fawnsley was present, scratching disconsolately with his fountain pen at a document thick with legalese, like a sick hen scrabbling for a piece of stray corn in the dirt.

'Took your time getting here,' he said, in lieu of a greeting

'What do you mean by that?' I replied. 'I've only been gone for one night. I'm not a miracle worker.'

Fawnsley tapped the calendar on his desk. It was made of

various blocks of ivory that could be turned to change the day, the month, and the year. The calendar read 15 October.

'Your calendar is wrong,' I said.

'My calendar is never wrong,' he answered.

I sat down heavily in a chair by the wall. I had lost a week. It wasn't possible. It simply wasn't possible. I had taken the train on the 8th. I had the ticket in my pocket. I had kept it so that Quayle wouldn't question my expenses. I searched my pockets and my wallet for the ticket, but it was gone.

'You look ill,' said Fawnsley.

'Trouble sleeping,' I said. I stared at the calendar. Not possible. Not possible.

Fawnsley chewed a question silently in his mouth. I could actually see his jaws working.

'You're not . . . ?'

He trailed off. The shadow of Craiglockhart hung over us as surely as if the military psychiatric hospital itself lay outside Quayle's chambers, and the sun was setting behind it.

'No,' I said. 'I'm fine.'

He didn't look as though he believed me. I tried not to look as though I cared.

'Did you get my telegram?' he asked.

'I did. Ten thousand pounds: a man could buy a lot with that kind of money.'

'Well, have you discovered what the man in question *did* buy with it?'

'Since you only informed me about it this morning, I may need a little more time,' I said.

Again, Fawnsley gave me that look. I corrected myself. I didn't want Fawnsley reporting back to Quayle that I was troubled, or unreliable. I needed the money.

'Sorry,' I said, making the best of a bad situation. 'I meant that I have only this morning received some information, based on what was contained in the telegram.'

'And what is this great leap?'

'I think Maulding might have spent the money on books.'

'*Books?*' squawked Fawnsley. 'He could buy a whole bloody library of books for ten thousand pounds.'

'He already has a library,' I said. 'When a man has as many books as Maulding, he stops being interested in the ones that are easy to acquire, because he already has them. Instead, he starts seeking out rare volumes, and the rarer they are, the more they cost.'

'And what kind of rare volumes are we talking about?'

But before I could reply Fawnsley was considering his own question.

'Surely it's not literature of a depraved nature? He never struck me as the type.'

'It depends upon what one means by "depraved", I imagine.'

'Don't come the philosopher with me, man. You know precisely what I mean.'

'If you're referring to works of an erotic nature, then, no, I don't think that was Maulding's weakness. He had some volumes of that type in his library, but not many. He did seem to have developed something of a fascination with the occult, though, and I couldn't trace all of the books on the subject that he had acquired. Most of them appear to be missing, although I admit that I might have missed a couple on his shelves. There are only so many titles that one man can examine at a time.'

'Occult? Erotica? You've become quite the expert, haven't you, and all that in just a week? Clearly, our money is being well spent. We may not have Maulding, but you're improving your education by leaps and bounds.'

There it was again: a week, a week.

'It's just common sense. Tell Quayle I'll be in touch when I have something more solid to offer him.'

'What about receipts?' said Fawnsley.

'You'll get them.'

'I should hope so. We're not made of money, you know.'

'I never thought that you were, Mr Fawnsley,' I said. 'If that were the case, you'd invest in a better suit of clothes, and the manners to go with it.'

Fawnsley seemed about to say something in reply, but decided against it. I knew what he thought of me already. Through a half-open door, I'd once overheard him carefully trying to steer Quayle away from hiring me shortly after I'd left Craiglockhart. I'd done some work for Quayle before the war, much like the work that I was doing now, but back then Fawnsley was merely a junior clerk. His predecessor had been a chap of the old school named Hayley, who was wounded at Sevastopol and drank port with his lunch.

'He wasn't even a proper officer,' Fawnsley had protested, a reference to the fact that I had been promoted from the ranks. 'Worse, he is a broken man!'

And Quayle had replied, 'He was more of an officer than you or I, and a broken man can be fixed, especially one who wants to mend himself.'

That was why I was loyal to Quayle. He had faith in me. It also helped that he paid me for my services: not well, and not fast, but he paid.

'Goodbye, Mr Fawnsley,' I said, but he bade me no farewell.

It was already dark when I reached the address in Chelsea occupied by Dunwidge & Daughter, Booksellers. It lay in an area known as World's End, named after a pub at the western extreme of the King's Road. In the last century, this area had been something of an artists' colony: Turner, Whistler and Rossetti lived and worked there, and it still had something of a bohemian feel to it.

Dunwidge & Daughter, though, seemed intent on maintaining a discreet presence, and the only indication that the terraced house might shelter a business lay in a brass plate on the front door, engraved with a pair of interlocking letter 'D's. I rang the bell. After a minute, a bald man wearing a suit jacket and waistcoat over his otherwise bare chest opened the door. He held a cigarette in one hand and a brass candlestick in the other.

'Yes?' he said.

'Mr Dunwidge?'

'That's me. Do I know you?'

'No. I'm here on behalf of Mr Lionel Maulding, one of your customers,' which was not so much a lie as an approximation of truth. 'My name is Soter.'

'It's late, but I suppose you'd better come in if you're here on Maulding's business.'

He opened the door wider, and I stepped inside. The house was dimly lit, but reminiscent of Maulding's own home in the sheer numbers of books that lined the walls of the hall. A stairway led up to the next levels of the house, but Dunwidge directed me through a door on the right. It was one of two interconnected rooms that served as a kind of shop floor, with books on tables and shelves and, in some cases, securely locked away behind glass-fronted and barred cabinets.

'He send you with his shopping list, then?' asked Dunwidge. He put the cigarette in his mouth and gestured with his right hand. 'Well, hand it over. Let's see what he wants this time.'

I didn't answer. There was a table by the window in the main room, and on it rested an ashtray filled with cigarette butts. It was clearly where Dunwidge worked when he had no customers to trouble him. The rest of the table was taken up by various sheets of paper covered in handwritten symbols, part of some code that I could not decipher. I flicked through them, but they were all similarly arcane.

'What are these?' I asked.

'You might want to tell your Mr Maulding about those,' said Dunwidge. 'Very interested in them, he was, but I didn't have a full set of sixty folios to offer him, not then. They're Cipher Manuscripts. I suppose you could call them a compendium of magick.'

'What language is this?'

'English and Hebrew, mostly. It's a substitution cryptogram. It's not hard to interpret, once you find the pattern. This one came from a former Adeptus Major in the Hermetic Order of the Golden Dawn. Seems he had a falling-out with Berridge over at the Iris-Urania, and Crowley too. Can't say I blame him when it comes to Crowley. I won't have him in the house. He's a wrong 'un, and I should know: I've seen enough of them in this business. Once I'm sure that we have the lot, I'll let your Mr Maulding know. I'll give him a good price, he need have no fear of that.'

Dunwidge lit a fresh cigarette without offering me one, and peered at me suspiciously through the smoke.

'He usually comes down here himself, does Mr Maulding,' he said. 'Always struck me as a private sort. Unusual that he'd send someone else along on an errand.'

I turned to face him.

'Mr Maulding seems to have disappeared,' I said. 'I've been asked to find him.'

'I see,' said Dunwidge. 'Well, he ain't here.'

'When did you last see him?'

Dunwidge engaged in some ear-tugging and cheek-puffing. 'Oh, not for two or three months or more, I would have said.'

'Really?'

'At least.'

I reached into my pocket and removed a sheaf of receipts from Dunwidge & Daughter.

'That's odd,' I said, 'because all of these receipts are more recent than that.'

'Well, we do a lot of business by post.'

'I'm sure. Nevertheless, Mr Maulding made a number of visits to London in the last month, and he was not in the habit of travelling to the city more often than was necessary. He was a meticulous man. He kept train tickets, notes of meals eaten and taxis taken. I've gone through them all, and it seems that your premises was his destination on more than one of those occasions.'

I waited to be called on the lie, but Dunwidge buckled.

'I might be mistaken, of course,' he said. 'We get all sorts of people through here, at all sorts of hours. I might have missed him. My daughter, she deals with most of the customers. I'm more of a backroom boy myself. Always have been.'

'Is your daughter here, Mr Dunwidge?'

'Oh, she's about, right enough. I expect she'll be along in her own good time.'

He fussed with some books, straightening their spines so that they were aligned with the edge of their shelf. It was clear that he now regretted being the one who had answered the door to me.

'Do you recall what books Mr Maulding might have purchased?'

'Not off the top of my head. You'd be surprised how many books we sell. Lot of interest in our area, lot of interest.'

More fussing, more aligning, the tension knotting in his shoulders.

'But you keep records, I'm sure?'

'My daughter does. I'm a numbers man. I add up the takings at the end of the day and see it all safely to the bank in the morning.'

'A backroom boy *and* a numbers man,' I said. 'The only limit to your talents appears to be your memory.'

He didn't let the sarcasm bite, but merely smiled bashfully.

'I'm not as young as I used to be,' he said, and the smile twisted just slightly so that it became a thing more unpleasant, more knowing. 'My memory does tend to come and go, I'll admit, and that can be a curse, you know, but a blessing too.'

He glanced over my right shoulder, and I saw relief and, perhaps, a hint of fear on his face.

'Ah, here she is,' he said. 'I was wondering where you'd got to, my dear. Gentleman here has some questions about Mr Maulding.'

There came that sly grin again. 'You'll forgive me, sir, but your name has already slipped my mind.'

'It's Soter,' I said, as I turned to face his daughter.

What struck me first about her was her solidity. She was

certainly not thin, but neither was she fat. She had the bulk of one who had engaged in heavy physical labour for much of her life, and I felt that, if I were to poke her with a finger, there would be only a little give to her flesh before I encountered hard muscle. She was tall for a woman – five-eight or a fraction more – and might have been any age from 30 to 50. Her hair was a muddy brown, pulled tight in a bun and fixed with pins. Her face was largely unadorned, apart from a slash of lipstick that was rather too pale for her complexion and lent her an aspect of bloodlessness that belied her bulk. She wore a black dress with mother-of-pearl buttons which, although it was relatively tight, showed few curves. I might almost have said that there was a sexlessness to her, but that would not have been right. She was clearly a woman, but I would no more have considered seducing her than I would have considered seducing a statue of Queen Victoria herself. There was an unattractiveness to her that emanated from within. I had met plain women, even ugly women, whose physical shortcomings had been remedied by their spirit, their decency and kindness even effecting a kind of transformation upon them, softening the bluntness of their features. This was not such a woman. The blight was inside her and no restyling of her hair, no careful use of cosmetics, no pretty dresses could have made her any less unsettling than she was.

'I'm Eliza Dunwidge,' she said. 'Pleased to make your acquaintance, Mr Soter.'

And there was something in the way she said my name that made me believe she already knew of me, although I had not perceived a similar response in her father when first we met. That benighted man seemed to take courage in his daughter's presence, and was now looking at me with his arms folded and an expression of satisfaction on his face, as if to say, 'Now, here's the thing, and a pretty thing it is. She'll set you right, oh yes. She'll scatter the pigeons and come back with feathers in her mouth . . .'

As if in response to such imagined thoughts, Eliza Dunwidge's hands emerged from behind her back, as though ready to wring the neck of the nearest bird. They were thin and delicate, and entirely without lines or blemishes. They resembled the hands of a mannequin that had been fused to her own limbs. Their nails were perfect and gleamed as they caught the light in the room.

'Mr Maulding is a good customer,' she said. 'We always look forward to seeing him here.'

'Did he visit you often?'

'May I ask why you're enquiring after him? We maintain the utmost discretion when it comes to our clients. As you may have gathered already, we offer a very specialized service. There are those who frown upon what we sell, which is why we choose not to display our wares in a shop window on Charing Cross Road.'

'Mr Maulding is missing,' I said. 'He has not been seen for a week—'

I thought of the calendar on Fawnsley's desk, and added, 'or more. I've been employed by his lawyer to enquire into his condition.'

Eliza Dunwidge did not seem unduly taken aback by this announcement. Perhaps people disappeared around her on a regular basis. There might even be a section in the shop containing works alluding to such practices: *'People, Disembodiment of.'* Still, she found it in herself to say the appropriate words under the circumstances, even if she gave no sign that she meant them.

'I'm sorry to hear that,' she said. 'I hope that no harm has come to him.'

'As you say, he was a good customer. Wouldn't want to go losing too many of those, would you?'

Her head tilted slightly. She was examining me in a new light, although it wasn't clear if she liked what she saw.

'No, Mr Soter, I would not.'

'I', not 'we'. Interesting. It was easy to see who was the principal partner in this particular firm. They would have been better off naming their business Daughter & Dunwidge.

I moved away from her and paused in front of the locked cabinets.

'Are these valuable?'

She joined me. She did not use perfume, and her body gave off a musky odour that was not unpleasant.

'Every book is potentially valuable. It depends upon the person who wants it as much as the book itself. Value is linked to age, rarity, condition, and, of course, affection for the volume in question – or simply the desire to acquire it. Eventually, of course, some books acquire an agreed-upon value. The works in that cabinet are among them.'

'Do you sell many books with an agreed-upon value that might be higher than most?'

'Some.'

'What is the most expensive book that you have in stock?'

'Off the top of my head, there are some sixteenth-century occult volumes that we would price in the high hundreds, but the demand for them is low.'

'And the thousands? Do you have books that cost more than a thousand pounds?'

She shook her head.

'Oh no, not here. To sell a book worth that much, one would need to have a buyer to hand. We would not be in a position to make a speculative purchase of a book worth so much simply in the hope that we might be able to sell it on at a later date. It would bankrupt us.'

'But there are such books?'

'Yes, of course.'

'Occult books?'

There was a pause before she answered.

'A few. Not many.'

'Was Lionel Maulding looking for such a book?'

She was staring at me intently now. Her face didn't give much away, but I knew she was considering how much I might know, and how much she could give away, if anything, before she was obliged to start lying or clam up entirely. I understood, too, that she was a strong woman but also a vain one. I had felt her dislike of me from the moment we set eyes on each other. To be caught in a lie would humiliate her and wound her pride. To remain silent would be little better, for it would be a tacit admission that I was on the right track, and any further enquiries on my part would catch her on the back foot. Either result would also mean that I had won the first stage of whatever game was being played here.

So she went for the truth, or some of it.

'Yes, he was seeking a very rare book,' she said.

'What was it?'

'It's a work so unusual that it doesn't have a fixed title, or rather, it's known by a number of names, none of which quite captures the essence of it, which is apt under the circumstances. Mr Maulding wasn't sure at first that it even existed, but the nature of his researches meant that he had begun consulting books that were more and more obscure, and each obscurity led to further obscurities, like the branches of a tree growing thinner and thinner. Eventually, he was destined to find references to works that were more whispers than actual volumes, to books that contained within them the myths of books.'

I waited. She was enjoying herself now. Experts love a captive audience.

'The title by which he knew it, and one by which I had heard it described in the past, was the *Atlas Regnorum Incognitorum*, usually translated as the *Atlas of Unknown Realms*, although it has also been called the *Atlas of Geographical Impossibilities*, and the *Fractured Atlas*. It has no known author, and no confirmed genesis. It is mentioned in other texts, but without any specific references to its contents. It is a book of which only a handful have any knowledge, but which none have actually seen.'

'And what does it contain?'

'Maps of worlds, it seems. Worlds other than this one.'

'You mean planets? Mars and suchlike?'

'No, I mean realms of existence, universes beyond our own.'

'The multiverse,' I said, recalling something of what the young man at Seaford's had mentioned.

Again, I saw her reappraising me in her head, although I felt that I was operating under false pretences as I couldn't recall the name of the chap who had come up with the word to begin with, and I wasn't sure that I could explain the concept in any depth even if a gun was put to my head.

'Yes,' she said, 'I suppose you could call it that.'

'And how much would this book be worth, should a copy of it come on the market?'

'Ah, but that's the thing,' she said. 'There are no copies. There is only the original, and that, if it ever existed, has long been lost.'

'No copies? Why not?'

I could almost see the twists of her mind reflected in the tense movements of her body. We were reaching the limits of what she was prepared to share, for now. She settled for her first lie, but I smelled it on her. Even her body odour changed, growing more bitter.

'One can't duplicate what one cannot see,' she said. 'To create a copy would require the presence of the original. Despite some lengthy searches, we were unable to meet Mr Maulding's needs.'

I inhaled the scent of the untruth, and touched my tongue to my lips to test its flavour. It stank of nettles, and tasted of copper.

'And if someone found out where this atlas was, and there was a buyer to hand, would ten thousand pounds cover the cost of it?'

'Ten thousand pounds would cover the cost of many things, Mr Soter,' she said, and followed it with a strange remark, if one could ascribe degrees of strangeness to a conversation that had been peculiar as soon as it had begun.

'Ten thousand pounds,' she said, 'may even buy a soul.'

She excused herself, informing me that her father would see me out. She stamped her way slowly up the stairs. A door opened and closed again above our heads, and then the house was quiet around us.

But I could sense her listening.

'Hope that was helpful to you,' said Mr Dunwidge.

'Somewhat,' I replied. 'Tell me, are there other booksellers in London who deal in similar material?'

'None like us,' he said, 'but I can give you some names. I don't see why we should be the only ones to have the pleasure of your company.'

He scribbled a handful of addresses on a sheet of notepaper, but he insisted on escorting me to the door before he handed over the list.

'Bye, now,' said Mr Dunwidge as he released me back into the night. 'Mind how you go.'

'I'll be seeing you again, I think,' I said.

'I'll let my daughter know,' said Mr Dunwidge. 'She *will* be pleased.'

And he closed the door in my face.

VII

I spent much of the following day working through the names on Dunwidge's list, but gained little from the experience. I was familiar with some of the businesses already, having seen their receipts among Maulding's records, but in every case it appeared that Maulding's dealings with them had been relatively minor, and involved few volumes of significant value. When I raised the title of the *Atlas of Unknown Realms*, I was met variously with blank stares or denials of its possible existence. Meanwhile, any mention of Dunwidge & Daughter elicited largely negative responses, underpinned by what I thought might have been a degree of unease.

Seaford's was still doing business when I arrived, for it stayed open later than most stores of its kind in order to cater to the students whose formal studies absorbed all the hours of daylight. I asked after Young Mr Blair and was told that he was fetching his hat and coat, and would be leaving by the front door. I waited for him there, night now fully descended, the fog embracing the city. I blew my nose to clear it of some of the filth, and wondered, not for the first time, what the air in the city was doing to my lungs. Those I could not purge so easily.

Young Mr Blair emerged from the shop like an infant being pushed from the womb, forced from a warm, familiar place into the cold, hostile world without. He took a final, fond glance back at the interior before placing a cloth cap on his head, carefully adjusting it so that as much of his ears as possible might be covered. His brown leather briefcase, weathered but not worn, rested by his right leg, his umbrella by his left. I could see him wrestling with the apparent familiarity of my face as I approached before the light of recognition illuminated his features. There was a benignity to him that I liked, a happy disengagement from the futilities and ugliness of life's toil that one encountered in those who had discovered a way to take something for which they had only love and gratitude, and make it their means of support.

I greeted him, and asked if I might walk with him for a time, to which he assented with a nod and what I thought were the words 'Of course' and 'Pleasure, dear fellow', although they were so interspersed with various 'ums' and 'ahs' and unintelligible phrases that it was difficult to be sure. Together we headed towards Tottenham Court Road and on to Oxford Street. As we passed the first of the Lyons Tea Rooms he sniffed wistfully at the air, and required little convincing to enter.

A Gladys took an order for tea and sandwiches, and while we waited for them to arrive Young Mr Blair sat with his hands clasped in his lap and a pleasant smile on his face, taking in the bustle and life around him. It must have constituted quite the racket compared to the near monastic silence of Seaford's, but Young Mr Blair basked happily in it all. I could see no ring on his finger, and I could not imagine that the junior members of staff spent much of their leisure time with Young Mr Blair once Seaford's closed its doors. With the passing of his nemesis, Old Mr Blair, he was now the most senior bookseller, and there would have been few peers to keep him company, even if they could have understood more than a fraction of what he was saying.

I recalled that wistful look he had cast back at the store as he left it. Seaford's was his true home. Wherever he laid his head at night was merely an adjunct to it. When away from the shop, I suspected that Young Mr Blair was sometimes rather lonely.

So we ate our sandwiches and drank our tea, and when Young Mr Blair had cleaned his plate by licking an index finger and dabbing it on the china so that not even a single crumb might escape, I suggested some apple tart with whipped cream. I raised a hand to the passing Gladys, and Young Mr Blair, with only a token effort at resistance, agreed that, yes, some tart would be very nice, and so we continued eating, and had our teapot refilled, and it was while we were letting the food settle in our stomachs that I raised again the subject of Dunwidge & Daughter.

Young Mr Blair puffed his cheeks, and scratched his chin, and drummed his fingers on the table, like a man contemplating the purchase of an item of whose provenance and quality he was profoundly distrustful.

'Dreadful woman,' he said at last, as if the conclusion had ever been in doubt. 'Quite, quite dreadful.'

I made it clear that I was not about to disagree with his assessment, and then explained something of my quandary: a mutual acquaintance (at this Young Mr Blair tapped a finger to his nose and winked theatrically) had sought a book from Dunwidge & Daughter (frown, more puffing of cheeks, 'appalling woman'), but the work was so obscure that they were unable to source it. Under such circumstances, I asked, to whom might our mutual acquaintance have turned?

Young Mr Blair considered the question.

'Occult?' he asked.

'Yes.'

'Bad stuff. Ought to have stayed away from it.'

'Probably.'

'Rare?'

'Very.'

'Expensive?'

'Very, very.'

'Maggs,' said Young Mr Blair decisively. 'Maggs is the man.'

'Does he have a first name?'

'Might do. Never uses it. Rotten fellow.'

He leaned across the table and whispered, 'Maggs the Maggot,' and nodded his head solemnly.

'Is he a bookseller?'

'Oooooh, no, no, no.'

Young Mr Blair appeared quite offended at the suggestion, as though by even implying such a thing I had besmirched the reputation of his trade.

'Book *scout*,' he corrected.

'I don't know what that is.'

'Looks for rare books. Buys 'em cheap – widows and suchlike, don't know any better – and sells 'em on to booksellers. Won't have him in the shop. Thief, um? Cheat, um? But he can find 'em. Can find anything if it's got a cover on it. Knows his books, does Maggs. Doesn't love 'em, though. That's the thing of it. You have to love 'em. No point to it otherwise.'

Young Mr Blair rubbed his right thumb against the middle and index fingers of his right hand in an unmistakable gesture.

'All about this, you know? Money, um? Nothing else. Bad as the woman. Ought to marry her!'

He laughed at his joke, and glanced at his pocket watch.

'Must be off,' he said.

He withdrew a wallet from the inside pocket of his jacket, but I waved it away.

'A thank-you,' I said. 'For your help.'

'Oh,' he said, and I thought that his eyes went moist. 'Oh, my dear fellow. Most kind.'

'Just one last thing,' I asked, as he began gathering his belongings. 'Where would I find this Maggs?'

'Princelet Street,' he said. 'By the synagogue. Don't know the number. Have to ask. Again, most kind, most kind.'

He tapped my arm.

'Beware of Maggs,' he said solemnly. 'Doesn't love books. Might have done, once, but something happened. Occult. Bad books, bad business. Understand?'

I didn't, not then, but I thanked him once more. We shook hands, and he headed into the night.

Princelet Street: that was in Whitechapel, close to Spitalfields. I knew that part of the city well, and from what I could recall there were two synagogues on Princelet Street: the Princelet Street Synagogue and the Chevrah Torah. I looked at my watch. It was after eight. I could go back to my lodgings, or I could try to find Maggs the book scout. Like Young Mr Blair, or the domestic vision that I had of him, there was little for me at home, and I realized that I might well have been projecting my own loneliness onto the old bookseller.

No matter. I decided to go after Maggs.

VIII

If it was true to say that nobody in Whitechapel had a bad word to say about Maggs the book scout, then it was only because nobody I encountered appeared to want to waste any words on him at all. I began asking about him in the vicinity of the Chevrah Torah, but was directed gruffly to the Princelet Street Synagogue further along the way. There, questions about Maggs were greeted with dark looks and, in one case, a veritable fountain of rheumy spittle that missed my boot by an inch. Eventually, an old Chasidic man wearing an ancient *spodik* on his head directed me to a lane that smelled of cat piss and stagnant water. There a doorway stood open, revealing a veritable warren of small apartments. A young woman, who might well have been a tart, stood smoking outside.

'Do you live here?' I asked her.

'Live – and work,' she said, and the way she tipped her head in the direction of the stairs removed any doubts that I might have had about her profession. When I didn't bite, she sucked deeply on her cigarette and ran her soft pink tongue over her lips.

'You a copper?'

'No.'

'You look like a copper.'

'Is that a good thing?'

'Not around here.'

'I'm trying to find a man named Maggs. I was told that he lives nearby.'

'He in trouble, then?'

'Why would you say that?'

'Because men who look like you don't go asking after men like Maggs unless there's trouble involved.'

'And what kind of man is Maggs?'

'He's the kind of man I wouldn't roll with if his cock was dipped in gold and he gave it to me after for a doorstop.'

It was an arresting image.

'I've been struggling to find anyone who might say something pleasant about him,' I said. 'When he dies, it's likely to be lonely by the graveside.'

'Shouldn't have thought so. Lot of people will show up just to make sure that he's dead.'

'They offer dancing shoes for such occasions, I believe.'

She smiled. 'If they don't, I'll make do with what I have.'

'Is he about, this Maggs?'

'Think so. He came in earlier, I believe. I heard him going up. He coughs a lot, does Maggs. Coughs, but doesn't die.'

'You really don't like him, do you?'

'He looks at women like he's planning to slice them and sell them by the pound. He stinks because he's bad inside. He'd steal the smell from a corpse, and he wouldn't spare a penny if it would save a life.'

She finished the cigarette and tossed it into the shadows.

'Number nine, top of the stairs,' she said.

'You, or him?'

'Him. I'm in number five, if you change your mind.'

'I won't, but thank you anyway.'

'Why? Because you're too good for a tart?'

'No, because the tart's too good for me.'

I found some money in my pocket, and I slipped her what she would have charged for a roll. As with the boy from the post office, I didn't ask for a receipt: Fawnsley and Quayle would just have to take it on trust.

'You don't have to do that,' she said, and her voice was softer than it had previously been.

'You've saved me that much in time,' I said.

The money vanished.

'Watch out for Maggs,' she said. 'He carries a knife.'

'Why?'

'For protection, but from what I couldn't say.'

Maggs, it seemed, belied the impression that some might have had of the book world as a place filled with the shy and the studious.

'Thank you for the warning,' I said.

I was about to leave her when a thought struck me. I took the picture of Lionel Maulding from my pocket and showed it to her.

'Have you ever seen this man around here?'

She held the picture in her hand and stared at it for a long time.

'I think so, but he was older than he is in that picture.'

'When was this?'

'I can't be sure. Not as long ago as a month, but not as short as a week.'

'Was he coming to see Maggs?'

'Well, he weren't coming to see me.'

She handed the picture back to me, hitched up her skirts to prevent them from dragging in the foul water of the lane, and went off to seek some business elsewhere. I watched her go. She was pretty in a hard way, but if she stayed in her current trade then the prettiness would fade and the hardness would take over, moving from the surface to the heart like ice on a lake. In another life I might have gone with her. I would have paid my money as much for her company as for any physical pleasure that I might have derived from it.

Before the war, perhaps: before High Wood.

As I climbed the stairs to Maggs's rooms, I began to form a narrative in my mind. Maulding approaches Dunwidge & Daughter as part of his search for the *Atlas*. When they can't help him, he looks elsewhere, and finds his way at last to Maggs. He's offering a lot of money for the book, more money than Maggs has ever seen before, but Maulding has led a sheltered life, and Maggs has not. Maggs sees the possibility of greater wealth than he has ever imagined. He lures Maulding with the promise of the book, and then takes his life.

Maggs, the book scout, with knife in hand.

Maggs, the murderer.

All very neat, all very tidy, which meant that it probably hadn't happened that way. But if the girl was right, then Maulding had been here, which made Maggs a link in the chain of events that had led to Maulding's disappearance.

I reached the door of number nine, and knocked upon it. There was no reply. I called Maggs's name and knocked again. The door, when I tried it, was locked, but a locked door is more the promise of security than security itself. I removed my wallet of picks, and it was the work of a minute before the door was open.

Inside was darkness. The drapes were drawn, and I could hear no sounds of occupancy, no movement, no snores. I called Maggs's name one more time before I entered, mindful of the reputation of the man I was seeking, wary of his knife.

I stepped inside, and was immediately in a large single room, furnished with a sagging couch and some mismatched chairs. The rest was books, but after time spent in Maulding's home, and the premises of both Seaford's and Dunwidge & Daughter, I was growing inured to the sight of so many volumes crammed into every available space. There was a smell of unwashed clothes and unwashed skin, but beneath it was the stink of burning meat: pork, or something like it. The paintwork was relatively new, but I thought that I could discern writing beneath it, as though some act of vandalism had been imperfectly obscured.

An open door by the empty bedroom led into a small kitchen. There was a man seated upright at a table, his back to me. He wore a waistcoat over a grey shirt that might once have been white, and his feet were bare. He was balding, and wisps of hair clung to his pate like gossamer threads caught on stone.

'Mr Maggs?' I said.

Maggs, if Maggs it was, did not move. I slipped my hand into the pocket of my coat and gripped my cosh, but as I drew nearer to the figure I could see that his hands were resting flat upon the table, and there was no weapon in sight.

I stopped when I was a few feet from the door. The man remained still. He was either holding his breath, or he was dead. I moved into the kitchen, and the reason for his stillness was confirmed.

The corpse at the table had no eyes, and his sockets now extended so far into his head that, had I a torch to hand, I felt sure that I could have shone the light into the holes and glimpsed the inside of his skull. I leaned closer, and thought that I smelled burning from the twin orifices, as though a pair of hot pokers had been pushed into his brain, searing as it went. I tested his flesh. There was stiffness, but no decay, not yet. This man was not long dead.

On the table before him, resting between his hands, was an envelope. I picked it up and looked inside. It contained £500, an enormous sum of money for one such as Maggs, yet there it rested. Where had it come from? I looked again at the envelope. It was cream, and of good quality, with a gentle ridging to the paper. I recalled the desk at the firm of Dunwidge & Daughter, with its pens and papers. In my wallet I still had the list of names given to me by Dunwidge. I unfolded the list and set it beside the envelope. The paper was the same.

And then I heard a scuttling behind me. I turned, expecting to see a rat, but instead I glimpsed a wriggling, jointed carapace, with sharp pincers, disappearing behind the stove. Once I had recovered from my shock at the sight of it, I seized a broom from the corner of the kitchen and went down on my knees. The floor was sticky, and had not been washed in years. I peered into the murk beneath the stove, and detected signs of movement. Grasping the broom by its bristles with one hand and placing the other halfway along its length, I stabbed at the presence in the shadows. I felt the top of the broom strike something that writhed as it was pinned to the wall. I pressed harder, but the thing broke free. It moved to my right, but now it was trapped in the corner, and I had it. I stabbed at it, over and over, until its struggles ceased, then used the broom to push its remains into the light.

It was about seven or eight inches in length, its body armoured like that of a lobster. Its carapace was a milky red, as though it had somehow survived being boiled in a pot, and I counted twelve pairs of jointed legs, each leg spurred with a vicious curving spike at the first joint. The pincers were at the rear of its body, increasing their resemblance to those of an earwig that had first struck me back at Maulding's house, but the multiple eyes at the other end were more like those of a spider: two large black orbs were positioned above its jaws, with a cluster of smaller organs scattered around them in what seemed like a random manner. The jaws themselves were lined with twin rows of small, sharp teeth that curved inwards, and surrounding them, corresponding to the main points of a compass, were four clawed extrusions for cutting and tearing.

I was reluctant to touch the thing, for small, translucent hairs covered its frame, and even in death they seemed to be releasing a milky fluid that I felt a profound desire to avoid. There was heat coming off it too, as strong as the flame on a stove, although it was gradually decreasing in intensity. I moved it so that I could look more closely at its mouth, and thought that I glimpsed something caught behind those curved teeth. A knife and fork lay on a dirty plate on the kitchen sideboard, and I used them to force the creature's jaws farther apart to examine more clearly what lay within. It was white, but with hints of colour, almost like a small egg, almost like—

I dropped the knife and fork and stumbled away from the creature, my gorge rising. I had seen so much that was awful in life. I was surprised at my capacity to be revolted by anything, but revolted I was.

Lodged in the creature's mouth was an eyeball, and I could only assume that it had once belonged to the unfortunate Maggs. I looked again at the corpse in the chair, and back to the creature on the floor. I felt again its diminishing heat, and smelled the stink of burning from the eyeless sockets in Maggs's head and the twin channels that had been seared through his brain. I had thought that something like a hot poker had twice been forced into his skull, but now I feared I was mistaken. Was it possible instead that something hot had worked itself *out* of his head, burning as it went, until at last it emerged into the light?

But why had he not moved? Why had he not struggled against it? Why was his body sitting upright in a chair, his hands placed on the table before him like a man waiting patiently for his evening meal to be served? And this thing, this abomination, was too big to have been accommodated by that narrow channel. Could it have grown so much already, swelling in its new environment? But how could such a creature grow? It must have shed its skin. Somewhere on the floor, perhaps. If I looked closely . . .

I was about to return to my knees, ready to find proof of my theory, when I paused. There were *two* holes in Maggs's head, two channels burned through his brain. This creature, if it had emerged from inside the book scout, having somehow implanted itself in his head, could only have created one of them, which meant—

Which meant that there was another of these horrors somewhere in Maggs's rooms. I froze and listened carefully for the telltale sound of it. Using the broom, I poked in the corners of the kitchen and under the sideboard. I then made my way into the main living areas and searched them carefully, even dragging the sheets from the bed and stripping the mattress from its base, but I could find no sign of another creature. It was not among the piles of books, nor was it hiding on top of the dusty shelves. If I was right about the source of the second injury to Maggs's skull, then, somehow, the creature had escaped.

I returned to the kitchen. Maggs had not moved, nor would he ever again, and the money was still in its envelope. So, another narrative, linked to the first: Maulding approaches Dunwidge & Daughter and they, in turn, introduce him to Maggs, although now Maggs is working on their behalf and is not a lone operator. Maggs either finds the book that Maulding is seeking and in return receives a finder's fee from Dunwidge & Daughter; or, more likely, he convinces Maulding that the book is in his possession, Maulding brings the money, and once the money is safely in his hands, Maggs disposes of Maulding for the Dunwidges, and gets paid £500 for his efforts. But where did the creature and its now-missing twin appear from, and how did a similar creature come to be in a bathtub in Lionel Maulding's house?

I looked at Maggs, as though he might give me the answer.

And Maggs, it seemed, tried to do so, for his lips began to move. His chin shifted, and his lips parted, but instead of words a quartet of claws emerged, forcing his already stiffening mouth wider, and I heard his jaw cracking with the force of it. The head of the second creature appeared through the gap, its own maw pulsing redly as it chewed on some unknown fragment of Maggs's innards.

I attacked it with the broom handle, striking at Maggs's face so hard that I felt his teeth shatter under the impact, and the broom itself broke in two. Maggs's body toppled and fell to the floor, landing on its back. The blow had caused the creature to retreat into his mouth, seeking the safety of his gullet, but I was not to be denied. I could see its dark eyes gleaming in Maggs's throat, so I took the sharp end of the broken broom and forced it again and again between the dead man's jaws, beating at it until his palate and his tongue were reduced to so much meat, and his teeth had been knocked entirely from his head, and the mess of the creature inside him was barely distinguishable from the general ruin.

And then I wept.

IX

I don't know how long I stayed that way, seated in a corner of the filthy kitchen with Maggs's body lying beside me on the floor. During that time, it seemed that I fell in and out of my earlier life – no, not life, but lives, for in each one was a different man: a son, a husband, a father, a soldier, a patient, and now a soul adrift. I felt and heard again the broom handle striking Maggs's flesh, and then it was no longer a broom handle but a rifle, and the bayonet at its tip was lodged so hard in the breastbone of the man in the mud before me that I had to place my right foot on his chest in order to wrench it free. I was crouched down at Crucifix Corner, beside the pitted figure of the tortured Christ,

High Wood in the distance, Death Valley before me, with the shelling, the endless shelling. I was standing over a crater on a September morning, watching as the first of 47 men from the London battalions was interred in the grey mud, enveloping their forms so that they became part of it, presaging the greater decay to come.

And then I was broken, and the world itself became a fragmented place.

Craiglockhart: a nurse was wheeling me into a small, private room where a chaplain and a brother officer were waiting, and someone was whispering the impossible to me, tales of a raid by Gotha bombers on 13 June, of a woman, and a girl, and a boy, buried in rubble.

Finally, I was standing by another hole in the ground, and more bodies were being lowered into it. I had not been permitted to see their remains before the coffin lids were screwed down, as though I had never before witnessed human beings reduced to raw meat and shattered bone by bombs, as though what I imagined could be any worse than the reality of the damage done to them.

If I am not a husband, not a father, not a soldier, then what am I?

Who am I?

I should have called the police, but common sense prevailed. Maggs's face was terribly damaged, and I was responsible. The dead creature on the floor had finally cooled. As it did so it turned to a dried husk, and when I touched it with my shoe it fell apart as though it were made from ashes. The one lodged in Maggs's throat had disintegrated in a similar fashion, coating the dead man's mouth and gullet with flakes of dark matter. If the police came, I did not doubt that I would be charged with the mutilation and murder of the book scout. I remembered the girl who had directed me to his rooms. She did not know my name, but she would be able to describe me without any trouble, and I didn't believe that I had paid her enough to buy her silence. Maggs was a scrawny man, and, were we in a more isolated place, I could have carried his body from the house and disposed of it, but I could hardly walk through the streets of Spitalfields and Whitechapel with Maggs's remains hanging over my shoulder.

There came a knocking on Maggs's door. I ignored it, but it came again, and I heard a woman's voice, a familiar one, calling out from the other side.

'Sir? Sir? Are you all right?'

It was the girl from the lane.

'Sir?' she said again.

I got to my feet. If I ignored her, she might well take it upon herself to call the police. I had no choice but to answer the door.

I opened it about halfway: just enough to let her know that I was safe while preventing her from seeing into the rooms behind me. She looked both relieved and puzzled.

'I was worried,' she said. 'Mr Maggs—'

'Has a reputation,' I finished for her. 'Undeserved, I might add, or no longer applicable.'

'Is he all right?' she asked. 'You didn't have to hurt him, did you?'

'No. Actually, he's just under the influence.'

I made a gesture of drinking, for I had seen the empty bottles of cheap gin piled up in a corner by Maggs's bed. The girl nodded in understanding.

'That'd be him,' she said. 'I don't know if he's better with or without it. It's as little as makes no difference.'

'Well, I'll put him in his bed, and turn him on his side so that he doesn't choke in the night, and then I'll be on my way,' I said.

'You look ill,' she said. 'Are you sure you're feeling yourself?'

'Now that you mention it . . .'

There was sweat on my face. I could taste it on my lips.

'Why don't you come down to the Ten Bells,' she said. 'A whisky will sort you out. It'll be on me, for your kindness earlier.'

I was tempted to refuse, to get as far away from there as quickly as I could, but a drink sounded good, and not the poor stuff that Maggs was in the habit of imbibing. Neither did I want to look in any way suspicious by fleeing the scene.

'You know, I'll take that drink,' I said, 'Just let me see that Maggs is fixed, and I'll be with you shortly.'

'Do you want some help?'

'No, I can manage.'

'Right then. I'll wait for you downstairs.'

I smiled, and closed the door. I returned to the kitchen and looked at Maggs. There was nothing to be done about him for now, but we were not far from the river. If I waited until the city was quiet, I could perhaps carry him to the bank under the pretext of his being the worse for drink, as long as I kept his face covered, and then dump him in the Thames. It might be days before he was found, and there was the possibility of the damage to his face being ascribed to his time in the water, or the propeller of a boat. In the meantime, I took the envelope of money from the table and placed it in my pocket.

In case you take me for a thief, let me say that I did not intend to keep it, but to pass it on to Quayle for safekeeping. It was Lionel Maulding's money – of that much I was certain – and, if it were left in these rooms, it would eventually find its way into the pockets of another. Quayle would look after it. Quayle would know what to do. For a moment, I was almost tempted to seek his help, to tell him of what had transpired in Maggs's kitchen, but I feared that he would not believe me, and might even hand me over to the police.

Quayle was cunning and careful, but he was not actively dishonest, or certainly not when it came to the possibility of a killing. I believed that it would pain him to turn me in ('He was never the same after the war, poor fellow'), and he might even act on my behalf if it came to a trial, but he would not shelter me if he thought me guilty of murder.

I went downstairs and joined the girl, who told me that her name was Sally. I walked with her to the Ten Bells on Commercial Street. The bar enjoyed a certain notoriety for its associations with Annie Chapman and Mary Kelly, two victims of Jack the Ripper, although any number of local establishments might have boasted of a similar connection. It didn't seem appropriate to discuss the murders with Sally, and she didn't bring them up. We talked instead of her life, steering clear of her profession, and I told her a little of myself, but not too much, and I did not give her my true name. After an hour, some women of her acquaintance appeared, and I made my excuses.

By then, Sally was tipsy. She tried to kiss me as I left, and asked me to return to her rooms with her. I declined, but promised I would seek her out on another night. She saw the lie, though, and the hurt in her face pained me. She was a good girl, and I had not been with a woman in so very long, not since my other life.

I left money at the bar, and ordered a round for her and her friends. She watched me depart, regarding me with dark, wounded eyes. I wonder now what became of her, but it is too late. It is too late for all of us.

X

So when did I begin to suspect that I was going mad? When the first of those creatures appeared in the bathtub, perhaps, or when that entity comprised of stars and exploded, frozen darkness appeared to me in the night? Yes, I came close to doubting my sanity then, although they were real to me, of that I was convinced. Was it when I met Fawnsley, and he told me that a week, not a day, had passed since his telegram to me? Possibly then. Yes, perhaps that really was the start of it. The presence of two more of those strange, segmented crustaceans in Maggs's rooms was simply further proof that, if I were being tormented by my imagination, then it was in a most profound way, and my grip on reality was weakening so much that eventually all doubt would cease, and I would be well advised to end it all with a bullet while some clarity of thought still remained.

But I truly began to fear for my reason when I returned to Maggs's quarters, buoyed with Dutch courage and ready to throw his corpse into the Thames, and found that the book scout was gone. His body no longer lay on the kitchen floor.

And that was not the worst of it. The very rooms themselves had changed: the position of his furniture, the distribution of his books, even the arrangement of his lodgings – all were different. The kitchen was now to the left as one entered, not to the right. The unmade bed was on the other side of its room. The bookshelves were gone, and the books were now arranged in neat, formal piles, like the beads on an abacus.

'No,' I said aloud. 'This is not possible.'

But it was. It had happened. I could see it with my own eyes.

I checked the pocket of my coat. The envelope was still there. I looked at the palms of my hands, and saw the marks left upon them by the broom handle. I felt giddy, and the whisky was curdling something in my stomach. There was a chair by the window, and I sat down on it and tried to compose myself.

I had been seated for only a few seconds when I detected movement in the shadows of the lane below. I stayed very still, hidden by Maggs's filthy, fly-speckled lace curtains, and watched as Dunwidge, adrift from his daughter's anchorage, slipped away into the night.

XI

So this, I think, is how it transpired.

Eliza Dunwidge was woken by a noise from the rooms below, the rooms that housed those wonderful books. Many of the

most valuable were now packed in boxes, safely stored for trans-
portation, and she and her father would have the rest ready to be
moved within the next 24 hours. Well, they would when her
father eventually returned. He should have been back by then,
but he was a man of nocturnal habits, and she was not about to
begin worrying about him at this stage of her life.

The sound came again: the faint shifting of a body against
leather, the creaking of wood. Perhaps her father had come
home unbeknownst to her, but he always made a point of telling
her that he was back, whatever the hour.

No, there was someone else downstairs.

She removed a baton from beneath her bed. It had once
belonged to a Liverpool policeman who was dismissed from the
force during the 1919 police strike, and died soon after. His uniform he had surrendered; his baton he had not. Eliza Dunwidge
had acquired it from his widow, along with a small library of
occult volumes that had been bequeathed to the officer by his
grandfather, and of whose value he and his family were ignorant. Eliza had made the widow a more than fair offer for the
books, given that she could have bought the lot for a fraction of
what she paid. Eliza was not in the habit of cheating people,
though. She knew the nature of books better than most. Books
had histories, and history was a form of remembering.

And occult books were better at remembering than most.

Carefully she descended the stairs. She heard the crackle of
logs burning, and saw the light from the flames reflected upon
the walls. She panicked then, fearing that the house was on fire,
and the books in danger. She entered the room quickly, her
thoughts only on saving her volumes.

'Hello, Miss Dunwidge,' I said. 'I was wondering when you
might join me. I have a nice little blaze going here, for it's a cold
night out.'

I tore another handful of pages from the book in my hand,
and added them to the fire in the grate. The volume was entitled
The Book of Ceremonial Magic by Arthur Edward Waite,

originally published in London in 1913, although this was apparently a later, private printing, according to the introduction. I had chosen it because the pages were large, and of good quality paper. They burned very well.

Eliza Dunwidge let out a shriek and prepared to descend on me with the baton, but the screech and the advance died simultaneously when I showed her the gun. It was a Luger with a four-inch barrel that I'd taken from a German corpse at Crucifix Corner. I had never had cause to use it, but I'd returned to my rooms to collect it following my talk with old Dunwidge. I'd caught up with him on Commercial Road, and encouraged him to return to Maggs's rooms with me. He had proved less cooperative at first than I might have hoped, but I had found ways of convincing him to help me with my enquiries.

'I don't know,' he had said, over and over. 'I don't know. Don't ask me.'

But he did know something, just not enough.

'It's the *Atlas*,' he said at last, after I'd been forced to bruise him a little. 'It's the *Atlas*. The world is no longer the same.'

Which was why I was back at the premises of Dunwidge & Daughter. I placed the police baton by the side of my chair: it seemed safer for both Eliza Dunwidge and me if I had it. I told her to sit down and she did so, wrapping her dressing-gown around her in case a glimpse of her flesh might sire lascivious thoughts in me. I asked her about the baton, mainly out of some concern that she or her father might enjoy some connection with the police, which would not have been helpful. Her description of its history put my mind at ease on that score.

Keeping the gun trained loosely on her, I used my left foot to shift a box of books nearer to me. I examined a couple while Eliza watched me anxiously. They looked much older than the Waite volume, and were carefully wrapped.

'You seem to be leaving,' I said. 'Relocating to bigger premises, perhaps, thanks to Lionel Maulding's money.'

'We're moving to the country.'

'May I ask why?'

'The city isn't safe any more.'

'It certainly wasn't safe for Mr Maggs. In fact, it had a very bad effect on him at the end.'

She didn't blink, but her father's presence at Princelet Street left little doubt about her involvement in whatever had led Maggs to his fate. The old man claimed ignorance of what had become of Maggs. He had not entered the rooms, he said. He had not moved the body. He said that he did not even know there was a body until I told him of it. Strangely, I believed him.

'You paid Maggs five hundred pounds, a great sum of money for a man like him,' I said. 'Why?'

Still she said nothing.

I picked up the first book from the box at my feet and tossed it on the fire.

'No!'

She rose from her seat, and even when I raised the gun from my lap it was all that she could do not to attempt to rescue the book from the flames.

'I will shoot you, Miss Dunwidge,' I warned. 'I'll shoot you in the foot, or the knee, because I don't want to kill you. But it will hurt. It will hurt a lot. You should also know that I have your father. His continued good health, recently undermined, is in your hands.'

In truth, I had only been forced to slap her father twice on the face before he became more amenable to conversation, and he had made me feel ashamed of my behaviour when he started to cry, but his daughter didn't need to know that. I had learned, though, that he was his daughter's creature, but had been privy to few of her recent dealings with Maggs. She had simply dispatched him to inform Maggs of my interest in Lionel Maulding, and encourage him to leave London for a time for fear that my enquiries would eventually lead me to his door.

'He's an old man,' she said, and the mention of him was enough to make her resume her seat.

'And if you start cooperating with me, he'll live to be older still.'

She swallowed hard.

'Please don't burn any more books,' she said.

'I won't if you'll talk to me, Miss Dunwidge. Just tell me about the five hundred pounds. Tell me the truth about the *Atlas*.'

And in the light and heat of the burning volumes, she did.

XII

She spoke to me as if to a child.

'The book is rewriting the world,' she said.

Under other circumstances I might almost have laughed in her face, but her expression brooked no such mockery and, truth be told, I was already inclined to believe her. After all, I had seen the change in Maggs's rooms, and had listened to the pained, desperate testimony of her father.

'How? How can a book rewrite the world?'

'Look around you, Mr Soter. Books are constantly changing the world. If you're a Christian, you have been changed by the Bible, by the word of God, or what was left of it when it was finally wrung through the hands of men. If you are a Muslim, look to the Koran; if a Communist, to Marx and Engels. Don't you see? This world is forever being altered by books. *The Communist Manifesto* was published in 1848, less than a century ago, and *Das Kapital* is younger still, yet already Russia has fallen to them, and other nations will soon fall too.'

'But those are ideas,' I said. 'The books communicate them, and the ideas take hold in the minds of men. The books themselves are not responsible, no more than a gun can be culpable for the bullet that it fires, or a blade for the wound that it inflicts. It is men who fire bullets and wield knives, and men who change the world. Books may inspire them, but they are passive objects, not active ones.'

She shook her head.

'You're a fool if that is what you truly believe. A book is a carrier, and the ideas contained within its covers are an infection waiting to be spread. They breed in men. They adapt according to the host. Books alter men, and men, in their turn, alter worlds.'

'No, that's—'

She leaned over and placed her hand upon my arm. Even seated in the warmth of the fire, her touch chilled me to the bone. I felt a physical pain, and it was all that I could do not to recoil. This woman was unnatural.

'I can see that you believe me,' she said. 'You are altered in aspect since last we met. Tell me of Maggs. Tell me what you saw.'

How could she know of Maggs, I wondered. Yet somehow she did.

'There were holes burned in his skull through the sockets in his eyes,' I said. 'There were creatures, arthropods or crustaceans, but not like anything I have seen or heard of in this world. I believe it was these horrors that bored their way out of Maggs's head, emerging through his eyes. I destroyed them both.'

'Maggs,' she said, and there was a hint of sorrow to her voice. 'He hated books, you know. He saw them only as a source of wealth. He loved only the hunt and not the object of it, but he had not always been that way. He had come to fear them. It happens, sometimes, to those in our particular trade: not all of the books that we handle are beautiful inside and out. We breathe in the dust of the worst of them, fragments of their venom, and we poison ourselves. That is what happened to Maggs. He sourced books, and the stranger the better, but he would not read them. Yet I believe that his curiosity about the *Atlas* overcame his fear: he looked upon it, and something in it took root in his brain.'

'How did he find it?'

'He had always been seeking it, hunting rumours and whispers. Maggs was a scout unlike any other, and he wanted to achieve what others before him had failed to do. Then Maulding came to me. I tried to dissuade him from looking for the *Atlas*, but Maulding had begun to lust after it too. If Maggs was a scout unlike any other, than Maulding was a unique collector. It was a combination of forces, a perfect conjunction of circumstance: it was the book's opportunity, and it chose to reveal itself.'

'You speak of it as though it were alive,' I said.

'You still don't understand,' she said. 'Books are not fixed objects: they transmit words and ideas. Their effect on each reader is unique. They put pictures in our minds. They take root. You saw Maggs. You saw what might happen to a man who underestimates a book, especially one like the *Atlas*.'

I looked at the fire. There were still books burning there. I smelled the leather bindings of them charring in the heat. Their pages curled inwards as they took flame, as though in agony.

'You were speaking of the *Atlas*,' I said.

'Maggs found it at last in the most unlikely of places: in the collection of a spinster in Glasgow, a God-fearing woman who did not even seem aware of its existence, and could not tell him how she had come by it. It had hidden itself away amid worthless reprints. It would not allow itself to be read, not until its time had come. Then Maggs found it and knew it for what it was, and he contacted me. He asked if I could find a buyer for it, not knowing that the buyer, too, had revealed himself. But the *Atlas* knew. The *Atlas* was ready for both of them.'

'So you paid Maggs a finder's fee, and passed the book to Maulding.'

'Yes.'

'You didn't cheat him?'

'No. I am scrupulous about such matters.'

'You are moral?'

'Not moral. Afraid.'

I let that go.

'Did you look at it?' I asked.

'No.'

'Why not?'

'Again, because I was afraid.'

'Did you even see it?'

'Briefly, when Maulding came to collect it.'

'What did it look like?'

'It was perhaps two feet by a foot and a half, the binding a deep red, the spine ringed with gold loops. Two words had been burned into the cover: *Terrae Incognitae*. Unknown Lands.'

'What was the binding? Leather?'

'No. I believe it was skin.'

'Animal?'

For the second time, she shook her head.

'Not . . . human?'

'Again, no. I don't believe that the binding was of this world, and the book *pulsed* beneath my hand. I could feel the warmth of it, the sense of something like blood pumping through it. It did not want to be held by me, though, only by Maulding. He was meant to have it. In a way, the book was always his.'

It seemed extraordinary. I believed that she had found the *Atlas* and sold it to Maulding, but the rest I found harder to accept: a living book, a book with intent, a book that had hidden itself away until the perfect moment, and the perfect owner, came along.

'If what you say is true, then why now? What changed to cause the book to act?'

'The world,' she said. 'The world has altered itself without the book's impetus. Evil calls to evil, and the circumstances are right. You more than anyone should know this to be true.'

And I understood.

'The war,' I said.

'The war,' she echoed. '"The war to end war", isn't that how Wells put it? He was wrong, of course: it was the war to end worlds, to end this world. The fabric of existence was torn: the world was made ready for the book, and the book was ready for the world.'

I closed my eyes. I heard the wet, heavy sound of bodies being dropped into a crater, and my own cries as they brought me the news of my dead wife and children. I saw twisted remains being carried from the ruins of a farmhouse, a whole family killed by a single shell, children born and yet to be born brought to an end in fire and rubble. She was not mistaken, I thought: if this is all true, then let the book take the world, for whatever emerged in its aftermath could be no worse than what I had already seen. The landlord's wife had been right: I did not believe that the war had purged the earth of poisoned seeds. Instead, they had germinated in spilled blood.

'Who wrote this book?' I asked. 'Who made it?'

She looked away.

'The Not-God,' she said.

'The devil?'

She laughed: a hoarse, unlovely sound.

'There is no devil,' she said. 'All of this –' she waved a hand at the occult books, boxed and unboxed, and she might as well have been consigning every one of them to the flames '– is so much smoke and mirrors, mere amusements for the ignorant. They have as much bearing on reality as does an actor capering on a stage dressed in a cloak and horns, and waving a pitchfork. The thing that created the book is greater and more terrible than any three-headed Christian god. It has a million heads, and each head a million more. Every entity that rages against the light is part of it, and is born of it. It is a universe unto itself. It is the great Unknown Realm.'

'What are you saying? That, through this book, some entity wants to transform this world into a version of its own?'

'No,' she said, and now the sternness left her face, and it glowed with a zealot's light, making her appear more ugly than before. 'Don't you grasp it? This world ceased to exist as soon as the book was opened. It was already dying, but the *Atlas* disposed of its remains and substituted its lands for ours. This is already the Unknown Realm. It is as though a distorting mirror has become not the reflection of the thing, but the reality of it.'

'Then why can't we see the changes?'

'You *have* seen the changes. Why, I do not know, but soon others will too. Somewhere deep in their psyches, down in the dirt of their consciousness, they probably sense it already, but they refuse to acknowledge what has occurred. To recognize it will be to submit to the truth of it, and that truth will eat them alive.'

'No,' I said. 'Something can still be done. I'll find the book. I'll destroy it.'

'You can't destroy what has always been.'

'I can try.'

'It's too late. The damage has been done. This is no longer our world.'

I stood, and she rose with me.

'I have one more question,' I said. 'One more, and then I'll leave you.'

'I know what it is,' she said.

'Do you?'

'It is the first and last question, the only question that matters. It is "Why?" Why did I do it? Why did I collude with the book? Why, why, why?'

She was right, of course. I could do no more than nod my assent.

'Because I was curious,' she said. 'Because I wanted to see what might occur. But like Maggs, like Maulding, I think that I was merely serving the will of the *Atlas* whether I knew it or not.'

If 'why' was the first and last question, then 'because I was curious to see what would happen' was the first and last answer. A version of it had been spoken to God Himself in the Garden of Eden, and it was always destined to be the reason for the end of things at the hands of men.

'I tell you,' I said, 'that I will find a way to stop this.'

'And I tell you,' she replied, 'that you should kill yourself before the worst of it comes to pass.'

She retreated from me until she was against the fireplace, the mantel at her shoulders. Her dressing-gown ignited behind her, the material blooming red and orange around her legs. Then she turned her back to me, revealing her naked body already blistering in the heat, the material adhering to her skin, and before I could move she threw herself face-first into the blaze. By the time I dragged her from the hearth her head was a charred mess, and she was already dying. Her body trembled in its final agonies as the books around her burned in sympathy.

I left them all to the flames.

XIII

As I walked away from the Dunwidge home, I heard the sound of screaming and shouting, and windows breaking. Before I had gone barely half a mile, the noise of the fire engines was ringing in the distance.

I had no cause to return to my lodgings. I had a gun, and I had left some spare clothing at Maulding's house. My business in the city was concluded. There was only one more task to be accomplished before I returned, and so I made my way on foot to Chancery, and the chambers of the lawyer Quayle.

I was perhaps a mile from my destination when I had the sensation of being followed. I turned and saw a little girl wearing a blue-and-white dress on the opposite side of the road from me, but about 30 feet behind. She had her back turned to me so that I could not see her face. Then, from the shadows between the street lamps, again at a similar distance but this time on the same side as myself, a boy emerged, walking backwards. He wore short trousers, and a white shirt. His movements were jerky and unnatural, and I was reminded of a moving image slowly being projected and simultaneously rewound.

Somehow the boy, like the girl, seemed to realize that he had been spotted, and he ceased all movement with one leg still suspended in the air. It was only then that I noticed his feet were bare, and strangely deformed. I was reminded of limbs I had seen in the trenches, swollen by gangrene or distorted by the breaking of bones. The girl's feet also were bare, but she was splay-footed, giving her the aspect of a large, pale penguin.

'Go away,' I said, then, louder: 'Go away! Go home. This is no hour for children to be abroad.'

But even as I spoke, I felt that any home they had was far, far from this place; or, if Eliza Dunwidge had spoken true, this was now their home, and had always been, and I was the stranger, the intruder.

I did not want to give my back to them, so I too began to walk backwards, and a peculiar sight we would have presented had there been anyone to see us, but there was no one. And as I moved, so too did the boy and the girl, and I heard their joints crack as they came, as though in that short time ice had formed on their limbs. The boy advanced with his irregular, loping gait, his feet twisting beneath him, while the girl waddled, her knees at an angle from the side of her body, and now she was not so much a penguin as a toad that had somehow managed the feat of walking upright, an impression reinforced by her girth, for she was a swollen child.

Eventually I ran. I confess it: I turned tail and fled. I could hear them coming after me, their feet slapping faster on the ground, and I prayed that someone might appear, a fellow night traveller who would force them to leave me be, or confirm, at least, that I was not yet completely mad. But I saw nobody: no people, no cars, not even a horse and cart. The city slumbered, or perhaps there was no city left, and the London that I had once known was entirely gone, replaced by a shadow of itself in which dwelt only deformed children and eyeless men.

I was still running when I noticed the absence of pursuit.

They were gone. I stopped, my hands on my knees, and gasped deep, painful breaths. My lungs were not as they once were. I had gone to France a young man, but now I was an old one in all but years. Ahead of me was the West End: there, at least, would be people, even at this hour, and dawn could not be far away. I cast one final glance behind me to ascertain that I was alone, then turned to be on my way.

They were there, of course. I should have known it. I had read enough ghost stories in my time, and passed an hour or two with the penny dreadfuls. The children, if that was what they were, had circled me just as troops in wartime will do, seeking the advantage in coming at the enemy from an unexpected direction. They were now only ten feet ahead, their backs still to me, but slowly they began to revolve – yes, revolve, as a weight suspended on a line will revolve – until I saw their faces at last.

Monstrous offspring, foul beasts: a random scattering of small black eyes cast over the upper part of their features, a dozen or more, like raisins in dough; no nose on either, but twin slits divided by a thin stretch of septum; and their mouths were lipless grimaces drawn back over jagged, rodentine teeth, with sharp protuberances at either side like the venomous jaws of a spider.

I did not pause. I did not think. An elemental fear had overcome me. I pointed the gun at the girl's face, and pulled the trigger. The bullet took her in the forehead and exited in a stream of fluid that was not red but yellow, like the innards of an insect. She fell back without a sound, but the boy let out a shriek from somewhere deep within. He sprang at me, and I shot him too, but the fury of his reaction took me by surprise and the first bullet hit him in the shoulder, twisting him and sending him to the ground, so that I was forced to finish him off as he squirmed beneath me, his jaws clicking as though, even in his dying, he desired to consume me.

When I was done with them, I dragged their remains into an alley and hid them behind overflowing bins that stank of rotting meat. There was no time for police, no time for explanations. I had to find the book: to find it, and destroy it.

XIV

Fawnsley arrived first, as he always did. It was shortly after eight. I had spent hours waiting, curled up in a corner of that dreary court-yard, the closed doors surrounded by their dark, shuttered windows seeming to me like the faces of great sleepers. I had tried to break into Quayle's offices, but the lock had resisted my ministrations. Quayle, I now knew, was miserly in all things but his own security.

I approached Fawnsley from behind as he searched for his keys, but the shadow on the door revealed my presence to him. He turned to face me, and his already pale features grew sud-denly greyer.

'You,' he said. 'Why are you here?'

His voice trembled and the keys jangled in his hand as he tried to find the lock without taking his eyes from me.

'I came to see Quayle. There is something I need from him.'

'You have no business in this place.'

'You are wrong. I have important business, more important than you can realize. I know what happened to Maulding, or think I know. I am close now. I can stop this. The world is changing, but I can make it right again.'

'I don't know what you're talking about,' said Fawnsley. 'It's been weeks, man, weeks! We gave you money, and then you van-ished. Not a word, not a single word. I warned you when last you came to me. I explained what was expected of you.'

His bullish note struck false with me. There was something else here, something that I didn't understand, but I was dis-tracted by his words. I did not want them to be true.

'What do you mean "weeks"? I came to you not days ago.'

'Nonsense. It's now November twelfth. You're raving. Look at yourself, man. Look what you've become.'

I tried not to let my fear show. I tried not to let the last of my reason slip away.

'It is not me,' I told him. 'It is the world. Look at what the world has become, and then see what it has done to me.'

I watched Fawnsley regain some degree of control, as though the mere pretence of bravery had been enough to fool even himself. His hand stopped shaking, and his unease was moderated by his instinctive cunning.

'Perhaps you should come inside,' he said. 'Warm yourself. You know where the pot is. Make yourself some tea, and take your rest. I will go and find Mr Quayle. He is at the Sessions House today, but he will come if I tell him of your, um, agitation.' He swallowed hard. 'He is most fond of you, despite all that has transpired.'

The Sessions House was the name commonly given to the Inner London Crown Court in Southwark. It was some distance from Quayle's offices, and it would take time and effort for Fawnsley to travel there and return with Quayle. The Fawnsley I knew would go to no such effort for me. He would barely have troubled himself to cross a street to help me if I stumbled.

I showed him the gun, and a dark stain appeared on his trousers.

'No,' he said. 'Please don't.'

'Tell me,' I said, 'and tell me true.'

I poked the gun hard into his ribs in case he still had any doubts about the gravity of his situation.

'The police,' said Fawnsley. 'They're looking for you. They say that you killed a man in Cheapside. They found the body in the basement of a tenement, and a woman, a whore, said that she remembered you. They wish to talk to you about other matters too: a fire, and—'

The words caught in his throat, and he could not go on.

'Speak!' I said.

Fawnsley began to weep. 'Children,' he said. 'There are dead children.'

'They were not children,' I said. 'Am I the kind of man who would kill a child?'

Fawnsley shook his head, but he kept his eyes from mine.

'No, sir,' he said. 'No, you are not.'

'Inside,' I said.

He managed at last to turn the key in the lock and open the door.

'Don't kill me,' he said. 'I won't tell.'

'Just do as I say,' I told him, 'and I'll see that you're unharmed.'

'Anything. Whatever you require: money, food. Only ask.'

I forced him up the stairs, recalling the last time I had been there, when the world was fractured but had not yet come apart entirely.

'I need neither,' I said. 'I just want to look at your files on the Maulding house.'

XV

I left with that which I had sought. The business of the Maulding family had been in the hands of Quayle and his predecessors for generations, and Quayle's grandfather had handled the purchase of Bromdun Hall at the beginning of the last century. It was good fortune that the meticulous records of the firm included a detailed drawing of Maulding's house, but I thought that I was due a little good luck at last.

I bought a copy of the *The Times* on High Holborn. It was dated 12 November. Fawnsley had not been lying. I had never really thought that he was.

The city seemed to close in on me as I walked, so that only the will of God prevented its buildings from toppling down and burying the populace under rubble. It might have been a blessing for some, for the men and women on the streets struck me as particularly restive and churlish, oppressed by a lowering sky and an unseasonable heat that had arisen in the early hours.

Some way past Chancery Lane, an omnibus had misjudged the corner and struck a deliveryman's cart, seriously injuring his horse so that the poor animal lay whinnying miserably on the ground, one of its back legs broken so badly that the femur had erupted through its coat. The omnibus was a B-type, similar to the hundreds that were requisitioned for battlefield use as troop carriers and mobile gun emplacements, even pigeon lofts to house the birds used for communication on the front. The Omnibus Company had begun to phase out the B-types in favour of the K and the S, and it was a wonder that this relic was still functioning, so battered did it appear. I had not come across one in a year. It was already an anachronism.

An old man smoked a cigarette at the scene, a large suitcase by his side.

'Been travelling this route for most of my life, and I never seen the like,' he said. He had a nicotine croak. 'You'd believe the man had never been behind a wheel before, but he's been working the buses since Tilling sent the first one out of Peckham, and that's neither today nor yesterday.'

'1904,' I said.

'That's right.'

'I grew up there. I remember.'

The driver did indeed have the look of experience about him, but he was clearly badly shaken by what had occurred. He was speaking softly with the carter while a policeman took notes. I pulled my hat low on my face, and looked to the pavement.

The old man took a long puff on his cigarette, and inclined his head disdainfully.

'I heard him say that he'd swear the road had narrowed. I think he's been drinking.'

There were more policemen approaching now at a run. With them was a young gentleman in a stained tweed suit. In one hand he carried a black bag, in the other a crude-looking gun.

'That'll be the police veterinary,' said the old man. 'About time too. If I'd had a gun, I'd have put the creature out of its misery myself.'

Instinctively my hand went to the gun in the pocket of my coat. The old man looked at me peculiarly.

'Are you feeling all right?'

'I'm fine,' I said. 'It's . . . it's the horse, that's all. I don't like seeing an animal in pain.'

'It'll end soon enough,' said the old man, and as if in answer to him I heard the report of the gun, unnatural in the still London air. I closed my eyes. I thought I could smell the horse's blood.

'You ought to sit down before you fall down,' said the old man.

'No,' I said. 'I believe I'll be on my way.'

'Please yourself.'

I lost myself in the crowd, but I was dizzy and ill, and I feared the streets. I took the Twopenny Tube to Liverpool Street, and there boarded a train. By late afternoon I was back in Norfolk. Bromdun Hall was silent and locked. I tried my key in the door, but it would not open. I broke a pane of glass in a window of the study and thus gained access. I did not go upstairs, for I felt safer in the ground floor rooms. I found some stale bread in the kitchen, and ate it with black tea.

I almost started work there and then, but the depredations of the preceding hours had begun to tell on me. I lay on the couch in the study with my coat as a blanket. I do not know for how long I slept, only that the texture of the light had altered when I woke. The night was the colour of molasses, and the dark had substance. I could feel it as I raised my hand against it, as though the nature of gravity had changed and the atmosphere was conspiring to suffocate me.

I heard an unpleasant scraping sound coming from nearby, like nails on a blackboard. It was that which had roused me. I searched for its source, and saw a shape move against the window. The scraping sound came again. Slowly, my movements still hampered by the very air, I approached the window. I had my gun in my hand, three bullets left in its chambers.

There were parallel scratches on two of the panes, and the glass was stained with a black fluid like squid ink. I looked out at the grounds beyond but there was no moon visible in the sky, and no stars shone. The blackness was so thick that I might as well have been underwater, and it would not have surprised me had a liquid darkness begun to pour through the broken pane and fill the room, slowly drowning me.

The broken pane: if I had gained access to the house by slipping my hand through the gap and opening the latch, then whatever was out there could have done the same. Why, then, scrape and scratch?

The answer came first as sound, then as form. I discerned a single deep inhalation from without, quickly followed by smaller, faster sniffs as something in the darkness caught my scent. A grey wrinkled form pressed itself against the glass in a gesture of dreadful longing, its thin limbs splayed, the loose skin that hung from them cracked and oozing, its fingers like sharp, jointed needles. It was about the size of a man, but hairless and eyeless, its flat nose twitching as it smelled me. And then its mouth, indiscernible until now, slowly opened, toothless and red, and from deep in its jaws an appendage shot forth, less a tongue than a fleshy tube, its opening ringed with tiny barbs. It struck the glass hard, leaving more of that black residue.

The sniffing came again, and the creature changed position, lowering itself to the shattered pane, its left hand blindly exploring the window until it found the gap and pushed its way through, blocking it entirely.

I prepared to shoot, then paused. What else might be out there? What other horrors might I draw to me with the noise? And the bullets: so few left, and no chance of securing more in this place.

I searched for another weapon. There was a letter opener on Lionel Maulding's desk. The blade was dull, but the end was sharp. I stabbed hard at the creature's arm and, although no blood or viscera came forth from the wound, I saw its mouth widen in soundless agony. I jabbed at it again and again as it struggled to pull its hand back, tearing its flesh still further against the sharp edges that still clung to the frame, until at last it was free. It retreated into the dark, and was gone.

There were wooden shutters on the windows. It was clear from the dust and dead insects upon them that they had not been used in some time, but I pulled them closed and secured them, and did the same with the other windows. I did not sleep, but waited for the coming of dawn. When at last light began to seep through I came close to weeping, for a part of me had feared that I might never see daylight again, so black was the night. I opened the shutters. There was a mist upon the grass, and the sun washed the dark clouds with red.

I thought that I had never seen anything so beautiful.

XVI

I began my work as soon as morning had secured its grip on the world. I checked the measurements of the rooms on the plans of the house before pacing those same quarters, checking my own reckoning against the original dimensions. It was my good fortune to have started with the study – that, or the final gasp of logic and rationality in a world that appeared to be coming apart at the seams. Quite simply, the study was not as long as it should have been, and it was clear that the shelves at the western end of the room had been set about seven feet away from the wall. Still, it was the work of an hour or more to determine a means of access to whatever lay behind, and I resorted, in the end, to emptying the shelves to a height of almost six feet before the mechanism revealed itself: a simple lever hidden behind an ornately bound first volume of Gibbon's *The History of the Decline and Fall of the Roman Empire* – quarto sections, 1776, I noted, for this book business was, I admit, starting to rub off on me.

I moved the lever, and a section of shelving opened with an audible click. I paused before widening the gap, uncertain of what might be revealed to me: a stink of corruption; another of those foul burrowing creatures, its body burning with an awful heat; or a glimpse of the maelstrom itself, a pathway between universes? Instead, when curiosity inevitably got the better of me, I saw only a smaller version of the room I already occupied, furnished with a square table and a single straight chair. There was a candle on the table, unlit. I found my matches and put one to the wick, for the door did not open fully, either by design or a fault in the mechanism, and I had barely been able to squeeze my way inside. In the flickering light of the candle, Lionel Maulding's occult library was revealed to me, volume upon volume, most of them old and having about them, even in appearance, the taint of the forbidden and unclean.

I paid them little heed, though, for it was the book on the table that most interested me. It was as Eliza Dunwidge had described it: a large bound work covered in a material that was obviously hide of some kind. I could see wrinkles and scars upon it and, God help us, what might even have been a tracery of veins. Worse, the book's surface did seem to throb with life, but that might simply have been a function of the candle's imperfect light combined with the nature of its binding and the tale told to me by Eliza. Still, I was reluctant to touch it. With its red covers and its yellowed page edges, it reminded me uncomfortably of a mouth. There was, too, the memory of Maggs the book scout, and the channels burned in his head by whatever the book had seeded in his brain.

But the *Atlas* called to me. I had come so far. I wanted to know. Somewhere in its pages lay the truth: the truth of what had befallen Lionel Maulding, but more importantly an answer to what was happening, or had already happened, to my own world.

I opened the book. I looked inside.

It was blank. How could it not be? After all, it had transferred its contents to this realm, overwriting all that had once existed, like a palimpsest that slowly, surely overwhelms the original.

And from somewhere both nearby yet immeasurably far away, I swear that I heard laughter, but it was the laughter of the damned.

XVII

I burned the book. I set fire to it in the fireplace of Maulding's library, laying it flat upon the wood and coals once I was certain that the blaze had reached the required intensity. The book sizzled and hissed and popped, more like meat roasting than paper burning. At one point it emitted a loud, whistling sound that was almost like a scream, but it ceased as the binding blackened. It stank as it was consumed. It smelled like decayed flesh finally consigned to the crematorium, but I had smelled worse.

I don't know how long I sat there, using a poker to move the book and stir the fire, until it coalesced into a ruined mass which would burn no further. I dozed for a time, and dreamed of the *Atlas* as it might once have been, with intricate maps of worlds unlike this one, its territories marked with the images of beasts and demons, its intricate cartography the work of the Not-God. But those pages were empty because all that they had once contained had been fed into this world like sand falling through an hourglass. Now there was nothing left, and the process of transformation had begun. Where Lionel Maulding was, I could not say. Perhaps, like Maggs, he had begun to die the moment that he opened the book, and its ideas had gestated in his head before erupting and, finally, consuming him.

But there was another narrative too, of course, even if I retreated from it just as assuredly as I desired to turn my back on the possibility of one world infecting and corrupting another: the book had never existed. It was a fraud perpetrated by the Dunwidges with the collusion of Maggs, and that unfortunate's death had been carefully staged in order to maintain the pretence, and ensure his silence. I, too, had colluded in it. I had played my role. I had allowed myself to be manipulated.

But what of those burrowing creatures, or the exploded thing in the hallway of this very house? What of the deformed children that had followed me through the streets, or the grey wraith at the study window? What of days – weeks – lost, according to Fawnsley? What of—

Everything?

For there was a third narrative, was there not?

It was late afternoon. Mrs Gissing had not appeared, nor Willox. I left the Maulding house, my possessions in my overnight bag, and walked to the station. The train to London was due. I would return there. I would go to Quayle. Whatever answer he gave me, I would accept. If there was a cell and a noose at the end of it, it could be no worse than this.

There was nobody at the ticket office when I reached it, and I detected some sounds of confusion from the platform. I followed the noise and found the stationmaster remonstrating with prospective passengers, his assistants beside him, all of them looking troubled.

'What's happening here?' I asked of no one in particular.

'The train from London didn't arrive this morning,' said a portly woman. 'The train to London came and went, right enough, but nothing from the city.'

She indicated the stationmaster.

'Old Ron here is as ignorant as the rest of us, but I have to get to London. My daughter's about to have her first child, and I swore to her that I'd be with her to help her through it.'

I was bigger and taller than the rest of those gathered, and eased my way through the crowd until I was face to face with the stationmaster. He was nearing the end of his time: grey-haired, overweight, and with a handlebar moustache that increased his resemblance to an old walrus.

'Explain,' I said to him, and something in my tone silenced those around me, and brooked no opposition from the functionary.

'It's like I've been telling these people, sir: we've had no trains arrive since this morning, and all the lines are down. I can't get through to anyone to find out what's going on. I sent one of the lads down to Norwich on his bicycle to see if he could find out anything, but he hasn't come back yet. I can give you no more.'

I stood on the platform and looked to the south-west. It might have been a trick of the light, but it seemed that the sky was darker down there, and tinged with red, even though sunrise was long past. It resembled a great conflagration seen from a distance. I glanced at the station clock, and watched the minute hand move.

'The clock,' I said.

'What about it?' said the stationmaster.

I continued to stare at the clock face. It was just gone noon, and the minute hand had shifted, but it was inching closer not to one but to twelve in this backwards realm.

The clock was running in reverse.

I left them and returned to Bromdun Hall. I have closed the shutters, and barricaded the doors. There is food here, and water. The sky is darkening, and it will not be light again. There are noises coming from upstairs, and from the grounds. I have closed the door to Lionel Maulding's secret study. From behind it, I can hear the splintering of reality, like ice cracking on a frozen lake.

It is the coming of the Not-God.

I have three bullets.

I will wait.

5. And In Darkness Shall We Dwell

The drapes had been allowed to fall, hiding the chambers of the lawyer Quayle from the night, and from any prying eyes that might have been inclined to wander in the direction of the lighted window. But to do so would have required the watcher to make his way into the tiny courtyard off Chancery Lane, and nobody entered that place unless for business with Quayle. In addition, to see into Quayle's rooms would have required somehow gaining entry to one of the buildings that brooded over the courtyard, their upper levels ever so slightly overhanging the lower in the Dutch manner, for they were narrow indeed, and any furniture they contained had been hauled in through the windows by means of the vicious-looking hooks that protruded from the gables.

Nobody could quite recall how the houses in the courtyard came to be built in this fashion, or who had been responsible for their construction. Peculiarly, neither was there any memory of the hooks being used for the purpose of hoisting furniture, and a search of the records of relevant businesses would have found no recent receipts or dockets relating to the delivery of anything, furniture or otherwise, to any of the buildings, Quayle's excepted. The question of their ownership was nebulous, and someone with sufficient time and energy might have trawled deeds and registries only to conclude that, whoever had possession of them, he or she was identifiable only as a client of the lawyer Quayle.

That esteemed gentleman was currently to be found at his massive black oak desk, his paperwork set aside, and a small glass of sherry by his right hand. Seated across from him on an upright chair, and contenting himself only with tea, was a detective from Scotland Yard named Hassard. Fawnsley, Quayle's clerk, was gone. He had slipped away shortly after the detective's arrival, presumably to his own lodgings, although there were those who would have been surprised to learn that he dwelt anywhere other than beneath Quayle's roof, so omnipresent was he, and so disinclined to leave his master's presence.

'Hassard,' said Quayle. 'That's a Huguenot name, is it not?'

'The Low Countries,' said the detective.

He was young, with hair that had turned prematurely grey. He seemed to regard Quayle's coiffure somewhat dubiously, for the lawyer retained a suspiciously dark thatch for his years.

'There was a Peter Hasaret, if I recall correctly, who fled the persecutions in those lands in the sixteenth century,' said Quayle.

'I believe that we are among his descendants,' said Hassard.

'He was burnt alive.'

'Again, so I understand. You seem well versed in Huguenot history, Mr Quayle.'

'The origins of this firm lie in a partnership between the original Quayle and one Couvret, a gentleman of that faith,' explained the lawyer. 'It ended badly. Couvret died.'

'Murdered, wasn't he?'

Quayle permitted himself a raised eyebrow, and regarded the detective as though perceiving him in a new, and not entirely welcome, aspect.

'Disembowelled, to be exact,' Hassard continued.

Quayle's other eyebrow briefly threatened to take flight and join the first, but he somehow managed to restrain it.

'I am not the only one who appears well versed in history,' said Quayle. 'I shall save you the trouble of further precision by admitting that my ancestor, the founding Quayle, was long suspected of being involved in Couvret's murder, although no proof ever emerged that would have led to a conviction.'

'Which would have been unfortunate for the firm,' said Hassard.

'Most,' agreed Quayle.

He sipped his sherry. Hassard made another attempt to drink his tea, but it was a little strong for his liking, and so thick and tarry as to be almost reluctant to depart the cup. He abandoned it, and opened his notebook.

'About Mr Soter,' he began.

'Yes?'

'Can I assume that you have not heard from him?'

'Not a word.'

'It's a most unusual business.'

'It is.'

'His manuscript has been examined by a number of different experts, including a military psychiatrist. If it is a suicide note, it's not like any that they've seen before.'

'I was permitted only to view a transcript,' said Quayle. 'Although it contained clear intimations of Soter's willingness to end his life, one assumes that such an act would have resulted in a body.'

'Which is why we continue to look for him,' said Hassard. 'He's wanted for questioning about five deaths: those of Eliza Dunwidge and her father; the book scout, Maggs; and two street children.'

'My understanding was that Maggs remained missing,' said Quayle, 'and the only account of what might have befallen him was contained in Soter's manuscript.'

'We dragged a body from the Thames last night. It's in a bad way, but we're pretty certain that it's Maggs. That makes five.'

'What of the intruder that Soter claimed tried to crawl in the window of Maulding's home?'

'A phantasm from a troubled mind, perhaps,' said Hassard. 'Although Maulding's window was broken, we found no signs of man or beast in the grounds of Bromdun Hall. No, there are just five victims with whom Soter had an association, but that should be enough to put the noose around his neck.'

'You appear quite convinced of his guilt.'

'The manuscript strikes me as self-serving, such as that nonsense about the insects in Maggs's room, and the disappearance of the body. Soter seemed to be trying to imply that old Dunwidge might have been involved in disposing of Maggs's remains, but Dunwidge isn't around to ask any more. Soter made sure of that. He beat him to death, and dumped his corpse in the basement of Maggs's lodgings.'

'So you claim.'

'He remains the most likely suspect, unless you can point us to another.'

'He was a disturbed man, but a hero once. The war broke him.'

'The war broke many, but they didn't all become murderers.'

'No, they did not. But it is necessary to understand the circumstances that might have given birth to one.'

'If you say so.'

Quayle sighed. Perhaps the detective was not so worthy of his interest after all.

'About those children,' said Quayle.

Hassard shifted in his seat.

'What of them?'

'I hear that they were . . . unusual.'

'They had rickets, if that's what you mean.'

'Something worse than rickets. I was informed that they were almost mutated.'

'That's nonsense.'

'Really? Is it also nonsense that you have so far failed to identify them, and that they were without parents or guardians, and no one has come forward to claim their bodies?'

'That's true,' Hassard admitted. 'But it doesn't make them any less dead. If I may be so bold, Mr Quayle, you seem almost inclined to doubt that Soter did anything wrong at all.'

'I'm a lawyer,' said Quayle. 'My duty is to question.'

'And mine is to find a murderer, and perhaps his accomplice.'

'Accomplice?'

'Someone entered Maulding's home before the police were summoned by the housekeeper. Soter, in his manuscript, claims to have barricaded the doors of the house before locking himself in Maulding's secret library, but the front door was open when the housekeeper arrived, as was the library itself. The doors to both had been broken from the outside. We found marks.'

'What kind of marks?'

'We thought at first that they might have been made by a crowbar, but now a rake appears more likely, or some implement with tines capable of scratching wood. We've questioned the groundsman, but he was at home throughout, and his family corroborates his statement.'

'Tines,' said Quayle thoughtfully. He raised his right hand before him, and stretched the fingers, examining the neatly cut nails. If Hassard noticed the gesture, he said nothing about it.

'And the book of which Soter wrote,' said Hassard, 'the one that he claimed to have burned?'

'Yes,' said Quayle. 'The *Fractured Atlas*.'

'We found no traces of it in the fire.'

'It was a book,' said Quayle. 'Books burn.'

'Yes, I suppose that must be it.'

Hassard tapped his pen on his notebook.

'Do you think that Soter was mad?' he asked Quayle.

'As I told you, I think he was disturbed.'

'If his manuscript is to believed, he thought that clocks were running backwards, and the dimensions of this world were altering. He ascribed some dread purpose to a derailment that blocked two tracks and brought down the lines.'

'I remember a different Soter, a better one.'

'Did you know that, some weeks earlier, he'd gone to the home of General Sir William Pulteney and kicked up quite the racket? It's lucky that the general didn't end up a victim too.'

'I did not, but Soter didn't care much for Pulteney. In that, at least, he was not deluded or insane.'

'Maulding's nephew didn't take that view when I spoke with him.'

'Mr Sebastian Forbes,' said Quayle, with no particular fondness. 'He stands to inherit a great deal of money, once the details of Maulding's estate are finalized.'

'Mr Forbes is of the opinion that, as executor of his uncle's will, you're dragging your feet on making sure that he gets what is rightfully his.'

'Really?' said Quayle. 'How odd. I think it's safe to say that Mr Forbes will get what's his when the time is right.'

Hassard appeared about to say something in reply, then bit his tongue and put away his notebook.

'Are we finished?' asked Quayle.

'For now.'

'I'm sorry that I couldn't be of more help to you.'

Hassard managed a smile.

'Are you really?'

'You're very cynical, even for a detective.'

'Perhaps. One final question does strike me, though.'

'Ask it.'

'Do you believe that Soter is dead?'

Quayle considered.

'I believe that Soter will not be found alive on this earth,' he said at last.

'That's an interesting reply.'

'Isn't it, though?' said Quayle. 'Come, let me show you out. Those stairs can be tricky.'

The night deepened. At last even the thin halo of light visible around the edge of Quayle's drapes was extinguished, and the lawyer himself appeared in the courtyard. He crossed the cobblestones, unlocked the door directly across from his office, and closed it gently behind him. He had not even bothered to check if he might have been observed, for he was sensitive to every minor change in his environment.

After all, he had been there for a very long time, and before him stretched infinity.

He ascended the narrow staircase, and entered his comfortable lodgings: a dining-room, a living-room-cum-library, a small kitchen, and a bedroom dominated by a massive oak bed of the same hue and vintage as the desk in his office. Again, had that mythical figure, the man with time on his hands and a particular interest in the lifestyle of the lawyer Quayle, been permitted entry, and enjoyed sufficient perspicacity, he might have noted that the square footage of the rooms, taken together, rather seemed to exceed the available space within the walls. Most of the volumes on the shelves were legal tomes, although interspersed among them were occult volumes of the most unique kind, including books named but never seen, and treatises cursed by the Church from the moment their existence became known.

Only one book was not shelved. It stood on a reading stand, its cover charred, its pages blackened. Just as Quayle entered, a section of the cover appeared to extend itself, if only by a fraction of an inch, covering a space that had previously been bare board. The *Atlas* was reconstituting itself.

Quayle set aside the sheaf of papers he had brought with him, and took off his jacket and scarf. He approached a door set into the shelves, one which, had an intruder succeeded in opening it, would have revealed only a blank wall. But Quayle knew better than anyone the strangeness of the universe, and that what one saw did not always bear an accurate relation to what was actually being seen. He withdrew a key from his trouser pocket, inserted it into the keyhole, and turned it. Although he gave only a single rotation to the key, yet from behind the door came the sound of many locks working, and it seemed to echo over and over, gradually receding as though a near infinite number of doors were slowly being unsealed.

Quayle seized the handle and twisted it. He opened the door outwards, revealing the naked man who hung suspended before him, seemingly unsecured, floating against the blackness of space beyond.

Lionel Maulding never stopped screaming, but he made no noise in that place. Quayle watched for a few moments as a section of skin unpeeled itself from Maulding's scalp and slowly tore a narrow strip through his forehead, along his nose, then his lips and his throat, moving steadily and evenly down his chest and belly . . .

Quayle looked away. He had seen the show before. He had even timed it. It took about a day for Lionel Maulding to be reduced to muscle and bone, veins and arteries, and then the process of rebuilding would commence. It seemed to Quayle that this was at least as agonizing for Maulding as the mutilation that necessitated it, but Quayle was entirely without pity for the man. Maulding should have known. There was nothing in the occult volumes that were his obsession to suggest the end to his explorations would be a pleasant one.

Beside Maulding hung Soter. His eyes were closed. His eyes were always closed, as were his ears, and his mouth, and his nostrils, all sewn shut with thick catgut, the same material that joined his arms to his body, and his legs to each other. Imprisoned inside that still form was Soter's consciousness, trapped in a hell that resembled High Wood, for after a man had been through such suffering, there was little else that could be invented to torment him further. For Soter, Quayle did feel something like pity. Quayle was not human, even by the low standards of his profession, but some iota of humanity had infected him after all this time.

Behind these two figures hung hundreds of similar forms: men and women suspended like the husks of insects in a great web. Some had been there for so long that Quayle could not even remember their names, or what they might have done to merit this end. It didn't matter. It was, Quayle supposed, all a question of perspective.

Deep in the blackness beyond the bodies, red veins were

visible, like the fractures in volcanic rock. The universe was sundering, its thin shell cracking. In parts it was almost transparent. Quayle watched a massive form press itself against the barrier, a being to which entire galaxies appeared only as froth on the surface of a distant lake. He glimpsed jointed legs, and jaws within jaws. He saw jagged teeth, and a mass of black-grey eyes like frogspawn in the depths of a pond.

Even after all this time, Quayle trembled in the presence of the Not-God.

Crowding behind it were others, so many others, not so great as the first but all waiting for the rifts to open and admit them. It would take time, of course, but time was nothing to them, or to Quayle. The world had been rewritten. The book had done its work, but when it was restored it would commence a new narrative, and the first chapter would tell of the creation of another kind of universe.

Quayle turned away. He locked the door behind him, went to his kitchen, and prepared a fresh pot of tea.

Then he sat, and watched the *Fractured Atlas* grow.

Razorshins

My grandfather's name was Tendell Tucker, and he was a hard man. He ran liquor for King Solomon during Prohibition, taking care of the road runs from Canada through Maine, and down to Boston. Mostly he answered to Dan Carroll, who was Solomon's partner, because my grandfather preferred dealing with the Irish to working with the Jews. He never said why. He was just that kind of fella.

A lot of people don't know it, but Dan Carroll was a cautious man, which might explain why he lived so long. During Prohibition, most of his shipments came ashore from boats at night, and were met by trucks that brought his booze to warehouses for distribution, but he liked to cover his bets when he could. He wasn't a gambler, not like Abe Rothstein, or even King Solomon himself. Carroll would calculate his outlay, and the potential profit to be realized from each shipment, then split it accordingly. So if he'd invested $30,000 in Canadian liquor, and was looking at a return of $300,000, he would work out how many cases were needed to cover his initial costs, and then run them into Boston separately, usually in specially converted Cadillacs. That way, if the coast guard came sniffing, or the feds, and a shipment was seized, he wouldn't be out of pocket.

That was where my grandfather came in. He was born in Fort Kent, just on the border between Maine and Canada, so he knew the country and the people. He ran the road crews for Carroll: recruiting drivers, checking that the cars were well maintained, and greasing palms to make sure that the local cops stayed out of the way. 'There were more cops than criminals in the bootleg business,' my grandfather used to say, and he was right, just as it always amused him that the politicians who passed the Volstead Act were first in line for the illegal booze that resulted from it.

Dan Carroll trusted my grandfather. A harsh word was never spoken between them.

And King Solomon?

Well, King Solomon wasn't the trusting kind, which was how the trouble began.

You have to understand something about Maine. Back in the nineteenth century, it was considered the drunkest state in the Union. The Mayor of Portland, Neil Dow, was a Quaker, and a founding member of the Maine Temperance Society. Consequently, he didn't much care for the reputation that the state had acquired. Hell, he only needed to take a walk from the lower end of Congress Street to Munjoy Hill to see what his city had become. That's a distance of about a mile, and in Dow's time it boasted about 300 establishments where a man or woman could get a drink. You didn't even have to step off the sidewalk: grocers prepared rum punch in tubs outside their stores, and served it up in tin cups. Eventually Dow had enough, and just about single-handedly forced through a prohibition law in 1851. It stood for nearly five years, until the Rum Riot of 1855 led to shooting and killing, and put the kibosh on both prohibition and Dow's reputation. So, you know, Maine's relationship with liquor was kind of complicated, to say the least, even before the Volstead Act came to pass.

And my grandfather did well out of Prohibition, like a lot of people who saw opportunity in a flawed law, and had the determination and organization to take advantage of the situation. Organization was the important word, because Prohibition created organized crime: with so much money to be made, order and discipline were crucial. My grandfather understood that, and so did Dan Carroll. He paid my grandfather generously for his work, and gave him a cut of any shipments that made it safely to Boston, which was most of them. But then, in January

1933, King Solomon sent a man named Mordecai Blum to Maine.

Blum arrived at my grandfather's house in Portland the day before he was due to travel to Vanceboro to pick up eighty cases of premium whisky that were coming across the border from McAdam. My grandfather knew that Blum was on his way: Dan Carroll had called ahead to warn him. There had been a falling out between Carroll and Solomon over a shipment that had gone astray. The story was that a boat went down in Machias Bay, but some of the liquor subsequently turned up in a garage owned by Bill Sellers, who worked for Carroll. Anyway, Carroll claimed to have known nothing about the deception, and Sellers ended up in a hole in the ground, but it cast a shadow over the working relationship between Solomon and Carroll for a time. For my grandfather, that shadow was Mordecai Blum's.

Blum was a squat, humourless man, with small, lifeless grey eyes that peered out from under heavy lids. His head was long and oversized, and did not narrow at the neck. It looked, my grandfather recalled, like a huge thumb protruding from the collar of his shirt. He was abominably hirsute: my grandfather caught a glimpse of him in his drawers while he was shaving, and swore that only his face and the palms of his hands were hairless. The rest of his body was entirely covered with a wiry black pelt, so that his skin was barely visible through it.

Blum radiated a kind of primitive power, and it was known that he did Solomon's killing for him. 'Motke the Mortician', that was what Dan Carroll called Blum, and he advised my grandfather to keep a close eye on the man, and not to turn his back on him, if he could help it. Carroll didn't think my grandfather was in any immediate danger, not if he was straight, which he knew my grandfather to be. Tendell might have been a criminal, but he was an honest one, if that isn't a contradiction in terms. In any case, he was smarter than to steal from Dan Carroll, and could account for every case of liquor that passed through his hands. Still, he did not share Carroll's faith in Blum's ability to distinguish between honesty and dishonesty, or his willingness to do so. My grandfather knew that the death of Sellers was not enough to satisfy King Solomon, and he had no desire to be sacrificed as an example to others.

My grandfather and Blum drove up to Vanceboro together, mostly in silence. Blum wasn't a talkative individual, and my grandfather preferred to keep his own counsel with strangers. He did learn that Blum didn't touch alcohol of any kind. Apparently wine and hard liquor disagreed with Blum's insides, and he didn't even care much for the taste of beer. Here they found some common ground. Tendell's own father had been a drinker of the worst stripe, a foul and physically abusive man who died a violent death at the hands of some lobstermen he'd crossed down on Commercial Street. He was gutted with a gaff, and left hanging from a wharf bitt. Personal experience, therefore, had left Tendell with a distrust of men who couldn't hold their liquor, and an innate caution in his own consumption. I never saw him drink more than one glass of rum or whisky at a single sitting, and even a beer would have gone flat by the time he got around to finishing it.

Eventually they reached Vanceboro, where the cars and drivers were waiting for them. Shortly after 10 p.m. a pair of trucks arrived from across the border, and the process of transferring the whisky to the Cadillacs began. Blum took no part in it. He watched the work, and then interrogated the Canadian drivers, who had been doing the run for four or five years and disliked their honesty being called into question. They might have been crooks too, but they were straight, and stole no more than they believed to be their due. Blum had a little notebook, and in it were recorded details of every run that had been made in the previous twelve months. He went through each one with the drivers, cross-checking what they could recall of their shipments with what my grandfather and Dan Carroll had ultimately delivered to Boston. When he wasn't satisfied with their answers, he would place a question mark beside the relevant entry in his notebook. My grandfather watched it all without comment, even though Blum was effectively implying that he might be a liar, and alienating the Canadian drivers in the process. Snow clouds gathered above them, and my grandfather was anxious that they should be on their way, but Blum would not be rushed. So it was that the first flurries had begun to fall by the time they were done, and their little convoy had not travelled more than ten miles when the road ahead was lost to them.

'We need to find shelter,' said Tendell. 'We don't want to get stuck out on this road with liquor in back.'

'I thought your bribes kept the police quiet,' said Blum. He removed his notebook from his pocket and began reciting various sums of money, and quantities of liquor, that Tendell had listed as bribe expenses over the preceding months.

Tendell was tempted to point out that Blum's questioning had delayed them, and otherwise they might have been a little farther ahead of the storm, and closer to a town, but he saw no sense in alienating Solomon's man.

'I can pay off cops,' said Tendell, 'but not the prohis, at least not the new ones who've only been up here since November. Some of the old guys, maybe, but the Bureau has started sending us true believers, and they frown on bribery. They're no fools, either. They know that we take these roads.'

'So what do you suggest?'

'A guy named Wallace lives not far from here. He has a barn that he lets us use from time to time. It'll cost us a case of liquor, but it'll be worth it. We can wait out the snow there. If needs be, Wallace has a tractor and a plough blade. He'll help us get us back on the road tomorrow.'

Blum didn't look happy at the thought of spending a night in the North Woods, but Tendell couldn't imagine a situation where Blum would look happy about anything. His demeanour didn't seem to allow much for positive emotions.

'A whole case?' said Blum. 'That sounds like a lot.'

'He's taking a risk, plus he does a little bootlegging and

moonshining of his own on the side. My guess is that he'll take what we give him and turn it into five times as much rotgut.'

'All the more reason to bargain him down.'

'He's not the bargaining type.'

'Everybody's the bargaining type. You just need to find the right leverage.'

Tendell glanced down at Blum's massive hands. He was closing and unclosing the fists, as though already preparing to use his own particular negotiating skills on the unfortunate Wallace.

'Listen,' said Tendell softly. 'This is my country, and my people. You leave the talking to me. In a day or two you'll be back in Boston, but Wallace and those like him will still be here, and I need them on my side. You understand?'

Blum turned his head lazily, and stared at Tendell from beneath those swollen lids. He reminded Tendell of the big cats in the Franklin Park Zoo, seemingly relaxed to the point of somnolence, until someone put meat before them.

'You know King Solomon?' asked Blum.

'I know him.'

'He doesn't trust you.'

'Yeah? And there I was thinking you'd come all this way to give me a prize.'

'I don't trust you either.'

'I'm sorry to hear that.'

'You can tell it to the King.'

Blum turned away. Tendell tightened his grip on the steering wheel. He'd never killed a man, never even come close, but he thought that he had it in him to kill Motke Blum if the opportunity arose, and fuck King Solomon.

Tendell pulled over to the side of the road, jumped out of the car, and went to inform the rest of the drivers about the change of plan.

'Fuckin' Wallace,' said Riber, the big Dane. 'Freeze our balls off, we will.'

Conlon and Marks, the other two drivers, nodded in agreement. Wallace lived a notoriously hardscrabble existence, even by the standards of the north-east.

'We can't keep driving,' said Tendell, 'not in this.'

'What about the Jew?' asked Conlon.

Although they hadn't spent much time with Blum, they had heard the questions he'd asked of the Canadians, and knew the problems he was trying to cause. He hadn't yet got around to questioning them, but he would.

'He's not happy about it,' said Tendell. 'But he can walk back for all I care.'

'Be a shame if something happened to him,' said Marks.

'If something does,' said Tendell, 'then King Solomon will kill us all.'

'He's a rat,' said Conlon.

'He's got nothing to rat about. We're clean. Danny knows it. This is all just for show.'

They grumbled a little more, but the cold and the snow put a quick end to it. When Tendell got back in his car, he saw that Blum had his Colt pistol in his lap.

'You going hunting?' asked Tendell.

'You were out there for a long time.'

'We were taking the night air. It's good for the constitution. Why don't you put the gat away? Nobody here has a beef with you.'

'Really? I got good hearing, me. I don't think your friends like me.'

'They don't have to. They only have to put up with you, just like I do.'

The gun disappeared beneath the folds of Blum's coat. Tendell resumed driving.

'You don't like Jews,' said Blum, after they had travelled for a mile or more, Tendell taking it slowly, unable to see more than a few feet ahead of him in the snow. It was a statement, not a question.

'I like Jews plenty,' said Tendell. 'I deal with them, drink with them, even fucked a few Jewish women in my time. It's not about that.'

'Then what is it about?'

'You're King Solomon's man, and you're looking for an excuse to put a bullet in my head, because the King wants to discourage others from doing what he thinks Sellers did.'

'There's no doubt about it. Sellers fucked the King over.'

'And Dan Carroll, too.'

'The King is not so sure.'

'Then the King is wrong.'

Blum's breath plumed and lost itself against the windshield, as though trying unsuccessfully to escape the hostile confines of the car.

'The King used to think that he and Carroll were alike,' said Blum. 'But he was wrong. The Irish run the police, the fire department, the councils. They have power. The Jews, they don't have power, not like that. We are not the same.'

'You think that situation is going to get better with you coming up here and pissing everyone off with your questions?'

'Do you play chess?'

'No. I never much cared for games.'

'It's a pity,' said Blum. 'Games are a reflection of reality, and chess is war on a board. The King and Dan Carroll are jostling for position. Those men behind us are pawns. They are the first to get wiped away in any conflict. Men like us, we are knights, bishops, rooks. If we are careless, we get taken by a pawn, but mostly we are vulnerable to those most like ourselves.'

'And Sellers? What was he?'

'He was a pawn who thought he could be a king.'

The two men exchanged no further words until they came to the turn-off that led to Wallace's place. There was no sign, and no gate, merely a gap in the tree line. A narrow trail, distinguishable only by its absence of growth, wound down through the woods to where a farmhouse became visible behind a veil of white. It wasn't much to look at, but lights burned in its windows, and smoke and sparks flew from its chimney. Behind it stood a big barn, and some smaller outbuildings. Farther back in the woods, Tendell knew, was Wallace's still.

The old man himself appeared in the doorway as they approached. He had a shotgun in his hands, although he did not raise it. Tendell halted while they were still a ways off, and identified himself.

'You can come on down,' said Wallace, and only then did Tendell lead the convoy into the yard. He put the brakes on and told Blum to stay where he was – 'He's nervous around strangers.' – then went to speak with Wallace. The homesteader was in his late seventies, with long white hair and a beard to match. His boots were unlaced, and he was wearing a big wool coat with a fur-lined collar over tan moleskin trousers and a navy sweater. Tendell noticed that the hammers of the shotgun were cocked, and Wallace didn't appear in any hurry to ease them back down.

'We need shelter for the night, Earl.'

'What do you have?'

'What do you think?'

Wallace squinted past him at the figure in the passenger seat.

'Who's that with you?'

Tendell didn't bother looking back.

'One of King Solomon's men. I got Conlon, Marks, and Riber, too.'

'You tell Solomon's man to stay where he was?'

'Yes.'

'Well, he didn't listen.'

Tendell heard gravel and snow crunching beneath boots as Blum joined them. He exchanged a look with Wallace. It said all that needed to be said about Blum.

'How you doing?' asked Blum.

'Just fine,' said Wallace.

He stared at Blum, who was stamping theatrically in the

falling snow, his hands buried in the pockets of his coat. Tendell was sure that the Colt was gripped in one of them.

'You got something wrong with your feet?' Wallace asked.

'I'm cold, is all.'

'Then you should have stayed in the car.'

'We got a problem here?' said Blum, looking from Wallace to Tendell.

'Jesus,' said Tendell. 'No, we got no problem, right, Earl?'

Wallace appeared inclined to disagree, but common sense prevailed. He eased the hammers down on both barrels of the shotgun, and cradled the weapon in his arms.

'The usual fee,' he said. 'One case.'

Tendell heard Blum draw in a breath as if to speak, but he'd had enough of him by that point. He turned, and raised the index finger of his right hand in warning. Blum didn't like it, but he held his tongue.

'One case,' Tendell agreed.

'You'll have to move the tractor,' said Wallace. 'Otherwise, the barn's empty. I got stew on the stove, and bread to soak. Coffee's brewing, too.'

'That's hospitable of you, Earl.'

Wallace glared at Blum.

'Damn Christian, even,' he said, then retreated into his cottage.

Tendell let Riber supervise the storage of the Cadillacs, and instructed him to bring in a case of whisky as Wallace's payment. He didn't want to leave Blum alone with Wallace. Who knew what Blum might say? Wallace was both proud and ornery, and even the promise of a case of liquor might not be enough to assure them of a place to stay for the night if he felt slighted in any way.

Wallace's house was divided into two rooms: a kitchen and living area, with a fire burning at one end, and a small bedroom at the other. Even with the fire, the main room was icy. They'd have to sleep on the floor, although Wallace could be relied upon for some cushions, and maybe a rug or spare blanket. Nevertheless, Riber was right: a cold night they'd have of it, and no mistake.

Blum took in his spare surroundings: a rough-hewn oak table, a quartet of chairs, three of which showed few signs of use, and a pair of overstuffed armchairs by the fire. The floor was stone, with animal skins covering most of it. No pictures adorned the walls, and the only books on the single shelf were a Bible and some Sears Roebuck catalogues. Blum made no comment on any of it. Instead he asked politely if it was okay to sit. Wallace gave his assent, and Blum pulled one of the dining chairs to the side of the fire. He warmed his hands, and did not speak for a time.

With the cars safely stored away, the other three men joined them, Riber carrying Wallace's case of liquor. Wallace opened it on the table and checked that the seals were intact before taking the box outside and storing it safely away in one of his outbuildings.

Conlon had a bottle in his coat pocket. He raised it questioningly to Tendell.

'You can take it out of my share,' said Conlon.

'No, I'll cover it,' said Tendell.

Cups were found. Tendell accepted only a splash. Blum declined, barely shifting his attention from the fire. Wallace returned from his errand, but did not partake. Tendell struggled to recall ever seeing the old man imbibe. The other four raised their cups to one another and drank. Tendell helped Wallace to find bowls for the stew, and some spoons.

'Does King Solomon's man have a name?' Wallace asked my grandfather quietly.

'Blum,' said Tendell.

'Motke Blum?'

'The same. You heard of him?'

'Lots of people have heard of him. He's no good.'

Tendell didn't bother arguing. Wallace went outside to relieve himself, as though the confirmation of Motke Blum's identity had raised the unconquerable desire to piss on something.

Wallace placed the pot of stew on the table. It was mainly vegetables and potatoes, with grey meat of some kind dotted throughout. The bread was freshly baked, though, and still warm to the touch.

'What's the meat?' asked Blum.

'Squirrel mostly,' said Wallace. 'Some beef chuck, too, but not so much that you'd notice. Can't guarantee it's kosher, though.'

He spoke seriously. He'd been paid, and saw no reason to be impolite, whatever he privately thought of King Solomon's man.

Blum shrugged. The stew was hot, and he was cold. They ate by the fire, Wallace and Tendell taking the armchairs. The talk was general, and mostly local gossip: tales of errant husbands and shrewish wives; of births and deaths; of those who were thriving and those who had fallen on hard times. No direct mention was made of Wallace's own illegal activities, but he did tell them that the prohis had been through the area just a week earlier, and found nothing.

'They have a lead?' asked Tendell.

'Fishing,' said Wallace. 'I hear they got themselves a grid. They keep a big map on the wall over in Houlton, and they pick a square, search it, then mark it off.'

'A map, you say?' said Tendell.

'Up there for all to see, if they have a mind to look.'

'Which some folks will.'

'I believe so.'

'And those kind of folks might be inclined to keep their ears open as well as their eyes.'

'Be fools not to.'

Tendell smiled. 'With all those eyes and ears open, it'd be a shock if the prohis found anything on one of those searches.'

'That it would be,' agreed Wallace.

Half the bottle was gone. Riber's chin was already on his

chest, and he was snoring. Conlon and Marks weren't far behind him. Blum was drinking coffee from a tin cup, the fire reflected in his eyes. The snow continued to fall.

'What do you reckon on the snow?' asked Tendell.

Wallace raised his eyes to the ceiling, as though he could see through it to the heavens above.

'It's down for the night, but not beyond,' he said. 'Come daylight, you should be all right. I'll clear the trail, and tow you if needs be. The main roads are your own concern.'

'I'm grateful to you.'

Wallace stood. 'I'll be going to my bed. There's bacon in the morning for those who want it, porridge for the rest. Throw some more logs on the fire, keep it lit.'

He looked at Blum.

'There is one more thing,' he said. 'I'll be wanting an extra bottle from you.'

Blum tore his attention from the fire. 'You've been paid as agreed,' he said.

'It's not for me. You'll leave it outside, by the fence.'

Blum frowned. 'What are you talking about?'

'It's a full moon tonight, though you can't see it,' said Wallace, 'and there's life in the woods. A bottle will send it on its way.'

'I'll see to it,' said Tendell.

'The fuck you will,' said Blum. 'What nonsense is this?'

'Superstitions,' said Tendell. 'Old lore. Doesn't matter. It'll be taken care of. You don't need to worry yourself with it.'

Blum pointed beyond the walls, to where the barn stood.

'That's King Solomon's whisky,' he said. 'Dan Carroll may be transporting this shipment, but the King's money paid for it. I've kept quiet while you handed over a case to this man, because it's coming out of your share, just like the bottle that was opened, but I won't stand by and see another bottle dumped into the woods because of a fairy story.'

'I told you,' said Tendell. 'I'll take care of it. I'll take the hit.'

'No,' said Wallace. Belligerence had now crept into his tone.

He indicated Blum with a flick of his chin. 'He must do it. If this is King Solomon's whisky, and he is King Solomon's man, then it comes from the King's share, and the King's man must make the payment.'

'Come on, Earl . . . ' said Tendell.

'No! If he won't pay, then you can all get the hell out of my house, and off my land. Those cars can't stay here unless payment is made.'

'This is a fucking joke,' said Blum.

'It's no joke,' said Wallace. 'You make the choice. You pay the woods, or you go.'

Blum shook his head in disbelief. He rose from his chair, and began buttoning his coat. Suddenly his right hand lashed out, and caught Wallace a heavy blow to the belly. Before anyone could react, Blum had landed another punch to the side of the old man's head, knocking him to the floor, and then proceeded to kick him where he lay. Tendell was the first to reach Blum and push him away. Blum stumbled over a chair, but kept his feet. He was about to turn on Tendell, but Riber, who had been woken by the argument, blocked his way.

Tendell examined Wallace. He was bleeding from the mouth, but he was conscious.

'You okay, Earl?'

Wallace muttered something, but Tendell couldn't understand it. He looked up at Blum to remonstrate with him, and saw that the Colt was back in his hand. Those dead eyes were now bright with rage. Riber was unarmed, and had raised his arms, but he did so while looking over his shoulder at Tendell for guidance.

'You know who I am?' said Blum. 'I am Mordecai Blum. I am King Solomon's man. When I speak, he speaks. When you lay a hand on me, you lay a hand on the King. You understand?'

'What the fuck?' said Conlon.

Tendell saw him move towards his coat, beneath which lay his gun. Tendell shook his head, and Conlon stopped.

'You shut up,' said Blum. 'You just shut your fucking mouth.'

'All this, over a bottle?' asked Marks.

'No,' said Blum. 'All this on a point of principle. This is King Solomon's liquor. It stays in the barn, and not a bottle more is touched until it's unloaded in Boston.'

Wallace mumbled again. His eyes fluttered.

'Help me get him to a chair,' said Tendell to Marks. 'We need to watch over him, and keep him warm. He may have concussion or something. And you' – he directed his gaze once again to Blum – 'put the gun away. I told you already: there's no need for it here. Jesus, he's just an old man.'

Marks assisted Tendell in getting Wallace into a chair. They put a blanket over him, and Conlon found a clean towel, dampened it, and used it to wipe away the blood. Wallace's upper lip was split, and one tooth had sheared off at the gum. They found it on the floor. Tendell threw it into the fire.

Conlon, Riber and Marks stood in one corner, watching Blum. It was clear that, given the chance, they would inflict damage on him. Blum had lowered the gun, but he still held it in his hand.

'What's done is done,' said Tendell, although it pained him to say it. 'You three, get some sleep. Blum, for the last time, put the fucking gun away. You see anyone else here waving a gun?'

Blum had calmed down, and the anger was gone from him. He put the gun back in the holster beneath his arm, and took the chair beside Wallace.

'I did not mean to hurt him so badly,' he said. 'But it is the King's liquor.'

'Next time, just take a fucking deep breath and walk away.'

Blum wiped his right hand across his mouth, smearing his face with some of Wallace's blood.

'What did he mean about the woods?' asked Blum.

'Nothing.'

'Tell me.'

'It's an old bootlegger's myth,' said Tendell. 'At the full moon, you leave a bottle for Razorshins.'

'Razorshins? What is Razorshins?'

'What does it matter?'

'I'm curious.'

'Now you're curious? Fuck you. Go to sleep.'

Tendell went into Wallace's bedroom and found some cushions, pillows and spare blankets. He distributed them to his men, keeping one pillow for himself, then lay down on a bearskin rug with his coat over him. He saw Blum pour himself another cup of coffee. He closed his eyes.

Tendell was not a superstitious man – he was not even particularly religious – but he understood the necessity of being tolerant of the convictions of others, especially when those individuals were doing one a favour, even if it did come at the cost of a little whisky. He knew that those who lived and worked in the North Woods had their own mythologies. They did not harm grey jays because they believed them to be the reincarnated spirits of deceased woodsmen, and white owls were regarded as omens of ill luck, to the extent that there were woodsmen who avoided the areas in which they dwelt. Tendell had also spent time with men who claimed to have glimpsed the wendigo, the Indian spirit, although such tales invariably involved dark references to cannibalism, and were less to be believed than tolerated.

Razorshins was not new to Tendell, for there were men of his acquaintance who claimed that their fathers and grandfathers had long paid obeisance to it, leaving out jugs of moonshine once a month so that it wouldn't interfere with their stills. During the previous century, a handful of scalpings and mutilations in the region, blamed on rogue natives, were later secretly ascribed to Razorshins. Nobody had ever seen the creature, so no one could say for sure, but Tendell knew of Maine moonshiners, men who were no fools, who swore that they had left out jugs, and came back in the morning to find them empty or gone, and unfamiliar tracks in the vicinity: almost skeletal, they said, the feet strangely narrow, with six toes and, some said, a kind of spine or spike at the heel.

Tendell opened his eyes. Blum was still seated by the fire, sipping coffee. Beside him, Wallace moaned in his sleep. The old man would live, but they'd never be welcome on his land again, no matter how much liquor they offered. Blum had pissed on that patch for sure.

Tendell closed his eyes again, and tried to sleep.

He was woken by a groan from over by the fire. He saw Blum on his feet, clutching his guts. Tendell tried not to smile. If a man wasn't used to eating critters, it could do funny things to his digestion. He heard Blum break wind loudly, and swear. Around him, the others snored.

Tendell raised himself up on an elbow.

'You better get to the outhouse before you gas us all,' he said.

'That fucking stew,' hissed Blum. 'It's tearing up my insides.'

'You're just not used to rich food, I guess,' said Tendell. He glanced at the window. 'Can't tell for sure, but it looks like the snow's stopped. That's something.'

Blum had removed his boots. He pulled them on, wrapped his coat around him, and staggered to the door.

'You see my hat?' he asked.

'No,' said Tendell, 'I got no idea where your hat is.'

'It's cold.'

'You better hurry, or you're going to shit yourself.'

Blum took one last look around for his missing hat, then resigned himself to managing without it.

'You might want to reconsider that bottle, while you're out there,' said Tendell, but Blum did not reply. He stepped into the cold, and pulled the door closed behind him. One of the drivers stirred in his sleep, but none appeared to wake.

'Tendell.'

The voice was Wallace's.

'You okay, Earl?' asked Tendell.

He got up and walked over to the fire to check on the old man. The flames were dying. He placed a log on them, positioning it so that it would burn and not smother.

'Lock the door,' said the old man.

Tendell thought that he had misheard.

'Say what?'

'Lock the door. Do it now. There isn't much time.'

'What are you talking about? Blum's out there.'

'And he's not alone. Listen! Do you hear it?'

Tendell listened, but heard nothing.

'It's all quiet,' he said.

'No, it's not.'

And then the sound came: the faintest pressure on snow, the crunching of fallen flakes, and something else – a clicking, like bone striking on bone.

Tendell left Wallace and walked to the window. The sky had cleared, and the woods glowed in the moonlight. He could see the barn where the Cadillacs were locked away, and to the right of it the little outhouse in which Blum was doing his business, the only marks on the snow his footsteps leading up to it.

'I can't—' said Tendell.

He saw it. He might have ascribed the movement to the breeze, had there been a breeze, to branches moving and casting shadows, but the night was entirely still. He struggled to comprehend what he was looking at, because the creature kept to the woods as it worked its way towards the outhouse, but the closest comparison he could find was to a massive stick insect, or a praying mantis. It was seven feet tall at least, and the colour of buttercream gone sour. It was almost without flesh, for Tendell could count every bone beneath the skin that draped its body. Its knee joints bent backwards, so that it leaned forwards as it walked. Its arms were raised before it, the hands probing at the air, the fingers long and ending in curved talons that clicked against one another. Bone spikes protruded from behind the knee and ankle, and from its elbows and wrists. A ragged line of them ran down its spine like the plates on dinosaurs that Tendell had seen in natural history museums. Its head was curved like the blade of an axe, a similarity that was confirmed when it turned towards the window, revealing a face no wider than Tendell's closed fist, and a mouth filled with sharp, fishlike teeth. It had no eyes, or none that Tendell could discern, but its nostrils were massive and wet, and sniffed at the night.

'Lock it!' said Wallace.

'What about Blum?'

At that moment, Blum emerged from the outhouse, still buttoning his pants.

'Blum!' Tendell rapped at the window. 'Blum!'

He heard movement behind him as the other drivers began to wake.

'Keep quiet,' said Wallace. 'You must keep quiet.'

Blum looked over, squinting at the window. A shadow fell across him, and his hands dropped to his sides as he saw what was coming for him. His trousers fell to his ankles. He tried to run, and there came a sound like the hissing of a scythe, and suddenly Blum was lying on the snow, his right leg entirely severed below the knee.

Blum let out an animal cry.

Tendell turned to get to the door, but Riber stood in his way, just as he had earlier come between Blum and Wallace. Behind him, Conlon had moved to secure the cottage.

'We have to help him,' said Tendell.

'We can't,' said Riber.

'If you go out there, you'll die,' said Wallace from the chair. 'We may all die yet.'

Tendell tried to slip by Riber, but he was no match for the Dane, who pushed him back.

'No,' said Riber.

Tendell again looked out the window. Blum was trying to drag himself through the snow, trailing blood behind him. The creature towered above him, and as Tendell watched it began slashing at Blum with its arms and legs, tearing through the fabric of his coat to leave bloody gashes in its wake. And all the time Blum kept crying out, over and over, until finally the creature grasped his hair in its left hand, and its right spur scalped him with a single swipe.

Tendell looked away. When he turned back, the creature was holding Blum's body upside down by the left leg. It swung him, and Blum was tossed into the darkness of the forest, but the creature remained staring at the house.

Tendell saw that Riber, Conlon and Marks were now all armed.

'Guns won't do any good,' said Wallace. 'Just get away from the windows. Come to the fire.'

The four men did as he said, but nobody set aside a gun. A shadow passed across the nearest window, and then the door was tested. They heard a tapping against the wood of the walls, and a scratching at the glass by the far window. Finally there was silence, until a crashing noise came from outside.

'It's in the barn,' said Tendell.

Glass broke. Metal was crushed, and wood splintered, then all was quiet again. Ten minutes went by, then fifteen, until Tendell found the courage to approach the window.

'I think it's gone,' he said.

'No,' said Wallace. 'It's still out there. It's waiting.'

'For what?' asked Riber.

'For one of us to go out. I think,' said Wallace, 'that sometimes it forgets how much it likes blood.'

None of them moved from the fire, until at last dawn came. The night departed, and with it went Razorshins.

They found some of Blum's remains in the forest, but identifying them as such would have been a problem for anyone unfamiliar with the manner of his passing. They buried what was left of him in the woods.

'What'll we tell King Solomon?' asked Conlon.

'Nothing,' said Tendell. 'My orders were to drop Blum off in Portland. As far as anyone here is concerned, that's what I did.'

'The King won't believe it.'

'Let that be Dan's problem.'

One of the Cadillacs was damaged beyond repair, but most of its cases were salvageable. They redistributed them among the remaining cars, and Tendell used Wallace's plough attachment to clear a path to the road, for Wallace himself was too weak to help. They left him with two more cases for his trouble, but he didn't thank them, and Tendell never spoke with him again.

It was only as they were leaving that Tendell saw Motke Blum's hat. It was lying by a fence post, beside an empty bottle. Around it were narrow, six-toed prints.

Tendell did not mention it to the others.

The disappearance of Motke Blum caused friction between Dan Carroll and King Solomon that threatened to erupt into violence, but later that same year two gunmen named Burke and Coyne put an end to the King in the men's room of Boston's Cotton Club, while Big Dan Carroll rode his luck, just as he always had, and eventually passed away in 1946 at the age of 63.

Shortly before Dan died, my grandfather shared with him the real story of Motke Blum's death. By then Carroll was a shell of the man he once had been, but he still had his mind.

'You should have told me the truth,' Carroll said.

'You'd have believed me?' asked my grandfather.

'I always believed you,' said Carroll. 'The only time I didn't was when you said that you left Blum in Portland, but it seemed better to accept your story and live with it, than start poking holes in it and bring King Solomon down on us all. And, you know, the King might also have believed you, too, had you told him.'

'Why do you say that?'

'Because the day before the King died, someone left a bottle on his doorstep. Inside it was a human scalp, preserved in Canadian liquor. I always wondered about that. You think Wallace sent it?'

'Probably.'

'You know that Blum killed his cousin?'

'No, I never heard that.'

'He lived in New Hampshire. Made moonshine, and got ambitious. Blum was sent to bust up his still, and busted him up too. He wasn't supposed to kill him, but he went too far.'

Carroll shifted on his sick bed, and, like an old dog, found a patch of sunlight in which to warm himself.

'You think Wallace knew that Blum was coming north?'

'I believe he did.'

'And the storm?'

'Good luck, or something more,' said Carroll. 'That snow came down real sudden. Took everyone by surprise, from what I can remember.'

'Wallace wasn't no shaman.'

'Wasn't he? Maybe he didn't have to be. You ever wonder what he did with all that liquor you gave him? He sure didn't drink it. Wallace was tee-total all his life.'

'He had a still.'

'If he did, he never sold anything from it.' Carroll eyed my grandfather. 'I thought you knew everything there was to know about those people up there. I reckon you might have been mistaken.'

'Damn,' said my grandfather.

'Yeah, damn,' said Carroll. 'Everyone, and everything, requires payment. Even King Solomon knew that.'

Carroll's eyes began to close. He was nearing his final rest. This would be the last conversation that my grandfather had with him.

'You ever go up there again, Tendell?' he asked. He did not look at my grandfather as he spoke.

'No, not after what happened.'

'I'd say that was very wise of you,' said Carroll. 'You think it's still in those woods?'

'I reckon so.'

'What do you think it's doing?'

And my grandfather remembered Wallace's words to them, after Razorshins had scalped Motke Blum.

'Waiting,' he said. 'Just waiting.'

On *The Anatomization of an Unknown Man* (1637) by Frans Mier

The painting titled *The Anatomization of an Unknown Man* is one of the more obscure works by the minor Dutch painter Frans Mier. It is an unusual piece, although its subject may be said to be typical of our time: the opening up of a body by what is, one initially assumes, a surgeon or anatomist, the light from a suspended lamp falling over the naked body of the anonymous man, his scalp peeled back to reveal his skull, his innards exposed as the anatomist's blade hangs suspended, ready to explore further the intricacies of his workings, the central physical component of the universe's rich complexity.

I was not long ago in England, and witnessed there the hanging of one Elizabeth Evans – Canberry Bess, they called her – a notorious murderer and cutpurse, who was taken with her partner, one Thomas Shearwood. Country Tom was hanged and then gibbeted at Gray's Inn fields, but it was the fate of Elizabeth Evans to be dissected after her death at the Barber-Surgeons' Hall, for the body of a woman is of more interest to the surgeons than that of a man, and harder to come by. She wept and screamed as she was brought to the gallows, and cried out for a Christian burial, for the terror of the Hall was greater to her than that of the noose itself. Eventually, the hangman silenced her with a rag, for she was disturbing the crowd, and an end was put to her.

Something of her fear had communicated itself to the onlookers, though, and a commotion commenced at the base of the gallows. Although the surgeons wore the guise of commoners, yet the crowd knew them for what they were, and a shout arose that the woman had suffered enough under the law, and should have no further barbarities visited upon her, although I fear their concern was less for the dignity of her repose than the knowledge that the mob was to be deprived of the display of her carcass in chains at St Pancras, and the slow exposure of her bones at King's Cross. Still, the surgeons had their way for, when the noose had done its work, she was cut down and stripped of her apparel, then laid naked in a chest and thrown into a cart. From there, she was carried to the Hall near unto Cripplegate. For a penny, I was permitted, with others, to watch as the surgeons went about their work, and a revelation it was to me.

But I digress. I merely speak of it to stress that Mier's painting cannot be understood in isolation. It is a record of our time, and should be seen in the context of the work of Valverde and Estienne, of Spigelius and Berrettini and Berengarius, those other great illustrators of the inner mysteries of our corporeal form.

Yet look closer and it becomes clear that the subject of Mier's painting is not as it first appears. The unknown man's face is contorted in its final agony, but there is no visible sign of strangulation, and his neck is unmarked. If he is a malefactor taken from the gallows, then by what means was his life ended? Although the light is dim, it is clear that his hands have been tied to the anatomist's table by means of stout rope. Only the right hand is visible, admittedly, but one would hardly secure that and not the other. On his wrist are gashes where he has struggled against his bonds, and blood pours from the table to the floor in great quantities. The dead do not bleed in this way.

And if this is truly a surgeon, then why does he not wear the attire of a learned man? Why does he labour alone in some dank place, and not in a hall or theatre? Where are his peers? Why are there no other men of science, no assistants, no curious onlookers enjoying their penny's worth? This, it would appear, is secret work.

Look: there, in the corner, behind the anatomist, face tilted to stare down at the dissected man. Is that not the head and upper body of a woman? Her left hand is raised to her mouth, and her eyes are wide with grief and horror, but here too a rope is visible. She is also restrained, although not so firmly as the anatomist's victim. Yes, perhaps 'victim' is the word, for the only conclusion to be drawn is that the man on the table is suffering under the knife. This is no corpse from the gallows, and this is not a dissection.

This is something much worse.

II

The question of attribution is always difficult in such circumstances. It resembles, one supposes, the investigation into the commission of a crime. There are clues left behind by the murderer, and it is the work of an astute and careful observer to connect such evidence to the man responsible. The use of a single source of light, shining from right to left, is typical of Mier. So, too, is the elongation of the faces, so that they resemble wraiths more than people, as though their journey into the next life has already begun. The hands, by contrast, are clumsily rendered, those of the anatomist excepted. It may be that they are the efforts of others, for Mier would not be alone among artists in allowing his students to complete his paintings. But then, it could also be the case that it is Mier's intention to draw our gaze to the anatomist's hands. There is a grace, a subtlety to the scientist's calling, and Mier is perhaps suggesting that these are skilled fingers holding the blade.

To Mier, this is an artist at work.

III

I admit that I have never seen the painting in question. I have only a vision of it in my mind based upon my knowledge of such matters. But why should that concern us? Is not imagining the first step towards bringing something into being? One must envisage it, and then one can begin to make it a reality. All great art commences with a vision, and perhaps it may be that this vision is closer to God than that which is ultimately created by the artist's brush. There will always be human flaws in the execution. Only in the mind can the artist achieve true perfection.

IV

It is possible that the painting called *The Anatomization of an Unknown Man* may not exist.

V

What is the identity of the woman? Why would someone force her to watch as a man is torn apart, and compel her to listen to his screams as the blade takes him slowly, exquisitely apart? Surgeons and scientists do not torture in this way.

VI

So, if we are not gazing upon a surgeon at work, then, for want of another word, perhaps we are looking at a murderer. He is older than the others in the picture, although not so ancient that his beard has turned grey. The woman, meanwhile, is beautiful;

let there be no doubt of that. Mier was not a sentimental man, and would not have portrayed her as other than she was. The victim, too, is closer in age to the woman than the surgeon. We can see it in his face, and in the once youthful perfection of his now ruined body.

Yes, it may be that he has the look of a Spaniard about him.

VII

I admit that Frans Mier may not exist.

VIII

With this knowledge, gleaned from close examination of the work in question, let us now construct a narrative. The man with the knife is not a surgeon, although he might wish to be, but he has a curiosity about the nature of the human form that has led him to observe closely the actions of the anatomists. The woman? Let us say: his wife, lovely yet unfaithful, fickle in her affections, weary of the ageing body that shares her bed and hungry for firmer flesh.

And the man on the table, then, is, or was, her lover. What if we were to suppose that the husband has discovered his wife's infidelity? Perhaps the young man is his apprentice, one whom he has trusted and loved as a substitute for the child that has never blessed his marriage. Realizing the nature of his betrayal, the master lures his apprentice to the cellar, where the table is waiting. No, wait: he drugs him with tainted wine, for the apprentice is younger and stronger than he, and the master is unsure of his ability to overpower him. When the apprentice regains consciousness, woken by the cries of the woman trapped with him, he is powerless to move. He adds his voice to hers, but the walls are thick, and the cellar deep. There is no one to hear.

A figure advances, the lamp catches the sharp blade, and the grim work begins.

IX

So: this is our version of the truth, our answer to the question of attribution. I, Nicolaes Deyman, did kill my apprentice Mantegna. I anatomized him in my cellar, slowly taking him apart as though, like the physicians of old, I might be able to find some as yet unsuspected fifth humour within him, the black and malignant thing responsible for his betrayal. I did force my wife, my beloved Judith, to watch as I removed skin from flesh, and flesh from bone. When her lover was dead, I strangled her with a rope, and I wept as I did so.

I accept the wisdom and justice of the court's verdict: that my name should be struck from all titles and records and never uttered again; that I should be taken from this place and hanged in secret and then, while still breathing, be handed over to the anatomists and carried to their great temple of learning, there to be taken apart while my heart beats so that the slow manner of my dying might contribute to the greater sum of human knowledge, and thereby make some recompense for my crimes.

I ask only this: that an artist, a man of some small talent, might be permitted to observe and record all that transpires so the painting called *The Anatomization of an Unknown Man* might at last come into existence. After all, I have begun the work for him. I have imagined it. I have described it. I have given him his subject, and willed it into being.

For I, too, am an artist, in my way.

A Haunting

The world had grown passing strange. Even the hotel felt different, as though all of the furniture had been shifted slightly in his absence: the reception desk moved a foot or two forward from its previous position, making the lobby appear smaller; the lights adjusted so that they were always either too dim or too bright. It was wrong. It was not as it had once been. All had changed.

Yet how could it be otherwise when she was no longer with him? He had never stayed here alone before. She had always been by his side, standing at his left hand as he checked them in, watching in silent approval as he signed the register, her fingers tightening on his arm as he wrote the words 'Mr & Mrs', just as he had done on that first night when they had arrived for their honeymoon. She had repeated that small, impossibly intimate gesture on their annual return thereafter, telling him, in her silent way, that she would not take for granted this coupling, this yoking together of their diverse aspects under a single name. She was his as he was hers, and she had never regretted that fact, and would never grow weary of it.

But now there was no 'Mrs', only 'Mr'. He looked up at the young woman behind the desk. He had not seen her before, and assumed that she was new. There were always new people here, but, in the past, enough of the old had remained to give a sense of comforting familiarity. Now, as his electronic key was prepared and his credit card swiped, he took time to take in the faces of the staff and saw none that he recognized. Even the concierge was no longer the same. Everything had been altered, it seemed, by her departure from this life. Her death had tilted the

335

globe on its axis, displacing furniture, light fixtures, even people. They had died with her, and all had been quietly replaced without a single objection.

But he had not replaced her with another, and never would.

He bent down to pick up his bag, and the pain shot through him again, the impact so sharp and brutal that he lost his breath and had to lean for a moment on the reception desk. The young woman asked him if he was all right and he lied and told her that he was. A bellhop came and offered to bring his bag to the room, leaving him with a vague sense of shame that he could not accomplish even this simple task alone: to carry a small leather valise from reception to elevator, from elevator to room. He knew that nobody was looking, that nobody cared, that this was the bellhop's purpose, but it was the fact that the element of choice had been taken from him which troubled him so. He could not have carried the bag, not at that moment, even had he wanted to. His body ached, and his every movement spoke of weakness. He sometimes imagined his insides as a honeycomb, riddled with spaces where cells had collapsed and decayed, a fragile construction that would disintegrate entirely under pressure. He was coming to the end of his life, and his body was in terminal decline.

He caressed the key card in the ascending elevator, noting the room number on the little paper wallet. He had been in that same room so many times before, but always with her, and once more he was reminded of how alone he was without her. Yet he had not wanted to spend this, the first wedding anniversary since her death, in the house that they had once shared. He wanted to do as they had always done, to commemorate her in this way, and so he made the call and booked the suite that was most familiar to him.

After a brief struggle with the electronic lock – what was so wrong with metal keys, he wondered, that they had to be replaced by unappealing pieces of plastic? – he entered the room. All was clean and neat, anonymous without being alienating.

He had always liked hotel rooms, appreciating the fact that he could impose elements of his own personality upon them through the simple act of placing a book on a nightstand, or leaving his shoes by the foot of the bed.

There was an easy chair in a corner beside the window, and he sank into it and closed his eyes. The bed had tempted him, but he was afraid that if he lay down he might not be able to rise again. The journey had exhausted him. It was the first time that he had travelled by plane since her death, and he had forgotten what a chore it had become. He was old enough to remember a time when it had not always been so, and an element of glamour and excitement remained. On the flight down he had dined off paper, and everything that he ate and drank tasted of cardboard and plastic. He lived in a world composed of disposable things: cups, plates, marriages, people.

He must have slept, for when he opened his eyes the light in the room had changed and there was a sour taste in his mouth. He looked at his watch, and was surprised to see that an hour had passed. There was also, he noticed, a bag in the corner, perhaps brought by the bellhop while he was napping, but it was not his.

Silently he cursed the young man. How difficult could it be to bring up the correct piece of baggage? It wasn't even as if the lobby had been very busy when he checked in. He got to his feet and approached the offending item. It was an unopened red suitcase, and lay on a stand beside the closet. It struck him that perhaps he might have missed it when he entered the room, wearied by his trip, and it had been there all along. He examined it. It was locked, with a green scarf tied around the handle to help distinguish it from similar items on airport carousels. There was no name apparent, although the handle was slightly tacky to the touch where the airline label had been removed. He glanced in the trash can, but it was empty, so he could not even use a discarded tag to identify its owner. And yet the case seemed oddly familiar to him . . .

The telephone in the bathroom was closer than the phone on the other side of the bed. He decided to use this one before pausing and looking again at the bag. He experienced a brief surge of fear. This was a big hotel in a large American city, and was it not possible that someone might deliberately have abandoned the case in one of its rooms? He wondered if he might suddenly find himself at the epicentre of a massive terrorist explosion, and saw his body not disintegrating or vaporizing, but instead shattering into countless pieces like a china statue dropped on a stone floor, fragments of his being littering the remains of the suite: a section of cheek here, an eye, still blinking, there. He had been rendered fundamentally flawed by grief; there were cracks in his being.

Did bombs still tick? He could not say. He supposed that some – the old-fashioned kind – probably did. Just as he had relied upon his windup alarm clock to wake him for his flight that morning (he lived in fear of power cuts when he had a plane to catch, or a meeting to make), then perhaps there were times when only a straightforward, ticktock timepiece with a little keyhole in the back would do the trick if failure was not an option.

Carefully he approached the bag, then leaned in close to it and listened, holding his breath so that any telltale sounds would not be masked by his wheezing. He heard nothing, and instantly felt silly. It was a misplaced case, and nothing more. He would call reception and have it taken away.

He stepped into the bathroom, hit the light switch, and stopped, his hand poised over the telephone. An array of toiletries and cosmetics was carefully lined up beside the sink, along with a hairbrush, a comb, and a small vanity case. He saw moisturizers, and lipsticks, and in the shower stall, a bottle of green apple shampoo alongside a container of jojoba conditioner. Blonde hairs were caught in the hairbrush.

They had given him an occupied room, one that was already temporarily home to a woman. He felt anger and embarrassment, both on her behalf and his own. How would she have reacted had she returned to her suite to find an elderly man snoozing in an armchair by her bed? Would she have screamed? He thought that the shock of a woman yelling at him in a strange bedroom might have been enough to hasten his mortality, and he was momentarily grateful that it had not come to such a pass.

He was already composing a tirade in his head when he heard the main door open, and a woman stepped into the room. She was wearing a red hat and cream mac, both of which she discarded on the bed along with two shopping bags from a pair of chichi clothing stores. Her back was to him, and her blonde hair was tied up loosely at the back of her head, held in place by a leather clip. Now that the coat was gone, he saw her lemon sweater and her white skirt, her bare legs and the tan sandals on her feet.

Then she turned and stared straight at him. He did not move. He felt his lips form a word, and he spoke her name, but she did not hear him.

No, he thought, this is not possible. This cannot be.

It was her, yet not her.

He was looking not at the face of the woman who had died barely a year before, her features heavily lined by old age and the depredations of the disease that had taken her, her hair thinning and grey, her body small, almost birdlike, where she had shrunken into herself during those final months, but at the face of another who had lived by that name in the past. This was his wife as she once was, as she had been before their children were born. This was his beloved as a young woman – thirty, perhaps, but no more than that. And as he gazed at her, he was taken aback by her beauty. He had always loved her, had always thought her beautiful, even at the end, but the photographs and memories could not do justice to the girl who had first entranced him, and about whom he had felt as never before or since about a woman.

She moved towards him. He uttered her name again, but there

was no response. As she reached the bathroom he stepped aside, performing a neat little dance that left him outside the room and her inside. Then the door closed in his face, and he could hear the sounds of clothing being removed and, despite his astonishment, he found himself walking away to give her a little privacy, humming a tune to himself as he always did in moments of confusion or distraction. In the short time that he had been asleep, the world appeared to have changed once again, but he no longer had any understanding of his place in it.

He heard the toilet flush, and she emerged, humming the same tune. She cannot see me, he thought. She cannot see me, but can she somehow hear me? She had not responded when he called her name, yet now here she was, sharing a song with him. It might have been coincidence, and nothing more. After all, it was one of their mutual favourites, and perhaps it was hardly surprising that, when she was alone and content, she would hum it softly to herself. He had, by definition, never seen her alone. True, there were times when she had been unaware of his presence for a time, allowing him to watch as she moved unselfconsciously through some of the rhythms and routines of her day, but such occasions were always brief, the spell broken by her recognition of his presence, or his belief that there were vital matters to which he had to attend. But truly, how important had they been? After she died, he would have given up a dozen of them – no, a hundred, a thousand – for just one more minute with her. Such was hindsight, he supposed. It made every man wise, but wise too late.

None of this was relevant. What mattered was that he was looking at his wife as she had once been, a woman who could not now be but somehow was. He went through some of the possibilities: a waking dream, perhaps, or a hallucination brought on by tiredness and travel. But he had smelled her as she passed, and he could hear her now as she sang, and the weight of her footsteps left impressions on the thick carpet that remained visible for a moment before the strands sprang back into place.

I want to touch you, he thought. I want to feel your skin against mine.

She unlocked her suitcase and began unpacking her clothes, hanging blouses and dresses in the closet and using the drawer on the left for her underwear, just as she did at home. He was so close to her now that he could hear her breathing. He spoke her name once more, his breath upon her neck, and it seemed to him that, for an instant, she lost her place in the song, stumbling slightly on a verse. He whispered again, and she stopped entirely. She looked over her shoulder, her expression uncertain, and her gaze went straight through him.

He reached out a hand and brushed his fingers gently against the skin of her face. It felt warm to the touch. She was a living, breathing presence in the room. She shivered and touched the spot with her fingertips, as though troubled by the presence of a strand of gossamer.

A number of thoughts struck him almost simultaneously.

The first was: I will not speak again. Neither will I touch her. I do not want to see that look upon her face. I want to see her as I so rarely saw her in life. I want to be at once a part of, and apart from, her existence. I do not understand what is happening, but I do not wish it to end.

The second thought was: if she is so real, then what am I? I have become insubstantial. When I saw her first, I believed her to be a ghost, but now it seems that it is I who have become less than I once was. Yet I can feel my heart beating, I can hear the sound my spittle makes in my mouth, and I am aware of my own pain.

The third thought was: why is she alone?

They had always arrived together to celebrate their anniversary. It was their place, and they would always ask for this room because it was the one in which they had stayed that first night. It did not matter that the decor had changed over the years or that the suite was, in truth, identical to half a dozen others in the hotel. No, what mattered was the number on the door, and the memories that the sight of them evoked. It was the thrill of returning to – how had she once put it? – 'the scene of the crime', laughing in that low way of hers, the one that always made him want to take her to bed. On those rare occasions that the room was not available, they would feel a sense of disappointment that cast the faintest of shadows over their pleasure.

He was seeing her in their place, but without him. Should he not also be here? Should he not be witnessing his younger self with her, watching as he and she moved around each other, one resting while the other showered, one reading while the other dressed, one (and, in truth, it was always he) tapping a foot impatiently while the other made some final adjustment to hair or clothing? He experienced a sensation of dizziness, and his own identity began to crumble like old brickwork beneath the mason's hammer. The possibility came to him that he had somehow dreamed an entire existence, that he had created a life with no basis in reality. He would awake and find that he was back in his parents' house, sleeping in his narrow single bed, and there would be school to go to, with ball practice afterwards, and homework to be done as daylight faded.

No. She is real and I am real. I am an old man, and I am dying, but I will not let my memories of her be taken from me without a fight.

Alone. She had come here alone. Or alone, for now. Was there another on his way, a lover, a man familiar or unknown to him? Had she once betrayed him in this room, in *their* room? The possibility was more devastating to him than if she had never existed. He retreated, and the pain inside him grew. He wanted to grasp her arms, to demand an explanation. Not now, he thought, not at the very end, when all that I have been waiting for is to be reunited with her at last; or, if there is nothing beyond this world, to lose myself in a void where there is no pain, and her loss can no longer be felt but merely absorbed into the greater absence beyond.

He sat heavily in the chair. The telephone rang, but whether in his world or hers, he did not know. They were layered, one on top of the other, like twin pieces of film, each containing a different actor. His wife, her shoes now discarded, skipped across the floor to the bed and picked up the receiver.

'Hello? Hi. Yes, everything's fine. I got here okay, and they gave us our room.' She listened. 'Oh no, that's too bad. When do they think they'll be able to fly you out? Well, at least you won't miss the entire stay.' Silence again. He could hear the tinny voice on the other end of the line, and it was his own. 'Well, it makes sense to stay at an airport motel, then, just in case. It won't be as nice as here, though.' Then she laughed, sensual and throaty, and he knew what had been said, knew because he had said it, could almost remember the exact words, could recall nearly every minute of that weekend, because now it was coming back to him and he felt a flurry of conflicting responses to the dawning knowledge. He felt relief, but also shame. He had doubted her. Right at the close, after all their years together, he had thought of her in a way that was unworthy. He wanted to find a way to apologize to her, but could not.

'I'm sorry,' he whispered, and to acknowledge his fault aloud gave him some relief.

He went through his memories of that time. Snow had hit the airport, delaying all flights. He had been cutting it pretty tight that day, for there were meetings to attend and people to see. His was the last flight out, and he had watched the board as it read 'delayed', then 'delayed' again, and finally, 'cancelled'. He endured a dull evening at an airport motel so that he would be close enough to catch the first flight out the next morning, if the weather lifted. It had, and they spent the next night together, but it was the only occasion on which they had found themselves apart on the eve of their anniversary, she in their room and he in another, eating pizza from a box and watching a hockey game on TV. Recalling it now, it had not been such a bad night, almost an indulgence of sorts, but he would rather have spent it with her. There were few nights, over the entire forty-eight-year history of their marriage, that he would not rather have spent by her side.

There was something else about that night, something that he could not quite remember. It nagged at him, like an itch in his recall demanding to be scratched. What was it? He cursed his failing memory, even as another emotion overcame him.

He was conscious of a sense of envy towards his younger self. He was so brash then, so caught up in his own importance. He sometimes looked at other women (although he never went further than looking) and he occasionally thought of his ex-girlfriend, Karen, the one who might have been his wife. She left to attend a small, exclusive college in the north-east with the expectation that he would follow, when instead he went elsewhere, choosing to stay closer to home. They had tried to make it work at a distance, but it had not, and there were moments in the early years of his marriage when he had thought about what it might have been like to be married to Karen, of how their children might have looked and how it might have been to sleep each night next to her, to wake her in the dark with a kiss and feel her respond, her hands upon his back, their bodies slowly entwining. In time, those thoughts had faded, and he dwelt in the present of his choosing, grateful for all that it – and she – had brought him. But that same young man, carefree and careless, would arrive the next morning, and take his beautiful wife to bed, and he would not yet understand how fortunate he was to have her.

She hung up the phone and sat on the bed, running her fingers across the stone of her engagement ring before tracing circles around the gold band that sat below it. She stood and then, as he remained in his chair, aware now of flurries of snow falling outside, she drew the curtains, turned on the bedside lamps so that the room was lapped by warm light, and began to undress.

And it was given to him to be with her that night, both distantly yet intimately. He sat on the bathroom floor as she bathed, his cheek against the side of the tub, her head resting on a towel, her eyes closed as the radio in the room played an hour of Stan

Getz. He was beside her as she sat on the bed in a hotel robe, a towel wrapped around her head, painting her toenails and laughing at some terrible comedy show that she would never have watched had he been present, and he found himself laughing along with her as much as with it. She ordered room service – a Cobb salad, with a half-bottle of Chablis – and he saw the fingerprints she left upon the chilled glass. He followed the words on the page as she read a book that he had given her, one that he had just finished and thought she might like. Now he read along with her, the contents of the book long since forgotten, so that together they both discovered it anew

At last, she removed the towel and shook out her hair, then took off the robe and put on a nightdress. She climbed beneath the sheets, turned out the light, and rested her head upon the pillow. He was alone with her, her face almost luminescent in the dark, yet pale and indistinct. He felt sleep approach, but he was afraid to close his eyes, for he knew in his heart that she would be gone when he awoke, and he wanted this night to last. He could not take being separated from her again.

But the itch was still there, the sense that there was an important, salient element to this that he could not quite recall, something linked to a long-forgotten conversation that had occurred when he had finally found his way to this room. It was coming back to him; slowly, admittedly, but he was discovering more pieces of that weekend in the cluttered attic of his memory. There had been lovemaking, yes, and afterwards she had been very quiet. When he looked down at her, he saw that she was crying.

'*What is it?*'

'*Nothing.*'

'*It can't be nothing. You're crying.*'

'*You'll think I'm being silly.*'

'*Tell me.*'

'*I had a dream about you.*'

Then it was gone again. He tried to remember what that

dream had been. It was relevant, somehow. Everything about that night was relevant. Beside him, his young wife's breathing altered as she descended deeper into sleep. He bit his lip in frustration. What was it? What was he failing to recall?

His left arm felt numb. He supposed that it was the position in which he was resting. He tried to move, and the numbness became pain. It extended quickly through his system, like poison injected into his bloodstream. He opened his mouth and a rush of air and spittle emerged. He experienced a tightness in his chest, as though an unseen presence were now sitting astride him, constricting his breathing and somehow compressing his heart so that he saw it as a red mass grasped in a fist, the blood slowly being squeezed from it.

'*I dreamt that you were beside me, but you were in distress, and I couldn't reach you. I tried and tried, but I couldn't get to you.*'

He heard her voice from afar, the words returning to him as an echo. He had held her, and stroked her back, touched by the strength of her feelings yet knowing in his heart that he thought her foolish for responding to a dream in this way.

She moved in her sleep, and now it was he who was crying, the pain forcing tears from the corners of his eyes.

'*I dreamt that you were dying, and there was nothing I could do to save you.*'

I am dying, he thought to himself. At last, it has come.

'Hush,' said his wife. He looked at her, and although her eyes were still closed her lips moved, and she whispered to him: 'Hush, hush. I am here, and you are here.'

She shifted in the bed, and her arms reached out and enfolded him in their embrace. His face was buried in her hair, and he smelled her and touched her in his final agony, his heart exploding deep within him, all things coming to an end in a failure of blood and muscle. She clasped him tightly to herself as the last words he would ever speak emerged in a senseless tangle.

Before the darkness took him.

Before all was stillness and silence.
'Hush,' she said, as he died. 'I am here.'
My god, I love you so.
Hush.
Hush.
And he opened his eyes.

Lazarus

I

He wakes in darkness, constricted by bonds. There is stone beneath him, and the air that he breathes is rank and still. He seems to recall that he has heard a voice calling his name, but it is silent now. He tries to get to his feet, but the bonds around him hinder his movements. There is no feeling in his legs. He cannot see, and he struggles to breathe through the cloth on his face. He begins to panic.

There is a sound, stone upon stone. Light breaks, and he shuts his eyes against it as it pierces the fabric. Now there are hands on him, and he is raised from the stone. Fingers gently remove the coverings. He feels tears upon his cheeks, but they are not his own. His sisters are kissing him, and speaking his name.

'Lazarus! Lazarus!'

Yes, that is his name.

No, that is not his name.

It was once, but Lazarus is no more, or should not be. Yet Lazarus is here.

A man stands before him, his robes covered in the dust of many miles. Lazarus recognizes him, beloved of his sisters, beloved of himself, but he cannot speak his name. His vocal cords have atrophied in the tomb.

The tomb: he stares down as the last of the grave wrappings are torn from his body, and a sheet is thrown over him to hide his nakedness. He looks behind him at the stone that has been removed from the mouth of the cave.

Sickness: he was ill. His sisters mopped his brow, and the

physicians shook their heads. In time they believed him to be dead, so they wrapped him in bandages and laid him in a cave. A mistake was made, and now it has been rectified.

But this is a lie. He knows it even before the thought has fully formed. Some great wrong has been committed in the name of pity and love. The one whom he recognized, the beloved, touches him, and calls his name. Lazarus's lips move, but no sound comes forth.

What have you done? he tries to say. What have you taken from me, and from what have I been taken?

II

Lazarus sits at the window of his sisters' house, a plate of fruit untouched before him. He has no appetite, but neither can he taste any of the food that has been given to him in the days since his return. He still struggles to walk, even with the aid of a pair of sticks, but where would he go? This world holds no beauty for him, not after the tomb.

Lazarus does not remember what happened when his eyes closed for the last time. He knows only that he has forgotten something, something very important and beautiful and terrible. It is as though a roomful of memories has been sealed up, and what was once known to him is now forbidden. Or perhaps it is all merely an illusion, just as it seems to him that the reality of his existence is obscured by gauze, a consequence of the four days spent lying on the stone, for his eyes now have a milky cast to them, and are no longer blue, but grey.

His sister Martha comes and takes the plate away. She brushes his hair from his forehead, but she no longer kisses him. His breath smells foul. He cannot taste the decay in his mouth, but he knows that it is there from the expression on her face. Martha smiles at him, and he tries to smile back.

Outside the window, women and children have gathered to

gaze upon he who was once dead, but is dead no longer. They are amazed, and curious, and—

Yes, fearful. They are afraid of him.

He leaves the window, and staggers to his bed.

III

Lazarus can no longer sleep. He is terrified of the darkness. When he closes his eyes, he smells the fetid air of the tomb, and feels the bandages tight around his chest, and the fabric blocking his mouth and nostrils.

But Lazarus is never tired. He is never hungry, or thirsty. He is never happy, or sad, or angry, or jealous. There is only lethargy, and the desire for sleep without the necessity of it.

No, not sleep: oblivion. Oblivion, and what lies beyond it.

IV

On the third night, he hears footsteps in the house. A door opens, and a woman appears. It is Rachel, his betrothed. She had been in Jerusalem when he woke, and now she is here. She runs her hands across his brow, his nose, his lips. She lies beside him and whispers his name, anxious not to wake his sisters. She leans over to kiss his lips, and recoils, but her fingers continue to move down over his chest and his belly, finding him at last, stroking, coaxing, her face slowly creasing in confusion and disappointment.

She leaves, and never returns.

V

The priests summon Lazarus. He is brought before their council, and made to stand below the dais of the high priest, Caiaphas.

Lazarus's voice has returned, but it is an imperfect thing, as though his throat is coated with grit and dirt.

'What do you recall of the tomb?' they ask, and he replies, 'Nothing but dust and darkness.'

'In the four days that you lay dead, what did you see?'

And he replies, 'I do not remember.'

Caiaphas dismisses the rest, so that only he and Lazarus remain. Caiaphas pours wine, but Lazarus does not drink.

'Tell me,' says Caiaphas. 'Now that the others have gone, tell me what you saw? Did you glimpse the face of God? Does He exist? Tell me!'

But Lazarus has nothing to offer him, and eventually Caiaphas turns his back and tells him to return to his sisters.

It is not the first time that Lazarus has been asked such questions. Even his sisters have tried to find out what lies beyond the grave, but in response he has been able only to shake his head and tell them what he told the priests.

Nothing. There is nothing, or nothing that I can remember.

But no one believes him. No one wants to believe him.

VI

Caiaphas calls another council, but this time Lazarus is not present.

'Is there no sign of the one who summoned him from the tomb?' he asks, and the Pharisees reply that the Nazarene has hidden himself away.

Caiaphas is displeased. With each day that goes by, he grows more resentful of Lazarus. The people are unhappy. They have heard that Lazarus can remember nothing of what he experienced after his death, and some have begun to whisper that there is nothing to remember, that perhaps the priests have lied to them. Caiaphas will not have his power challenged.

He orders the stoning of three men who were overheard

discussing Lazarus in this manner. They will serve as an example to the others.

VII

Lazarus burns his hand on a hot iron. He does not notice until he tries to release his grip, and instead leaves a patch of skin behind. There is no pain. Lazarus would find this curious, except that Lazarus no longer finds anything curious. The world holds no interest for him. He cannot taste, or smell. He does not rest, and instead experiences every day as a kind of waking dream. He stares at his raw, bleeding palm, then explores it with his fingers, tentatively at first before finally tearing at the flesh, ripping it apart until the bones are exposed, desperate to feel anything, anything at all.

VIII

A woman asks Lazarus if he can contact her son, who died in his sleep two days before, and with whom she had argued before he went to bed. A man asks him to tell his dead wife that he is sorry for being unfaithful to her. The brother of a man lost at sea asks Lazarus to find out where his brother buried his gold.

Lazarus cannot help them.

And all the time, he is confronted by those who question him about what lies beyond, and he cannot answer. He sees the disappointment in their eyes, and their suspicion that he is lying.

IX

Caiaphas is troubled. He sits in the darkness of the temple, and prays for guidance, but no guidance comes.

In the case of Lazarus and the Nazarene, there are only so many possibilities that he can consider.

i) The Nazarene is, as some whisper, the Son of God. But Caiaphas does not like the Nazarene. On the other hand, Caiaphas loves God. Therefore, if the Nazarene really is the Son of God, then Caiaphas should love him too. Perhaps the fact that Caiaphas does not love the Nazarene means that the Nazarene is not, in fact, the Son of God, for if he were, then Caiaphas would love him too. Caiaphas decides that he is comfortable with this reasoning.

ii) If the Nazarene is not the Son of God, then he does not have the power to raise the dead.

iii) If the Nazarene does not have the power to raise the dead, then what of Lazarus? The only conclusion to be drawn is that Lazarus was alive when he was placed in the tomb but, had he been left there, he would most assuredly be dead by now. Thus, Lazarus *should* be dead, and his continued refusal to accept this fact is an offence against nature, and against God.

Caiaphas decides that he is no longer quite as troubled as before, and goes to his bed.

X

Rachel is released from her obligations to Lazarus, and marries another. Lazarus watches from an olive grove as the bride and groom arrive at the wedding feast. He sees Rachel, and remembers the night that she came to him. He tries to understand how he should feel at this time, and counterfeits envy, grief, lust, and loss, a pantomime of emotions watched only by birds and insects. Eventually he sits in the dirt and puts his head in his hands.

Slowly, he begins to rock.

XI

The Nazarene returns in triumph to Bethany. The people hope that he will give them answers, that he will tell them how he accomplished the miracle of Lazarus, and if he is now prepared to do the same again, for there have been further deaths since last he came to that place, and who is he to say that the grief of Martha and Mary was greater than that of another? A woman whose child has died carries the infant in her arms, its body wrapped in white, the cloth stained with blood and tears and dirt. She holds up the corpse, and begs the Nazarene to restore the infant to her, but there are too many others shouting, and her voice is lost in the babble. She turns away, and makes the preparations for her child's funeral.

The Nazarene goes to the house of Martha and Mary, and eats supper with them. Mary bathes his feet with ointment and dries them with her hair while Lazarus looks on, unspeaking. Before the Nazarene leaves, Lazarus asks for a moment with him.

'Why did you bring me back?' he asks.

'Because you were beloved of your sisters, and beloved of me.'

'I do not want to be here,' says Lazarus, but the people have gathered at the door, and the Nazarene's disciples pull him away, concerned that there may be enemies among the crowd.

And then he is gone, and Lazarus is left alone.

XII

Lazarus stands at a window, listening to the sound of Rachel and her husband making love. A dogs sniffs at him, and then licks his damaged palm. It nibbles on his tattered flesh, and he watches it blankly.

Lazarus stares at the night sky. He imagines a door in the

blackness, and behind that door is what he has lost. This world is an imperfect facsimile of what once was, and all that should be.

He returns home. His sisters no longer speak to him. Instead, they gaze at him with cold eyes. They wanted their brother back, but all that they loved of him remains in the tomb. They wanted fine wine, but all they received was an empty flask.

XIII

The priests come for Lazarus again, arriving under cover of darkness. They make a great deal of noise – enough, he thinks, to wake the dead, were the dead man in question not already awake – but his sisters do not come to investigate. This time he is not brought before the council, but is taken into the desert, his arms tied behind his back, his mouth stuffed with a rag. They walk until they come at last to the tomb in which he had once been laid. They carry him inside, and place him on the slab. The rag is removed from his mouth, and Lazarus sees Caiaphas approach.

'Tell me,' Caiaphas whispers. 'Tell me, and all will be well.'

But Lazarus says nothing, and Caiaphas steps back in disappointment.

'He is an abomination,' he tells the others, 'a thing undead. He does not belong among us.'

Once again, Lazarus is bound with bandages, until only his face remains uncovered. A priest steps forward. In his hand he holds a grey stone. He raises it above his head.

Lazarus closes his eyes. The stone falls.

And Lazarus remembers.

Holmes on the Range:
A Tale of the Caxton Private Lending Library & Book Depository

The history of the Caxton Private Lending Library & Book Depository has not been entirely without incident, as befits an institution of seemingly infinite space inhabited largely by fictional characters who have found their way into the physical realm.

For example, the death of Charles Dickens in June 1870 precipitated the single greatest mass arrival of characters in the Caxton's history. Mr Torrans, the librarian at the time, at least had a little warning of the impending influx, for he had received a large quantity of pristine Dickens first editions in the post a few days earlier, each carefully wrapped in brown paper and string, and without a return address, as was traditional. No librarian had ever quite managed to figure out how the books came to be sent; old George Scott, Mr Torrans's predecessor, had come to the conclusion that the books simply wrapped and posted themselves, although by that stage Scott was quite mad, and spent most of his time engrossed in increasingly circular conversations with Tristram Shandy's Uncle Toby, of which no good could possibly have come.

For those unfamiliar with the institution, the Caxton came into being after its founder, William Caxton, woke up one morning in 1477 to find a number of characters from Geoffrey Chaucer's *Canterbury Tales* arguing in his garden. Caxton quickly realized that these characters – the Miller, the Reeve, the Knight, the Second Nun, and the Wife of Bath – had become so fixed in the public imagination that they had transcended their literary origins and assumed an objective reality, which was problematical for all concerned. Somewhere had to be found for them to live, and thus the Caxton Private Lending Library & Book Depository was established as a kind of rest home for the great, the good and, occasionally, the not-so-good-but-definitely-memorable, of literature, all supported by rounding up the prices on books by a ha'penny a time.

Of course, Mr Torrans had been anticipating the appearance of the Dickens characters long before the death of the author himself, and the subsequent arrival of the first editions. Some characters were simply destined for the Caxton from the moment that they first appeared in print, and Mr Torrans would occasionally wander into the darker realms of the Caxton, where rooms were still in the process of formation, and try to guess which figures were likely to inhabit them. In the case of Dickens, the presence of a guide to the old coaching inns of Britain provided a clue to the future home of Samuel Pickwick, and a cheap bowl and toasting fork would serve as a reminder to Oliver Twist of the terrible early start to life that he had overcome. (Mr Torrans was of the opinion that such a nudge was unnecessary under the circumstances, but the Caxton was mysterious in its ways.)

In fact, Mr Torrans's only concern was that the characters might include rather more of the unsavoury sort than he would have preferred – he was not sure what he would do if forced to deal with a Quilp, or a Uriah Heep – so it came as a great relief to him when, for the most part, the influx was restricted to the more pleasant types, with the exception of old Fagin, who appeared to have been mellowed somewhat by the action of the noose. Hanging, thought Mr Torrans, will do that to a man.

But the tale of the Dickens characters is one for another time. For the present, we are concerned with one of the stranger stories from the Caxton's annals, an occurrence that broke many of the library's long-established rules and seemed destined, at one point, to undermine the entire delicate edifice of the institution . . .

* * *

In December 1893, the collective imagination of the British reading public suffered a shock unlike any in recent memory with the publication in the *Strand Magazine* of 'The Final Problem', in which Arthur Conan Doyle killed off his beloved Sherlock Holmes, sending him over a cliff at the Reichenbach Falls following a struggle with his nemesis, Professor Moriarty. The illustrator Sidney Paget captured the hero's last moments for readers, freezing him in a grapple with Moriarty, the two men leaning to the right, clearly on the verge of falling, Moriarty's hat already disappearing into the void, foreshadowing the inevitable descent of the two men.

The result was a disaster for the *Strand*. Twenty thousand people immediately cancelled their subscriptions in outrage, almost causing the collapse of the periodical, and for years after staff would refer to Holmes's death only as 'a dreadful event'. Black armbands were said to have been worn by readers in mourning. Conan Doyle was shocked by the vehemence of the public's reaction, but remained unrepentant.

It's fair to say that Mr Headley, who by that point had succeeded Mr Torrans as the librarian upon the latter's retirement, was just as shocked as anyone else. He was a regular subscriber to the *Strand*, and had followed the adventures of Holmes and Watson with both personal and professional interest: personal in the sense that he was an admiring, engrossed reader, and professional because he knew that, upon Conan Doyle's death, Sherlock Holmes and Dr Watson would inevitably find their way to the Caxton. Still, he had been looking forward to many more years of their adventures, and so it was with no small amount of regret that he set aside the *Strand* after finishing 'The Final Problem', and wondered what could have possessed Conan Doyle to do such a thing to the character who had brought him both fame and fortune.

But Mr Headley was no writer, and did not profess to understand the ways of a writer's mind.

* * *

Let us step away from the Caxton for a moment, and consider the predicament of Arthur Conan Doyle in the year of publication of 'The Final Problem'. In 1891, he had written to his mother, Mary Foley Doyle, confessing that 'I think of slaying Holmes . . . and winding him up for good and all. He takes my mind from better things.' In Conan Doyle's case, those 'better things' were historical novels, which he believed more worthy of his time and talents than what he described as the 'elementary' Holmes stories, the choice of that word lending an unpleasing ambiguity to Holmes's own use of the term in the tales.

Here, then, was the apparent reason for killing off Holmes, but upon Conan Doyle's death a peculiar piece of manuscript was delivered to the Caxton Private Lending Library, tucked into the 1894 first edition of *The Memoirs of Sherlock Holmes*, the volume that concluded with 'The Final Problem'. It was written in a hand similar to Conan Doyle's own, although with discernible differences in capitalization, and with an extensive footnote relating to the etymology of the word 'professor' that was untypical of the author.

Attached to the manuscript was a letter, clearly written by Conan Doyle, detailing how he woke one morning in April 1893 to find this fragment lying on his desk. According to the letter, he wondered if it might not be the product of some form of automatic writing, for he was fascinated by the possibility of the subconscious – or even some supernatural agency – taking control of the writer in order to produce work. Perhaps, he went on to speculate, he had arisen in the night in a semiconscious state and commenced writing, for aspects of the script resembled his own. Upon the discovery of the manuscript he examined his right hand and discerned no trace of ink upon it, but was astounded to glance at his left and find that both the fingers and the edge of his palm were smudged with black, a revelation which forced him to seek the comfort and security of the nearest chair.

Good Lord, he thought, what can this mean? And, worse,

what consequences might it have for his batting? Could he somehow be transforming into an ambidexter or, God forbid, a favourer of the left hand, a sinister? Left-handed bowlers on the cricket pitch were one thing – they were largely harmless – but left-handed batsmen were a nuisance, necessitating the rearrangement of the field and causing all kinds of fuss, bother and boredom. His mind reeled at the awful possibilities should his body somehow be rebelling against him. He might never be able to take the crease for Marylebone again!

Gradually Conan Doyle calmed himself, and fear gave way to fascination, although this lasted only for as long as it took him to read the manuscript itself. Detailed on its closely written pages was a conversation between Sherlock Holmes and Professor Moriarty, who had apparently taken it upon themselves to meet at Benekey's in High Holborn, a hostelry noted for the privacy offered by its booths and the quality of its wines. According to the manuscript, Moriarty had instigated the meeting by way of a note delivered to 221B Baker Street, and Holmes, intrigued, had consented to sit down with the master criminal.

In his letter, Conan Doyle explained what he found most troubling about the contents of the manuscript upon first perusal: he had only begun writing about Moriarty days earlier, and had barely mentioned him in the course of the as-yet-untitled story. Yet here was Moriarty, seated in Benekey's, about to have the most extraordinary conversation with Sherlock Holmes.

Extract from the manuscript (Caxton CD/ MSH 94: MS)
Holmes regarded Moriarty intensely, his every nerve aquiver. Before him sat the most dangerous man in England, a calculating, cold-blooded, criminal mastermind. For the first time in many years, Holmes felt real fear, even with a revolver cocked in his lap and concealed by a napkin.

'I hope the wine is to your liking,' said Moriarty.

'Have you poisoned it?' asked Holmes. 'I hesitate even to touch the glass, in case you have treated it with some infernal compound of your own devising.'

'Why would I do that?' asked Moriarty. He appeared genuinely puzzled by the suggestion.

'You are my archnemesis,' Holmes replied. 'You have hereditary tendencies of the most diabolical kind. A criminal strain runs in your blood. Could I but free society of you, I should feel that my career had reached its summit.'

'Yes, about that archnemesis bit . . .' said Moriarty.

'What about it?' asked Holmes.

'Well, isn't it strange that it's never come up before? I mean, if I'm your archnemesis, the Napoleon of crime, a spider at the heart of an infernal web with a thousand radiations, responsible for half that is evil in London and all that kind of thing, and you've been tracking me for years, then why haven't you mentioned me before? You know, surely it would have arisen in conversation at some point. It's not the kind of thing one tends to forget, really, is it, a criminal mastermind at the heart of some great conspiracy? If I were in your shoes, I'd never stop talking about me.'

'I—' Holmes paused. 'I've never really thought about it in that way. I must admit that you did pop into my mind quite recently, and distinctly fully formed. Perhaps I took a blow to the head at some stage, although I'm sure Doctor Watson would have noted such an injury.'

'He writes down everything else,' said Moriarty. 'Hard to see him missing something like that.'

'Indeed. I am lucky to have him.'

'I'd consider it a little annoying myself,' said Moriarty. 'It's rather like being Samuel Johnson and finding that, every time you lift a coffee cup, Boswell is scribbling details of the position of your fingers and asking you to say something witty about it all.'

'Well, that is where we differ. It's why I am not a scoundrel.'

'Hard to be a scoundrel when someone is always writing down what one is doing,' said Moriarty. 'One might as well just toddle along to Scotland Yard and make a full confession, thus saving the forces of law and order a lot of fuss and bother. But that's beside the point. We need to return to the matter in hand, which is my sudden arrival on the scene.'

'It is somewhat perturbing,' said Holmes.

'You should see it from my side,' said Moriarty. 'Perturbing isn't the half of it. For a start, I have an awareness of being mathematically gifted.'

'Indeed you are,' said Holmes. 'At the age of twenty-one you wrote a treatise on the binomial theorem, with a European vogue.'

'Look, I don't even know what the binomial theorem is, never mind how it might have gained a European vogue – a description that makes no sense at all, by the way, when you think about it. Surely it's either the binomial theorem or it isn't, even if it's described in a French accent.'

'But on the strength of it you won a chair at one of our smaller universities!' Holmes protested.

'If I did, then name the university,' said Moriarty.

Holmes shifted in his chair. He was clearly struggling. 'The identity of the institution doesn't immediately spring to mind,' he admitted.

'That's because I was never chair of anything,' said Moriarty. 'I'm not even very good at basic addition. I struggle to pay the milkman.'

Holmes frowned. 'That can't be right.'

'My point exactly. Maybe that's how I became an ex-professor, although even that doesn't sound plausible, given that I can't remember how I was supposed to have become a professor in the first place, especially in a subject of which I know absolutely nothing. Which brings me to the next matter: how did you come to be so expert in all that stuff about poisons and types of dirt and whatnot? Did you take a course?'

Holmes considered the question.

'I don't profess to be an expert in every field,' he replied. 'I have little interest in literature, philosophy, or astronomy, and a negligible regard for the political sphere. I remain confident in the fields of chemistry and the anatomical sciences, and, as you have pointed out, can hold my own in geology and botany, with particular reference to poisons.'

'That's all well and good,' said Moriarty. 'The question remains: how did you come by this knowledge?'

'I own a lot of books,' said Holmes, awkwardly. He thought that he could almost hear a slight question mark at the end of his answer, which caused him to wince involuntarily.

'Have you read them all, then?'

'Must have done, I suppose.'

'Either you did or you didn't. You have to recall reading them.'

'Er, not so much.'

'You don't just pick up that kind of knowledge off the street. There are people who've studied dirt for decades who don't know as much about it as you seem to.'

'What are you implying?'

'That you don't actually know anything about dirt and poisons at all.'

'But I must, if I can solve crimes based entirely on this expertise.'

'Oh, *somebody* knows about this stuff – or gives a good impression of it – but it's not you. It's like me being a criminal mastermind. Last night, I decided that I was going to try to commit a perfectly simple crime: jeweller's shop, window, brick. I walk to jeweller's, break window with brick, run away with jewels, and don't look back.'

'And what happened?' asked Holmes.

'I couldn't do it. I stood there, brick in hand, but I couldn't throw it. Instead I went home and contrived an elaborate plan for tunnelling into the jeweller's involving six dwarfs, a bald man with a stoop, and an airship.'

'What has an airship got to do with digging a tunnel?' asked Holmes.

'Exactly!' said Moriarty. 'More importantly, why do I need six dwarfs, never mind the bald man with the stoop? I can't think of any situation in life where the necessity of acquiring six men of diminished stature might arise, or none that I care to bring up in public.'

'On close examination, it does seem to be excessively complicating what would otherwise be a fairly simple act of theft.'

'But I was completely unable just to break the window and steal the jewels,' said Moriarty. 'It wasn't possible.'

'Why not?'

'Because I'm not written that way.'

'Excuse me?'

'It's not the way I was written. I'm written as a criminal mastermind who comes up with baroque, fiendish plots. It's against my nature even to walk down the street in a straight line. Believe me, I've tried. I have to duck and dive so much that I get dizzy.'

Holmes sat back, stunned, almost dropping the revolver from his hand at the realization of his own true nature. Suddenly, it all made sense: his absence of anything resembling a past; his lack of a close familial bond with his brother, Mycroft; the sometimes extraordinary deductive leaps that he made, which baffled even himself.

'I'm a literary invention,' he said.

'Precisely,' said Moriarty. 'Don't get me wrong: you're a good one – certainly better than I am – but you're still a character.'

'So I'm not real?'

'I didn't say that. I think you have a kind of reality, but you didn't start out that way.'

'But what of my fate?' said Holmes. 'What of free will? If all this is true, then my destiny lies in the hands of another. My actions are predetermined by an outside agency.'

'No,' said Moriarty, 'we wouldn't be having this conversation if that were the case. My guess is that you're becoming more real with every word the author writes, and a little of it has rubbed off on me.'

'But what are we going to do about it?' asked Holmes.

'It's not entirely in our hands,' said Moriarty.

And with that he looked up from the page . . .

* * *

And that was where the manuscript ended: with a fictional character engaged in a virtual staring contest with his creator. In his letter, Conan Doyle described letting the papers fall to the floor, and in that moment Sherlock Holmes's fate was sealed.

Holmes was a dead man.

Thus began the extraordinary sequence of events that would come to imperil the Caxton Private Lending Library & Book Depository. Conan Doyle completed 'The Final Problem', consigning Holmes to the Reichenbach Falls and leaving only his trusty Alpinestock as a sign that he had ever been there at all. The public seethed and mourned, and Conan Doyle set out to immerse himself in the historical fictions that he believed would truly make his reputation.

Mr Headley, meanwhile, went about the business of the Caxton which, for the most part, consisted of making pots of tea, dusting, reading, and ensuring that any of the characters who wandered off – as some of them were inclined to do – returned before nightfall. Mr Headley had once been forced to explain to an unimpressed policeman why an elderly gent in homemade armour seemed intent upon damaging a small ornamental windmill that stood at the heart of Glossom Green, and had no intention of having to go through all that again. It was difficult enough trying to understand how Don Quixote had ended up in the Caxton to begin with, given that his parent book had been written in Spanish. Mr Headley suspected that it was something to do with the proximity of the first English translations of Cervantes's work in 1612 and 1620 to their original publication in Spanish in 1605 and 1615. Then again, the Caxton might simply have got confused. It did that, sometimes.

So it came as some surprise to him when, one Wednesday morning, a small, flat parcel arrived at the Caxton, inexpertly wrapped in brown paper, and with its string poorly knotted. He opened it to find a copy of that month's *Strand Magazine* containing 'The Final Problem'.

'Now that can't be right,' said Mr Headley, aloud. He had already received his subscription copy, and had no use for a second. But the nature of the parcel, with its brown paper and string, gave him pause for thought. He examined the materials and concluded that, yes, they were the same as those used to deliver first editions to the Caxton for as long as anyone could remember. Never before, though, had they protected a journal or magazine.

'Oh dear,' said Mr Headley.

He began to feel distinctly uneasy. He took a lamp and moved through the library, descending – or ascending; he was never sure which, for the Caxton's architectural nature was as individual and peculiar as everything else about it – into its depths (or heights) where the new rooms typically started to form upon the arrival of a first edition. No signs of activity were apparent. Mr Headley was relieved. It was all clearly some mistake on the part of the *Strand*, and the paper and string involved in the magazine's delivery only coincidentally resembled those with which he was most familiar. He returned to his office, poured himself a mug of tea, and twisted up the newly arrived copy of the *Strand* for use in the fireplace. He then read a little of Samuel Richardson's epistolary epic *Clarissa*, which he always found conducive to drowsiness, and settled down in his chair for a nap.

He slept for longer than intended, for when he woke it was already growing dark outside. He set kindling for the fire, but noticed that the twisted copy of the *Strand* was no longer in the storage basket and was instead lying on his desk, entirely intact and without crease.

'Ah,' said Mr Headley. 'Well.'

But he got no further in his ruminations, for the small brass bell above the office door trilled once. The Caxton Private Lending Library didn't have a doorbell, and it had taken Mr Headley a little time to get used to the fact that a door without a doorbell could still ring. The sound of the bell could mean only one thing: the library was about to welcome a new arrival.

Mr Headley opened the door. Standing on the step was a tall, wiry man, with a high brow and a long nose, dressed in a deerstalker hat and a caped coat. Behind him was an athletic-looking gent with a moustache, who appeared more confused than his companion. A slightly oversized bowler hat rested on his head.

' "*Holmes gave me a sketch of events*",' said Mr Headley.

'I beg your pardon?' said the man in the bowler hat, looking even more confused.

'Paget,' said Mr Headley. '"The Adventure of Silver Blaze", 1892.' For the two men could have stepped straight from that particular illustration.

'Still not following.'

'You're not supposed to be here,' said Mr Headley.

'Yet here we are,' said the thinner of the two.

'I think there's been a mistake,' said Mr Headley.

'If so, it won't be resolved by forcing us to stand out here in the cold,' came the reply.

Mr Headley's shoulders slumped.

'Yes, you're right. You'd better come in, then. Mr Holmes, Doctor Watson: welcome to the Caxton Private Lending Library and Book Depository.'

Mr Headley lit the fire, and while doing so tried to give Holmes and Watson a brief introduction to the library. Initially there was often a certain amount of shock among new arrivals, who sometimes struggled to grasp the reality both of their own physicality and their fictional existence, as one should, in theory, have contradicted the other. Holmes and Watson seemed to have little trouble with the whole business, though. As we have already seen, Holmes had been made aware of the possibility of his own fictional nature thanks to the efforts of ex-Professor Moriarty, and had done his best to share something of this understanding with Watson before his untimely demise at the hands of his creator.

'By the way, is my archnemesis here?' asked Holmes.

'I'm not expecting him,' said Mr Headley. 'You know, he never seemed entirely real.'

'No, he didn't, did he?' agreed Holmes.

'To be honest,' Mr Headley went on, 'and as you may have gathered, I wasn't expecting you two gentlemen either. Characters usually only arrive when their authors die. I suspect it's because they then become fixed objects, as it were. You two are the first to come here while their author is still alive and well. It's most unusual.'

Mr Headley wished that there was someone he could call, but old Torrans was long dead, and the Caxton operated without the assistance of lawyers, bankers, or the institutions of government, or at least not with the active involvement of any of the above. Bills were paid, leases occasionally secured, and rates duly handed over to the authorities, but it was all done without Mr Headley having to lift a finger. The workings of the Caxton were so deeply ingrained in British society that everyone had simply ceased to notice them.

Mr Headley poured the two guests some tea and offered them biscuits. He then returned to the bowels – or attic – of the library, and found that it had begun to create suitable living quarters for Holmes and Watson based on Paget's illustrations, and Watson's descriptions, of the rooms at 221B Baker Street. Mr Headley was immensely relieved, as otherwise he would have been forced to make up beds for them in his office, and he wasn't sure how well Holmes might have taken to such sleeping arrangements.

Shortly after midnight, the library finished its work on 221B, complete with a lively Victorian streetscape beyond the windows. The Caxton occupied an indeterminate space between reality and fiction, and the library was not above permitting characters access to their own larger fictional universes, should they choose to step outside their rooms for a time. Many, though, preferred either to doze – sometimes for decades – or take the occasional constitutional around Glossom village and its environs, which at least had the merit of being somewhere new and different. The inhabitants of the village tended not to notice the characters unless, of course, they started tilting at windmills, talking about witches in a Scottish accent, or enquiring about the possibility of making a suitable marriage to entirely respectable single, or even attached, gentlemen.

Once Holmes and Watson were ensconced in their quarters, Mr Headley returned to his office, poured himself a large brandy, and detailed the events of the day in the Caxton's records, so that future librarians might be made aware of what he had gone through. He then retired to his bed, and dreamed that he was holding on by his fingertips to the edge of a precipice while the Reichenbach Falls tumbled thunderously beneath him.

After this mild hiccup, the life of the library proceeded largely without incident over the following years, although the activities of Holmes and Watson were not entirely unproblematical for Mr Headley. They were fond of making forays into Glossom and beyond, offering to assist bemused officers of the law with investigations into missing kittens, damaged milk churns, and the possible theft of a bag of penny buns from the noon train to Penbury. Their characters having ingrained themselves in the literary affections of the public, Holmes and Watson were treated as genial eccentrics. They were not alone in dressing up as the great detective and his amanuensis, for it was a popular activity among gentlemen of varying degrees of sanity, but they were unique in actually being Holmes and Watson, although obviously nobody realized that at the time.

There was also the small matter of the cocaine that found its way into the library on a regular basis. Mr Headley couldn't pin down the source of the drug, and could only conclude that the library itself was providing it, but it worried him nonetheless. God forbid that some perspicacious policeman might detect evidence of narcotics use on Holmes, and contrive to follow him back to the Caxton. Mr Headley wasn't sure what the punishment might be for running a drug den, and had no desire to find out, so he begged Holmes to be discreet about his intake, and reserve it for the peace and quiet of his own rooms.

Otherwise, Mr Headley was rather delighted to have as residents of the library two characters of whom he was so enamoured, and spent many happy evenings in their company, listening as they discussed the details of cases about which he had read, or testing Holmes's knowledge of obscure poisons and types of tobacco. Mr Headley also continued to subscribe to the *Strand*, for he generally found its contents most delightful, and had no animosity towards it for publishing Holmes's last adventure since he was privileged to have the man himself beneath his roof. He tended to be a month or two behind in his *Strand* reading, though, for his preference remained books.

Then, in August 1901, this placid existence was disturbed by a most unexpected development. Mr Headley had taken himself away to Clackheaton to visit his sister Dolly, and upon his return found Holmes and Watson in a terrible state. Holmes was brandishing the latest copy of the *Strand* and demanding loudly, 'What's this? What's this?'

Mr Headley pleaded, first for calm, and then for the offending journal, which was duly handed over to him. Mr Headley took the nearest chair and, once he had recovered from his surprise, read the first instalment of *The Hound of the Baskervilles*.

'It doesn't mention my previous demise,' said Holmes. 'There's not a word about it. I mean, I fell over a waterfall, and I'm not even wet!'

'We'll have to wait and see,' said Mr Headley. 'From my reading, it seems to be set prior to the events at the Reichenbach Falls, as otherwise Conan Doyle would surely have been forced to explain your reappearance. Don't you have any memory of this case, Holmes – or you, Doctor Watson, of recording its details?'

Both Holmes and Watson told him that the only details of the *Hound* of which they were aware were those they had read, but then admitted that they were no longer entirely certain whether those memories were the result of reading the first instalment, or if their own personalities were being altered to accommodate the new story. Mr Headley counselled caution, and advised Holmes and Watson not to over-react until they learned more about the tale. Mr Headley made some discreet enquiries of the *Strand*, but the magazine's proprietors were tight-lipped about the return of Holmes to their pages, grateful only for the spike in subscriptions brought by his reappearance, and Mr Headley's efforts were all for naught.

So he, along with Holmes, Watson, and the British reading public, was forced to wait for the arrival of each new monthly instalment of the story in order to try to discern Conan Doyle's intentions for his creations. As time went on, though, it became clear that the story was indeed historical in nature, preceding the events of 'The Final Problem'. As an experiment, Mr Headley withheld the conclusion from Holmes, and then questioned him about its contents. Holmes was able to describe in detail how Rodger Baskerville had embezzled money in South America, taken the name Vandeleur, and opened a school in Yorkshire that closed following a descent into infamy, all of which was revealed in the final part of the story that Holmes had yet to read. From this they were able to establish that Conan Doyle, by revisiting his characters, was effectively creating new memories for Holmes and Watson which, although mildly troubling for them, was not a disaster.

Nevertheless, Mr Headley was unable to assuage a growing sense of impending doom. He began to keep a very close eye on the *Strand* and similar journals, and paid particular attention to any and all rumours about Conan Doyle's literary activities.

The rumblings began in the autumn of 1903. Mr Headley did his best to keep them from Holmes until, at last, the October edition of the *Strand* was delivered to the Caxton, and his worst fears were realized. There, handsomely illustrated by Paget, was

'The Adventure of the Empty House', marking the return of Sherlock Holmes, albeit initially disguised as an elderly book collector. Mr Headley read the story in the back office of the Caxton, with the door locked and a desk pushed against it for added security, locked doors being no obstacle to any number of the library's residents, Holmes among them. (Mr Headley had endured a number of awkward conversations with the Artful Dodger who, the librarian was convinced, was stealing his biscuits.)

To be perfectly honest, the explanation of how Holmes had survived the incident at the Reichenbach Falls strained Mr Headley's credulity, involving, as it did, the baritsu martial art and a gravitationally unlikely ability to topple from a cliff yet somehow land on a path, or perhaps not fall and just appear to land on a path, or appear to fall and—

Never mind. Some business about Tibet, Lhasa, and Khartoum followed, and dressing up as a Norwegian, and it all made Mr Headley's head hurt, although he admitted to himself that this was due in part to the potential consequences of this Sherlock Holmes's return for the Caxton's Holmes. He would have to be told, of course, unless he was already aware of it due to a sudden change in his memories, and a previously unsuspected ability to speak Norwegian.

Mr Headley felt that he had no choice but to visit the rooms of Holmes and Watson to find out the truth for himself. He moved the desk, unlocked the door, and headed into the library, stopping off in the dictionary section along the way. He found Watson napping on a couch, and Holmes doing something with phials and a Bunsen burner that Mr Headley suspected might not be entirely unrelated to the production of narcotics.

Mr Headley took in the dozing figure of Watson. One additional unpleasant piece of information contained in 'The Adventure of the Empty House' was that Watson's wife, Mary, seemed to have died. This might have been more awkward had it not been for the fact that the Watson living in the Caxton had no memory of being married at all, perhaps because his wife hadn't figured much in the stories, or not in any very consequential way, and therefore hadn't made much of an impact on anyone involved. Still, Mr Headley would have to mention Mary's demise to him. It wasn't the sort of thing one could brush under the carpet.

For now, though, his main concern was Holmes.

'Everything all right, Mr Holmes?' asked Mr Headley.

'Is there any reason why it shouldn't be?' Holmes replied.

He didn't even look up from his workbench. A sweet, slightly spicy scent hung in the room. It made Mr Headley's head swim.

'No, no, none at all. Um, is that a drug I smell?'

'I'm experimenting', said Holmes, quite tartly, and, thought Mr Headley, not a little defensively.

'Right, of course. Just, er, be careful, please.'

There was a vent in the wall behind Holmes's head. Mr Headley wasn't entirely certain where it led, but he still lived in fear of that mythical policeman sniffing the air and, once he'd recovered his senses, organizing a raid.

Mr Headley cleared his throat and enunciated, as clearly as he could:

'Goddag, hvor er du?'

Holmes looked at him peculiarly.

'What?'

'Lenge siden sist,' said Mr Headley.

'Are you feeling all right?'

Mr Headley glanced at the small Norwegian phrase book in his hand.

'Jo takk, bare bra. Og du?'

'Are you speaking . . . Norwegian?'

Watson woke.

'What's all this?' he asked.

'Headley appears to have struck his head,' Holmes explained, 'and is now under the impression that he's Norwegian.'

'Good Lord,' said Watson. 'Tell him to sit down.'

Mr Headley closed his phrase book.

'I haven't hit my head, and I don't need to sit down,' he said. 'I was just wondering, Mr Holmes, if by any chance you spoke Norwegian?'

'I have never had any cause to learn the language,' said Holmes. 'I did wrestle with *Beowulf* in my youth, though, and obviously there are certain similarities between Old English and Norwegian.'

'Have you ever heard of a Norwegian explorer named Sigerson?' asked Mr Headley.

'I can't say that I have,' said Holmes. He was now regarding Mr Headley with a degree of suspicion. 'Why do you ask?'

Mr Headley decided to sit down after all. He wasn't sure if it was good or bad news that the Caxton's Holmes had not begun producing new memories due to the return of his literary self. Whichever it was, he could not hide the existence of the new story from Holmes. Sooner or later, he was bound to find out.

Mr Headley reached beneath his jacket and removed the latest edition of the *Strand*.

'I think you should read it,' he told Holmes.

He then turned to Dr Watson.

'I'm sorry to have to tell you this,' said Mr Headley, 'but your wife has died.'

Watson considered the news for a moment.

'What wife?'

The three men sat in Mr Headley's office, the copy of the *Strand* lying on the table before them. The occasion called for something stronger than coffee, so Mr Headley had broken out his bottle of brandy and poured each of them a snifter.

'If he's me,' said Holmes, not for the first time, 'and I'm him, then I should have his memories.'

'Agreed,' said Mr Headley.

'But I don't, so I can't be this Holmes.'

'No.'

'Which means that there are now two Holmeses.'

'It would appear so.'

'So what happens when Conan Doyle eventually dies? Will this second Holmes also show up here?'

'And the second Doctor Watson,' added Watson, who was still perturbed to have discovered that he was once married, an arrangement of which he had begun to dredge up some vague memories, possibly dating back to *The Sign of the Four*. 'I mean, we can't have two of us – er, four of us – trotting about. It will just be disconcerting.'

'And which of us would be the real Holmes and Watson?' added Holmes. 'Obviously, we're the originals, so it should be us, but it could be a messy business explaining that to the rival incumbents for the positions, so to speak. Worse, what if this new Holmes and Watson usurp us in the public imagination? Will we just cease to exist?'

They all looked rightly shocked at this possibility. Mr Headley was very fond of this Holmes and Watson. He didn't want to see them gradually fade away, to be replaced at some future date by alternative versions of themselves. But he was also concerned about what the arrival of a new Holmes and Watson might mean for the Caxton. It could potentially open the way to all kinds of calamitous conjunctions. Suppose non-canonical versions of characters began to appear on the doorstep, making claims for their own reality and sowing unrest? The result would be chaos.

And what about the library itself? Mr Headley understood that an institution as complex and mysterious as the Caxton must also, on some level, be extraordinarily delicate. For centuries, reality and unreality had remained perfectly balanced within its walls. That equilibrium might now be threatened by Conan Doyle's decision to resurrect Holmes.

'There's nothing else for it,' said Holmes. 'We shall have to go to Conan Doyle and tell him to stop writing these stories.'

Mr Headley blanched.

'Oh no,' he said. 'You can't do that.'

'Why ever not?'

'Because the Caxton is a secret establishment, and has to remain that way,' said Mr Headley. 'No writers can ever know of its existence, otherwise they'd start clamouring for immortality for their characters and themselves. That has to be earned, and can only come after the author's death. Writers are terrible judges of these things, and if they knew that there was a kind of pantheon for characters here in Glossom, then we'd never hear the end of it.

'Worse, imagine what might happen if the Caxton's existence became public knowledge? It would be like London Zoo. We'd have people knocking on the doors day and night, asking for a peek at Heathcliff – and you know what he's like – or, God forbid, a conversation with David Copperfield.'

There was a collective sigh. It was widely known in the Caxton that to ask David Copperfield even the simplest of questions required one to set aside a good portion of one's day to listen to the answer.

'Nevertheless,' said Holmes, 'I can see no other option for us. This is our existence that is at stake – and, perhaps, that of the Caxton too.'

Mr Headley drained his glass, and paused for only a moment before pouring himself another generous measure.

Oh dear, he thought. Oh dear, oh dear, oh dear.

Preparations for the journey were quickly made. Mr Headley locked up the library, having first informed a few of the more balanced residents of the reason for the trip, even though he knew that his absence would barely be noticed by most of the others. They could spend weeks and months – even years – in slumber, only waking when a publisher reissued their parent book in a new edition, or when a critical study caused a renewal of interest in their existence.

'Please try not to attract too much attention,' pleaded Mr Headley, as he paid for three first-class tickets to London, although even as the words left his mouth he realized how pointless they were. After all, he was boarding a train with two men, one of whom was wearing a caped coat, a deerstalker hat, and shiny new shoes with white spats, and could not have looked more like Sherlock Holmes if he had started declaring loudly that—

'The game is afoot, Watson!' shouted a cheery voice from nearby. 'The game is afoot!'

'God give me strength,' said Mr Headley.

'Your friend,' said the ticket clerk. 'Does he think he's, you know . . . ?'

'Yes,' said Mr Headley. 'In a way.'

'Harmless, is he?'

'I believe so.'

'He won't go bothering the other passengers, will he?'

'Not unless they've committed a crime,' replied Mr Headley.

The ticket clerk looked as though he were seriously considering summoning some stout chaps in white coats to manage the situation, but Mr Headley grabbed the tickets before he could act and hustled his charges in the direction of the carriage. They took their seats, and it was with some relief that Mr Headley felt the train lurch and move off without anyone appearing to haul them away.

Many years later, when he had retired from the Caxton in favour of Mr Gedeon, the new librarian, Mr Headley would recall that journey as one of the happiest of his life, despite his nervousness at the impending encounter with Conan Doyle. As he watched Holmes and Watson from his seat by the door – Holmes on the right, leaning forward animatedly, the index finger of his right hand tapping the palm of his left when he wished to emphasize a point, Watson opposite him, cigar in hand, one leg folded over the other – Mr Headley felt as though he were part of one of

Paget's illustrations for the *Strand*, so that he might have stepped from his own life into the pages of one of Conan Doyle's adventures. All readers lose themselves in great books, and what could be more wonderful for a reader than to find himself in the company of characters that he has long loved, their lives colliding with his own, and all being altered by the encounter? Mr Headley's heart beat in time with the rhythm of the rails, and the morning sun shone its blessings upon him.

Sir Arthur Conan Doyle stepped from the crease at Marylebone Cricket Club, his bat cradled beneath his right arm. He had enjoyed the afternoon's out-of-season practice, and felt that he had acquitted himself well, all things considered. He was by no means good enough for England, a fact that troubled him only a little, but he could hit hard, and his slow bowls were capable of disconcerting batsmen far more capable than he.

Conan Doyle had also largely forgotten the shock caused some years earlier by the apparent somnambulistic use of his left hand to write a scrap of Holmesian manuscript. For many months after he had approached the cricket field with a sense of trepidation, fearing that, at some inopportune moment, his left hand, as though possessed, might attempt to take control of his bat, like some horror out of a story by Hauff or Marshe. Thankfully, he had been spared any such embarrassment, but he still occasionally cast his left hand a suspicious glance when his batting went awry.

He changed, made his farewells, and prepared to travel to his hotel, for he had work to do. Initially he had returned with a hint of resignation and a mild sense of annoyance to writing about Sherlock Holmes, but 'The Adventure of the Empty House' had turned out better than anticipated: in fact, he had already begun to regard it as one of the best of the Holmes stories, and the joy and acclaim that greeted its appearance in the *Strand*, combined with the honour of a knighthood the previous year, had reinvigorated Conan Doyle. Only the continued ill health of his beloved Toulie still troubled him. She remained at Undershaw, their Surrey residence, to which he would travel the following day in order to spend the weekend with her and the children. He had found another specialist to consult about her condition, but secretly he held out little hope. The tuberculosis was killing her, and he could do nothing to save her.

Conan Doyle had just turned onto Wellington Place when a small, thin man approached him. He had the look of a clerk, but was well dressed, and his shoes shone in the sunlight. Conan Doyle liked to see a man taking care of his shoes.

'Sir Arthur?' enquired the man.

Conan Doyle nodded, but didn't break his stride. He had never quite grown used to the fame brought upon him by Holmes, and had learned at an early stage of his literary career never to stop walking. Once you stopped, you were done for.

'Yes?'

'My name is Headley,' said the man. 'I'm a librarian.'

'A noble profession,' said Conan Doyle heartily, quickening his pace. Good God, a librarian. If this chap had his way, they might be here all day.

'I have some, er, colleagues who are most anxious to make your acquaintance,' said Mr Headley.

'Can't dawdle, I'm afraid,' said Conan Doyle. 'Very busy. If you drop a line to the *Strand*, I'm sure they'll see what they can do.'

He made a sharp turn to the left, wrong-footing Mr Headley, and quickly crossed the road to Cochrane Street, trying to give the impression of a man with life or death business to contract. He was almost at the corner when two figures stepped into his path, one of them wearing a deerstalker hat, the other a bowler.

'Oh Lord,' said Conan Doyle. It was worse than he thought. The librarian had brought along a pair of idiots who fancied themselves as Holmes and Watson. Such men were the bane of his life. Most, though, had the common decency not to accost him on the street.

'Ha ha,' he said, without mirth. 'Very good, gentlemen, very good.'

He tried to sidestep them, but the one dressed as Holmes was too quick for him, and blocked his way.

'What the devil do you think you're doing?' said Conan Doyle. 'I'll call a policeman.'

'We really do need to talk, Sir Arthur,' said Holmes – or 'Holmes', as Conan Doyle instinctively branded him in his mind. One had to nip these things in the bud. It was why inverted commas had been invented.

'We really do not,' said Conan Doyle. 'Out of my way.'

He brandished his walking stick at his tormentor in a vaguely threatening manner.

'My name is Sherlock Holmes—' said 'Holmes'.

'No, it isn't,' said Conan Doyle.

'And this is Doctor Watson.'

'No, it's not. Look, I'm warning you, you'll feel my stick.'

'How is your left hand, Sir Arthur?'

Conan Doyle froze.

'What did you say?'

'I asked after your left hand. I see no traces of ink upon it. You have not found yourself writing with it again, then?'

'How could you know of that?' asked Conan Doyle, for he had told no one about that unfortunate experience of April 1893.

'Because I was at Benekey's. You put me there, along with Moriarty.'

'Holmes' – or now, perhaps, Holmes – stretched out a hand.

'I'm very pleased to meet you at last, Sir Arthur. Without you, I wouldn't exist.'

The four men sat at a quiet table in Ye Olde Cheshire Cheese off Fleet Street, to which they had travelled together in a hansom cab. Mr Headley had done his best to explain the situation to Conan Doyle along the way, but the great man was clearly still trying to fathom the reality of the Caxton and its characters. Mr Headley could hardly blame him. He himself had needed a long lie-down after old Torrans had first revealed the nature of the Caxton to him, and he could only imagine how much more traumatic it might be for Conan Doyle with the added complication of witnessing his two most famous creations lunching before him on pea soup. Conan Doyle had settled for a single malt Scotch, but it looked like another might be required before long.

At Conan Doyle's request, Holmes had dispensed with the deerstalker hat, which now hung on a hook alongside his long coat. Without it, he might simply have been a regular client of Ye Olde Cheshire Cheese, albeit one with a certain intensity to his regard.

'I must admit, gentlemen, that I'm struggling with these revelations,' said Conan Doyle. He looked from Holmes to Watson and back again. Almost involuntarily, his right hand moved, the index finger extending, as though he wished to poke them to confirm their corporeality, the sound of Watson slurping his soup notwithstanding.

'It's hardly surprising,' said Mr Headley. 'In a way, they're a testament to the power of your imagination, and the depth of your creations. Never before in the Caxton's history has a writer lived to see his own characters come to life.'

Conan Doyle took another sip of his whisky.

'If more writers did,' he replied, 'it might well be the death of them.'

Holmes set aside his soup.

'Sir Arthur,' he said, 'Mr Headley has explained the situation to you as best he can. It's most difficult and worrying, and we can see only one solution to the problem. I appreciate that it might place you in an awkward position, but you must stop writing about Sherlock Holmes.'

Conan Doyle shook his head.

'I can't,' he said. 'I've reached an agreement with *Collier's Weekly*. Not only that, but the public will see me hanged if I've raised their hopes of more adventures only to shatter them within a month. And then, gentleman, there is the small matter of my finances. I have a sick wife, two young children, and houses to maintain. Would that my other literary endeavours had brought me greater success, but no one mentions Rodney Stone in the same breath as Holmes and Watson, and I cannot think of the reviews for *A Duet* without wanting to hide in my cellar.'

'But the more Holmes stories you write, the more likely it is that you'll bring a second Holmes – oh, and Watson—'

'Thank you, Holmes.'

– 'into being,' said Holmes. 'Would you want a second Sir Arthur wandering the streets, or worse, moving into your home? Think of William Wilson. You might end up stabbing yourself with a sword!'

Mr Headley leaned forward.

'Sir Arthur, you now know that the fabric of reality is far more delicate than you imagined,' he said. 'It may be that the consequences of two versions of Holmes and Watson having a physical presence might not be so terrible, whatever the personal or professional difficulties for the characters involved, but there is also the possibility that the entire existence of the Caxton might be undermined. The more the reading public starts to believe in this new incarnation of Holmes, the greater the chance of trouble for all of us.'

Conan Doyle nodded. He suddenly looked tired, and older than his years.

'Then it seems that I have no choice,' he said. 'Holmes must fall again, and this time he cannot return.'

Dr Watson coughed meaningfully. The others looked at him. The good doctor had finished his soup, for it was a pea-based delicacy of the highest order, but all the while he had been listening to what was being said. Dr Watson was much wiser than was often credited. His lesser light simply did not shine as brightly next to the fierce glow of Holmes.

'It seems to me,' he said, 'that the issue is one of belief. You said it yourself, Mr Headley: it is readers as much as writers who bring characters alive. So the solution . . .'

He let the ending hang.

'Is to make the new Holmes less believable than the old,' Holmes concluded. He patted Watson hard on the back, almost causing his friend to regurgitate some soup. 'Watson, you're a marvel.'

'Much obliged, Holmes,' said Watson. 'Now, how about pudding?'

Sir Arthur Conan Doyle never visited the Caxton Private Lending Library, although an open invitation was extended to him. He felt that it was probably for the best that he kept his distance for, as he told Mr Headley, if he needed to spend time with the great characters of literature, he could simply pick up a book. Neither did he ever again meet Holmes and Watson, for they had their own life in his imagination.

Instead he carefully set out to undermine the second incarnation of his creations, deliberately interspersing his better later stories with tales that were either so improbable in their plots and solutions as to test the credulity of readers to breaking point – 'The Adventure of the Sussex Vampire' being among the most notable – or simply not terribly good, including 'The Adventure of the Missing Three-Quarter', 'The Adventure of the Golden Pince-Nez', or 'The Adventure of the Blanched Soldier'. He even dropped in hints of more wives for Watson, whom he didn't actually bother to name. The publication of such tales troubled him less than it might once have done, for even as he tired of his inventions he understood that, with each inconsequential tale, he was ensuring the survival of the Caxton, and the continued happiness of his original characters.

Yet his strange encounter with the Caxton had also given Conan Doyle a kind of quiet comfort. In the years following his meeting with Holmes and Watson, he lost his first wife, and, in the final weeks of World War I, his son Kingsley. He spent many years seeking proof of life after death, and found none, but his knowledge of the Caxton's existence, and the power of belief to incarnate fictional characters, to imbue them with another reality outside the pages of books, gave him the hope that the same might be possible for those who had been taken from him in this life. The Caxton was a world beyond this one, complete and of itself, and if one such world could exist, then so might others.

Shortly after Conan Doyle's death in July 1930, copies of the first editions of the Holmes tales duly arrived at the library, including *The Memoirs of Sherlock Holmes* with its enlightening manuscript addition. By then Mr Gedeon was the librarian, and he, Holmes, and Watson endured a slightly nervous couple of days, just in case the plan hatched by Watson and enacted by Conan Doyle had not worked, but no new incarnations of Holmes and Watson appeared on their doorstep, and a strange warm gust of wind blew through the Caxton, as though the great old institution had just breathed its own sigh of relief.

A small blue plaque now stands on the wall of the Caxton, just above the shelf containing the Conan Doyle collection. It reads: 'In Memory of Sir Arthur Conan Doyle, 1859–1930: For Services to the Caxton Private Lending Library & Book Depository.'

I Live Here

This is a true story. I've changed one or two small details, but no more than that. It seemed appropriate that, in the discussion of supernatural fiction to follow, I should somehow manage to sneak in something which is not quite fiction at all.

Writers are, in general, solitary beings. Oh, we mix with friends, and family, and one another. Some of us even manage to form relationships that last long enough to produce offspring. There is always a part of us, though, that prefers to be alone. We keep it walled off. It is this hidden aspect that enables us to be writers.

There was a time when publishers were content to permit writers to be themselves – that is, to let them write, and make no demands upon their time other than the occasional interview with a suitably serious literary journal or newspaper, or the signing of some pages for a limited edition to be sold through subscriptions, or a lunch with an editor during which wine would be drunk, complaints aired, and rivals belittled.

Now, though, writers are expected to be salesmen and hucksters. We have to promote our wares. We are enjoined to meet our public. Some writers are very good at this, and are happy to do it. Personally, I don't mind the promotional aspect of the job, just as long as it doesn't take up too many hours, for the more hours that I spend away from my desk, the less I write.[1] Overall,

---

1 Mind you, I've become better at writing on the road, if only out of necessity. When I started out as a writer, I was probably a little precious about the whole business, and felt that I couldn't work unless I was at my own

I suspect my readers would prefer to have more of my books to read than the dubious pleasure of my company, but I find that the demands on my time increase commensurately with the number of titles I produce, and I could now spend an entire year merrily promoting my books in various countries, if the mood took me.

For some writers, such touring is a way of bringing in extra income from appearance fees, workshops, and unspent *per diems*. For others, it's simply a break from routine, a chance to see a new city at a publisher's expense, and perhaps catch up with friends and colleagues in exotic surroundings. Again, all of this presupposes that the writer in question enjoys such affairs, and is capable of putting on a bit of a show for the public. This is not always the case. There are writers who should not be allowed out of the house, and should never, under any circumstances, be permitted to meet their public, for it does neither party any favours.

I have seen some writers behave desperately poorly towards their readers, and spent time with others who simply don't know how to behave at all. At a French literary festival I once sat between two American writers of mystery novels with Western settings, neither of whom had the good manners or common

---

desk, and even then I rarely produced more than 1000 words a day, after which I'd require a bit of a lie-down until one of the servants woke me with a restorative brandy and a freshly ironed copy of the evening paper. Now I can write just about anywhere – the middle seat of airplanes, noisy coffee shops, even under the gaze of a TV camera, as I did when a documentary crew was filming in my home. The only thing guaranteed to distract me is a conversation on a cellphone, which is why, in *Bad Men*, my fifth novel, a man is brutally beaten and then shot to death for having the temerity to use a cellphone when a pair of killers are trying to read their newspaper. I wrote that section on the same day that someone had disturbed my reading and writing in a coffee shop by engaging in very loud conversation with someone in Yemen. I'm nothing if not passive-aggressive.

sense to remove his cowboy hat in the lovely converted church in which the session was taking place. I watched as a future winner of the Man Booker Prize turned to his fellow panellists and said, 'Don't you just hate all . . . *this*?' while gesturing disdainfully at a small, damp audience, of which I was a part, that had come out on a miserable night to listen to them speak. In a children's bookstore, I sat with two authors who had collaborated on a series of cynically created but moderately successful books for young adults and listened while they whispered scornfully to each other about their readers.

But no matter: that's not the point of this tale, and writers will, in turn, have stories of drunken members of the public interrupting readings, or rubbishing their efforts, or taking the opportunity offered by audience questions to shill their own self-published work. I have, at various times, been followed through the dark streets of Birmingham by an over-enthusiastic reader, who later wrote to tell me that she'd never stalked anyone before, and was happy that I was her first; been mistaken for the writers Ian Rankin, Michael Connelly, Joe Connelly, and James Patterson, all of whom, I would venture to suggest, are slightly older gentlemen than I, bear no physical resemblance to me whatsoever, and are not even Irish; had water poured over my head, and wine spilled on my nice new trousers; and been kicked in the face by a bookseller in Glasgow who was very anxious that I should take a look at her new shoes. In the end, it's enough to accept that authors now have to publicize their books in a way that their predecessors in a gentler age did not, and one might as well approach the task with a degree of good humour and good-will, and remember that there are far worse ways to earn a living.

So it was that, some years ago, my publicity tour took me to a city in the north-east of England. Quite often, I'll drive myself around on such jaunts, as the journeys between signings offer a little welcome alone time. On this occasion, my publisher's northern sales rep was driving me, which was fine as I have huge affection for him, and he's good company on a long trip. The event was to take place in a city centre library, and was scheduled to start long after most of the shops had closed for business, so the streets were quiet as we made our way to the venue.

The event itself was largely unremarkable, as these things go. There were no fights. Nobody died. I read a little, and talked more, and those in attendance appeared to have a good time – or were polite enough to keep it to themselves if they didn't – and bought some books afterwards. When I visit bookstores and libraries to talk, I'm acutely aware that people have other things that they could be doing instead, and I try to make the evening pass as entertainingly as possible. If nothing else, I'd like people to leave with a feeling of pleasant surprise at how painless the whole business was, and have them consider attending another at some point in the future, rather than have them vow to cut their own feet off before they ever again darken the doors of a literary event.

Finally, when I thought that the members of the public had all departed, an older lady, who had been waiting quietly in a corner, approached the table at which I was seated. A younger woman, clearly in attendance to offer some form of moral or even physical support, hovered uncertainly behind her.

'Mr Connolly?' said the older lady. 'I have a question to ask.'

It was late, and I was signing books for the local bookshop, but I can multitask to some degree. I told her that I'd be happy to answer any questions she might have, if I could. She seemed nervous, frightened even. I rarely have that effect on people. I try not to, to be honest. It's bad for sales.

'I've read your books,' she said, her voice shaking, 'and I've enjoyed them a great deal. I have a difficulty, and I was hoping that you might be able to help me with it.'

She was very serious. She did not smile. I set aside the book that I was signing.

'Go on,' I said.

'There is a house here in the town,' she said. 'Something bad lives inside it. It's dangerous. It hates everything, but it hates children most of all. I live near this house. I watch it, and I do my best to keep children away from it, but I'm getting old, and I'm going to die soon. Somebody has to watch that house when I'm gone. What I was wondering is: do you have any knowledge of such things, or would you be aware of anyone who has?'

She waited for a reply. I looked at the sales rep standing beside me. He looked at me. We both then looked at the old woman.

Here's the thing: on occasions such as this, one tends to assume that people may be slightly mad. It's terrible, I know, but it's true. Perhaps 'mad' is the wrong word. 'Eccentric' might be more appropriate.

Except that this woman didn't look mad. I know that it's not easy to judge, and I'm no expert. Quite frankly, if we could spot madness just by looking in someone's eyes then a great many tragedies might be averted. But the woman appeared to be in full possession of her wits, as far as I could tell. She was also definitely very, very scared.

'Are you talking about an exorcist?' I asked.

'No,' she said. 'We've had the house blessed, but it did no good. I don't think that this presence is ever going to leave. I suppose I was hoping that you'd know if there were "watchers" – you know, people who guard old, dangerous places.'

But I didn't, of course, because I'm not really that kind of person.

I'm this kind of person.

I am frequently asked if I believe in the supernatural, but my direct experience of any realms beyond this one is minimal to the point of non-existence. I consider myself to be a healthy sceptic: it may be that ghosts exist, but I've never seen one. On the evening that my father's body was taken to the church to await its funeral Mass and burial the next morning, the inhabitants of our house – which included my mother and brother, along with a visiting aunt and uncle – were woken in the dead of night by the sound of loud snoring. My father was a terrible snorer, and this was snoring on a quite epic scale. My mother, brother, aunt and uncle gathered on our landing to listen to it. I was the only person who was not there, as I was fast asleep. I later suggested that it might have been me that they heard, although my mother assured me this was not the case. I was quite relieved, as I didn't want to be labelled the kind of snorer who could wake an entire house, even if it meant entertaining as an alternative explanation the possibility of some intervention from the afterlife. Anyway, what I'm saying is that even when my own childhood home may or may not have experienced some form of paranormal visitation, I remained completely unaware of it. It may be that any number of ex-girlfriends are right, and I am just unusually insensitive.

My interest in matters ghostly is largely literary in origin. I have been fascinated by stories of the supernatural ever since childhood. Initially, I hunted down anthologies aimed at younger readers, including works that claimed to be nonfiction but strained the credulity of even my pre-teen self, but I quickly progressed to more adult fare.

During the writing of this little essay, I returned to the bedroom of my childhood home in Rialto to look for evidence of my juvenile fascination with the uncanny.[2] On the shelf by my bed, I found the following:

The Pan Book of Horror Stories (1959), edited by Herbert van Thal
All editors of volumes of horror stories should have surnames like 'van Thal'. Herbert van Thal was born Bertie Maurice van Thal, but Bertie – or Maurice – van Thal doesn't have quite the same ring about it and, if nothing else, Herbert (or Bertie) had a

---

2 I should say that my bedroom remains very much as it did when I left Rialto some decades ago. I like to think that my mother has preserved it as a shrine to my genius, just in case any scholars of my work decide they need to immerse themselves in the details of my early life, although I rather suspect she'd be quite happy if I'd just clear all the rubbish out so she can put it to better use.

fairly sure knowledge of the trappings of the uncanny. The Pan collections run to thirty volumes, although van Thal edited only the first twenty-five before death put an end to his anthologizing. The first is still probably the best, featuring stories by Bram Stoker ('The Squaw') and Muriel Spark ('The Portobello Road') among others. As the covers became more lurid – which is saying something, as they were never exactly understated to begin with – the quality of the tales inside grew steadily worse. They also, if I remember correctly, became a bit seedy, but I may just have been easily shocked. Still, this book was certainly among my first introductions to supernatural fiction, and I therefore owe van Thal a debt of gratitude. Incidentally, my friend Professor Darryl Jones, himself a fine anthologist of supernatural fiction, assures me that van Thal was also known as the ugliest man in London, which, if true, seems strangely appropriate.

The Hammer Horror Film Omnibus (1973)/*The Second Hammer Horror Film Omnibus* (1974), both by John Burke
During my childhood and early adolescence, horror films were a staple of BBC2's Saturday night television programming. This invariably took the form of a double bill, the first of which was typically an earlier Hammer horror with, therefore, little or no nudity, while the second tended towards the more adult. I was, unfortunately, cursed with parents who didn't really go out much at weekends, and their interest in watching horror films on a Saturday night was less than zero. In fact, my first exposure to the Hammer oeuvre came through my best friend at the time, whose family had a holiday home in Rush, Co. Dublin.

I never quite understood why a family would bother buying a holiday home that was only about half an hour away from where they lived. It seemed to defeat the whole notion of holidays as being a break from the norm. Then again, my father disliked holidaying in any location a) to which he could not drive; and b) which might cost him money, so most of my summers were spent in my grandmother's cottage near Ballylongford, Co. Kerry, where my father could holiday for free while keeping a close eye on his car.

Anyway, Dan's parents (let's call him Dan, because that was his name) were considerably more liberal than my own mum and dad, especially when it came to the viewing habits of their three children, so they were quite happy to let us all sit up and watch 1966's *Dracula, Prince of Darkness* on their small black and white portable television.

The film, as you may already have guessed, was a revelation to me. I had never seen anything like it before, and it is still one of my clearest movie-watching recollections, even after almost forty years. I still believe that *Dracula, Prince of Darkness* is the best of Christopher Lee's outings as the Count, helped by the fact that Lee had not yet begun to tire of his association with the role, although the absence of Peter Cushing, who graced *Dracula* (1958) as Van Helsing, is regrettable. It should be noted that the film also made a strong impression on Dan, although not entirely a favourable one: he endured a spectacular nightmare as a consequence of watching it, during which he wet the bed, although it would have been more distressing for me if I'd been on the lower bunk. I like to think of it as a lucky escape.

All of this occurred in the days before home video recorders. These were also the days before colour television, at least for anyone I knew. Oh, and my parents never owned a video recorder, so the first time I ever had movies on demand was when I left home and bought my own TV and VCR. Therefore the only way to relive a movie-watching experience during my childhood was to hunt down the novelization of a beloved film and reread it at will. Thus it was that *The Second Hammer Horror Film Omnibus* was a godsend, featuring, as it did, not only *Dracula, Prince of Darkness* in prose form, but also three other Hammer films that I had not yet seen – and wouldn't get to see for many years to come.

Among these was *The Reptile*, which, like *Dracula, Prince of Darkness*, was released in 1966. (This was a pretty good year for

Hammer, as it also saw the appearance of *Rasputin: The Mad Monk*, featuring Christopher Lee in the title role, and the possibly not-entirely-historically-accurate *One Million Years B.C.*, starring Raquel Welch in a fur bikini.) Many years later, I would write a story entitled 'Miss Froom, Vampire', which was produced for BBC Radio 4 by my friend Lawrence Jackson.[3] Lawrence persuaded Jacqueline Pearce, who had starred as the unfortunate Anna in *The Reptile*, to read the story. By that point Pearce was better known for playing the evil Servalan in the BBC science fiction series *Blake's 7*, and for appearing in a state of quite spectacular nakedness in Michael Radford's 1987 film *White Mischief*.

I was fortunate enough to attend the recording of the story in London, and to be able to confess in person the extent of the crush I'd had on Jacqueline for the best part of twenty-five years. Even in her seventh decade, and recovering from cancer, she was splendidly glamorous, and marvellous company. I don't think I'd ever met an actress of the old school before, all 'Darling!' and theatrical anecdotes, and I was distinctly overwhelmed. I took her to dinner at Hakkasan off Tottenham Court Road, and it remains one of my most cherished experiences. She now lives on an animal sanctuary in South Africa. In fact, I've just dropped her an e-mail between writing that last sentence and starting this one. She's a link to my earliest affection for the supernatural, and if nothing else comes of this odd little essay, it has at least led me to get in touch with her once again. (Her reply has just come through, and begins 'Darling Heart!' God, she's a star.)

Since we're on the subject of *Dracula*, it would be churlish to continue without making some reference to its creator, Bram Stoker. I've only recently noticed that at No. 30 Kildare Street

---

3 Originally the stories were to be broadcast late at night, but someone at the BBC had the bright idea of putting them on in the early afternoon slot, just as parents were bringing their children home from school. There were, I believe, complaints.

– across from the stop where I occasionally catch a bus home[4] – is a plaque celebrating the fact that Stoker once lived there, which I hadn't realized, as most of the focus on Stoker in Dublin tends to revolve around his birthplace in Clontarf. The plaque on No. 30 was, as I subsequently learned, erected by the Bram Stoker Society, which was formed in 1980 around the corner in Trinity College, Dublin, which was Stoker's alma mater – he graduated in 1870 with honours in science – and, indeed, my own.

A word about the Bram Stoker Society: when I was studying at Trinity, which was from 1988 to 1992, the Bram Stoker Society was notorious for the depth of its devotion to the great man, to the extent that if you were taking the college air, and inadvertently confessed to a modest affection for Stoker's work, there was a genuine fear that members of the Bram Stoker Society would descend like birds of prey and spirit you away to some dark room where you would be forced to watch endless Hammer reruns until you clawed your eyes from your head. Even to mention in passing that your grandfather was a stoker on a ship raised the possibility of having a symposium spontaneously organized around you.

---

4 People of my acquaintance occasionally express surprise that I still take the bus, assuming that, at a certain point, I must surely have felt obliged to abandon such nonsense and hire a chauffeur. In fact, a former neighbour of mine was quite shocked to hear that I caught the bus into the city, and seemed to regard taking public transport as being on a par with pimping one's offspring, or trapping pigeons for food. I was once catching the bus into Dublin city centre shortly after Christmas, and took the only available seat beside an older lady who, I couldn't help but notice, kept casting sideways glances at me. Eventually she tapped me on the arm and said, 'The old books not doing so well, are they?' I think I was rendered speechless for a moment, before I managed to puff out that I was on the bus not because I had fallen on hard times, but because I quite liked taking public transport, to which her immortal reply was, 'Ah, you do, yeah', spoken in a tone of what I can only describe as aggressive disbelief.

In their defence, the members of the Bram Stoker Society were engaged in a fairly thankless task. At that time, Trinity College – and possibly Dublin city as a whole – was happy to trumpet its connections to former alumni such as Oscar Wilde and Samuel Beckett, whose work could safely be regarded as literature. (Actually, the university's English Department wasn't even very keen on allowing students to study writers who weren't already dead and buried, and therefore unlikely to tarnish their legacy by producing a late period work promoting pederasty or white supremacy.) Stoker, by contrast, was a whole different kettle of slightly wrong-smelling fish. If Trinity College had an attic, his legacy would have been stored there. It is to the credit of the Bram Stoker Society that its members persevered in the face of a general lack of enthusiasm for the promotion of Stoker's literary works, even if they did make folk a bit nervous in the process.

Stoker's writing career is problematical, though. To borrow a baseball metaphor, he knocked the ball out of the park with his fifth novel, *Dracula* (1897). Unfortunately, to extend the metaphor, it was his only ball, and he never quite managed to find it again. He subsequently tried to capitalize on the boom in Egyptology with *The Jewel of Seven Stars* (1902) and, um, the boom in stories about women who are secretly giant serpents with *The Lair of the White Worm* (1911), but I recall both as being fairly joyless reading experiences, although *The Lair of the White Worm* at least has the merit of being completely bonkers whereas *The Jewel of Seven Stars* is just dull. As for *The Lady of the Shroud* (1909), in which the titular heroine feigns vampirism for reasons which were not entirely clear to me when I read the novel, and probably weren't entirely clear to Stoker either, the less said the better.

This is not to say that Stoker's post-*Dracula* career is entirely without interest. 1914 saw the posthumous publication of *Dracula's Guest and Other Weird Stories*, which collected a number of Stoker's best works of short fiction, including 'The

Judge's House' (1891), 'The Squaw' (1893) and 'Dracula's Guest' itself, which was deleted from an early draft of *Dracula*, and was probably originally written as the novel's opening chapter.

But Stoker can be forgiven a lot simply for the gift of *Dracula*, and the book has aged well. It uses the structure of the epistolary novel – a form that somehow managed to survive the exquisite tedium of Samuel Richardson's *Pamela* (1740) and his later *Clarissa* (1748), a book so long that even starting it is to laugh in the face of one's own inevitable mortality – but adapts it to include newspaper cuttings, and Dr Seward's recordings to his phonograph, which, even now, give it a curious modernity, and suggest a fragmentary approach that resonates with some of the literary experiments of the next century.

Francis Ford Coppola, in his unfairly maligned 1992 film of the novel, captures this sense of technological development by referencing the early days of cinema. Unfortunately, no amount of innovation or directorial experimentation can save Coppola's *Dracula* from two deeply awful acting performances. The second-worst comes from Keanu Reeves, who has never before or since more justified the generally unfair epithet 'Canoe Reeves', and less inhabits the role than has it whittled out of him. But he is put in the ha'penny place by Anthony Hopkins as Van Helsing who, over the space of two hours, produces more ham than a slaughterhouse, and appears to be preparing for his bewildering effort in *Legends of the Fall* two years later, in which, as Colonel William Ludlow, he gives the Academy of Motion Picture Arts and Sciences just cause to reclaim the Oscar that he previously won for *The Silence of the Lambs*.[5]

---

5 I'm tempted to argue that winning the Best Actor Oscar for playing Dr Hannibal Lecter was the worst thing that could have happened to Hopkins in terms of his craft, since – with a couple of honourable exceptions, namely *The Remains of the Day* and *Shadowlands* – it appeared to lead him to assume that there really was no such thing as overacting, and caricature and character amounted to more or less the same thing in Hollywood.

If we were to pinpoint a flaw in Stoker's novel, it would be that the early chapters are so wonderful that the middle and later sections pale somewhat by comparison. The novel is at its best when dealing with Jonathan Harker's arrival in Transylvania, and his early experiences in Dracula's castle, including his first meeting with the Count, and his later glimpse of Dracula crawling headfirst down the sheer wall of his castle as he sets off to hunt. There then follows Harker's seduction by three female vampires, which is interrupted by the return of Dracula, who throws them an infant in a sack upon which to feed. Finally, with Chapter 7, we have the high point of the novel: the wreck of the *Demeter*, the Russian vessel carrying Dracula to England.

The searchlight followed her, and a shudder ran through all who saw her, for lashed to the helm was a corpse, with drooping head, which swung horribly to and fro at each motion of the ship.[6]

The Silence of the Lambs is one of the few films at which I've shed a tear, although I should point out that it was less a question of content than circumstance. I'd just returned from the United States to see my father, who was dying of cancer in hospital, and I felt the urge to hide away somewhere dark afterwards. My then-girlfriend suggested we go to see a movie, and *The Silence of the Lambs* was the only film that happened to be starting at the right time. So we went to the Screen cinema, where I burst into tears about halfway through the show, thereby becoming, I believe, the only person to have wept at *The Silence of the Lambs*. Anyway, we'll come back to Lecter anon.

6 Here Stoker is directly referencing Henry Wadsworth Longfellow's poem 'The Wreck of the *Hesperus*'. ('A frozen corpse was he./Lashed to the helm, all stiff and stark . . .') I know this because Mr Buckley, my first secondary school English teacher, drummed the poem into us with the aid of the business side of a wooden duster liberally applied to the knuckles of those who failed to recall that it was, without doubt, the schooner *Hesperus* that sailed the wintry sea, and the skipper had, quite naturally, taken his little daughter to bear him company. Thanks to the Christian Brothers, I

Stoker then decides to push Dracula largely into the wings for much of what follows, leaving us for company the lunatic entomophage Renfield; Harker's distressed fiancée, Mina Murray; the faux Europeanisms of Van Helsing; and an increasingly peakéd Lucy Westenra. *Dracula* without Dracula is a lot less fun than *Dracula* with Dracula, and these sections drag a bit, before a race back to Transylvania for the grand finale, which Stoker had originally intended to conclude with Dracula falling into a volcano, although sanity subsequently prevailed.

Interestingly, a similar problem exists in Mary Shelley's *Frankenstein; or, The Modern Prometheus* (1818), but since Shelley was only nineteen when she commenced writing it, and it was her first attempt at a novel, a little leeway should be permitted. (In 2014, I was fortunate enough to see Shelley's original manuscript of *Frankenstein* as part of a British Library exhibition entitled *Terror and Wonder: The Gothic Imagination*, and what was most striking about it was that it seemed to have been written in a school jotter, and so resembled a student's English essay homework.)

To read Shelley's novel, even two centuries later, is to be amazed at the depths of this young woman's imagination. Contemporary critics had never encountered anything like it before, and struggled to put it in perspective. The reviewer in *The British Critic* acknowledged that the writing had power 'but this power is so abused and perverted, that we should almost prefer imbecility . . . we must protest against the waking dreams of horror excited by the unnatural stimulants of this later school; and we feel ourselves as much harassed, after rising from the perusal of these three spirit-wearing volumes, as if we had been over-dosed with laudanum, or hag-ridden by the night-mare'.

---

can also recite in its entirety Shylock's 'Mercy Speech' from *The Merchant of Venice*, which amounts to my party piece. Everything else I learned, including the entire physics curriculum and all history with the exception of Operation Barbarossa, I've completely forgotten.

Blackwood's Edinburgh Magazine was kinder, being impressed with 'the author's original genius and happy power of expression', although the reviewer remained under the misapprehension that the author was male, since the book was first published anonymously.

Frankenstein opens brilliantly, as the Walton expedition sails farther and farther north until it becomes trapped in ice, whereupon Victor Frankenstein is discovered on an ice floe, and begins to tell Robert Walton his tale, which Walton in turn recounts to his sister in England. *Frankenstein*, like *Dracula*, is mostly written in epistolary form – a hallmark of English gothic fiction is its use of letters, documents, or fake historical records as a means of encouraging readers to suspend disbelief – but what is most striking is how little of the book is familiar. So much of the imagery associated with Frankenstein and his creation comes to us not from Mary Shelley, but from cinema. Shelley doesn't even inform us of how Victor Frankenstein animates the creature. We're led to assume that electricity plays some part, if only because Frankenstein tells of seeing an oak tree destroyed by lightning when he was a boy, and the impression made upon him by the demonstration of such power, but that's all we get. There is no great creation scene, no lightning striking a rod and coursing through the monster's frame, no cries of 'It's alive!' All of that comes from James Whale's 1931 film. Shelley, instead, gives us this, from Chapter II:

It was on a dreary night in November, that I beheld the accomplishment of my toils. With an anxiety that almost amounted to agony, I collected the instruments of life around me, that I might infuse a spark of being into the lifeless thing that lay at my feet. It was already one in the morning; the rain pattered dismally against the panes, and my candle was nearly burnt out, when, by the glimmer of the half-extinguished light, I saw the dull yellow eye of the creature open; it breathed hard, and a convulsive motion agitated its limbs.

* * *

It's dramatic in its way, but far more understated than its cinematic equivalents – and there have been many screen efforts to depict the monster's birth. We don't even learn how Frankenstein came by the necessary body parts to form his creature, and its appearance is very different from the iconic form of Boris Karloff, complete with flattened head and bolts through the neck. Shelley's monster is eight feet tall, but:

His limbs were in proportion, and I had selected his features as beautiful. Beautiful! – Great God! His yellow skin scarcely covered the work of muscles and arteries beneath: his hair was of a lustrous black, and flowing; his teeth of pearly whiteness; but these luxuriances only formed a more horrid contrast with his watery eyes, that seemed almost of the same colour as the dun-white sockets in which they were set, his shrivelled complexion and straight black lips.

He is also, as we soon learn, superhuman, gifted not only with incredible strength but great speed and agility too, which enable him to flee after he has been rejected by his creator. Then there is his intelligence, which is where the novel takes a bit of an odd turn in its second volume. Frankenstein travels to the Swiss Alps, where he meets his creation again. We learn that the creature has spent many months hidden in a lean-to adjoining a cottage, and through listening to its inhabitants, and reading stolen books, has learned how to speak.

Leaving aside the fact that nobody appears to have spotted the eight-foot tall monster living in the shed, the creature's linguistic advances are pretty remarkable. Unfortunately, he turns out to be a Chatty Cathy, and once he gets started there's no shutting him up as he tells Frankenstein of his many happy hours of shed-dwelling. The novel itself also veers into more conventional territory, as the monster regales his creator with a tale of star-crossed lovers and perfidious Turks, before at last getting down to the main business of the evening, his desire that Frankenstein should create a mate for him, at which point the novel gets interesting all over again in a sexually peculiar way, and reminds us that, yes, it is being written by a precociously gifted teenage girl – a teenage girl, what's more, who was already pregnant with the poet Percy Bysshe Shelley's first child at the age of sixteen or seventeen, Shelley having left his own pregnant wife Harriet for Mary and fled with her to France.

Although that child died shortly after birth, Mary quickly conceived another, despite Shelley's attempts to pimp her to his friend Thomas Jefferson Hogg. Then, still unmarried but calling herself 'Mrs Shelley' instead of Mary Godwin, she ended up at the Villa Diodati in Switzerland in the company of Shelley, Lord Byron – who had himself fled England to avoid an array of financial and sexual scandals, including an affair with his half sister, Augusta Leigh, leaving behind a wife and at least one child – and Byron's personal physician, John Polidori, later to write *The Vampyre*. With each invited by Byron to create a ghost story, Mary, unable to sleep one night, and desperate to meet the poet's challenge, came up with the idea for *Frankenstein* in the course of a 'waking dream', even if the manuscript clearly shows that her lover made editorial suggestions and changes further along the path to publication.

Percy Shelley drowned in 1822 – although by then his attentions had progressed from Mary to Jane Williams: he and Byron were fickle in their affections, to say the least – and his remains were burnt on the beach at Viareggio with Byron in attendance. A year after Mary Shelley's death in 1851, her box-desk was found to contain, among other items, a silk parcel containing some of Shelley's ashes and the remains of his heart.

Frankenstein connects with a later piece of English gothic, Robert Louis Stevenson's *Strange Case of Dr Jekyll and Mr Hyde* (1886), through science and dreams. Like Shelley's novel, Stevenson's 'shilling shocker', or 'crawler', was at least partly conceived as the consequence of a nightmare. One night in

1885, Stevenson's wife, Fanny,[7] was startled by her husband's cries, and woke him, as a dutiful wife would. Stevenson was none too happy at his dream being interrupted, as she had just pulled him out of the story's first scene of transformation. Stevenson, though, was made of stern stuff, and the first draft of the tale is reputed to have taken him no longer than three days to write.

---

7 Apropos of not very much at all, I once had a great-aunt named Fanny, now long deceased, who occupied a floor of one of the last of Dublin's old tenements, on Camden Row. She was a tiny lady who lived in a television-free flat with her brother, surrounded by stuffed birds, and smoked huge amounts of Woodbine cigarettes that had stained her fingers and hair bright orange. (I think she may be partly responsible for the appearance of the villain known as the Collector in my Charlie Parker novels.) She also grew smaller and smaller as she got older, so it may be that she isn't in fact dead at all but has just become so tiny that we can no longer even see her, and somewhere overlooked trails of Woodbine smoke at carpet level testify to her continued existence.

Anyway, every few weeks Great-Aunt Fanny would come to our house for dinner, and one of these visits coincided with the first broadcast on the BBC of 'Salem's Lot, Tobe Hooper's adaptation of the Stephen King novel, starring David Soul. (Since 'Salem's Lot made its first TV appearance in the US in November 1979, I figure the BBC must have shown it early in 1980, although I'm open to correction on this.) As will be revealed later in this little piece, I loved 'Salem's Lot, and had already read the novel by the time the TV adaptation appeared, so I was primed for one of its big shocks, which is the first appearance of the Nosferatuesque vampire Barlow as he enters a prison cell to get his fangs into Ned Tibbets. It's one of the great TV reveals, and Reggie Nalder, the partially disfigured Austrian actor who played Barlow, is genuinely terrifying in the role. But while I may have had my prepubescent loins girded in preparation for this moment, the more elderly loins of Great-Aunt Fanny, who happened to be sitting in a nearby armchair, remained resolutely ungirded. I can still hear the sound of her dropped teacup shattering on our tiled fireplace as she lapsed into shock.

Scientifically, *Frankenstein* is indebted to the flourishing study of medicine, and in particular the fascination with the inner workings of the human body that would ultimately lead to the practice of 'burking', the commission of murders in order to secure bodies for the dissection tables. Burking takes its name from William Burke who, with his accomplice William Hare, killed sixteen people in the vicinity of Edinburgh in 1828, and sold the corpses to Dr Robert Knox for dissection. Burke was hanged for his crimes, while Hare was released after turning King's evidence, after which little is known about him. Burke was publicly dissected following his execution, and his skeleton is now displayed in the Anatomy Museum of the University of Edinburgh Medical School.

Stevenson's novel, meanwhile, takes its cue from a neo-Darwinian theory of degeneration: that civilization contains within itself the seeds of its own decay. While examining the duality of man it suggests that, having evolved from primitive beings, their violent atavistic urges remain part of our makeup, waiting for a catalyst to cause them to emerge. It was a tenet of the earliest works of criminal anthropology, among them those of Cesare Lombroso, who took the view that 'the germs of moral insanity and criminality are found normally in mankind in the first stages of his existence'.

Although Stevenson also nods to the epistolary tradition by using letters to impart knowledge to the reader, they're simply part of a larger narrative. What struck me most forcibly when rereading *Dr Jekyll and Mr Hyde* was how slowly the nature of the relationship between Jekyll and Hyde is made apparent. We are by now familiar with the basic thrust of the story – scientist experiments with a potion to unleash his inner primitive in order to separate it from his higher being:

If each, I told myself, could but be housed in separate identities, life would be relieved of all that was unbearable; the unjust might go his way, delivered from the aspirations and remorse of his more upright twin; and the just could walk steadfastly and securely on his upward path, doing the good things in which he found his pleasure, and no longer exposed to disgrace and penitence by the hands of this extraneous evil.

But a contemporary reader approaching the story for the first time would have done so with little or no idea of what linked Jekyll to Hyde, and it's really only in 'Henry Jekyll's First Statement of the Case', which closes the book, that the truth is revealed. The rest is given to us in flashes, and accounts from a number of narrators and witnesses, each of whom can, of necessity, supply only an incomplete version of events. It's a classic slow reveal.

In 1888, Jekyll and Hyde found their way to the London stage, and the performances at the Lyceum Theatre coincided with the Whitechapel murders of prostitutes committed between August and November of that year, five of which were attributed to the killer known as Jack the Ripper. Suddenly Stevenson's work took on a chilling relevance, with an editorial in the *Pall Mall Gazette* noting that 'There certainly appears to be a tolerably realistic impersonification of Mr Hyde at large in Whitechapel.'

While it was initially assumed that someone capable of committing crimes of such barbarity had to be of a coarse and impoverished nature[8] – 'we should not be surprised if the murderer in the present case should not be slum bred', the editorial harrumphed – it didn't take long for the flaws in that reasoning to be questioned, with the *Pall Mall Gazette* backpedalling furiously just a few days later, suggesting helpfully that 'The Marquis de Sade, who died in a lunatic asylum at the age of seventy-four . . . was an amiable-looking gentleman, and, so, possibly enough, may be the Whitechapel murderer.'

---

8 Or an actor, which is pretty much the same thing: Richard Mansfield, who portrayed Jekyll and Hyde at the Lyceum in 1888, was briefly a Ripper suspect because of the convincing nature of his performance.

So just as the outwardly respectable Henry Jekyll housed within him the murderous Edward Hyde, it now entered the realms of possibility that Jack the Ripper might be a man of some sophistication and breeding. This has given rise to an entire industry devoted to speculation about suspects as diverse as Sir John Williams, Queen Victoria's surgeon, named as the killer as recently as 2013 by an author claiming to be the descendant of his final victim, Mary Kelly; and, perhaps most spectacularly and wrong-headedly, the artist Walter Sickert, who, in 2001, was fingered by the mystery writer Patricia Cornwell as the culprit largely on the basis that his paintings were kind of sleazy. Cornwell was duly accused of 'monstrous stupidity' for tearing apart a Sickert canvas in order to prove her theory, although not being much of a fan of Sickert's work myself – I know what I like, wouldn't have it on the wall at home, etc. – the only good thing that can be said to have come out of Cornwell's efforts is that there is one less Sickert painting in the world.

And thus it is that from *Strange Case of Dr Jekyll and Mr Hyde* – and the image of the Ripper as a savage hiding behind the façade of a gentleman – we can trace a slightly wavy line to Thomas Harris, and the creation of the cannibal psychiatrist Dr Hannibal Lecter, he of *The Silence of the Lambs* and making-this-author-cry fame. As it happens, Anthony Hopkins was the first actor to win the Best Actor Oscar for a horror film since Fredric March, who won the award in 1932 for the lead role in – yes, you guessed it – *Dr Jekyll and Mr Hyde*.

Tales of Mystery & Imagination (1908), by Edgar Allan Poe
Sorry, that was rather a long digression, and we're now back at my childhood bookshelves. The Poe anthology is, I think, one of only two books that I salvaged from my grandmother's house in Kerry before it was sold and demolished after her death. The other is a paperback copy of *Let's Hear It for the Deaf Man* (1972), the first Ed McBain book I ever encountered and also, I

believe, the first mystery novel I ever read.[9] I have a strong suspicion that Poe may have been my introduction to more grown-up supernatural storytelling, as I have a memory of struggling as a child with his prose style. My grandmother's library thus provided the genesis of my literary career, as right from my first novel, *Every Dead Thing*, I was fascinated by the possibility of combining the rationalist traditions of the mystery novel with the anti-rationalist underpinnings of supernatural fiction.

Of course, this didn't entirely meet with the favour of mystery fiction's more conservative rump. The mystery community – readers, writers, critics – has its own equivalent of those people who instinctively file objections to planning permission on the grounds that they would very much prefer things in general to remain the same, regardless of whether or not the proposed changes might actually be for the better. It's not even true to say that they have a definition of what mystery fiction is; instead, they simply know what it isn't. They have always had a particular hatred for the mixing of genres, to the extent that a mystery novel set, say, in the Old West, will automatically be categorized as a Western, while a mystery set in the future is science fiction. English historical settings seem to be okay, presumably on the grounds that the glories of the Empire appeal to their natural conservatism.

---

9 It is also the only novel of which I can say with certainty that my father read it too. My father wasn't a huge reader of fiction, but each summer he would choose one book from my grandmother's shelf as his holiday reading. He once made the mistake of selecting the distinctly weighty *I, Claudius* by Robert Graves, which took him two entire summers to read, and I suspect the slighter *Let's Hear It for the Deaf Man* might have been a reaction to this previous error. We fought over that book, as the cover and title attracted my attention. My dad, though, never read another McBain, while I hunted down all of the 87th Precinct series, and in *Every Dead Thing* I even named a character Fat Ollie as a doffing of the cap to the writer who introduced me to mystery fiction. Unfortunately, McBain took this amiss, and threatened to sue me, but we made up before he died.

These self-appointed guardians of the mystery genre's past, present, and future reserve a particular hatred for any hint of the supernatural, a hostility that finds its most famous expression in the set of ten rules of detective fiction formulated by Father Ronald Knox in 1929, the second of which reads, 'All supernatural or preternatural agencies are ruled out as a matter of course.'[10]

Now I wasn't writing novels in which 'The ghost did it', but was merely trying to explore some of the possibilities inherent in William Gaddis's suggestion that 'you get justice in the next world, in this world, you have the law' (*A Frolic of His Own*, 1994). I was curious about that disparity between law and justice, the difference between our imperfect human system of justice and the possibility of a Divine justice, and the implications that the existence of the latter might have for the origins of evil. I was also interested in creating new forms, hybrids of existing traditions, because I believed that in experimentation lay progress.

I was reminded, too, that the little collection of Poe salvaged from my grandmother's house contained stories of both mystery and the supernatural, for *Tales of Mystery & Imagination* housed, in addition to narratives of outright horror, two of the three

---

10 Knox (1888–1957) also frowns on twins, doubles, detectives who themselves commit crimes, excessive use of secret passages, and Chinamen. The last, it should be noted, can be taken as a general rap on the knuckles for those writers of the Sax Rohmer school who leaned heavily on the threat of the 'Yellow Peril' for their plots. Knox might have been well advised to couch this rule (No 5) in slightly less bald terms than 'No Chinaman must figure in the story,' which is open to some degree of misinterpretation. Even more regrettably, Knox, in his 1928 essay 'Studies in the Literature of Sherlock Holmes', gave birth to a school of mock-critical writing underpinned by the assumption that Holmes, Watson, Poirot and the like were all real people, which is found inexplicably amusing by the kind of individuals who only refer to Agatha Christie as 'Miss Christie' and think everything stopped being funny when music halls closed.

Dupin mysteries, in which a French amateur detective investigates a number of baffling crimes. The most famous of these remains 'The Murders in the Rue Morgue', in which the solution to a brutal double murder involves – and I'm giving a little away here, but not much – an orangutan, which suggests that even Poe recognized the absurdity of the purely rationalist approach.[11]

When I was putting together *Nocturnes*, my first collection of supernatural prose, I tried to write a Poe-esque tale entitled 'The Bridal Bed', but I left it out of the main volume because I discovered that it's a lot harder than it first appears to write like Poe. As with Raymond Chandler, his mood and style are so distinctive that to imitate him risks descending into pastiche. I later relented and included it in the paperback edition, but I think I had the decency to apologize for it.

Poe stood beside a volume of H.P. Lovecraft stories on my grandmother's shelf. I still have no idea how the Lovecraft got there. Poe's presence I could almost understand, as he came in the form of an old hardback and so fitted in with the general look of her library, but the Lovecraft was a relatively new Panther paperback edition, possibly of *The Lurking Fear and Other Stories*, although I can't swear to it. I could only assume that one of my older cousins had left it, but I had just two older cousins, neither of whom struck me as the type to bother with Lovecraft. It was, in its way, all very Lovecraftian – or perhaps, more correctly, M. R. Jamesian (of whom more later).

---

11 Poe, it's safe to say, was not the most rational of men, and certainly had his demons. In his biography of the writer (*Poe: A Life Cut Short*, 2009), Peter Ackroyd recounts an incident in which a dirty and dishevelled Poe left his mortally ill wife in order to remonstrate with another young woman to whom he may once have been unofficially engaged, and who had since married someone else. 'Poe,' as Ackroyd informs us, 'then minced up some radishes with such fury that pieces of them flew around the room. He drank a cup of tea, and departed.' It is, somehow, the detail about the radishes that is most disturbing.

Whatever its origins, I struggled with the Lovecraft even more than I did with the Poe, and I remain a Lovecraft agnostic to this day. It has always seemed to me that Lovecraft's imaginative reach frequently exceeds his literary grasp by some distance. Even his most famous novella, *At the Mountains of Madness*, falls down when it comes to putting words to his odd vision of the universe, plagued by gibbering horrors from the beyond. There's far too much 'I cannot bring myself to describe the terrible vision that met my eyes . . .' followed by 'Oh, all right, I'll have a go' for my liking. As the story's narrator puts it at one point, 'I might as well be frank – even if I cannot bear to be quite direct', ignoring the fact that frankness without directness is like an arrow without a point on the end. I'll grant that his best tales manage to exceed the sum of their parts, although Michel Houellebecq's *H.P. Lovecraft: Against the World, Against Life* (2005), an attempt at reassessment and rehabilitation, left me distinctly cold. Then again, that may just be a natural – and, to my mind, eminently understandable – response to anything Houellebecq writes. Remember: it's not bias if you're right.

As it happens, I'm quite gratified that I took the writing of this piece as an opportunity to return to my childhood home. (My mother is gratified too, as I'm leaving with a couple of boxes of books, my old teddy bear, and some model cars. Not only is her ceiling now in less danger of collapsing on top of her, but she may also be optimistic about the possibility of my severing the apron strings entirely, and wholeheartedly embracing adult life, bless her.) I was a child who loved books, and I am an adult who is the product of books. There, in my old bedroom, the history of my childhood reading remains in dusty limbo. I really must encourage my mum to think about putting a plaque upon the wall of the house, and charging people to visit.

Strangely absent from those shelves, though, was M. R. James, and it is James who remains my favourite writer of supernatural fiction—

But perhaps I should qualify that statement before we go any further.

My first explorations of longer supernatural fiction came in the form of the novels of Stephen King. I started with the afore-mentioned *'Salem's Lot* (1975), followed by *The Shining* (1977), which was given to me by Eamonn Sweeney, the boy I sat next to for one year in primary school, so we're talking about 1979 at the latest. Eamonn Sweeney thought that *The Shining* was the most frightening book ever written. He was wrong, of course: that honour went to *'Salem's Lot*, but *The Shining* certainly was interesting, if a little lengthy.[12] When I reviewed *Doctor Sleep*, King's sequel to *The Shining*, for *The Irish Times*, I calculated that I had read more than fifty of King's books, which is an awful lot of one writer's work to have consumed.[13]

I should confess that King and I had a slight parting of the ways around 1986's *It*. It wasn't anything that he had done, and the split wasn't final. I just wanted to see other writers. I would still read the books as soon as they came out, but I did so at one remove. Some point of connection had been lost, and I couldn't understand why.

I think that I may have an answer now. In 1986 I had just turned eighteen, and my relationship with horror as a genre was changing. Horror fiction, when read in adolescence, offers

---

12 As it happens, *The Shining* is only eight pages longer than *'Salem's Lot*, but I'd argue that it *feels* longer. One of King's gifts is his ability to take a large cast of characters and move easily among them all without sacrificing tension, which he does particularly well in *'Salem's Lot*. It may simply be that the claustrophobia of *The Shining* didn't appeal to me as much as a boy. I really should reread it, but there are just so many books that I have yet to read.

13 I've missed some e-books, I've never been able to get to grips with *The Dark Tower*, his extended fantasy series, and *Faithful*, his nonfiction book about baseball and his beloved Red Sox, written with Stewart O'Nan, remains unopened because it's a nonfiction book about baseball.

a means of exploring the darkness and complexity of the adult world. It's only superficially about vampires, or werewolves, or ghosts. What it does is enable young people to ascribe a name – zombie, ghoul, monster – to the unnameable, to give form to formless terrors, and in that way come to terms with them.[14] King's fictions are particularly suited to these explorations, in part because he writes so well about childhood and adolescence (which is not to say that the books themselves are childish or adolescent, not at all). But once we enter young adulthood, the need for such tools is less pressing. We begin dealing with the reality of sexuality, relationships, compromise, work, responsibility and, far in the distance, the shadow of mortality. As a consequence, horror fiction loses some of its immediacy.

But, in my mid-forties, I have new terrors to confront: the ageing of my body, concerns for my children, the reality of my

---

14 Some years ago, when I published *The Gates*, the first of my Samuel Johnson novels for younger readers, I was invited to discuss the book on BBC Radio 4's *Today* show with John Humphrys. For those of you outside the UK who may be unaware of him, Humphrys is a formidable broadcasting figure, the kind of chap who eats errant politicians for breakfast and spends the rest of the day sucking the marrow from their bones. Anyway, it turned out that *The Gates* had come to Humphrys's attention because his son was reading it, and Humphrys Senior decided that the book's climactic description of the Devil was a bit much for chaps of Humphrys Junior's vintage. While he was quite nice about it all, it was clear that he believed no good could come of reading This Sort of Thing, even if the Samuel books are intended to be at least as funny as they are scary. I did try to draw an analogy with old folktales, and explained to him that if you take the element of fear and threat out of such stories then you deprive them of power and meaning, but he wasn't really having it. Still, I emerged from the whole experience with only a couple of minor bruises, and it's not often that a writer gets to argue such a case on the flagship current affairs show of the world's leading broadcaster. In your face, J.K. Rowling.

own death. I was immortal when I first read King; I feel absurdly vulnerable now. With all that in mind, I find myself affected anew by King's later works. They are the writings of a man who has suffered grievously himself. In 1999, King was struck by a minivan while walking in Lovell, Maine. He endured life-threatening injuries that left him with an addiction to pain medication, which he has since overcome, and caused him to consider giving up writing entirely. (As for the driver of the minivan, one Bryan Edwin Smith, he died one year after the incident, on 21 September 2000, the date of Stephen King's 53rd birthday, which is the kind of thing that usually only happens to people in Stephen King novels.)

I was careful to use the term 'horror fiction' earlier in order to distinguish it from general supernatural fiction. There is a lazy tendency to assume that horror, ghost, and supernatural stories are all one and the same, but a tale of ghosts or the supernatural may not necessarily be horrific. The horror genre is the only one to be named after an intense feeling with largely negative connotations: to be horrified is to be disgusted, even repelled. This is why supermarkets avoided stocking horror fiction on their shelves for many years, and booksellers hid their horror sections away at the back of stores, there to be discovered by largely amiable young men and women with only mildly concerned parents. The horror genre had a hint of the illicit and the shameful about it, but that was the whole point. As Woody Allen once said about sex, it's only dirty when it's done right. The clean, glittering vampires of the *Twilight* novels are the stuff of romance, but Stoker's Dracula – a child-killer, a pollutant, a thing of dirt and rats – is a true creature of horror.

The effectiveness of a piece of horror, though, is dependent on revelation, on what is seen and felt. As King admits in *Danse Macabre*, 'I recognize terror as the finest emotion . . . and so I will try to terrorize the reader. But if I find I cannot terrify him/her, I will try to horrify; and if I find I cannot horrify, I'll go for the gross-out. I'm not proud.'

I was once asked to offer a definition of a tasteful horror story. The only answer I could come up with is that a tasteful horror story is one nobody would want to read. Taste really has no part to play in horror. Rather, like physical pain, it's a question of what one is capable of enduring, and it's no coincidence that horror fiction frequently explores John Donne's assertion that 'The concavities of my body are like another Hell for their capacity', a quotation that I used at the start of *Every Dead Thing*. At its most effective, horror fiction is tied up with the fragility of the human form, with injury, pain, and ultimately, death. In that sense, all great horror is body horror; it's why Thomas Harris's *The Silence of the Lambs*, with its details of mutilation and cannibalism, is not a thriller but a horror story. The body, horror fiction warns us, is a frail construct, and will betray us all in the end.

Since I've admitted to unforgivable gaps in my reading of King's output, I should also confess that I actually read very few modern supernatural novelists, King and a handful of others apart, so I can't *but* have been influenced by him. I even write about Maine, just as King does, although that's because I worked in the state when I was younger, and now have a house there. I also still think of myself primarily as a writer of mysteries, while King is at heart a horror writer, although I know that the question of genre hasn't really troubled him in a long time. What I'm trying to say is that I'm not some kind of insane stalker of King who has moved to Maine to be closer to my idol. I've simply read most of his books, and have therefore contributed something to his mortgage payments. (See the piece of guttering on the right of his house? I *own* that.)

So why don't I read many longer works of supernatural fiction? Well, I suspect it's because I feel that the short story is the ideal form for explorations of the supernatural. A short horror story can give us a glimpse behind the curtain, a brief hint of whatever lurks in the shadows, but it's under no particular obligation to provide an explanation, which renders the after-effect of the sighting all the more unsettling. On the other hand, if someone writes a novel that clocks in around the 1000-page mark, then some kind of explanation or conclusion is pretty much obligatory. The problem is that the explanation is generally going to be less interesting than the initial mystery. To put it simply, the question is more intriguing than the answer.

King's massive 2009 novel *Under the Dome* (1074 pages, since you ask), the tale of a small Maine town sealed off from the rest of the world by a massive force field of unknown origin, is a master class in tension, a gripping depiction of an enclosed community gradually succumbing to violence and anarchy. King doesn't put a foot wrong until the very end, when he decides that some kind of revelation about the origin of the titular dome is required. Oddly enough, in this case it isn't: the dome is merely the catalyst for an investigation of the society trapped beneath it, and the variety of responses provoked by the town's containment. It doesn't really matter how the dome came to be there: it is the people scurrying around under it – fighting, fleeing, and killing – who are interesting. The explanation for the dome's presence, when it comes, smacks of an episode of *The Twilight Zone*. It's too flimsy to support the massive edifice above, and the novel almost collapses as a consequence.[15]

The fault, I would argue, isn't entirely King's, but lies with the genre. If I were a more vain man, I might formulate a rule entitled Connolly's Law: the effectiveness of a piece of supernatural fiction is inversely proportional to its length.

This is not to say that there are no great horror novels – King's output alone disproves this – but there are far fewer than one might expect, and many are relatively slight, to the extent that some might more correctly be termed novellas: *The Haunting of*

---

15 Even Homer nods occasionally. And let me just stress that I love King's work, and am very fond of the man himself. In the end, we can learn more from the occasional missteps of a great writer than from the qualified successes of poorer practitioners.

Hill House by Shirley Jackson (200 pages, in my edition); *Frankenstein* by Mary Shelley (221 pages); *I Am Legend* by Richard Matheson (170 pages); *The Turn of the Screw* by Henry James (128 pages); and *Strange Case of Dr Jekyll and Mr Hyde* by Robert Louis Stevenson (65 pages). On the other hand, freed from the constrictions of copyright – which, to be fair, bedevilled the efforts of our old friend Herbert van Thal – one could create many volumes of fine short supernatural fiction, and it is interesting just how many lists of the great horror novels have to be plumped up with anthologies of stories.[16]

I wonder, too, how much of my affection for short fiction in the genre is tied up with my exposure to compact instalments of supernaturally-themed television shows, which formed much of my youthful viewing, even more than old horror movies on the BBC. I grew up with *Tales of the Unexpected* and *Hammer House of Horror*, episodes of which lasted thirty minutes and an hour respectively. Even adaptations of longer novels were frequently doled out in small doses: I can still remember being

---

16 I admit that this is a contentious issue. The fine writer Robert Aickman noted that 'While the number of good ghost stories is very small indeed, the number of bad ones, as with bad plays, must be encountered professionally in order to be believed.' Aickman took the view that a great ghost story might emerge only once or twice in a writer's career, although the quality of his own output largely disproved his thesis, and the same might well be said for the short stories of M.R. James, Arthur Machen, Algernon Blackwood, Stephen King, and others.

Thanks to *Armchair Nation*, Joe Moran's excellent history of British television, I recently learned that Blackwood was an unlikely pioneer of television broadcasting. At the age of almost eighty he became a fixture of *Saturday Night Story*, in the course of which he would sit in a chair and tell a tale to viewers. The story in question would be made up as he walked the mile and a half from his Underground station to the Wood Green studios, for he refused to rehearse or use a script, and timed himself by the studio clock to finish dead on time.

terrified by the 1978 *Armchair Thriller* dramatization of Antonia Fraser's *Quiet As A Nun* which, although a thriller rather than a supernatural novel, owed a strong debt to the gothic tradition, and might have drawn an approving nod from Matthew Lewis, author of *The Monk* (1796), another work infused with a deep awareness of the potential eeriness of nuns.

Then there was ITV's *Sapphire & Steel* (1979–82), a science-fiction/fantasy hybrid so strange that it's almost impossible to conceive of how it came to be green-lit in the first place. To be fair, the show itself is almost impossible to understand, so at least a degree of consistency runs through the whole process. It featured Joanna Lumley, late of *The New Avengers*, and David McCallum, star of *The Man from U.N.C.L.E.*, as – well, this is where it all gets a bit difficult, as it's not entirely apparent *what* they are. They seem to be trans-dimensional agents of some sort, possibly in the employ of Time itself, but – and stay with me here – they're also elements, as in the Periodic Table of the Elements. We know this because, at the start of each show, a male voice informs us that 'Transuranic elements may not be used where there is life. Medium atomic weights are available: Gold, Lead, Copper, Jet, Diamond, Radium, Sapphire, Silver, and Steel. Sapphire and Steel have been assigned . . .'

Which doesn't clear things up at all, but never mind.

The cases investigated by Sapphire & Steel contained elements of the ghost story – creepy old houses, or an abandoned railway station apparently haunted by the spectre of a dead WWI soldier – and rarely ended up providing anything approaching a satisfactory explanation. I have never been one for drugs, but I suspect that the experience of watching *Sapphire & Steel* may be akin to smoking large quantities of pot before trying to read a science textbook.

Only later did I encounter anthology shows such as *Dead of Night*, a BBC series first broadcast in 1972, and then largely forgotten. Just three episodes survive, of which 'The Exorcism' is probably the best. In a similar vein was *Supernatural* (1977), in which aspiring members of the Club of the Damned were invited to tell a horror story as part of their membership application. If they failed sufficiently to frighten their peers, they were killed, which seems perfectly reasonable to me. (I think this principle should be applied across the board, starting with comedies that fail to provoke even a minor titter. Adam Sandler and Rob Schneider might as well just buy their own nooses and have done with it.)

Even children's television appeared to operate on the basis that the best way to deal with troublesome kids was to terrify them into catatonic silence. For *The Changes* (1975), the BBC adapted a trilogy of Peter Dickinson novels in which Britain reverts to a pre-industrial society following a signal emitted by all machinery and technology, and merrily included episodes featuring accusations of Satanism and witchcraft for pre-tea-time consumption. ITV gave us *Shadows* (1975–78), to which a number of heavyweight writers contributed, including J.B. Priestley and Fay Weldon. I don't recall much about it, to be perfectly honest, although I have a vague memory of an episode featuring a mobster and a pair of haunted shoes which, thanks to the wonders of the Internet, I now know to be 'Dutch Schlitz's Shoes'.[17]

Best of all was the same network's *Children of the Stones*, subsequently described as 'the scariest programme ever made for children', involving stone circles, Druids, black holes, people apparently being turned into standing stones, and theme music – composed by Sidney Sager – virtually guaranteed to cause anyone who had been exposed to the original show in their youth to revert to traumatized childhood upon hearing it again.

But I now realize that some of my earliest encounters with short-form horror on TV came in the guise of the BBC science

---

17 One summary of the episode being 'The villainous Mr Stabs is concerned that his hand-power has become almost exhausted.' Please insert your own puerile joke here.

fiction series *Doctor Who*. I was seven years old when season thirteen was first broadcast (starring Tom Baker as the Doctor) and a complete *Doctor Who* devotee. Seasons thirteen and fourteen of the show are regarded as 'Gothic Who', mostly due to the efforts of producer Philip Hinchcliffe and script editor Robert Holmes, who was a fan of 'an old sort of Hollywood horror', according to Hinchcliffe. But 'Pyramids of Mars' offered robots disguised as mummies, and an Egyptologist possessed by the ancient Egyptian deity Sutekh. 'The Brain of Morbius' rewrote *Frankenstein*, replacing the limbs of the dead with alien body parts. 'The Hand of Fear' tackled the horror sub-genre of tales of possessed limbs, exemplified by W. F. Harvey's short story 'The Beast with Five Fingers', while 'The Masque of Mandragora' harked back to Poe. This gothic era climaxed with 'The Talons of Weng-Chiang' (the final story of season fourteen, and the last before the original series began a steady decline), which combined Sherlock Holmes with *The Phantom of the Opera*, the 'Yellow Peril' tradition of Asian villains, a murderous toy with the cerebral cortex of a pig, and a giant rat.

Doctor Who had dabbled with horror prior to Hinchcliffe, although before my time. My introduction to the series came in the form of 'The Sea Devils', an episode of which I saw at my aunt's house in Dunblane in 1972, when I was just four, and which, with its famous sequence of the titular amphibians emerging from the sea, may have scarred me for life.

But one year earlier, the show had featured an adventure entitled 'The Daemons', in which an archaeological dig at the village of Devil's End unearths a horned beast known as Azal. Despite the title, and wary of offending religious sensibilities, the BBC backed away from describing Azal as a demon or, indeed, the Devil himself, although he couldn't have been more Satanic in appearance if he'd arrived clutching a big fork and wearing a pentagram-shaped hat on his head. Instead Azal is described as an alien, and only with the 2006 David Tennant-era episode entitled 'The Satan Pit' would the show explicitly attempt to engage with the subject again. Yet for all its perhaps understandable shuffling around Satanism, 'The Daemons' is fairly prescient, appearing months before the release of the famous British folk horror film *The Blood on Satan's Claw*, and two years before the high point of the genre, Robin Hardy's *The Wicker Man*.[18]

All of which brings us back to M.R. James, the greatest writer of short supernatural fiction that the genre has yet produced. James (1862–1936) was the provost of King's College, Cambridge and later of Eton College.[19] He wrote just over thirty ghost stories, many of them intended to be read aloud to friends and colleagues at Christmas time. James was a medieval scholar, and the central characters in his tales are often academics, antiquarians, or gentleman-scholars of a particularly fusty and reserved kind. (James's first anthology, published in 1904, was entitled *Ghost Stories of an Antiquary*.)

A typical James tale will find some such fellow poking around in an old church or library – examining an obscure carving ('The Stalls of Barchester Cathedral'), perusing an ancient volume ('Canon Alberic's Scrap-book'), or investigating rumours of hidden wealth ('The Treasure of Abbot Thomas') – and suddenly being confronted with a hideous entity linked to the object in question. What is most wonderful about James is the physicality of the roused spirits. When we think of ghosts it is often in an incorporeal way: ethereal wisps that float through walls or,

---

18 'The Daemons' also includes one of the most iconic lines in *Doctor Who* history when Brigadier Lethbridge-Stewart, of the alien-battling United Nations Intelligence Taskforce, is confronted by an animated church gargoyle named Bok. His response? 'Chap with the wings there . . . five rounds rapid.'

19 In a lovely piece of circularity, James knew the young Christopher Lee while he was at Eton, and Lee would later play James in the BBC television dramatizations of his readings.

in the case of poltergeists, entities with no form at all whose presence can only be discerned through their impact on terrestrial objects. James has no truck with that kind of nonsense: his horrors can be seen and touched. More worryingly, they can see and touch in turn. The unfortunate narrator of 'Abbot Thomas' recounts how he is 'conscious of a most horrible smell of mould, and of a cold kind of face pressed against my own, and of several – I don't know how many – legs or arms or tentacles or something clinging to my body'. Of John Eldred's demise in 'The Tractate Middoth', we are told that 'a little dark form appeared to rise out of the shadow behind the tree-trunk and from it two arms enclosing a mass of blackness came before Eldred's face and covered his head and neck'.

James seems to have had a particular horror of hair. (He was a notorious arachnophobe.) The demon that guards Canon Alberic's scrap-book is 'a mass of coarse, matted black hair', and Barchester Cathedral hides a being with 'rather rough and coarse fur'. Most unpleasantly of all, Mr Dunning in 'Casting the Runes' thrusts his hand beneath his pillow and feels 'a mouth, with teeth, and hair about it'. This image would have provided a therapist with regular income for many years had James chosen to present himself for treatment, but it doesn't take a committed Freudian to spot all manner of psychosexual confusion underpinning James's work. He was, in all probability, a closeted gay man at a time when society's tolerance for such forms of attraction was limited in the extreme. The main outlets for his repressed sexuality came in the form of extended bouts of wrestling with possibly like-minded gents on college floors, and in the squelching, tactile, hirsute horrors that found their way into his stories.

Then again, the nature of James's sexuality matters less than the power of the tales that he left behind. The world has seen plenty of repressed homosexuals, but few of them have bequeathed a body of work quite like James's. Perhaps more interesting is that his stories stand as dire prognostications of the danger of intellectual curiosity, a peculiar position for an academic to take.[20] Indeed, one of his tales is called 'A Warning to the Curious'. In James's world, it's entirely inadvisable to go poking one's nose into dark corners for fear that something may well poke one back.

But why isn't James on my childhood bookshelf? He is, in a sense: 'Casting the Runes' and 'Oh Whistle, and I'll Come to You, My Lad' are both contained in anthologies that I bought as a child, but my primary introduction to James came through the medium of television.

From 1971 to 1978, the BBC broadcast a series of television adaptations of supernatural short stories under the banner of *A Ghost Story for Christmas*. I was an altar boy in my local church, which meant that I served at Midnight Mass each Christmas Eve. (This being Ireland in the late seventies and early eighties, Midnight Mass was usually held at 9 p.m. in order to avoid an influx of drunks when the pubs closed at 11 p.m.) I was too young to catch the original transmissions of these dramatizations, but I was old enough to be able to watch the repeats. By the time I returned home from the service, my parents were either already in bed or happy to leave me to my own devices as long as I promised not to go into the living-room to peek at my Christmas presents. I would sit in the kitchen with a cup of tea and some chocolate, turn on our portable television, and take in 'The Ash Tree', 'Lost Hearts', or whatever other adaptation the

---

20 In his recent BBC documentary on James, Mark Gatiss suggests that Professor Parkin in 'Oh Whistle ...' is punished not for his curiosity but for his intellectual pride. It's an interesting reading, but does require that one takes a title like 'A Warning to the Curious' – admittedly a much later tale – as either ironically meant, or simply the product of a change in the James's philosophy. Oh, and Gatiss's 2013 directorial debut, in the form of a dramatization of James's story 'The Tractate Middoth' for the BBC, is worthy to stand alongside the best of the original TV adaptations of the author's work.

BBC happened to put my way.[21] Sometimes, if I was particularly fortunate, they'd also throw in a Laurel and Hardy short, which made it marginally easier for me to go up the dark stairs to bed afterwards.

In 2012, the aforementioned Professor Darryl Jones edited a definitive collection of James's work for the Oxford University Press. To celebrate its publication, we showed Jonathan Miller's 1968 adaptation of 'Oh Whistle . . .' (which lost the original 'Oh' to become simply 'Whistle . . .' for reasons that I've never understood) to audiences in Dublin and Belfast. What was surprising was just how effective it remained, anchored by a terrific performance by Michael Hordern as Professor Parkin, who stumbles across an old bone whistle inscribed with the words '*Quis este iste qui venit*' (Who is this who is coming?), a question to which, unfortunately, he is destined to learn the answer. Yes, the apparition, when it finally manifests itself, takes the form of a bedsheet on a wire, but it's Hordern's reaction to it that haunts the viewer, the sense that his world has been changed for ever, and he will never again rest peacefully in it.

So there we have it: a little piece of my reading and viewing history, and a pointer, perhaps, to the reasons why I write what I do.

And what of that old lady, and her tale of the house in which an entity apparently lingered, waiting to prey on children? Well, I couldn't help her much. I did refer her to a Hodder author who specializes in books on angels, but the whole

---

21 These adaptations were not limited exclusively to the work of M.R. James, and I defy anyone not to be profoundly unsettled by Andrew Davies's 1976 version of 'The Signalman' by Charles Dickens or, indeed, Leslie Megahey's beautiful 1979 interpretation of Sheridan Le Fanu's 'Strange Event in the Life of Schalken the Painter', which is infused with both a love of seventeenth-century Dutch art and a real sense of sexual transgression.

problem was outside my remit, and I don't think anything came of the referral.

Subsequently I returned to the same city to talk about a collection of essays on crime fiction that I'd co-edited, and the elderly lady was present again. This time I had travelled alone, so there was no rep with me. As on the first occasion, she waited until everyone else had left before approaching, and then produced a map showing an area of the town. On it was drawn the letter 'X', and beside the X were the words 'I live here'.

Naturally I assumed that the X in question marked her own house, and she was the one living there, but I was wrong.

'That's where it lives,' she said.

She was smiling. She had me, and she knew it.

'I have a car,' I said.

'You should go and see it.'

And I did.

It was a foul afternoon, damp and cold. As it turned out, the house in question stood on a street not far from the library. It wasn't hard to find as it was the only house still standing. The rest of the street had been given over to industrial buildings, interspersed with patches of waste ground to break the monotony. The house looked like it had once been part of a terrace of similar redbrick dwellings, but they were all gone now, and only this one remained, as though it had been dropped from space. It had two windows on the upper storey, a window and a door on the lower. Most of the panes were broken. The doors and windows were covered by wire grilles – too late to save the glass, but a deterrent to anyone who might have fancied a spot of breaking and entering – and behind the grilles were sheets of plywood, so it was impossible to see inside.

Was it unsettling? Slightly, even if only in its incongruity. This was no longer a residential street. Had anyone still been living in the house, the view from the windows would have been one of unsurpassed ugliness, a testament to what sometimes still passes for urban planning in Britain's more benighted cities. The house just looked lost, and slightly baleful. It didn't even have a garden any longer. No wall or fence separated it from the pavement. It was simply *there*.

But all stories like this should have an odd thing about them, shouldn't they, one little detail that leaves the reader with a shiver. Here is the odd detail: the plywood at one corner of the lower level was broken, or had rotted away, although a piece of dusty glass covered the gap. Written in the dust of the glass, as though by a finger, were three words:

I LIVE HERE

And they were written on the *inside* of the glass.

Even though no exclamation mark stood at the end of the declaration, I heard its emphasis in my head as I read the words. It was simultaneously a statement of fact, and a kind of threat, and a howl of anger and despair at the decay that surrounded it and at what it had itself become.

Did I see a ghost?

No.

Did I sense a presence?

No.

Does something squat in that old house, rippling with hatred, waiting to take its rage out on the children who play on the waste ground, roaming just beyond its reach? I don't know, but the woman who sent me there believed that the house was not unoccupied, and she appeared sincere, and sensible, and self-aware.

Eventually someone will knock it down, and that will probably be for the best. If an entity does haunt it, then it is tied to either a person or a place. I could see no people, and the only place was the house itself – its wood and bricks and broken glass, its floorboards and tiles and walls. Take them away, and there is nowhere for anything to hide.

I may be wrong, of course. After all, I make no great claims of insight on the subject. I don't think that I even want to know for sure. I still retain that image of Michael Hordern as Professor Parkin, sitting in his nightgown on his uneasy bed, his certainties about this world shaken, and his secret fears about the next confirmed. Better to remain uncertain, perhaps.

Better to heed the warnings to the curious.

Acknowledgements

I published the first volumes of *Nocturnes* back in 2004, so more than a decade has gone by in the interim. This second volume includes every piece of short fiction that I've written since then, some of which were commissioned – and, mercifully, accepted – by various editors.

I have a slightly unusual and ambivalent relationship with short fiction. What usually happens is that I will come up with an idea for a story – say, a tale of haunted shoes – and then won't write it unless an editor comes along and says, hey, we're looking for stories about shoes, at which point I'll leap from my chair and announce that I have just the thing. On the other hand, once I start writing short stories I find that I very much enjoy the whole process, and all of the previously unpublished stories in this anthology were written in an extended burst of activity lasting from late in 2013 to the end of January 2015.

'On *The Anatomization of an Unknown Man* (1637) by Frans Mier' first appeared in *The Irish Times* as part of a series of stories inspired by the Universal Declaration of Human Rights, so its existence owes much to Roddy Doyle, who asked me to write the tale (admittedly after someone else dropped out, but it was still very nice of him) and everyone at *The Irish Times* and Amnesty International who was involved with the project. Fintan O'Toole, literary editor of *The Irish Times*, also commissioned and published 'Mud' to mark the centenary of the start of World War I.

'The Caxton Private Lending Library & Book Depository' came about because Otto Penzler at the Mysterious Bookstore in New York asked me to contribute to his collection of

435

bibliomysteries, and then refused to leave me alone until I actually finished it. Del Howison and Jeff Gelb published 'A Haunting' in *Haunted: Dark Delicacies III*, and Christopher Golden, editor of *The New Dead*, kindly allowed 'Lazarus' to open that anthology. To celebrate its 300th edition, *Shortlist* magazine invited writers to produce a short story of exactly 300 words, which is how 'A Dream of Winter' came about. 'The Children of Dr Lyall' first appeared in *Oxcrimes*, an anthology of stories in aid of Oxfam. My friend and fellow author Mark Billingham asked me to become involved in a three-part radio broadcast for the BBC entitled 'Blood, Sweat and Tears'. Since he and Denise Mina immediately jumped on sweat and blood respectively, I wrote a story about tears, which became 'The Hollow King'. Thanks to Celia de Wolff, Penny Downie and all involved in the recordings for bringing it to life. Finally, Leslie Klinger, editor of *The New Annotated Sherlock Holmes*, saved my blushes by reading 'Holmes on the Range' before publication.

That leaves me to thank Sue Fletcher, my editor at Hodder & Stoughton, and all those responsible for publishing my books there, especially Carolyn Mays, Swati Gamble, Kerry Hood, Lucy Hale and Auriol Bishop; Breda Purdue, Jim Binchy, Ruth Shern, Siobhan Tierney, and all at Hachette in Dublin; Emily Bestler, my long-suffering American editor, and everyone at Atria/Emily Bestler Books, including Judith Curr, Megan Reid, and David Brown; and my beloved agent Darley Anderson and his team of exceptionally kind and talented people. Meanwhile, Ellen Clair Lamb looks after all of the nasty detail stuff that I can't be bothered with because I'm such a big shot, and Madeira James and the folk at Xuni.com make sure I can find myself on the internet.

Lastly, Jennie Ridyard is my best friend and coauthor, and Cameron and Alistair agree to continue living with us as long as we can keep them in the style to which they've become accustomed, which is why I thank you, the reader, for your support.